# little
# liar

# CLARE BOYD

# little liar

bookouture

Published by Bookouture in 2017
An imprint of StoryFire Ltd.
Carmelite House
50 Victoria Embankment
London EC4Y 0DZ
www.bookouture.com

ISBN: 978-1-78681-397-8
eBook ISBN: 978-1-78681-396-1

For Simon, Tilda and Joni

# PROLOGUE

The nurse washed me down. I was weak on my legs. The bloody flannel between my legs didn't embarrass me. I was flying as high as a kite. Delirious. Forgetful of what was to come.

My baby had black hair and blue eyes. He didn't have a name yet. He would need a good name. A name that symbolised a new start, the turning of a new leaf. He was change; he was joy; he was redemption.

When the two women came in, I didn't at first recognise their faces. One tall, one stout. Both were too solemn for the occasion. Their impassive expressions didn't reflect the magnitude of my achievement. Could they not see my miracle lying in his plastic cot? Could they not see that he was the most beautiful baby boy in the whole hospital? Could they not see the love etched into my eyes?

'It's time,' the tall one said.

A small piece of toast came up from my throat, whole, as though it had never been swallowed. It tasted poisonous.

'No.' I flung my body over the cot.

These two women were surely not evil enough to rip the beating heart from my chest. A sob rolled up from the depths of me. They couldn't have him. He was my flesh and blood. He was the only good thing left in my life. He was mine.

Disconnected, I heard a wail echo around the hot room and noticed it was my own. My body shook, electrified by a wave of agony.

'You remember what has been decided?' the tall woman said gently, like I was a child or an imbecile.

'If you fight it, you'll only make it worse,' the other woman said, almost in a whisper. I saw tears in her eyes. Her pity was unbearable.

I straightened my body, clinging to the edge of the cot with both hands, neck bent, transfixed by his tiny face. I had tried to prepare for this moment.

There was no way to prepare for hell.

His little gunky eyes were closed. He was the embodiment of peace and innocence. Two states of being that I had forgotten existed and would never feel again.

My hospital gown was damp where my breasts had leaked. They would leak empty. Like my soul.

I kissed his frowzy head and felt a yearning that was so penetrating it was as though I were dying.

As I watched his tiny little body leave the room in another woman's arms, I knew my life was over.

# CHAPTER ONE

Through the diamond-shaped panes of glass, I could see my mother at the stove under the warm kitchen light, stirring something. The children's colourful plastic mugs sat in waiting, bright and garish against the white backdrop.

My heart was racing and my palms were clammy. I hesitated, my keys dangling at the lock. I couldn't go in. Not yet. I needed five minutes.

Before I opened the front door, before the three-hour onslaught of the bedtime routine, I stepped back and climbed into the soft leather of my car and closed myself in, bracing myself.

When Rosie and Noah were very small, I would tell them that I was their sunrise and their moon; that I would always be there to kiss them in the morning and to tuck them up with a story at night. This week, I had left too early in the mornings to be their sunrise. But every evening, at six o'clock, I hurried on up the hill from the train station to be their moon, and every evening, the closer I got to home, the less I wanted to go back in.

Dog-tired and dried-out after a long day at work in the City, I felt as though I was about to step onto a stage to give the performance of my life, again, having had very average, if not appalling, reviews every night for ten years. In the mood I was in, I didn't know how I would get through tonight's drama without ad-libbing and strangling both my children in the Second Act, or at least wanting to.

I imagined all the other mothers out there wafting through bedtime, singing and laughing with their naughty little charges, and I wished with all of my heart that I was one of them. The thought of this mystical, capable breed made me want to shrivel up and die, to leave an inadequate puddle of blue suit and white shirt in the driver's seat: the vanishing act of a working mother.

I laid my head back against the smooth, cool headrest. Just a few more minutes would be all I needed to slow my heart.

The car faced our tall, black gates and dense hawthorn hedges, behind which our 1930s Arts and Crafts house dominated the small, grassy roundabout of Virginia Close. The five other houses that wrapped around the top end – or bulb – of the close were of the same era, mostly without extensions or big gates like ours, but equally as pretty, with their low-sloping roofs, solid red-brick walls and elegant casement windows. They faced each other like a circle of friends chatting. And I guessed our house was probably the least chatty of all five.

A fox darted out from the hedge. Its eyes glinted at me through the fog that had rested on the top of this hill and around the house like a lazy cloud for days since September had struck, shrouding a breezy, warm summer, which was gone overnight. The animal stopped and looked at me as though I was the imposter.

The muscles that gripped my womb began to cramp. The baby wasn't big enough to kick inside me, but it was enough to draw me back to my dawn and dusk responsibilities.

I eased out of the car and crunched across the gravel to my front door. I heard a rustle behind me. The fox was sloping away through the hedge into Mira and Barry's garden next door, where it would, no doubt, prey on their chickens and leave the feathery detritus of its massacre strewn across our lawn.

The moment my key entered the lock, I heard Rosie and Noah's feet pounding the wooden floors, and the thought of catching that first sight of them gave me butterflies. The locks clicked and sprang from the other side. I put my keys away and let Rosie open it herself. Before I could put my bag down or take off my coat, they had both bounded up like puppies, wrapping their arms around me to squeeze me with all their might.

I took Noah's face in my hands. 'Hello, my little one.'

His peachy skin and thick, blond eyebrows melted my heart. I buried my face into his neck and breathed him in, while Rosie clung to the back of me. Twisting around, I stroked her long, black hair and kissed her on the lips. 'Hello, beautiful. Good day at school?'

'Charlotte stole my rubber and then pretended she didn't,' she cried indignantly.

'That's shocking! Did you tell the teachers?'

Rosie shook her head earnestly. 'I don't tell on people, Mummy. I'm ten.'

'Mummy, come see,' Noah said, taking my hand and dragging me through to the kitchen. 'Look what we made!'

'Hi darling,' my mother said, pulling a pan of milk from the stove. Her movements were slow, as if the pan weighed ten tonnes. The purple of her veins pushed through the liver spots on the back of her hand, the veins like snakes around her bones, clinging to her skeleton for dear life.

'Hi Mum.' I kissed her on the cheek. She smelt of sugar and soap. Her blue eyes blinked too much, like a little girl might bat away her tears to be brave.

'Look, Mumma! We did these all by our own,' Noah exclaimed.

A pile of fresh chocolate muffins sat in the middle of the kitchen table, next to the cold cottage pie covered in plastic wrap that I had hoped they would have eaten by now.

'Wow, Noah, did you really make them all by yourself?' I corrected, avoiding eye contact with my mother in case the disappointment showed on my face. The mound of picturesque muffins had morphed in my head into thousands of grams of sugar, into piles of the evil white stuff, literally flowing over the edge of the children's recommended daily intake.

'Can we have another one?' Rosie asked, grabbing the biggest one from the cooling rack.

Before I had the chance to say no, my mother said, 'Just one more then.'

My look of incredulity fell dead onto the tiles behind my mother's back as she turned away from me.

'Thanks, Granny Helen!' Rosie cried, racing off before I could stop her.

'Rosie!' I called after her. 'Have you done your homework?'

'I told her she could do it after a bit of telly.'

My mother poured two large mugs of hot milk.

'Is the pie in?' I asked, feeling a throb in my temples.

'I was just about to put it on.'

Exhaustion rolled through my body. It was already a quarter past six. Supper and homework should have been done by now if we were to fit bath, stories and bed in before midnight. I downed a large glass of tap water.

My mother picked up the mugs. 'I'll just take these through and say goodbye to them.'

I had a pang of fear about our separation. I would be alone and I worried about how well I would cope, knowing how bad it could get.

When she returned from saying goodbye, she slipped on her coat and looked into her tiny handbag. 'Glasses. Phone. Keys. Good, I'll leave you to it,' she said.

'You don't want to stay for a cup of tea?'

Her gaze slipped across my face. I clicked through my flaws. My black hollow eye sockets, my frizzy black hair, lank at my shoulders, my paper-thin skin that never sees sunlight. When Peter first met me, he said that my features were beautifully unruly, that my smile was all teeth and cheekbones and eyebrows, like a mischievous child's. I had liked the idea that I might seem to him unrulier and less grown-up than I felt. Though that face, the one that he had fallen in love with, was a little past forty now, and I doubted it held the same charm.

'You're looking awfully thin, darling,' she said.

'No pregnancy glow then?' I laughed thinly.

'Are you working too hard?'

'I never thought I'd hear you say that.'

'I'd better go,' she said.

I hadn't wanted to be rude, or to throw us back to my teenage years. What I had really wanted was a warm hug.

When the door closed, I could have sworn I heard the sucking of air, as if I were being sealed into a vacuum. My eyes felt dry. A sense of isolation and dread slumped across my shoulders.

I imagined my office, shadowy and quiet. The documents in the centre of my desk, neatly placed by Lisa, ready for my meeting at nine o'clock sharp. Work life was strenuous, but I could predict the outcome, mostly.

In the television room, Rosie and Noah were curled up together in the corner of the wrap-around sofa, cosy under the faux-fur blanket. Their feet rested on the newly upholstered ottoman. They looked warm and comfortable together. Above their heads hung the oil painting I had bought Peter for his birthday last year. The figure's naked torso was thrust over her thighs, in dance or pain, I didn't know. The colours clashed. Her back was a series of huge, undisciplined arcs. I imagined the artist's arm must have tired from the bold brushstrokes. The work expressed something that resonated with me deep down. I wished we had more art across the expanse of white-washed walls in our open-plan house. From the outside, it was quaint and wonky, a stream of sweet peas climbing up the south-facing wall, while the inside was groomed and tweaked: clean lines, honed modernity, sleek, bleak cabinetry and silver-plated fittings.

'What are you watching?'

Neither of them looked away from the television. An annoying American accent whined out of the flat-screen.

'Hello, earth to Rosie,' I said more pointedly.

'Could you move, Mum. I can't see.'

A big part of me wanted to leave the two of them there. Peter would have told me to. He would have told me that Rosie could catch up with her homework tomorrow, and he would probably have nestled under the blanket with them. But I couldn't. Homework was important. Routines were important. Everyone knew they made children feel safe. I was not their friend, I was their mother.

I clapped my hands, making the decision. 'Upstairs both of you. Rosie, maths homework. Noah, reading books please. Come on, shipshape.'

They groaned and began to roll off the sofa.

'I hate fractions,' Rosie said.

'It won't take long and I'll have tea ready for when you're finished.' I clapped again, annoying myself as I did it.

But instead of going upstairs to her desk, Rosie nipped past me towards the kitchen, saying, 'I've just got to get something from outside.'

I followed her, leaving Noah, who turned the television back on.

At the back door, Rosie was putting on her wellingtons.

My jaw clenched. 'Rosie, what are you doing?'

I knew I shouldn't fear my daughter's potential to outwit me. A better mother might handle her more adeptly than I; but then again, I'd like to see them try.

'I've just got to get something.'

'What an earth do you need to get? It's dark out.'

'It's for Charlotte.'

'What is?'

'Never mind!' she called out behind her as she disappeared into the fog.

'Hurry up!'

Rankled by Rosie's rebellion, and worried about how I might claw back the lost homework time, I kept a close eye on the kitchen clock, hoping she would come back in of her own accord.

The pie would take three quarters of an hour, which was how long Rosie's homework should take, if she stopped wasting it by messing around outside.

After fifteen minutes, I shoved my own boots on and stormed out into the gloom, across the uninspiring expanse of lawn, which had always struck me as rather plain and boxy, underused and overshadowed by two high, wax-leaved hedges that blocked out our neighbours on either side. Behind the clumps and wisps of fog, I imagined the hedges as a rigid row of shoulder-to-shoulder sentries, keeping watch as I marched down to the bottom of the garden to do battle in the tangle of woods.

Rosie was sitting underneath the canopy of the oak tree on a sawn stump for a stool with her head-torch lighting her lap.

'Whatever are you doing?'

She ignored me and continued to work, head bent over a mass of leaves on her lap. Moving closer, I saw how she was twisting wool around dried oak twig cuttings.

'Come on, don't mess about, Rosie, I'm too tired,' I sighed. That overused phrase.

Under Rosie's spotlight, I watched her fingers work adeptly, her concentration unbreakable. I shivered, feeling the chill air circulate under the cotton of my shirt.

'Homework time, please, Rosie.'

'It'll only take a minute.'

'You've been out here for twenty.'

'Just two more minutes, please.'

As I waited, wondering if I should go back in or continue hustling her, I looked around at her den, her favourite place to be. I was touched by the care and attention she had taken to build this little world of hers. There was a blue tin kettle resting on a collection of twigs in a circular pit of stones, and an old wooden table laid with bark plates and twig knives and forks. From the tree, a plastic bucket dangled from a climbing rope.

'Does it still work?' I smiled, tugging at the pulley-system that connected with Mira and Barry's garden next door.

For the first time, Rosie's attention was on me. She looked up. 'I don't know.'

Rosie had discovered it on the first day we had moved in; left behind by the little girl who had lived here before us. At first, Rosie had secretly continued the previous owner's game, sending little posies of sweet peas to Mira in the bucket, which Mira had sent back filled with homemade biscuits in tinfoil and little notes attached. When we found out, I had agreed she could use it occasionally, with permission from a grown-up.

'Why didn't you let me use it?'

'I did!'

'Hardly ever!' she protested.

'I was worried it would bother them.'

'Why?' Rosie said, bending to her work again.

The rope was damp and mildewed. As I pulled it, the blue bucket bounced and bopped along the rope towards the shared hedge. Just as the bucket reached the top of the hedge, I pulled the other rope, reversing the movement and returning it safely home.

'Because people like their privacy, that's why.'

'But she lets Beth go through her garden to my camp.'

'Hmmm,' I said disapprovingly.

'She doesn't mind, it's the truth, Mum.'

Knowing it was a sticking point, I changed the subject. 'Come on, Rosie. Enough of that now. Time to go in.'

'But I need to do this before tomorrow.'

'No, you don't. Now come on.'

Rosie continued wrapping and tying. 'You don't understand, Mum. It's really important.'

'If you don't come now, Rosie, I'll ban your games this week.'

'Don't care.'

I braced myself for a fight. 'I won't tell you again.'

'Just two minutes.'

I stood there like a fool, wondering how to persuade her to come back inside, short of dragging her by the hair.

And then she raised her head, dazzling me with her head-torch, brandishing an intricate autumn wreath of oak leaves, which was dramatically backlit by the torch beam. I took it from her and rotated it round in my hands, admiring her work, charmed by its originality, distracted from the goal of getting her to do her maths homework, which suddenly didn't seem so important. 'Rosie, that is really beautiful,' I said, returning it to her.

'It's for Charlotte.'

'She'll love it.'

Hand-in-hand, we ambled back across the garden, the wreath crackling as it brushed against her knee.

I gave her hand an extra tight squeeze. I felt a pang of fear, as though my grip on her was tenuous, as though she had never really been mine to hold on to. They say that you only have temporary custody of your children, that they are not yours to own. How true this felt in that moment. She was her own little person with her own journey to make. How much influence I had over her narrative was anyone's guess.

'Can I do my maths after supper?'

'Okay. Just this once,' I said, knowing I'd been duped.

'Thanks, Mummy.'

'How d'you get away with it, eh?' I grinned, pinging off her head-torch and switching it off.

'Because you love me so much?' she asked cheekily.

'That's exactly why,' I agreed, laughing, and kissing the top of her head.

When Rosie and I were getting along, I felt at peace in the world. It was all I had ever wanted for us: to enjoy the journey as mother and daughter, to feel I was guiding her towards a happy future. And as we went back inside, I hoped the sense of calm would last.

# CHAPTER TWO

Mira sank into the hot steaming water. It was a little too hot. She liked it that way. Her skin prickled with pleasure as she slowly submerged her body up to her neck. The bubbles crackled in her ear. The water near-scolded her skin.

Her bath should have been the most peaceful time of her day, but there were antics next door. The raised voices were turning to screams. She put her book down on the towel and reached for her phone and earphones, forced to listen to the words instead of reading them, to block the noise out. The audio book had been Barry's suggestion.

He was probably sick of her complaining about next door, but Mira couldn't bear the screaming. A child in distress was the worst, most abhorrent, heinous sound for her. As if it wasn't bad enough to hear it at work, she thought, pressing her flannel into her eyes.

It was the only part of her job that she couldn't stomach. The tears in the playground, the fights, the yelps of joy, she didn't mind. It was the gut-wrenching screams that she found impossible; when a child was really hurting, inside rather than out. She believed she could tell the difference. If she had it her way, she would make it her business to keep every single one of those children at Woodland Primary happy, all the time.

Maybe it was because she didn't have her own children. If she had her own, she supposed she would worry only about her own. Although, that's what frustrated her most about the parents she had to deal with at school. It was all about what their own precious little Johnnys or Marys needed. There was very little concern about the bigger picture, for their community. Like the parents who parked on the zigzags every single morning, who didn't seem to care that a child might get run over because they obstructed the crossing, just as long as they were not late for work or for their yoga class. The culprits were usually the 'Down From London's or DFLs, as Mira and Barry called them. They made Mira cross. Really cross.

'Hello love? Are you decent?' Barry said, knocking, rat-a-tat-tat. He would always wait ten or so minutes before he came in for a chat, to give her time to read at least a few pages of her book. The earplugs were in her ears and the narrator was speaking but she realised she hadn't listened to a word of it.

Nudging the door open with one shoulder, Barry came in with a tray, which carried a tall glass of Prosecco that twinkled at her invitingly. Next to the glass, Barry had prepared a bowl of broken up bits of Curly Wurly chocolate bar. Her favourite.

'Here you go. Thought you'd need it after today,' he said, placing it on the chair by her head.

'Thanks, my dear. What a lucky wife I am.' She stretched her neck and puckered her lips to give him a wet, bubbly kiss.

He settled down in the wicker chair in the alcove by the small window. Beyond the flowered blind was the Bradleys' house, almost close enough to reach out and touch.

'So, how was it today?' Barry asked. His spectacles magnified his brown eyes and his grey hair was combed neatly to one side. Like a schoolboy, Mira thought.

'Seemed to go well. They asked loads of questions, and they smiled quite a bit, which I thought was a good sign. Patricia was in a tiz-woz though.'

'Well, it's her head on the line if you don't get "outstanding" again.'

'Whatever happened to "good"? Good doesn't seem to be good enough anymore.'

'It's all those mums like whatshername next door who come into this area with their big cars and expect all sorts of nonsense.'

'Gemma and Peter send their kids private.'

'Still. It's mums like her that cause all the trouble.'

As if on cue, a muffled yowl emanated from the Bradleys' marble-tiled family bathroom. Mira knew it had marble tiles because one of the tradesmen had shown her round the house before the Bradleys had moved in. She had lied to the plumber, introducing herself as Gemma's sister, which was laughable considering how different they looked. Mira was built big, with a round, tough body topped off by her short, blunt grey hair and ruddy tan. It was baffling to Mira that Gemma, with her wispy hair and skinny bottom, could be Head Honcho of Blah-Blah Department at some fancy bank. Amazingly, the plumber hadn't questioned their contrasting appearances. If she'd come in wearing a balaclava and carrying a swag bag, he probably wouldn't have cared. No respect for his client, plainly. She had guessed that Gemma had treated him badly, barked orders at him and forgot to make him tea. That was five years ago now, Mira mused, staggered by how quickly time flew.

'Funny how she never liked the blue bucket.'

'Seemed innocent enough.'

'Maybe they don't like you,' Mira said, blowing a mountain of bubbles at Barry.

'Thanks a bundle,' he laughed, wiping his glasses.

Submerging further into the water again, she asked, 'How was *your* day?'

'I did the roses at Lower Barn and Mrs Cranbourne hovered over me all day. Sometimes I wonder why she doesn't do them herself. Although, she is a love. Quite chatty.'

'Oh yeah? Pretty is she, too?'

'She's about hundred and five!'

Mira cleared the bubbles to see how her breasts were bobbing on the surface. Maybe this was why she liked baths so much. It was the only time when her body defied gravity and looked perky.

'I *feel* about a hundred and five sometimes,' she said.

'Well, you look about *twenty*-five,' Barry said, reaching out to wiggle her big toe. Mira wondered whether marriage-goggles, like beer-goggles, were a thing. Barry didn't seem to see her with any real clarity. In his eyes, she had stayed exactly the same since the day they married twenty years ago. She wasn't complaining. With her fiftieth birthday coming up next year, she was grateful for his marriage-goggles.

'Tell me about Mrs Cranbourne,' Mira said, adjusting the folded towel behind her head.

She liked his stories about his clients. It was vicarious curtain-twitching. Not that he was a natural raconteur. He would drone on and on sometimes, adding too much detail. She would dip in and out, piqued by certain facts: like Mr Ingham's habit of clipping his toenails into his wife's flowerpots when the sun was shining, and young Danny Clark's progress on the motorbike dirt-track that he was building for his five-year-old in his back garden, or Mrs Bloom's naked swimming.

A high-pitched, sustained wail rang out from the Bradleys' bathroom next door. *'You've hurt me, Mummy!'*

On and on she screamed.

Barry, usually impervious to the noises of next door, stopped speaking for a second and glanced at Mira nervously.

To Mira, the screaming sounded like fingernails down a blackboard. She put her hands over her ears. She could still hear her, as though it were her own scream. Her own scream. And then a splash and a race through the waves at Climping beach. Ten years old again. Exhilarated, terrified, chasing through the seaweed, squishy and slimy under her feet. A flash of sunlight bleached her memory.

Or was it the streetlight. Barry had flicked open the blind to peer out.

The split screen of Barry, here and now, and the other half, her past.

Mira spoke over her past, as it romped through one half of her mind.

'Should we be worried?' Mira said, releasing her hands.

The screaming continued, even louder now, as though the window had been opened. Mira's head throbbed. A pebble hard into her back. Her knees buckling into the brown stinking mush. Another pebble into her head. Her mother's laughter. Or was it her sister's?

'We've been through this, Mira love. It's just family life, that's all.' Barry let go of the blind.

'The poor little pet, she's in real distress. Do you think I should go round there?'

'Barbara's kids used to scream like that when they had their hair brushed. Don't you remember on that holiday in Cornwall?'

'But they were only little 'uns and Rosie next door must be at least eleven now, no?'

'Maybe so, but when Barbara...'

There was another rattling cry. And then a string of unintelligible admonishments from, she could only assume, Gemma Bradley. It was certainly a female adult shouting back. The tone of her voice was certainly nasty.

'Maybe we should sell up and move,' Mira said, meaning it this time.

'You can't escape families. They're everywhere.' He pushed his glasses up and rubbed his face under them. It made him look like he had no eyes.

'I'm sure some are quieter.'

*Mum would turn in her grave if we sold this house*, Mira thought, pre-empting Barry.

'Mum would turn in her grave if we sold this house,' Barry said.

'If we downsized, we'd have a few spare pennies. We could do that cruise around the fjords,' she said, believing she could really do it. Downsizing and holidays abroad had, in the past, seemed like an exhausting prospect, but maybe she could do it if she changed gear a little.

'Maybe when I retire,' Barry said.

'Yes,' she sighed, knowing they would never sell up and cruise in Norway. Barry's mother didn't haunt the house, but she certainly haunted Barry. The meddling old bag, Mira thought. However hard Mira had tried to live up to her expectations, Mrs Entwistle had never forgiven her for marrying her one and only son.

'And as for Barbara. Gee whizz, she would have a...' he began.

Mira wanted his talking to drown out Rosie's screaming, but it didn't. The noise entered Mira's bones. She slipped down into the bath until her head was covered. The water pressing on her eardrums, deadening the sound of Barry's monologue. She was surprised she could hear his words so clearly. Then she heard the bathroom door opening or shutting. She jumped, sitting up straight, feeling the cold air flare goose-bumps across her arms. Barry had left her. She patted her hair. It was bone dry, as was the skin on her cheeks. She could have sworn she had been under the water. The water was suddenly cold and she leapt out of the bath towards her warmed towel on the heated rail, knocking over the champagne glass.

Still dripping, unnerved, she padded downstairs, leaving wet footprints in the pink carpet.

She could hear Barry in the kitchen, clearing things away.

In Barry's study, or 'music room' as he called it, she stepped over his dusty guitar and his exercise bike and knelt on the floor in front of the chest of drawers. Quietly, so as not to alert Barry, she pulled open the drawer to find the large photograph album. The pink material covering the bindings was watermarked like ribbon. It was smooth under her fingertips.

The tissue paper separating the stiff pages rustled as she turned them. A few of the tiny plastic stickers that her sister had painstakingly fixed to the corners of the square instant snaps had come away from the paper. The photos dangled limply like her memories. She flicked through them, knowing exactly which photograph she wanted to look at.

*Climping Beach, 1976, Me, Mira and Mum* was written underneath it in her sister's spidery fountain pen writing. For some reason, when she looked at this faded photograph, her mouth felt dry and her heart beat faster.

It had been a happy day, hadn't it? Their smiles were in their eyes. Their skin brushed by sunlight. She could almost see her chest heaving after a swim in the sparkling sea that lapped at their feet. A flawless summer's day. The colour of her mother's jumper looked yellow in the photograph, but it had been orange back then, back in 1976. Bright orange and scratchy on Mira's face. The smell of the damp, hot wool on a summer's day came rushing back to her. Her mother was always cold. And that dress. Mira's only dress. She put her face closer to the photograph and squinted at the little dots over the white cotton, which she remembered as tiny, brown flowers. One of the thin straps would always fall off her shoulder, as it had in the photograph. She had forgotten about that dress.

The screaming was getting louder, like a siren in her ears, it never stopped. She ripped her towel from her body and buried her head in it.

Barry was behind her. She must have cried out.

'No, no, shush-shush, not this again, Mira, shush-shush,' Barry said, kneeling beside her.

Mira felt her nakedness keenly as though she was in front of a stranger. Perhaps she was the stranger. For twenty-five years, they had learned each other's rhythms and habits and moods, intimately, but there were times when Mira felt like a fraud. He saw her one way; she knew different. He had pigeonholed her as a good person, someone worth loving; she knew different.

Barry untangled the towel from her head, wrapped it around her, and held her.

For a moment, she was comforted, slumped into him, allowing his gentle rocking to soothe her. But he continued talking. 'Rosie's not yours to worry about. She's safe,' he said. 'You're safe, with me, here.'

His words irritated her, made her itch under his touch. She wriggled free of him and wiped her wet cheeks with the towel.

'This isn't about me, Barry. I have to go over there to check she's all right. Just to check.'

Barry scratched at the curly grey hairs sticking out of his shirt and sighed.

'Okay, love, if it'll make you feel any better,' Barry said, letting her go.

# CHAPTER THREE

Rosie and Noah had pushed me to the edge. They had fought over the soap in the bath; they had smeared toothpaste on their clean pyjamas; they had upended three toy boxes, twice; they had performed acrobats on their beds, messing up the sheets. I had barked orders at them in a low-level bad temper until they were both in bed, ten minutes or so before Peter was due home at nine o'clock.

After tidying the kitchen and preparing supper number two, I trudged upstairs to make sure that the children's lights were still out. Noah was splayed out, eyes half closed. I picked up his teddy and placed it in the crook of his arm and he smiled sleepily at me. In Rosie's room, I saw the glow of her torch under the duvet. The sense of failure was monumental. Every ounce of patience evaporated in an instant.

'What the hell do you think you're doing?'

'Nothing.'

I whipped back her covers and she quickly snapped the cover closed on her pink, plastic diary.

'It's nine-thirty!' I cried.

'I couldn't sleep.'

I pointed at the diary. 'Give it to me, please.'

The cheap, box-like contraption, sold as a 'Secret Teen Diary', contained a large pink notepad that was hidden behind a special battery-operated flip-door. It was her favourite possession. She wrote in it every day, delighting in the special code-pad that locked it up.

'I was just finishing the page, that's all.'

'I'm afraid you've pushed me too far this time,' I said, shaking my head, trying to take it out of her hands.

Rosie held on tight, wailing like a siren. 'I've got to put the light back in properly!'

I let go of it, allowing her to slowly and carefully press the mini plastic arm of the LED light into the slot above the diary door, and click the two pens into the side panel. Reluctantly, she handed it over.

'Right. This is confiscated for a week,' I said, putting the diary high on the top of her bookshelf.

She let out a scream of protest. 'You can't confiscate it, Mummy! I need it.'

I heard Noah's door slamming. He probably knew what was coming, just as I did.

Standing stock still, I closed my eyes and crossed my arms over my chest. Her small fists pummelled at my thighs and her finger-nails ripped at my shirt and her scream penetrated my brain like a thousand pinpricks.

Her temper had shot from zero to one hundred in seconds.

'Give it back!' she yelped, leaping up pointlessly at the top shelf where her diary lay. 'It's mine!'

As her piercing, high-pitched shrieking bore into me, I tried to disassociate. I dug my nails into my arms to counteract the pain Rosie was inflicting, to quell the panic that now mingled with the anger. I felt dizzy in the dark behind my eyelids. Opening them, I looked over Rosie's head to fixate on the pretty polka-dot curtains I had chosen for her.

During Rosie's tantrums, when she loathed me with such ferocity, I lost that reassuring sense that I was in charge of my own destiny. That wail of hers! How it cut into me. While in the grip of it, she personified absolute chaos, carnage, collapse.

'You can have it back in five days,' I said, reducing the sentence, wishing I had not started this, wishing I had let her continue writing in her diary all night.

'But I need it!' she yelled back.

The timer for my and Peter's supper rang out from the kitchen. I tried to prize her limbs from my body to walk downstairs, but she slid along with my steps.

I stopped walking, worried she'd hurl herself down the stairs. She circled me, tugging at me, hitting me, weakening the barrier of calm with every bruising throw of her fist. It was like the whole world stopped turning while that noise deafened me, echoed through the house, shaking the walls, piercing enough to break glass.

'You don't understand!' she wailed. She lunged at the wreath she'd made which was now lying on her beanbag, and hurled it at me. It whizzed past my head and hit the banisters behind me, leaves and acorns coming loose.

'That's a shame,' I said, picking it up and putting it back on her beanbag.

'It's your fault!'

'You threw it,' I said, wondering why I felt the need to qualify that.

She let out a shriek so loud it felt like my brain was splitting in two. '*I HATE YOU!*'

I tried to move away again, to get downstairs to turn the oven off, but it would have been dangerous to go near the stairs while she was thrashing about at my feet.

'Get out of my way,' I said through clenched teeth. She clamped her arms around my ankles and writhed on the floor.

'Daddy's supper's burning.'

It was like having a rabid dog snap and bite and growl at my feet, while the noise of her screaming was like a bird squawking as it circled around my head. Fear and powerlessness overwhelmed me, and then a biting resentment took chunks out of my sense of reason until it was physically painful to resist retaliating.

A black fog of rage rose from the pit of my stomach. I didn't know how to stop her.

'Get off me, Rosie.' I tried to prize her off my legs, but her grip was too tight. I pushed her body away from mine, but she lashed out, leaping up and slapping at my head. The more I struggled the tighter she coiled herself around me. I was trapped. It was suffocating. I couldn't breathe; I couldn't find a way out.

'THAT'S ENOUGH!' I bellowed, deep, guttural and frightening.

Violent images of my hand across her head flew into my mind. I wasn't the kind of mother who hit her children. But the image came again and again. Every obstructive twist of her body around mine as I tried to walk downstairs to where our supper would be burning brought another appalling image of my hand at her head, my loss of control, my physical power against hers. My mind wiped out the abhorrent thoughts and a more superficial fury consumed me.

I grabbed her by the arm and yanked her kicking and screaming back into her bedroom and onto her bed. I slammed the door, and held it shut. The panels bowed and cracked with each of her kicks. She pulled it open harder, and I slid along the carpet under her strength as I clung to the doorknob. I was completely out of control. As I tried to pull it closed again, her little arm shot through the gap and the door slammed onto it. I let go and she went flying onto the floor behind her.

'You hurt me Mummy!' she howled, cradling her arm, rolling around on the floor.

'Let me see?' I barked.

She stopped writhing to show me her arm. The small, raised welt on her wrist sent a shock of guilt through me.

'Can you move it?' I asked, just to make sure.

'It stings!' she cried, flapping her hand back and forth easily. It was clear the injury wasn't serious. Relief flooded through me.

'Into bed, Rosie,' I said, through gritted teeth, unable to show sympathy, unable to apologise, while she, too, was unable to back down. She resumed her rolling around. We were in deadlock.

I left her there and stormed downstairs, away from her.

The relentless screaming continued, emptying me out further, the stress killing me slowly, surely.

Dry-eyed, I was desperate to cry, to be weak, to collapse, but I clung with both hands to the edge of the kitchen sink, terrified that if I let go I would fly at her in a rage.

I would not cry. I never cried. I was Helen Campbell's daughter. Campbell women didn't do crying.

I thought of Mira next door. Her kitchen window was only a few feet away from ours. During the renovations, Peter and I had decided to keep our drafty Crittal frames for the aesthetic, in spite of the flimsy glass. Now I wished we had thick double-glazed PVC. There were lights twinkling through the thinning hedge that separated our houses. Sometimes I could hear Mira chatting to Barry. If she had been standing in her kitchen now, or feeding the hens down the side alley, she would have heard me shout like that. It was shaming. Heat crossed my cheeks.

And then I heard Peter's voice. He was home. I pressed my fingers into my eyeballs and heaved a deep, deep sigh of relief.

'What's going on here, then?' Peter said, jangling his keys. 'I could hear you all the way down the road.'

'Daddy! Come up here!' Rosie cried from the landing. Her hero.

I turned to see Peter perform an exaggerated march upstairs, swinging his arms like a soldier. 'What's all this racket about, young lady?' he hollered officiously.

Rosie giggled.

I turned the oven off and I saw how my fingers shook. The skin of the chicken breasts was blackened. It would be inedible. Still, I moved on autopilot and brought two plates out and laid the knives and forks and poured two glasses of water.

By the time Peter came down again, there was silence from Rosie's room.

He kissed me on the cheek, but I couldn't look at him.

'What's she up to now?' I whispered through clenched teeth, trying to control the tremor in my voice. I was raw from the after effects of rage. It still coursed through my veins, pumping my body with unwanted adrenalin. The flash of Rosie's red wrist sent a shiver of horror down my spine.

'She's in bed,' Peter said, matter-of-fact.

'Seriously? Why does she do it for you and not for me?'

'I told her I'd buy her a cream egg.'

I swivelled round and glared at him, our first eye contact of the day. 'You didn't!'

'Of course I didn't!' he laughed. His well-mannered bone structure and the arresting clarity of his light grey-blue eyes were like a tonic on my soul. His pale hair had recently begun to recede. I thought it rather suited him. The peak at the front was ruffled to the side. His straight brow and long straight nose were a T-shape, lending his face grace and straightforwardness.

That face of his; how I loved it.

He reached for the bottle of Chablis in the fridge and two glasses from the cupboard.

'Want one?' he said.

'I shouldn't.'

'A few sips won't hurt.'

'Go on, then. Just half,' I said, taking the glass gladly.

'Cheers big ears,' he said, taking two large gulps as he checked his phone.

The chilly acidic hit was instantly soothing.

'Why are you home so late?' It sounded like an accusation. I was still experiencing tremors of fury.

'M25.'

I felt bad. His commute in the car to and from his office every day was three hour round trip.

'Sorry. That tantrum was hell on earth.'

'It sounded like she was being murdered.'

'Look what she did!' I proffered my arm, showing him the red scratches.

'Maybe you should tell her she can't go to Charlotte's birthday party.'

'No, no, it's fine,' I said. Honestly, I felt responsible for Rosie's tantrum. I had confiscated her diary, which I knew was the one tool she used to get herself to sleep. I should have let it go. I had done it all wrong. I was the worst mother in the universe.

'But she's ten years old!' Peter cried.

'It's normal. I've read about it loads online.' I was back-tracking.

But Peter went on. 'If I'd treated my mum like that when I was her age I would have got a clip round the ear.'

I was unable to tell him how uselessly I had managed her, how I had trapped her wrist in a laughable struggle, how I had imagined my hand whipping Rosie across her cheek to stop her screaming. It was horrifying to have had the thought, and even worse to think that I might have done it if Peter hadn't arrived when he did.

'It might have been a sugar high. Mum gave them two massive chocolate muffins before supper.'

Perking up, Peter said, 'Do you think Rosie might be sugar intolerant? I read about it in the papers the other day.'

'You think?'

It was easier to blame the sugar.

'And she's under a lot of pressure at school,' I added.

Peter looked over his wine glass at me as he sipped. 'Yes, could be that.'

Both of us wanted to believe this.

'Or maybe it's the baby? We only told her last week. She might have been stewing about it.'

He laughed. 'Remember when Noah came along, her hugs were a little terrifying?'

Then Rosie's feet padded down the stairs. Instantly, my hackles rose.

Stay calm, let it go, I thought, taking another sip of wine, relying on it.

'Can I just say sorry?' she sniffed. 'I love you, Mummy.'

I kissed her head and drew her closer. Love for her returned to my heart like magic.

'I love you so much too, you silly thing,' I said, believing in her remorse.

She tightened her little arms around me.

My daughter was a livewire, she was unpredictable, but she was passionate and headstrong and beautiful, with her pastel-pink cheeks and straight hair down her back, as black as the night, and her huge eyes like a clear sky. The loathing and desperation I had felt only half an hour before were so far flung, so diminished, I wondered how it was possible to have felt that way at all.

# CHAPTER FOUR

*Dear Mummy,*

*Anne Frank writes Dear Kitty in her diary. I think Anne Frank pretends that Kitty is listening to her, even though she isn't really. I can pretend that you are listening to me too even though all you do is tell me off. What would you do if you found me writing this now? It was easy to get it down from the shelf. I just stood on my stool. Like DUH!*

*I wish I could fix that wreath for Charlotte. It broke when I threw it. Charlotte said that if she doesn't get a present from me tomorrow, she won't let me come to her birthday party. And it is a BOWLING PARTY and her mum is making her HOMEMADE CHOCOLATE FUDGE CAKE!*

*I wonder what it would be like to have a mummy who makes chocolate fudge cakes, like Charlotte's mummy? Granny Helen said to me that you choose your mummies and daddies. Noah believes her but I know she made it up. It is so silly. Even mummies and daddies don't get to choose their children. WEIRD. Would you choose me?*

*INVISIBLE INK ALERT: I think I would definitely choose Charlotte's mummy. She lets her play Strawberry Killer-Cakes on her phone at bedtime.*

*Better go. If you catch me, you will get cross with me ERRGAIN.*

*Love,*
*Rosie*

*P.S. I am sorry for screaming again.*
*P.P.S. I hate myself.*
*P.P.P.S. My wrist doesn't hurt so much now.*

# CHAPTER FIVE

At first, I didn't recognise her. She was backlit by the garage sensor lights. I thought I had let a stranger in through the gates. Her hair was wet and slicked back, when usually it stuck up at the top like a crew cut.

'Oh, hello Mira.'

'Hello Gemma, I was just dropping by because...' she began, but she didn't look at me, she looked past me, into the hallway behind me. 'I wondered if Peter was here?'

'Yes, he's watching telly. Do you want me to get him?'

I was desperate for her to leave, wished I'd never answered the doorbell. The last thing I needed was Mira. The noise of the gates opening and the gravel under her heavy step could rouse Rosie again, and if she started up again, I would shoot myself.

'Oh, right.' She paused as if listening out for him. She pulled her fleece tightly around her chest. 'It's just he offered to lend us the lawnmower. Ours is broken.'

'How is Barry working without a lawnmower?'

'Oh, most of his clients have sit-on-tops,' she replied absent-mindedly, moving from one foot to the other, taking another peek beyond me, into my house.

'Right. I'll just go get him.' I checked my watch, thinking it was rude of her to drop round so late to ask about the lawnmower. I had just put two salmon steaks in the oven, and I didn't want them to burn like the chicken had.

'Oh, okay, yes,' she replied, as if she wasn't quite sure why she was there all of a sudden.

And then I clicked. She must have heard my fight with Rosie. I felt the damp seep through my stretched sleeves, which were clenched in my fingertips, the wool sticky in my palms. This wasn't a casual visit from Mira. This wasn't to notify us that we had waited too long to cut the hedges; to tell us that we had left our bins out on the wrong day; to inform us that the house alarm had rung for an hour before the police had turned up; to inform us of how many lights we'd left on while we'd been away; to pass comment on how much fun we seemed to be having at the dinner parties we held. I could tell by her demeanour.

Generally, Mira was jolly, ruddy and chatty; the kind of woman who makes homemade biscuits to put in the blue bucket for the cheeky little girl next door. Now, in the murky glow of my half-lit hallway, she stood wide and seemed edgy. If I turned her away, or made excuses, I would look like I had something to hide. Did I have anything to hide?

'Would you like to come in for a glass of something? Peter has opened a bottle already.'

'Oh, okay, if it's not too late?'

'No, no, do come in.' *Yes, nine o'clock is too late when you have to get up at five thirty*, I thought.

She was looking around at the shiny fittings and furniture as though a nasty surprise lurked ready to jump out at her. I saw my house through her eyes. It was probably unnecessarily luxurious. Too much velvet and crisp linen; too many expensive surfaces and designer lines.

Mira sat down at the kitchen table, wobbling it. The unsettled flame of the scented candle let out a plume of black smoke.

'Lovely kitchen,' she said, taking a sip of wine.

'Thanks, we had it done last year by a dad at the kids' school. If you want to do yours, I'll text you his number, if you like, he's really good. He sourced really cheap work surfaces for us. I mean, usually they cost a fortune. Just let me know,' I droned, trailing off, knowing she wasn't the kind of woman to update her kitchen. She probably thought I was such a cliché.

'We've still got Barry's mum's kitchen. The cupboards are an ugly old mush green but they do the job.'

'Yes, of course, I'm sure. It doesn't really matter, does it? I mean, honestly, I never used to care about what my kitchen units looked like. Now, I don't know, it kind of seems like the thing to do round here. Like I might have fewer friends if I didn't have a nice kitchen,' I laughed, only half-joking. Her presence was unsettling me.

Mira cocked her head at me sympathetically, as if I had made a confession. I suppose I had, in a way. In this small town, the obsession with house renovations and the talk of it at dinner parties had probably got to me, on some level. Perhaps it had turned me without me noticing. I filled my empty wine glass with fizzy water, aware that the half-glass of Chablis had gone straight to my head.

'Well, we're all the same. I spent such a lot of money on new curtains from John Lewis for our lounge, to match our cushions, you know? And as soon as Barry had put them up I hated them. What a waste. Silly, isn't it?'

I was so grateful to her for being kind, I laughed, a little too loudly and enthusiastically, and relaxed a little. She grinned and took another sip of wine. Her hair was bouncing back as it dried, shooting up from her widow's peak.

'Yes, it is silly. Very silly,' I agreed. I decided that I had been paranoid to suspect she had come round because of Rosie. A fast-forward replay of my row with Rosie pricked my consciousness, but only briefly. All young children screamed, and Mira of all people would know this. At Woodlands, she would be surrounded by screaming children all day long.

'Gosh, sorry Mira, I was supposed to get Peter for you, wasn't I? He's in the den. You can't hear the doorbell from there. I'll be back in a minute.'

I nipped down the corridor, feeling swimmy from the wine. While pregnant with Rosie and Noah, I had never allowed myself more than a few sips of champagne on special occasions, and I was reminded of why.

Peter was lying stretched out on the sofa with his hand down his trousers, scratching his balls. The sound of racing cars screeched from the television.

'Peter, didn't you hear the doorbell?' I whispered.

'No, who was it?'

'It's Mira, from next door. She's here in the kitchen having a drink.'

'What? What the hell?' he said, sitting up and untwisting his shirt.

'She wanted to talk to you about borrowing our lawnmower.'

'Oh hell. Can't *you* talk to her about it?'

'I didn't know we even owned a lawnmower.'

'How d'you think Luke mowed our lawn? With nail clippers?' he asked, cocking an eyebrow at me, plainly amused, plainly half-cut already.

'Oh, stop it, I don't know, just come through will you?'

He padded after me in his socks with his empty wine glass in one hand.

'Hello Mira! What a lovely surprise!' he bellowed, pushing his hand into hers affectionately.

'Hello, Peter. Sorry, I'm not staying,' she said, not moving an inch.

'A drop more?' He topped up her glass and poured another one for himself. 'What were you two gassing about?' he asked, as though we were long-lost friends.

'Kitchens,' Mira laughed.

'Oh Lord. You don't want me to pay for another one, do you darling?' Peter said. The mischief lit his eyes. I was the one who had paid for the kitchen.

'No, no, I was just telling Mira how much I loved slaving over a hot stove for you darling, night and day. Filled with gratitude for all that you provide, my Lord and Master.'

Peter and I laughed together. The hell of bedtime, and Rosie, and my rage, slipped away into the background.

'Us women know how to keep our families happy, don't we just?' Mira laughed.

'Right, indeed,' Peter said, clapping his hands. 'Now, I'll just get you the keys for the shed. The code for the gate is 2211. So you can nip in to get it any time you like.'

'Oh, that is very kind, thank you,' Mira said, looking over to me as she stood up.

I forced out a smile out and nodded. 'Yes, of course, brilliant, that's fine,' I said, irritated by Peter's gesture. I didn't want her wandering into our home any time she liked. I hadn't even given the gate code to my mother, or Rosie.

'Mummy?'

My smile dropped away. Rosie appeared in the doorway in her pink nightgown like a ghostly apparition. I wanted to scream.

Mira turned to see who it was.

Peter caught my eye briefly. 'Rosie, darling. What are you doing up again? Come on, up to bed,' he said, trying to lead her away. Rosie wouldn't budge.

I pushed Mira's chair under the table and straightened it to match the other chairs. 'I'll see you to the door Mira. Off to bed, now, Rosie, poppet. Daddy'll take you up,' I said, trying to sound flippant, unfazed.

'But I want *you*, Mummy. I can't sleep.'

'Why can't you sleep, pet?' Mira asked, crouching down to her level.

'My wrist is hurting.'

'Oh dear. What did you do to it?' Mira said, pulling up her sleeve to inspect it.

The red groove looked angrier than before.

'Nothing,' Rosie said, glancing up at me.

My heart was in my mouth.

From her haunches, Mira twisted her head, still holding Rosie's arm, and frowned at me. The kitchen down-lighters cast long eyelash shadows on her cheeks, like clown tears.

'She slammed her bedroom door on her hand. Isn't that right, Rosie?' I said, looking to Rosie for confirmation.

Rosie looked up at me as though she was looking up at an ogre. Her blue eyes were wide, smudges of tiredness ringing them. Her skin glowed a frightening white. Her chin wobbled and dimpled.

Trying to hide my agitation and my guilt, I rolled my eyes at Mira, about to say, 'Look at this madam, with all her drama!'

Mira did not give me the chance to say anything. She dropped Rosie's arm and fled, towards the front door, past Peter who was pulling the shed key from the hooks in the boot room.

'I'll come by for the lawn mower tomorrow,' she said from behind her fingers, which were pressed to her mouth, and she disappeared into the gloom outside.

Peter emerged from the boot room dangling the keys on one finger. 'What an earth spooked her?'

'You shouldn't have given her the gate code,' I barked, storming past him. 'Get upstairs Rosie, or there'll be trouble. Up, up, up,' I said, smacking her bottom gently as she ran upstairs.

Before she turned the corner at the top of the stairs, I caught a satisfied smirk on Rosie's pretty little face.

*

Finally, after settling her again, Peter and I were at the kitchen table with our supper in front of us. I chewed with my head bent low, shattered.

'The one thing I dreaded most about moving out to the country was the idea of busybodies like Mira interfering in our business.'

'It's just good community spirit.'

I couldn't tell if he was serious or not.

Sometimes I regretted that Peter and I had moved out of London to this house. Technically it was perfect, a dream house, a dream location, tucked away in a bucolic market town in an expensive enclave of the Home Counties. Most days Rosie and Noah ambled to and from their school on their own, across the green expanse of the recreational ground, past cricket or tag-rugby matches, straight to our sweet garden gate at the bottom of the garden. They breathed clean air and their bellies were filled with fruit and vegetables and wholegrain. The crime-free fields of green were a hop-skip-and-a-jump down a country lane. The views of treetops and shimmering lakes – and the odd swimming pool thrown in – would be the backdrop to their childhoods. If suits of cotton wool were available at John Lewis, I would have clicked and collected, and wrapped them both up tightly in them. I worked bloody hard to pay for our exclusive spot on this hill. But often I loathed it and everything that it represented.

'We're extremely community spirited,' I protested. 'We have Vics and Jim two doors down for starters.'

'We only know them because we send our kids to the same private school,' he said, spitting 'private school' as though it was a dirty phrase, adding, 'New Hall Prep isn't exactly inclusive, let's face it.'

'It's a really good school,' I said, knowing Peter had never liked it. He thought they pushed them too hard. He had wanted Rosie to go to the picturesque Woodlands Primary on the green, with the forest school and the front door that was covered in children's colourful handprints, reminding him of the school he had been to as a child.

'But we lead such separate lives from all those other parents. We don't even see Vics and Jim that often, and they're our best friends.'

'We're all too busy paying for the school fees.'

I glanced over at the whiteboard, scribbled on in blue and red marker – blue for Noah, red for Rosie – to find an hour when we might have time to nip round to someone's, anyone's, house spontaneously. Unless we dropped an afterschool club or decided that homework could be skipped, there was no spare time. Even at the weekends, both children had tennis club on Saturday morning, followed by Rosie's tap class, and our family trip to the gym for swim-time, which would be followed by more homework. On Sundays, I would take Noah to mini-rugby training first thing, while Rosie and Peter would go on a bike ride. And then we'd head to our regular table at the pub in the next village, where we'd eat a roast next to the roaring fire, often with Vics, Jim and Beth, and usually play chess tournaments on the sofas afterwards, unless I had work to do.

Peter looked out of the window whimsically. 'It was like a free-for-all at my house growing up. Aunt Sophie lived two doors down and Uncle Teddy lived in the next street and my cousins ran into our garden through the back hedge.'

'Your family is weird.'

'I'm sure it was easier bringing up kids back then,' Peter reflected. 'When Granny Cilla lived with us, Mum used to nip over to Aunt Sophie's for a cup of tea and she'd leave me with Granny and I'd sneak out without her noticing and trike round to Mrs Denbigh's for some squash and a soggy digestive.'

'How old were you?'

'Four, five.'

'Couldn't your granny've got you a drink and biscuit herself?'

'She thought elves lived in the biscuit tin.'

'And your mum didn't worry about leaving you with her?'

'She was normal a lot of the time.'

'My worst nightmare,' I said, absent-mindedly, thinking about where the instructions were for the electric gate so that I could change the code.

'Having dementia?'

'That too. But living with my mum would literally be my second worst nightmare.'

'Probably hers, too,' he snorted.

I laughed. 'She's always said Jacs and I should stick her in a home if it comes to it.'

'Strange that,' Peter mused. 'You'd think she'd want to hang out with the kids and help out.'

'I don't need any help. I've got Harriet,' I said, flicking through the stack of manuals in the kitchen drawer.

I heard him open the fridge and pour more wine into his own glass.

'It might be a good idea to take a cake round to Mira or something. Show a bit of old-fashioned neighbourly spirit, no?' he said.

'Why don't you?'

'Go round?'

'Yes, if you're so keen.'

'Just thought it would be a nice thing to do, that's all.' He looked hurt and I wished I were more magnanimous.

'You know, I would go round but I'm always so knackered when I get home.'

'Maybe I will go round,' he mumbled as he padded off across the heated floorboards in his socks, probably to watch sport on television.

We both knew he wouldn't go round.

'Found them!' I cried triumphantly to myself, brandishing the instructions to nobody.

The night air was damp up my sleeves and licking my collar. My mobile phone torch lit the way to the black gates, which loomed larger in the dark. A bat flitted high in the sky above my head as I tapped away at the keypad. Mira could probably hear the blue neon keypad beep away as I reset the entry code, and I felt embarrassed at the thought of her watchful eye, as though she saw me in a way that no others saw me, as though she had found me out.

While both Peter and I had done anything and everything to keep her at arm's length up until now, Peter's fresh desire to make an approach unnerved me. I wondered if there was more to it. Just as a criminal with pockets stuffed with stolen goods might be particularly well mannered or chatty around a suspicious shopkeeper, I wondered whether Peter sensed danger.

# CHAPTER SIX

Mira felt her way through the shadows of furniture to the kettle, which she switched on in the dark. The rushing noise competed with the sound of blood coursing through her ears. A little girl from school had told her that without ears we wouldn't be able to stand up properly. She held her hands at her ears, to check, to find balance somehow. Her fingers felt cold, and she tucked them into her underarms, wet through her fleece. When the white steam from the boiling water billowed up into the ceiling, she pictured putting her fingers onto the spout to stop it.

At the foldout table, she cradled her mug. There was a stack of opened letters and bills lying in front of her. The knife that Barry had used to open them was lying on top. Barry would systematically slip into and slice through every envelope that came through the door, regardless of the addressee. It was a habit that infuriated Mira, but he insisted he couldn't read the small print of the names written on the front. Mira did not believe him. He liked to know everything. How little he really knew. There had been a time when she had intercepted the post every day. He hadn't known that, now, had he?

The tea tasted watery and too milky as she sipped it.

She reached into the pocket of her fleece for her mobile phone and scrolled through her contacts list. The *A*s, the *B*s, down to the *P*s. She stopped at 'Police Station', listed simply as 'Police Station', just as she had 'Health Centre' and 'School' and 'Hairdressers' listed. It wasn't necessary to call 999, was it?

Rosie's wrist had been soft and light in her hands. She had wanted to kiss her better. She had wanted to be sick onto Gemma's pristine shiny floors.

What was happening over there now?

Cold to hot, her mobile slipped with sweat. She knew PC Yorke worked nights on Mondays. If she talked to him, she could talk to him off the record, as a friend, describe what she had seen: her suspicions, her doubts. Did 'off the record' exist in a policeman's life? Were local policemen ever allowed to make their own judgment calls? He was part of a chain of command. He would lose his job if anything happened to the girl. Then again, if she told PC Yorke, she would be passing the responsibility over. It was an appealing thought.

But what would she tell him? What had she actually seen next door? Her heartbeat escalated. *What had she seen?* She had seen guilt in Gemma's eyes. She had seen fear in Rosie's.

She sipped her tea and listened out, as though her hearing could hone in on Rosie's bedroom. Dead silence. Deadened perhaps.

She felt a draft down the back of her neck from the open window. Then a numbing sense of cold engulfed her. A dress-strap fell from her shoulder. But when she touched her arm to pull it up, she realised she was still wearing the fleece she had put on earlier this evening. She was disoriented, fearful. Her mind was playing tricks on her, dragging her somewhere she didn't want to go, like the tides sucking at a pebble on the shoreline. The tides. The beach. What was her memory trying to retrieve? She wanted to push whatever it was back down, but she was unable to. A vivid recollection came to her of a thud against her bare right shoulder. A hot circle of pain. Another stone hit her lower back. Doubled over in agony. Her knees grazed by the sand, the tiny brown flowers of her dress flattened wet against them. The blur of the flowers through her tears.

She remembered covering her head with her arms, waiting for another attack.

'Get up! Your dress'll be wet for the party!' her mother had screeched. 'You stupid girl,' she had cried, pulling her to standing by a strand of hair. 'You stupid, stupid little girl!' Her mother's words echoed through the wind, around her head in gusts as she was dragged back over the dunes. Stumbling and tripping, she saw the Natterjack toads leaping away from her feet, scared away, free to escape. Her sister was scampering ahead, knowing she had got away with it.

Mira stood gasping at the open window of her kitchen, drinking in the fresh air, as though she had just experienced a surge of pain that was now subsiding.

It was still now. Blissfully silent.

She was too tired to make the call to PC Yorke tonight.

Her phone lay redundant on the kitchen table as she climbed the stairs up to bed. Her head lolled forward, the effort to raise it was too much for her.

The light was still on in the bedroom. Barry's detective novel was propped in his hands. His eyes were closed. She slipped under the covers next to him.

'Did I fall asleep?' he said, suddenly sitting bolt upright. 'I hadn't meant to fall asleep! What happened?'

'Don't worry, everything's fine. Nothing to worry about. Go back to sleep.'

He rubbed his eyes, but left his glasses on the side table. 'Did you ask them what was wrong with the girl?'

'Yes, yes, nothing to worry about,' she repeated. 'She hurt her arm in the door.'

'Oh phew. I was worried about you,' he said, before crashing down again. 'Come in for a cuddle.'

She lay blinking in the dark for hours, feeling his chest move up and down against her back, comforted by his ability to sleep deeply.

*

The next morning she found a Post-it note stuck to the kettle:

*Early start at Brook House. Talk later at bath-time. Barry x.*

She was restive, tense about last night, and she felt desperately disappointed that he wasn't there to talk to.

On the tin of teabags, she found another post-it note:

*Love you, Mira Meerkat.*

She smiled. It was the nickname the children in Year Two had given to her. On the first Forest School Tuesday of the winter term, she and the Forest Team Leader and fifteen seven-year-olds had sat on wood stools around the fire to choose forest names for each other. Little Oscar became Oscar Ostrich, and Bella was Bella Badger. When it was Mira's turn, she had worried they would choose Mira Moose, which she would not have been able to laugh about. The very thought of the nickname gave her a twinge of her old self.

'You old softie, Bazzer,' she said out loud, tucking the Post-it into her skirt pocket. 'Now, let's get that egg on,' she added.

Barry would snigger at her when he caught her talking to herself. He said she sounded completely bonkers.

When she saw her phone lying on the table where she had left it last night, she wondered if maybe she was. Gemma Bradley had come across as a charming, affable woman, albeit a little neurotic. Perhaps Rosie was simply a spoilt brat who made her mother's life a misery. Who was Mira to judge? She remembered how she had left their house. How rude she had been, flying out without a proper goodbye. What would Peter have made of her? With a shiver, she realised she must have looked like a loony, and not just in the quaint way Barry viewed her.

As she sat dipping her toast into her egg, dip, dip, dip, thinking more than eating, she heard children's voices next door. She charged up the stairs, knelt on the toilet seat and pushed open the window, just a crack, to see down into the Bradleys' back garden.

Peter Bradley was crouching at Rosie's feet, straightening her tie. She was sulking. He kissed her nose. Her smile was almost there, but not quite. Her cheeks looked tear-stained, unless they were the shadows from the apple tree. The little boy – Noah, she remembered he was called – struggled to put his rucksack on his back. Peter stood by the door in his suit, sipping his cup of coffee as he watched his children walk across the lawn to school.

Noah sped ahead, leaving Rosie slouching behind.

With a horrible start, Mira noticed Rosie was cradling one arm in the other. All the feelings of last night came rushing back. The lightness of Rosie's arm. The fear on the child's face. Somewhere inside her, she recognised this fear.

If she didn't do something about this, she would never forgive herself.

She ran downstairs, checking her watch, knowing she would be late for work if she made the call, knowing she had to make the call.

Her flesh trembled as she scrolled down.

The police station telephone rang and rang. Come on, pick-up. Pick-up! If she didn't do it now, she might lose her nerve. Barry would persuade her out of it. He might not understand what it was like to have a gut feeling about something, to feel with such certainty that something wasn't right. If she waited around for conclusive evidence, it might be too late.

She kneaded her fingers into her thigh, through the cotton of her skirt. Another memory was rolling up through her like nausea. She looked down at her knees. She saw small, wet prints. She saw salt water marks. She saw little brown flowers.

Then she remembered standing in the bathroom of the house she grew up in, at the plastic pink sink with the mirrored cabinet above it. The soap was too thin and it broke in two. She had rubbed it into the brown flowers of her dress until the salt marks had dissolved away. Her sister, Deirdre, had banged on the door. Mira had scrubbed until the skin on her fingers was sore. The dress was limp and sodden on the hanger, like a sad, deflated version of herself. She had run out of the bathroom, ignoring Deirdre's taunts, downstairs to the airing cupboard, where she had draped the dress carefully over the padded red cover of the boiler. It would be dry in time for the party and her mother wouldn't be angry with her.

Forty-five minutes later, she had opened the airing cupboard, ready to slip the warmed material on over her pants, only to find that it had fallen down into its own puddle on the floor. It was as wet as it had been in the sink.

In the car, her grubby corduroy flares and Airtex shirt had crawled with insects, or so she had imagined. She had wanted to rip Deirdre's velvet party dress at the sleeve.

'You're going to be the only one in the whole party who isn't dressed properly,' her mother had ranted as she manoeuvred their Ford Cortina out of their drive. Slumped in the backseat, Mira had watched the 1970s bungalows pass by her window. 'Always the same, you are, just like your father,' her mother had hissed.

Always the same, always causing trouble.

Mira hung up the phone and wiped a layer of sweat from her forehead.

The troublesome Mira had grown-up. The new Mira was a much-loved and relied-upon teaching assistant, loved by the children, loved by the staff, loved by Barry. She was Mira Meerkat, no less.

After work, when Barry was home, she planned to present her dilemma about Rosie Bradley to him, over a glass of something in a relaxing bath, where she could think straight. She would tell him every last detail of last night. If Barry decided she should call PC Yorke, then she would. Nothing was real until she had talked it through with Barry.

Having turned off her phone, she went straight into Barry's office, knelt at the chest of drawers and brought out the album. She opened it up to the page where Deirdre was digging a hole in the flowerbeds next to their mother's roses. Her blonde pudgy sister in red Mary Jane's and a home-knitted cardigan. She was adorable. Seeing her cheeky smile and chubby wrists made Mira feel better. It replaced the vile memory that had resurfaced. It hadn't been all bad when she was little.

Her mind had lost its sense of direction. It seemed to be taking her back, not forward. This horrible business next door had triggered something deep down inside her, and it was bringing to the surface things she'd rather forget. The memories that came to her now felt worse than the reality had been for her back then. Or were they nightmares? Could you have nightmares while awake? Was she going mad?

Stop that. Get over it, Mira, she told herself. Stop these destructive thoughts. Yes, her mother had been strict. So what. Bad memories were bound to pop up from time to time. There was nothing to be scared of.

Before she replaced the album, she noticed the three old Tesco carrier bags that were stuffed full of instant photographs from her childhood. She shuddered. She and Deirdre had found them under their mother's bed after she had died. Although Mira had insisted on taking them, she had never dared to open them. They had been sitting there in the drawer, knotted up, for ten years.

Decisively, Mira lugged each bag out of the drawer and dumped them onto the dining room table.

She heaved a ragged sigh, slurped her cold cup of tea and glared at the bags. 'There, now. I'm not scared of you, see?'

# CHAPTER SEVEN

All of the clothes were pretty. Pink lace trims. Cream faux-fur shrugs. White ruffled shirts. It was a risk to buy a dress for Rosie without her with me.

Nevertheless, I had decided that it was worth it to see the enchantment and surprise on her face when I presented it to her in a smart bag with ribbon and tissue paper. And it would be just in time for Charlotte's birthday party at the weekend. More than anything, I hungered to get rid of the unpleasant aftertaste of our row, to paper over the memory of our disorderly tussle. The skin across my whole body flushed as I thought of her rolling around on the floor holding her wrist.

I picked up the pink patent slip-ons. The shop assistant's ironed blonde hair flicked onto the leather of my handbag as she bent down to straighten the rows I had disrupted.

The minutes were ticking away. I had an hour before I was due back at work to meet my managing director for 'a little chat'. I was nervous about the meeting and flustered with indecision about the dress.

'They are our bestsellers,' the shop assistant said, pushing her tortoise-shell glasses onto her head.

The boutique was too quiet, exclusive, uncomfortably so. I was ready to bolt.

'Very lovely,' I replied politely.

A little girl's dream, surely. My mother had forced me to wear brown buckle-ups until I was twelve. Whenever Rosie had wanted patent leather shoes or slip-ons, I, too, had always said no. This time I would get her what she wanted. Was pink too babyish? Had she grown out of pink? I wasn't sure. I wasn't sure I knew what she liked. Although I pushed that thought aside.

In the baby section, I spotted an adorable stripy Babygro. My hand moved under my coat, to touch, to connect with that tiny six-week-old embryo. I imagined folding new Babygros into the drawers in the spare bedroom, which I would transform into a nursery, with fresh paint and soft rugs. I would reassemble the wooden cot I had used for Rosie and Noah and position it by the window with a view of the apple tree. I wanted to take care to tie the white waffle cot protector to the bars with proper little bows and position a colourful mobile above the changing table. My nesting instincts usually hit me towards the end of my pregnancies, but maybe I would give myself more time to fix the room up this time round.

I refolded the soft Babygro. This was about Rosie, not the baby.

My fingers danced across the dresses on the rail, and stopped at a blue polka-dot dress with a drop waist. I pulled it out, trying to imagine Rosie wearing it. She would look beautiful in anything I bought. I tried to think about what *she* would like. Did she like blue? What was her favourite colour? How awful that I didn't know. I cringed, layering the guilt.

My dithering was bothering me. At work, I was considered focussed and purposeful. I was trained to coolly assess corporate lawyers for the firm, grill them and charm them; analyse them with rigorous psychometric testing, run workshops and make notes on their behaviour. I was employed to recruit dependable workaholic sociopaths to head departments and make the corporate world go round. But I was flummoxed by the task of choosing a dress for my own daughter.

The shop assistant was refolding the Babygro I had just folded. I needed her help. 'Excuse me. I think I do need some help actually. I'm looking for a party dress for my ten-year-old.'

'Of course, madam. What is her colouring?'

'She has beautiful long black hair,' I smiled, warmed by the vision of her. 'And she has lovely pale skin. And big blue eyes.'

The shop assistant's head was cocked to the side. 'She sounds beautiful.'

'She is.' I was slightly embarrassed. All mothers thought their children were beautiful. This woman must have heard it a thousand times before.

'And what's she like?'

'Ummm, well,' I began. The question panicked me. 'She likes to be the boss,' I laughed.

'Okay, so she's quite sophisticated then.'

She walked straight over to a navy-blue dress that was hanging near the shop window. It had one long silk sleeve and the other was shoulder-less.

'It's very elegant...' I began.

'It was featured in *Teen Vogue* last month.'

'*I'd* wear it. But I think it might be a little too sophisticated for her.'

'They grow up too fast these days, don't they?'

'Yes, they do,' I agreed with a tingle of dread as I imagined Rosie as a teenager.

'What about this one?'

It was more like a sundress, with a white sweetheart bodice, detachable spaghetti straps and little daisies dotted across the skirt. It was the kind of dress I would have dreamed of wearing as a child. I took it from the shop assistant, felt the crisp cotton and noticed the yellow gauze that filled out the underskirt.

'Perfect. The yellow will look lovely with her dark hair. Have you got any shoes that might go with it?'

The woman helped me choose some silver slip-ons, and also persuaded me to buy a matching bag, white socks and even a children's perfume that smelt sickly like sweets. With the receipt, she added a packet of Love Hearts into the bag, which I removed as soon as I left the shop.

As I raced back to the office, I felt lighter, wishing I could go home early to give it to her now. Two fingers to you, Mira Entwistle, and to all your nasty judgements. How dare she check on us like that? She knew nothing about Rosie and me.

When I walked back into the office, swinging the pale grey shopping bag, my assistant gasped. 'I love Coco's. I bought my niece a little scarf in there once.'

I resisted the urge to unpick the sticker on the tissue paper to show her.

Lisa had impeccable taste. She wore black pencil skirts and silk blouses and very high heels, like a secretary in American romantic comedies. I had always felt rather plain next to her in meetings. My hair was cut well, but it never shone like hers, and my skinny legs got lost in my unfashionable suits. I resolved to make the time someday to take notes on where she bought her make-up and clothes so that I could refresh my tired, conservative wardrobe and buy some face creams or foundations that weren't supermarket brand for a change.

'I must be paying you too much, Lisa.' I winked at her.

'I wish,' Lisa retorted, leaping up and following me into my glass office.

She reeled off a list of all the people who had called while I was out and stuck the Post-its on my desk next to the various aphorisms I had written on a cluster of neon pink Post-it notes:

*Live life to the fullest!*

*If you don't believe in yourself, nobody else will!*
*Carpe diem!*
*It always seems impossible until it's done!*
*Failure will never overtake me if my determination to*
*succeed is strong enough!*
and so on.


'Have you managed to find out what this "little chat" with Richard is all about?'

'No,' Lisa shrugged, and avoided eye contact.

'Lisa?'

'Don't know a thing, honest.' A crinkle arrived on her flawless young forehead. 'Richard said two o'clock remember,' she added, swivelling away to tap at her keyboard.

It was obvious that Lisa was holding something back. She and Richard's secretary, Becky, were close friends, and wickedly indiscreet with each other.

'You're making me nervous,' I said, pulling on my suit jacket, feeling the heat in the room suddenly, wondering whether it had been wise to spend all that money on Rosie. Redundancies were a daily occurrence these days.

'Please don't be late for him, will you?' Lisa urged, waving me away with one hand.

Richard's office was five floors up on floor twenty-five.

Floor twenty-five was very different to floor twenty.

The vast room was open-plan with rows of desks where the bankers sat in front of their huge screens, scrutinising indecipherable columns of numbers and talking heatedly into headphone receivers.

I recognised some of the men I had employed for the company: Matthew Willoughby – 32, First from Bristol, requested a salary way past his pay-grade, scored four out of five on the performance grades, letting himself down on 'openness'; Jonathan Pressfield – 29, worked the trading floor from sixteen years old, just made redundant, two children to feed, three out of five, hence the redundancy. He wasn't ruthless enough. I liked him. He made the team a happier place, which was why I had originally hired him, against Richard's advice. I made a note to pass by his desk after this meeting to see how he was getting on.

Becky was not at her desk to act as gatekeeper to Richard, so I tried to lurk in plain view. Through his open door – the only door on the whole floor – he beckoned me in while still holding the phone to one ear. My throat felt tight and I wondered if any sound would come out when I said hello.

Did he look shifty? Did he look like a man who was about to sack me?

His hair was tamed into black, smooth waves across his skull. His cheeks looked buffed, as though he'd been given a rigorous face scrub from his mum, or his wife, who were probably interchangeable.

Richard wouldn't look shifty if he was about to shoot me in the head.

He hung up. 'Sorry about that. Hello Gemma, please, sit,' he smiled, beckoning me over to the Chesterfield sofa, incongruous within the modern glass office.

I sat at the other end and crossed my legs, and then uncrossed them. The leather creaked.

'So, how are the kids?'

'Great, yes.' I nodded, thinking 'get the fuck to the point!'

'Noah still playing tennis?'

To uphold good relations, Richard always held one key personal fact about his employees to trot out at appropriate moments.

'His serves are better than mine,' I replied.

'Good lad! Right, well, let's get to the point, shall we?'

Another nod was all I could manage.

He continued. 'You've probably heard the rumours that Cathy is leaving us?'

My palms tingled. 'Yes?'

'We wondered,' he began, jiggling his leather brogue in my direction, 'if you would consider filling her shoes?'

His smile had hit his eyes now. A rush of pride overshadowed any of the practical considerations about my undeclared pregnancy and I sat up poker-straight, as though called to attention. Cathy Knowles was Head of Recruitment across Europe. It was a significant promotion. My salary would leap.

'I would be delighted to,' I answered firmly, trying to sound measured.

He clapped his hands. 'That's great news. Now, I can't talk salaries or contracts yet, we'll have to go through the proper channels, as you well know. We'll be going ahead with the boring bloody process of advertising and interviewing externally, but I wanted to reassure you that, in my book, it's just a formality. We don't want to lose you to some headhunter while we fanny around with protocol, now, do we?'

'No fannying around,' I grinned. 'Thank you very much for the opportunity. I'm really looking forward to the challenge.' I was eager. My head spun. Although I knew the job wasn't quite mine until contracts were signed, I couldn't wait to tell Peter.

On the train back home, I thought practically about what a promotion would entail. I hadn't been honest with Richard about the baby. I had been swept up in the moment, desperate to enjoy the accolade. The promotion was flattering. No, it was more than that, it was what I had worked fifteen years towards. But if he knew I was pregnant, I doubted he would want to 'fanny around' finding maternity cover for me. I had six weeks to declare it before the three-month mark. I had to work out what this new job would mean for the baby, for the family, for me.

It meant longer hours. It meant working weekends. It meant regular trips abroad. It meant much more stress. And it meant even less time with the children. This baby would be my third child to experience nannies when very young.

I didn't know how to consolidate the two parts of me. The desire to make time for a pretty nursery clashed with my career ambitions. But hadn't I been managing the balance of home life and work life relatively well so far? Tiredness and stress were facts of everybody's life these days, weren't they? Maybe I could ask to work from home one day a week. Delegate some of the trips abroad? Rosie would be taking her eleven-plus next year. She would grow out of her tantrums, surely, and she would be taking herself off to school on a bus or train, or she might even board.

I stopped. I was getting ahead of myself. Once Richard found out about the baby, he might change his mind. Either way, it would be months before I was officially offered the role. Some upstart from another firm might interview so well they wouldn't be able to resist them. There was time to think about it, to work out the logistics, to talk to Peter about it. The train carriage shot through a tunnel and I shut down my ruminations, cutting them off like the tunnel had cut my view beyond the window.

I climbed the hill home without the usual dread. The paper-light dress had an invisible glow of love and contrition.

I checked the time. A quarter to eight, much later than usual due to the quarterly budget meeting. Harriet, the nanny, would be telling the children to brush their teeth and get into bed ready for story-time with Mummy.

'Helloooo-ooh!' I called up the stairs.

Noah came rushing at me, full of chatter.

Rosie was at the top of the stairs with a toothbrush in her mouth and her hip cocked to the side. 'Hi Mum,' she mumbled.

'Don't drop toothpaste on the carpet, Rosie!' I cried, immediately wanting to push the words back into my mouth and replace them with, 'Hello, darling! How was your day?'

'Hi,' Harriet said, sauntering out of Noah's room, folding one of his school jumpers. Her wide hips were swaying, and her full, permanently dry lips were humming. She was a rare combination of efficiency and calm. The children never ruffled her, or certainly never in front of me. Her voice remained at a level pitch, always. I envied her for it. Her bright red hair was a wonder to Noah, and he would twirl it in his fingers when she cuddled him. I hated watching it. He never did that to me. There were times when I wished she would get pregnant with her good-for-nothing boyfriend, and leave us to find someone they weren't so attached to. But then, of course, I feared it more than wanted it.

'How've they been?'

Before she answered, she followed me down the stairs and sat down next to a basket of clean clothes, folding as she spoke.

'All good. We had a run around on the rec for an hour after school and we saw Charlotte there,' Harriet said, wrinkling her nose.

'Rosie's going to her birthday party this weekend.'

'She's very rude.'

I looked at my watch, replying distractedly. 'Hmmm, yes, her mum spoils her I think... You can pop off a little early if you like?'

Usually I would ask Harriet to detail everything both Rosie and Noah had said, done and eaten. But tonight, I was impatient with her to leave so that I could give Rosie her present.

Harriet dutifully disappeared after saying goodbye to Rosie and Noah.

And I carried the dress up the stairs.

First, I said goodnight to Noah. Then I peered around Rosie's door. She was reading quietly in bed, just as she had been asked to do. I had the urge to drag Mira Entwistle from her horrible green kitchen and show her how contented Rosie could be. Maybe I should fling the window wide open so that Mira could eavesdrop on Rosie's giggles when she sees her new party dress.

'I've got something for you,' I said, coming in. Her face lit up.

I sat on her bed and handed her the bag. 'It's for Charlotte's party.'

'Oh!' she cried, squeezing her cheeks together in excitement, staring at the bag.

'Go on, open it.'

Laying the tissue paper package on the bed, she knelt down to open it.

I watched every tiny twitch on her face as she unfolded the sundress. She looked at it and didn't say a word. Was she simply speechless and overwhelmed?

'It's lovely,' she said, and folded it back into the tissue paper.

'Don't you want to try it on?'

'I'll try it on tomorrow,' she said.

My heart wanted to break.

'Don't you like it, sweetheart?'

'It's lovely, Mummy, I love it,' she said, reaching her arms around me for a polite hug. 'Thank you so much.' She then moved her hand over my pregnant belly. 'When is it going to kick, Mummy?'

'Not for another couple of months probably.'

Sometimes, it was easier to think about the baby in the abstract, as an unformed embryo, but when I imagined its legs and arms kicking, a flutter of panic danced through my chest. This baby was going to be real. It was going to need much more than a few designer Babygros and a pretty cot. We would be a family of five. Peter and I would be outnumbered. Why, again, had we thought we could handle another one?

'Did I kick a lot?'

'You kicked so much I am still black and blue inside,' I laughed.

She giggled. She loved hearing about being inside me, and about her birth. Her wonder reminded me of the miracle and privilege of being pregnant. We would handle the next one, just as we handled the other two. We would be okay. Third babies always slotted into the established family unit just fine. It was going to be fine.

'There are some other bits and bobs in the bag,' I said, hopefully.

She looked into the bag gingerly. When she brought out the silver slip-ons, bag and perfume, she seemed genuinely enthralled.

'Look!' she cried, hanging the bag over her pyjamas and slipping into her shoes. She paraded around in them pretending to be a fashion model. How I wished I had bought the blue dress. The yellow dress seemed babyish to me now that I saw Rosie in front of me, at ten years old, so tall, and only a few years away from puberty. I'd got it wrong. I had got her wrong.

I read the words of her bedtime book without engaging with them. I couldn't shift the disappointment.

'I'm sorry you don't like the dress,' I said when I kissed her goodnight.

'I love it, Mummy, I really, really do!' she said.

I wanted to believe her. 'You'll wear it to Charlotte's party then?'

There was a pause as she snuggled down with her bear.

'It's a bowling party Mummy,' she said, almost in a whisper.

The baby seemed to flip inside my belly, sending waves of sickness through me. A bowling party? Why the hell hadn't I known?

'Oh. No. Sorry,' I said, unable to offer more. I was mortified.

'It's okay, Mummy,' she said and she stroked my hand.

A ten-year-old, trying to reassure her mother. It was pitiful. And there, Mira seemed to be in the room with us again, watching me fail, and sneering at me for being utterly useless.

# CHAPTER EIGHT

*TOP SECRET*

*Dear Mummy,*

*I am so sad. I am the saddest girl in the whole wide world. I made you so sad and now I am so sad. I wish I liked the dress. It is very posh.*

*INVISIBLE INK ALERT: It was HORRIBLE, BABYISH, SILLY, STUPID, UGLY DRESS. I HATE IT. YUCK. If I wore that dress Charlotte would laugh at me, especially at a bowling party. How embarrassing. I would totally die.*

*The silver shoes and handbag are SICK (that means AWESOME). I don't like them... I LOVE THEM. I'll wear them with my skinny jeans and my black super sparkly bomber jacket that Auntie Jacks gave me for my birthday. You HATE, HATE, HATE that jacket. You have different taste to me. I think that's okay, but you don't. I hope you let me wear it. I will DIE if you don't. Maybe I'll scream so that Mrs E from next door comes over again. JUST JOKING.*

*INVISIBLE INK ALERT: Or am I joking?!!!!!!!!*

*I was listening to you and daddy talk about her after she left. You said she was a Nosey Parker. Two in the swear box mummy! She used to be very kind to send me those YUM SCRUM biscuits in the blue bucket. I loved the blue bucket. Maybe I'll start it up again. But I don't really want her to come over again. I'm a bit embarrassed that she heard me screaming. I wish I could stop myself. I wish I could delete the bad thoughts from my brain. Noah calls me pea-brain, but I have a massive brain filled with hundreds and thousands and a million-gazillion hundred worries. How do I make them stop?*

*Answers on a postcard! Daddy always says that. Silly daddy.*

*Night, night!*

*Five more sleeps until Charlotte's party.*

*Love,*
*Rosie*

*P.S. Please don't make me wear the dress to Charlotte's party. I am worried you will because it probably cost a gazillion pounds.*

# CHAPTER NINE

The clouds had gathered over the sun and the dark green wallpaper sucked up what little light there was left. Mira clicked on the lamp. The yellow glow seemed only to add to the murky atmosphere.

Deidre cackled as she flicked through the old photographs. From the moment Mira had allowed Deidre to rip into the Tesco bags, she realised it had been a mistake to ask her to help sort them through. Mira had wanted the moral support. It had seemed logical to enlist her sister, who was the only other person alive who had been there throughout her childhood. Perversely, this turned out to be exactly why she was the worst person for the job. Deidre had never helped her with anything.

Her laughter throbbed in Mira's head like the onset of a migraine. It rose, morphing into high-pitched screeching.

'Where's that screaming coming from?' Deidre said absent-mindedly, rustling around for another photograph.

Realising that her sister's laughing and the screeching were separate, Mira dropped the photograph she was holding and shot up from the dining room table.

The searing noise was definitely coming from a child's lungs.

'Next door. We hear it all the time.'

'Sounds like you as a child,' Deidre snorted.

Mira wanted to take her sister's pearls and hang her up by the light-fitting with them. If her sister had been privy to the endless nights of Rosie's distressing cries from next door, she would not be flippant. Neither had Deidre been part of the agonising debates that she and Barry had been having about Rosie's well-being, how they had talked in circles, discussing the various reasons to be concerned, analysing what they knew of the Bradleys, elaborating on and guessing about what they didn't know. Although their discussions would always end the same. Barry would persuade Mira that she did not have enough evidence to go to PC Yorke. 'Listen, she's not screaming tonight,' he had said each time, and Mira would stop moving in her bath and strain to hear noises from next door, only to hear nothing, which she should have been happy about.

'I'm just going to check something,' Mira said, abandoning her sister and the photographs.

Two at a time up the stairs, straight to her bedroom window, which had views out of the front of the house. She stood behind the curtain and had a diagonal view out, over the hedge, and down to the Bradleys' front driveway.

The electric gates were closing. Gemma was violently pulling Rosie by the arm across the gravel from their car to the front door. Noah jogged after them wailing.

'You're hurting me, Mummy!' Rosie yelled before their front door was slammed.

Mira's pulse raced as she slowly, thoughtfully descended back downstairs. Her mind was filled with abhorrent imaginings.

The dining room was stuffy, but she couldn't open a window for fear of hearing more next door.

There was hardly enough room to squeeze past her sister at the table to sit down. Barry's mum had left them the mahogany table with the house and it was too big for the room. Mira fantasised about slicing it up with a chainsaw.

'Gosh, what a mess,' Deidre said, dropping her zany red reading glasses from her head to her nose. She was fatter than ever. Her double-chin slanted down to her cleavage, the flesh bulging either side of the throttling string of pearls. She wore a purple nylon shirt that she would probably have liked to be silk. Mira had never owned anything silk and had no desire to.

'I'm going to sort them out and put them in here,' Mira said, sliding her hand over the smooth leather of the album.

Deidre ripped open the second bag. Her breathing had grown heavier, almost like snuffling.

'Oh my God, look at Dad's hair!' she guffawed.

Mira wanted to tell Deidre to leave them alone, or to snatch the bag out of her sister's fat hands.

Their father's hair was long to his shoulders, lank and greasy, just like his arms that hung from the sleeves of his towelling T-shirt.

'That was the fashion back then,' Mira said defensively.

When they were little, they would sit next to each other like this to eat tea, and their mother used to push them into the table too tightly. Mira had that same sense of breathlessness now.

She presented another photograph to Deidre, like a police-woman presenting the face of a suspect to a witness. 'Which one was this? He's in loads of photos. He must've been around more than the others.'

'Oh, shit a brick,' Deidre said. 'I'd forgotten about him.'

'He was one of Mum's boyfriends, wasn't he?'

'He was the one who came round a lot after Dad left. What *was* his name? He was Irish. Not Declan. Donagh? He was all right, I seem to remember.'

'Out of a very bad lot.' Mira remembered a steady flow of different men, but their faces were as memorable to her as those she saw in the supermarket every week.

'Hmmm,' Deidre said.

'So, if Dad left when I was eight, that means it was probably 1975,' Mira said, writing the date and name clearly on the back.

'You're not going to put *him* in the family album are you?'

'No, of course not,' Mira snapped, knowing that her sister was probably joking, but unable to laugh with her. 'I just wanted to be sure he wasn't some long-lost uncle or something, that's all.'

Deidre stopped, picked up a photograph that had slid from the second bag and gasped. 'Oh my God. There's me and...'

Deidre stopped.

Mira turned cold. She didn't know if she could look. Her sight blurred.

The white reflection across the glossy print floated in front of Mira's eyes, while the colours in the photograph itself were lost: the red of his jacket, the blue of Deidre's jeans, the brown of Mira's dress.

She snatched the photograph from Deidre and flipped it over quickly without looking at the front. But the images of the three of them seeped through, into her fingertips, rolling up into her head, like a ball with a message inside, cracked open to reveal backlit cut-outs of her sister in the crook of a boy's arm. Shadow faces. Banter. Nasty. Bad feelings. 'Come on, Mira. Come in for the shot.' Craig's voice. Mira staring at the white-painted blades of grass near her face, the shoes of the girl who held the camera crushing them. She looked up to her sister. Blinded by the sun. Her arm yanked by Craig, his hand tight on her upper arm. 'Come in for a cuddle,' hot in her ear. She had tugged at the back of her dress to hide her knickers. The brown flowers had faded after so many washes.

Whining. 'Mira hates photos.' Deidre's hip cocked to one side. Her new pencil skirt.

'What's wrong, scared you'll be shown up?'

Mira, being dragged in front of the camera, clutched at his side. Cheap aftershave, days old. Deidre's evil eyes, and her cackle.

'Say cheeeese!' the faceless photographer had called out.

The unnecessary flash, red-eye, and Craig's hand was under Mira's dress, squeezing her buttock. The shock. Like a bucket of cold water over her head. Her muscles froze, dumb-founded.

The hand was gone. Craig and Deidre, the perfect boyfriend and girlfriend, were kissing with tongues. His filthy hand was now under her sister's denim jacket. A sly wink at Mira over Deidre's shoulder.

'Are you still with us, Mira?' Deidre warbled.

'What?' Mira blinked, clearing her vision. The words at the nib of her pen were incomplete. She finished the information: *1981. Mira, 14, Deidre, 16, Craig Baxter.*

Another photograph was in her sister's hand.

'Did you ever take that dress off?' Deidre continued, glued to the next picture.

'Mum wouldn't buy me a new one.' The bitterness contorted her face.

Mira remembered the small messy stitches in the straps where she had extended them at the back, and how the bodice had flattened her growing breasts.

'You had a paper round, didn't you?'

As Deidre well knew, their mother had used Mira's paper round money for cigarettes and whisky. Mira didn't bother reminding her, feeling unable to stomach Deidre's challenge. The inevitability of her loyalty to their dead mother was tiresome. Unless Deidre really had forgotten in the way that Mira herself had forgotten so much.

'Another cup of tea?' Mira said, and moved out of the room, leaving Deidre talking to the photographs.

Mira had become weary of looking back. Please, no more faces she could not name. No more afterthoughts of a past she could not recall. Why, again, had she wanted to open those bags?

As she stood by the kettle, the screaming next door was ringing in the background like a distant alarm, waxing and waning on the wind. She didn't know how long she could bear to listen to it.

# CHAPTER TEN

'Can you show me how to get more jewels, Rosie?' Noah asked.

'Sure.'

The jolly bleep of the game filled the car as I drove them home from the bowling alley. I was grateful for five minutes of peace.

But then the chit-chat over the gaming turned nasty.

'No, not like that.'

'Give it to me, it's mine.'

'I'm just trying to show you.'

'Give it!'

'No!

And on it escalated, ruining my five minutes.

By the time I had parked up outside the gates, they were hitting each other.

'Stop fighting, you two.'

And then Rosie bit Noah's arm.

I frog-marched her from the car.

In the hall, I was down on my haunches. 'You never, *ever, ever* bite anyone, do you understand?'

'He hit me!' she wailed.

'Even so, you don't *bite* people. It is unacceptable.'

'La, la, la, la,' Rosie sang, dropping the present Charlotte's mother had given her onto the floor at my feet, and holding her hands over her ears.

My stomach was cramping with Braxton Hicks. I was at a loss. Why was she so impossible? Why did everything end in a fight? Why wouldn't she listen to reason? That same familiar bubbling anger was rising in my body.

'Rosie,' I said, grabbing her by the shoulders, feeling the power of my fingertips, holding back the urge to press away her remorselessness, to make her feel how Noah felt when she bit him. 'You'd better listen to me, young lady.'

She stuck her tongue out at me and sang louder.

I released her shoulders as though they were burning hot. If I continued holding them, I would have squeezed them too tightly.

Standing up, I took my coat off, wondering how to control my fury. I was a fully-fledged grown-up and I had no idea how to calm myself down, or what to do with my own daughter. I couldn't just leave it. She had bitten Noah's hand. More worryingly, she was showing no remorse. There had to be consequences.

'Okay, if you are rude to me one more time, I am going to confiscate your going-home present.' I snatched up the scented rubbers and pens from the floor.

She shrugged. 'So what?' The sparkles on her black bomber jacket glinted at me.

'Oh right, so that doesn't bother you. How about if I confiscate the new bag that I bought you?'

A smile flickered across her lips. 'I gave it away already.'

'What?' I whispered, noticing for the first time that she wasn't wearing it. At the bowling alley when I had picked her up, it had been too chaotic to notice anything.

'Charlotte wanted it, so I gave it to her.'

The hurt cut so deep, I reeled back from her, as though she was monstrous.

Quietly, through clenched teeth, I hissed at her, 'Go to your room.'

'No.' She looked over her shoulder, trying to be nonchalant, but I could sense she knew she was pushing me too far.

Louder this time. 'I said, *Go to your room.*'

'I don't want to.' She swung her arms at her side like a toddler, testing me to breaking point.

I walked towards her with my finger pointed right into her face. 'Get up those stairs or I'll never let you go on another play date with Charlotte as long as you live. Ten minutes! And don't you dare come out until I get you.'

And she ran. An ear-splitting scream erupting from her lungs as she slammed the door. I could hear her throwing things around in her bedroom. Each thud or crash came with a howl like a wolf at the moon. 'I hate you! I hate you! I hate you!' Again and again she repeated it. Each time she said it, I flinched, as though she was throwing something directly at my head.

*'And I hate you too,'* I whispered, dying inside a little as I said it, as if all the troubles in my life were her fault.

'Noah!' I called.

I found him at the computer, looking up pop songs on YouTube.

I scooped him up onto my knee and sat where he had been sitting in front of the computer.

'I think Rosie's had a little bit too much sugar at the party, don't you?' I said, but my voice was wobbling and my breathing ragged. 'How's your hand?'

He stuck it under his thigh, hiding it from me. 'It's fine, Mumma.'

A tear was still in place on his cheek, a perfect droplet suspended under his eye. I wiped it away.

'Let's have another look.'

'I don't want you to be more cross with Rosie.'

'I won't, I promise.'

My hands were still shaking as I held his; Rosie's wails were ringing through the house.

There were evil little red teeth marks, but the skin wasn't broken. I kissed it better.

'Let's put some loud music on so we can't hear that naughty big sister of yours screaming her head off. How about some Luther?'

'Yeah!'

The sounds of 'Never Too Much' blasted out of the computer as I pressed the volume up to maximum. On screen, the eighties New Yorkers were tapping their cowboy boots and white sneakers and busting moves to Luther Vandross on their Walkmans and ghetto-blasters. I felt Noah's little bottom wiggle to the music. I jumped up, holding his hands, and we bopped and pranced around, showcasing silly moves, throwing our arms and legs about like a pair of monkeys. Knowing I shouldn't lift heavy things, I threw caution to the wind and swung him up into the air and round and round in my arms, boogying away the blues. Rosie's screams might as well have been miles away in another country.

A parenting book had told me to ignore tantrums, and so here I was, ignoring her, ghetto-blaster style.

And then, cutting through the cranked up music, I heard a scream from Rosie that set my teeth on edge and my heart pounding. The pitch had changed. It suggested pain rather than attention-seeking. I dropped Noah's hands. 'Stay down here, Noah,' I cried, and bolted up the stairs and burst into Rosie's room.

She was on her knees in the middle of an explosion of shattered, shimmering glass, holding her bloody fingers up to me, tears streaming down her face.

The large framed photograph that had been hanging above her mantle-piece was on the floor, the glass broken in pointed splinters and shards. The professional shots of Rosie and me in the frame, cuddling and laughing against a white studio backdrop, were smeared in her blood.

'Oh my God!' I cried, terror splitting my brain in half.

I tip-toed through the glass to rescue her, reaching under her armpits to lift her up and over the smashed pane and onto the carpet in the corridor.

'I'm so sorry Mummy,' she whimpered, holding her palms out.

Frantically, I inspected her hands, back and front, and wrists, up and down her arms, her neck, her legs, back and front, up her thighs, for the source of the blood flow. There were two or three lacerations on her shins, and cuts on the thumb and forefinger of her right hand, and then a deeper cut through the centre of her left palm, which seemed to be the main source of the blood.

'Oh darling. It's okay now. You're all in one piece. That's all that matters. Come on, let's get it cleaned up,' I said, and I carried her to the bathroom, her chest heaving into mine as she cried and clutched at me.

The blood swirled through the running water in the sink like pink ribbons. I worried there was too much blood, that it needed stitches. I had another look to see how deep it was, imagining the five-hour wait at A & E. Peter was due back home any minute. He'd know what to do.

'Whatever were you doing in there?' I asked, pressing the towel into her palm to stem the flow. Her chest was heaving as she spoke. 'I was trying to put the glass back together on our picture.'

'You know better than to touch broken glass, Rosie!' I cried, wondering how the frame had fallen. Not wanting to ask, knowing she must have thrown something at it in her raging state.

Really, I didn't care what had happened or why, as long as the blood stopped flowing. I looked at it again, assessing it, coming to the conclusion that it probably didn't need stitches.

'It fell when teddy hit it. It's *all* my fault! I hate myself! I didn't mean to bite Noah. I am such a horrible, horrible big sister. I hate myself,' she sobbed, throwing her arms around my neck.

So, here was Rosie's remorse, finally. She came to it the hard way, but deep down I was relieved it had come to her in any way at all. It alleviated my more profound concerns about what kind of child I had given birth to, before the nurturing, before my mistakes.

'Come on, no more crying. Let's get a bandage on that cut. I think it looks much worse than it is.'

In a strange state of after-shock, I looked into the cupboard for the plasters and couldn't see them. Rosie's near-miss was racing through my mind as I stared blankly into the cupboard for the box that was right in front of me.

The doorbell rang.

'Hold on, that must be Daddy. He must've forgotten his keys. Stay there, I'll be right back, that's right, hold it tight on the cut.'

'Silly daddy,' Rosie sniffed.

Leaving Rosie on the loo-seat with her hand wrapped in a bloody towel, I floated downstairs, shaken to the core, hoping to see Peter at the door in his cycling gear, hoping for a big hug.

It was not Peter. It was Mira Entwistle.

Her mouth was open, about to speak.

A pink electronic diary and one silver shoe were in her hands. What was she doing with Rosie's things? What was she doing here?

'Those are Rosie's,' I said.

'They were lying over there,' Mira said, handing them to me, pointing to the gravel below Rosie's bedroom. I placed them inside on the side table, and went outside to look up to Rosie's bedroom windows, both of which were open.

Mira stepped back, one step at a time, as if she couldn't take her eyes off me. Her grey crew cut clashed with her ruddy complexion. Her body was thick-set, stocky and rounded. I wouldn't win a physical fight with her, but here she was, backing away from me, seemingly terrified. I was disoriented, baffled. After the shock of Rosie's accident, I couldn't put two and two together.

'I'm going to have to call the police,' Mira said.

Gemma laughed. '*What?*'

'I heard everything.'

'What did you hear, may I ask?' I said, straightening, crossing my arms, indignant.

'Everything.'

'If you are referring to Rosie's screaming, she had an accident, that's all. She's absolutely fine now,' I said, hiding the rising panic.

'Can I see her?'

'No, you absolutely cannot see her. She hardly knows you. You have no right to come barging in here scaring her. Could you please leave?'

Mira's fist jabbed repeatedly at the button for the gate. I was moving towards her, but the fear in her eyes stopped me in my tracks.

The gate closed her out and I was left quivering in the drive with the garden spinning around my head. Hormones were coursing through my body and I imagined my baby flipping about inside me like a dying fish.

The other silver shoe was suspended in a low bush.

I reached through the bare branches, and then whipped my arm back, jolted by the sight of my hands. My palms were covered in blood. I looked down at the rest of me. My white shirt was smeared with violent red swipes and smudges like an unravelled bandage.

'Oh God.'

I ran inside to see my face in the hall mirror. More blood, wiped down my neck. A patch on my upper lip.

'Mummy?' Rosie called.

'Oh shit,' I said to myself quietly, transfixed by my gory reflection. My palms were sweating. The wetness mixed with Rosie's blood as if I too were bleeding now.

Rosie called for me again. I was catatonic.

Noah ran out from the television den and stopped to gape at me. 'Mummy, you're bleeding!'

'Rosie cut herself,' I said blankly, still rooted to the spot.

'You can have one of my Mr Bump plasters,' Noah said.

'Thank you, Noah,' I smiled, knowing how special they were to him. If only a Mr Bump plaster could have fixed it.

'Can I have some orange juice?'

'Don't spill any.' Like it mattered.

And up I went, to dress Rosie's wound, wrap a bandage around the cotton wool and gauze. Fear throbbed at my temples. Mira can't have been serious about calling the police. I couldn't even bring myself to imagine what was going on in her head when she saw the blood on me.

I had been defensive and aggressive. If only I had let her in to see the broken glass, to see Rosie. If she had spoken to Rosie, she would have understood. She works at a school, she will know all about children's tantrums.

I decided the only thing to do was to go over there with the children and explain, or get Rosie to explain. Mira would believe me, and she'd certainly believe Rosie.

# CHAPTER ELEVEN

*TOP SECRET*

*Dear Mummy,*

*My diary did not break when I threw it out of the window! AND THE CROWD GOES WILD!*

*BUT BUTT-FACE, my hand is mega painful though :( and it stings like mad.*

*If it was on my other hand I would not have to do any homework and that would be AWESOME. :) ;).*

*Maybe I should cut my other hand. DOUBLE OUCH. NO WAY.*

*Now I have to go to Mira next door and tell her that I am okay. Maybe I should put a letter in the blue bucket like I did when I was little. She's nice to worry about me. Am I okay? Not really but you will never understand so what is the point in telling you?*

*INVISIBLE INK ALERT: I did not give my bag to Charlotte. I loved it so, so, so much. She forced me to give it to her. If I tell on her, she said she's going to cut off my ponytail when I'm not looking. I believe her too because she did that to her friend at her other school. MEAN CHARLOTTE. MEANIE MEAN MEAN.*

*The picture of me and you is broken and that makes me want to cry.*

*Better go, you are calling me and telling me to hurry up. Always shouting. Shouty, shouty mummy.*

*Love,*
*Rosie*

*P.S. No time for that!*

# CHAPTER TWELVE

'Gemma was covered in blood. We have to call the police,' Mira cried, charging around the house trying to find her phone while Barry and Deidre stood there staring at her.

'Stop running around like a blue-arsed fly. What do you mean, she was covered in blood?' Deidre barked.

'Blood was on her clothes and her hands! Blood. Covered in blood, like in a horror film.'

'I'd better go round there,' Barry said, putting down his mug.

'To check I'm not making it up?'

'No, Mira, to check the girl is okay.'

'Don't you think I tried? She wouldn't let me in! Don't you understand? That's why we need to call the police,' Mira cried.

Deidre pulled her phone out of her pocket and dialled.

'What are you doing?' Mira shouted.

'Calling the police!'

'I want to talk to PC Yorke. Where the bloody hell is my phone?'

Mira wanted to pull her own head off with frustration. Whirling around her mind were Rosie's chilling screams: *You can't make me, I hate you, you can't shut me in here, I hate you, I hate you, I hate you.*

'999 will send you to the same place, love,' Deidre said, with the phone to her ear.

'Yes, police, please... I want to report an incident at my sister's neighbour's house... We think a child is in danger... Immediate, yes, I suppose so... Mira? What's her name?'

'Rosie Bradley.'

'Gemma Bradley is the mother and Rosie Bradley is the daughter... domestic abuse of some sort... There was lots of screaming from Rosie... Mira, what's the other child's name?' she asked.

'Noah.'

'Noah... Well, the mother had blood all over her clothes and the girl... yes, Rosie... was screaming blue murder... Yes, hold on.... what number is her house?'

'Four.' Mira's voice came out gruffly. Even to her own ear, she sounded like a different person. The line she was crossing had changed her already.

Each and every detail of what she had seen and heard she relived, making sure she could clearly justify their 999 call.

Gemma's rough handling of Rosie out of the car, dragging her almost, was distressing in itself; Rosie's possessions being hurled with such force out of the window; the loud crash of what sounded like a big object being thrown, which possibly hit something, or someone; the blood-curdling cry from Rosie, followed by the inappropriate music. Or did she hear the music before the scream? Was Gemma trying to drown out Rosie's screams? Then the sudden quiet. The vision of Gemma, covered in blood, unaware or unashamed, had been appalling. The steely eyes, the haughty manner, the cold rebuttal. If she had nothing to hide, why ever would she not let her see Rosie?

There was nothing else for it. Anyone with a conscience would have to call the police. There was no time for doubt.

'Number four, Virginia Close, Denton... Number three... Mira, M.I.R.A., Entwistle, E.N.T.W.I.S.T.L.E. GU21 5XR... Uh huh... Okay. Thank you,' Deidre said, hanging up. 'They're sending out the next available unit,' she told them.

Deidre sat down at the kitchen table.

'Why did you have to use my name?'

'You think that woman next door won't know it's you?'

'You don't have to stay, you know,' Mira said, biting back much more.

'I can't leave you now,' Deidre said. 'Let's play Gin Rummy.' She pulled out a pack of cards from her handbag.

'Terrific idea,' Barry said.

Reluctantly, Mira sat down in front of the cards Deidre was dealing at the kitchen table and tried to focus on her hand.

The ticking of the clock was loud in her right ear. Every second was an hour.

While Deidre studied her cards, Mira stole glances at Barry, whose right eyebrow twitched. He studiously avoided looking at Mira. Since the call to the police, she had been unable to catch his eye. Clearly, he believed she had been wrong, Mira thought. As though it were a permanent state, Mira felt wrong in the face of what she believed to be right. She had always been wrong, about everything. Wrong. A wrong-un, as her mother had said once.

'You're a right wrong 'un, you are Mira Moose-face.'

Remembering that casual insult rushed Mira back to that sitting room, as though she was standing in front of her mother again. Mira recalled how her mother had been reclining on the sofa, licking her finger as she lazily turned the page of her tabloid, scolding her whilst flicking through the news. How repellent Mira had found her, in her pink leggings with the hole, and the thinning wires of hair around her forehead.

'He was the one who did it, Mum!' Mira had cried, defending herself.

'Why did you have to go tell *Deidre*? Just when she's happy with Craig, you've gone and upset her for no reason.'

'But his hand was in my pants! He's *horrible*. She should dump him for doing that!'

'Just because you're a jealous little minx?'

'I'm not *jealous* of Deidre going out with that *creep*!'

Mira had held back the tears. Nobody would care what she did or where she went. She marched down the lane, armed with a cigarette she had plucked at home from the splay in the glass tumbler: a bunch of flowers with no heads. Swollen with more anger than she knew what to do with, she lit a cigarette for the first time. The heady hit from the nicotine calmed her. With each inhale, she sucked back the wild, clanging anger that threatened to overtake her. The sullen, sulky Mira returned. Back to normal. The barriers in place.

Mira still kept a packet of cigarettes on top of the bookshelf in the lounge, for moments just like these. Barry would turn a blind eye when she had the odd one after a stressful day, but she would be too self-conscious to smoke around Deidre.

Twenty-two minutes after the call to the police, there were flashing lights outside the window. A blue film tinged the outdoors. Their front gate, the hedges, the grass, the sky, the very air they breathed changed colour. The blue turned the familiar into the unknown.

Mira placed her fan of cards neatly down on the table and took a deep breath.

Barry looked directly at her over his cards but his expression was inscrutable.

'Oh Lord, they're here,' Deidre said, leaping up with more energy than she had shown all day. She moved into the lounge to peer out of the window, which Mira knew would not give her a view of anything but the hedge.

If they wanted to see, they would have to go into their bedroom and look down over the hedge, but Mira didn't want to see any more.

When the police cars' lights switched off, the white sunshine blanched Mira's confidence.

# CHAPTER THIRTEEN

I was clearing up a murder scene, or so it seemed. I felt sullied as I picked up the pieces of glass and carefully placed them in the bin bag. Nothing could tidy away the unpleasant aftertaste of guilt. With a damp cloth, I gently wiped the blood from the prints of our smiling faces, and longed to go back to that day, when Rosie was three years old, and she had been difficult, yes, but less complicated. Had I been a better mother back then? Had I been a better person?

The doorbell rang. I hadn't heard Peter arrive. I had been at the back of the house in Noah's bedroom choosing an appropriate outfit for him for our visit next door. I had changed into clean clothes and the bloody shirt was already spinning around the washing machine.

I checked my watch, five past two. He had said he would be home at roughly two o'clock, give or take half an hour. Part of me had hoped he would get back in time to persuade me out of my visit next door. If I explained everything to Peter, I hoped he would think I was making something out of nothing, that our business was not Mira's, that he would forbid me to carry out the humiliating task of persuading Mira that I was not a child abuser. Deep down, I would know I had to do it anyway, but his blind loyalty would bolster me.

With the dustbin bag full of glass and the broken-up frame, I opened the door, distractedly, ready to launch into the story of the past hour to Peter.

Two dark figures in hats blocked my passage. Time stopped. The bin bag was suspended in the air between them and me. The synthetic smell from the bag brought bile onto my tongue and its heaviness felt like it might snap my arm from its socket.

The figure on the right spoke. 'Mrs Bradley?'

'Yes? Sorry, I'm just putting this out,' I said, panicking. I squeezed through them with the bin bag, in an attempt to be casual. I was so inappropriately casual that I probably looked unhinged. I imagined them making a note of it in their heads, building a picture, before the notebooks were brought out. A slither of glass poked through the bag and pierced my thigh as I carried it to the bin and I wanted to cry. I stared at the gates, willing Peter through them.

They allowed me to pass back across the threshold of my own home.

'Hello, I'm PC Yorke and this is PC Connolly, we've had an incident reported to us from your neighbour about some screaming and we're just here to check that everything's in order.'

It felt like my brain had caved in. The muscles around my womb clenched my baby, instinctively preparing for the danger ahead. It took every ounce of self-control I possessed to contain the panic. My first instinct was to tell them that they could not come in, that it was inconvenient, that I was outraged.

'I really think there has been a terrible misunderstanding,' I said, half-laughing, trying to convey how risible I thought them being here was. But I didn't move to let them in. My brain's messages to my body weren't working.

'Can we come in please?' The officer said, more sternly this time. 'We need to see your children to make sure they're safe.'

'They are absolutely safe. I'll get them for you,' I said, incredulous, standing aside to let them in. They followed me through the house to the kitchen. 'Rosie! Noah! Come in here, please!' I called out the back door, high-pitched, near hysterical.

They ran in, flushed, grinning from ear-to-ear, a little scruffy in their outfits contrived for Mira. They looked happy and well cared for, and I had a stab of pride.

'This is Rosie,' I said, noticing how both officers immediately clocked the bandage on her hand, 'and this is Noah.'

The children stared up at them agog, and looked over to me for reassurance.

'It's okay, the officers are here to make sure everyone is safe after the accident with the picture.'

'What's that?' Noah asked, pointing to the square black device in PC Connolly's hand.

'It's an MDT. A Mobile Data Terminal. We write in it,' PC Connolly said.

'Can I see?' Noah said.

'Noah,' I admonished.

'It's okay. Here.'

PC Yorke showed Noah the screen briefly, but his eyes were on the move, up and down the children's bodies, around my house, scanning for something. Neither officer made eye contact with me for more than a second.

'Hello,' PC Connolly said. Her blonde bob was flicked under either side of her wide jaw. She bent down to Rosie. Her voice was gentle and relaxed. 'What happened to your hand, Rosie?'

Rosie looked down at her hand and bit her lip, nervy and timid, she wouldn't answer.

I leapt in to save her. 'It is just a small cut under that big bandage! The picture frame fell off the wall and it shattered all over the floor, didn't it Rosie?'

Rosie was wide-eyed at me, as though I had lied, which was true, I had lied, sort of, to protect her. The picture frame hadn't just 'fallen off the wall'. When do picture frames just fall off walls? It sounded like the domestic abuse cliché, 'she just walked into a door'.

The female officer stood up and addressed me sternly. 'Could you please remain silent. We need to hear from your daughter.'

Taken aback, I looked searchingly at PC Yorke, whose finger seemed to point briefly at PC Connolly as he brushed it under his nose awkwardly. His flat, grey face was unreadable, like a concrete wall.

'Let's hear from you, Rosie? Tell me what happened,' PC Connolly said.

Rosie just stood there frozen to the spot, holding a strange faraway expression.

Both police officers glanced at one another, an all-knowing click of recognition giving away their obvious concern, and I wanted to smack them.

In spite of my fear of PC Connolly, I stepped in and wrapped my arms around Rosie. 'Come on, darling, it's okay,' I said, coaxing her. 'Go on. Tell them exactly what happened.'

'I don't want to,' she said, looking up at me. Her chin was dimpling.

'You have to, Rosie.'

'Am I in trouble?' she whispered, as though she and I were alone in the room.

'No, no, poppet, you are absolutely not in trouble. Just tell them how you cut your hand. Nobody is going to be cross with you.'

'I tell you what, why don't you show me where it happened? It might be easier to explain,' PC Connolly said, and she held her hand out to Rosie, who, much to my amazement released me, took it and led PC Connolly up the stairs. I could hear the beginning of what she said, before their voices were quiet.

I felt heady. My separation from her was a wrench I could hardly believe I was allowing. Everything about letting her walk upstairs with this stranger felt unnatural and wrong.

Noah pulled at my leg. 'Why is that police going upstairs with Rosie, Mummy?'

I was just about to answer, when PC Yorke did it for me. 'She's just making sure everything is safe for you and your sister.'

PC Yorke's portable radio let out a crackle of voices, distracting me from the angry retort that was building in my head. I was aggrieved by the imposition of these two officers in my home.

'Sorry about that.' He turned the volume down. 'Right, I'll need to take down a few details from you, if that's okay?'

I felt angry prickles cross my chest, which was probably flashing red, highlighting my discomposure. I placed my hand there, feeling my skin's heat throb into the pads of my fingertips.

'Noah, do you want to play outside?' I said.

Noah scampered off.

'Is it okay if we sit down?' I said.

His black uniform was thick and heavy with equipment around his belts, and his coat dwarfed my upholstered chair where he hung it. He shuffled far back from the table, as though giving himself space for the important task ahead. I pushed my torso tight into the opposite side of the table, prim, ready for a test. I had to adopt a practical approach, as I would in a boardroom meeting at work. I would answer his questions efficiently and without emotion. The facts would be gathered and they would leave us alone.

It was easy to do at first. He began by asking me for exact spellings of our names, our dates of birth, telephone numbers, the children's school, and lastly, our doctor's surgery. I didn't tell him I was pregnant. I'm not sure why. Perhaps because it was none of his business. Perhaps because I didn't want his sympathy. Perhaps because I wanted to protect my baby from his scrutiny.

'So, now we've got all that out of the way, let's talk about what happened,' PC Yorke said. 'We have established that Rosie has cut her hand, which you say doesn't need any medical attention?'

'No,' I said.

'We have reason to believe the incident with Rosie happened in her bedroom, is that correct?'

'Yes.'

'Were you with Rosie at the time?'

'No.'

'Where were you at the time?'

'I was in the study with Noah.'

'Could you please show me where that is?' he said, standing up.

We stood in the book-lined room and my eye was drawn through the French windows to the stone patio, where I caught sight of a robin dart from the hydrangea bush to a limp, wilting leaf on the dead rose vine. It bounced for a second and flew off.

'And what were you doing in here?'

'I was listening to music with Noah.' I pointed to the computer on the leather desk.

'Were you aware that Rosie was screaming while you were listening to music?'

'Yes. Well, yes.'

'But you decided not to check on her?'

'I've read that it's best to ignore a child when they're having a tantrum.'

His eyes flicked up from his device. Under his questioning stare, the advice I had read online shrivelled up as namby-pamby nonsense.

'At what point did you know that the picture fell off the wall?'

'After I heard the crash, and when her screaming sounded different.'

'At what point did you decide to go upstairs?'

'When I heard the crash.'

'So, you heard the crash, and her screaming sounded different. When you say "sounded different", can you describe the scream to me?'

'It became really high-pitched, I suppose.'

'And then what did you do when you heard this high-pitched scream?'

'I ran straight upstairs to check on her.'

'Could you call Noah in here, so I can talk to him please?'

'Is that really necessary? He's only six.' Stay calm, stay calm, I said to myself, co-operate, I have nothing to hide.

'I'm afraid it is important I talk to him. Could you get him please?'

I called Noah in from outside. 'Jump up onto the swivel chair a minute, poppet. PC Yorke has a few questions for you too,' I said, trying to sound upbeat, as though it was such a big treat to be interviewed by a police officer who suspected your mother might have intentionally harmed your big sister.

Noah sat twisting back and forth on the chair while I hovered in the corner, leaning into the bookshelf, fearing that my insignificant life was about to become as meaty as those behind the book spines.

PC Yorke crouched down to his level. 'So, Noah, what were you doing in the study with your mummy today?'

'Rosie was screaming like this WAH, WAH, WAH!' Noah, the showman, said, obviously deciding to play up the comedy for his audience, as he had a habit of doing.

'And when Rosie was going WAH, WAH, WAH, what was Mummy doing?'

'We were dancing to Luuuuuther!' He jumped off the chair and wiggled his bum.

I couldn't help smiling, and I caught PC Yorke smiling too.

'And then after you were dancing with Mummy, then what happened?'

'Mummy was really, really cross, like this,' he said, and he screwed up his face into his best angry-face grimace. 'And then she went like this,' he said, miming stomping out of the room and stroking his tummy, as I would do often, unconsciously connecting to my baby.

'I think you should be on the stage when you grow-up, eh?'

'Yeeeeeaaah!' Noah cried, doing a *tah-dah* with his arms. I began to cringe slightly. It was little over the top, possibly a reflection of his anxiety.

'Tell me, did you hear anything apart from Rosie screaming from upstairs?'

'Only this, WAH, WAH, WAH!' Noah screeched.

'All right, Noah. Calm down, please,' I said.

'Okay,' PC Yorke laughed. 'Did you hear anything else?'

Noah shrugged. 'Nope.'

'So, where did Mummy go then after she walked out of here?'

'Ummm. She went upstairs to Rosie's bedroom.'

'And what did you see there?'

'I was a good boy.' He became serious.

'You were a good boy, were you?'

'Yes, Mummy told me to stay down here and so I was good and I stayed here.'

'You stayed down here, did you. And did you hear anything while you were down here, being a good boy?'

'No.' He shook his head slowly and looked up at me.

'Good boy,' PC Yorke replied, standing up again. 'Okay, well done, Noah, thank you very much for answering all my questions.'

'Can I watch telly, Mummy?'

'Go outside for a bit. You can watch some later when Daddy's home.'

I checked my watch. It was a quarter to three. Three-quarters of an hour late. Of all days. Of all bloody days. I wanted to scream out of a window, across the tree-tops to bring him home, like a bird's call across a jungle.

PC Yorke tapped furiously into his device and walked out of the study, back down the corridor, towards the bottom of the stairs, and looked up, paused, tapped some more information, and back into the kitchen, where we sat down again. His command of my space was disconcerting. In another context, I imagined that it would be reassuring, say, if we'd been burgled, and he was on our side automatically.

'So, tell me what happened upstairs, Mrs Bradley.'

Again, the look of sympathy. It put me instantly on edge. Did he know more than I did before he had heard my story?

'I went straight into her bedroom and saw that Rosie was kneeling in the middle of all this broken glass and there was blood everywhere,' I said, pressing my fingers to my mouth. I noticed my top lip was sweaty.

'You saw blood. Where was the blood?'

Tap, tap, tap.

'On the photographs and on the mount, and on her hands.'

'What did you do when you saw this?'

'I lifted her out of the room away from the glass and then I carried her to the bathroom to clean her up. That's how I got covered in blood, but I hadn't noticed it on my clothes until Mira saw me,' I trailed off, trying to fight back the tears.

'And you found a cut on Rosie?'

'Yes, on her hand.'

'How do you think she cut her hand?'

'I don't know, when it fell maybe?'

'Was she hurt anywhere else?'

'I found several small cuts over her shins and knees where she'd knelt on the glass.'

'Where was the cut exactly on her hand?'

'On her palm.' I showed him on mine, and wished with all of my heart that the laceration had been mine.

'The left hand, then?'

'Err. Yes, left.'

'And your husband? Where is he now?'

'He's on a bike ride,' I answered, conjuring up the cheering image of Peter in his Lycra. 'He should be home any minute.'

'Were you aware that Rosie was throwing things out of her window?'

'No, I wasn't.' Embarrassment fired up my cheeks. I was her mother, I should have known. I should know everything about her and I felt that I knew nothing.

I could hear Rosie and PC Connolly's voices coming closer. My heart pounded.

When they came into the kitchen, I pushed out a smile, which slackened when I realised that PC Connolly was not smiling back. I had an urge to tear them apart.

I wanted Rosie to run towards me.

'Everything okay?'

'We had a very good chat, didn't we Rosie?' PC Connolly said.

'Hi Mum,' she said, barely looking in my direction. 'Can I go outside with Noah?'

'Of course.' And off she ran.

PC Yorke read out a rough outline of what we had discussed, and PC Connolly nodded and drew her forefinger across one eyebrow as if smoothing it. She sat down next to PC Yorke.

'Could we just go back a bit, Mrs Bradley? So, you say you cleared away the broken glass. Can you tell me where it is now?'

'It's all in that bin-bag I took out when you arrived.'

'And your clothes? We understand they were bloody? With Rosie's blood or your blood?'

'Rosie's. It's in the washing machine.'

'I see,' she said, looking over at PC Yorke.

'What? Would you need it as evidence or something?' I laughed.

'It helps us to build a picture of what happened.'

'I've told you what happened.'

'Yes. One more thing, Mrs Bradley, do you ever forcefully shut Rosie in her room?'

'I'm not even going to answer that.'

'It is important that you do, please.'

'No, of course I don't. Of course not. Anyway, there isn't a lock. You saw her door, didn't you?'

'But do you ever try to trap her inside?'

'How the hell would I do that?'

'You tell me.'

'I would never trap her inside her room. Sometimes I tell her to go to her room for time out.' As I said it, a flash came to me, of me pulling at her door. Her wrist. The welt. The dress. The bag. It would be impossible to explain.

PC Connolly nodded at me.

I repeated it. 'I would never trap Rosie in her bedroom.' I wanted to add, *Don't you understand? I love her*, and, *I would do anything to take back this afternoon*, but I knew the words would be lost on them.

'Have you or anyone else in the family had any history of involvement with children's social care?'

'For goodness sake. No, of course not. Look, quite frankly, I've had enough of this,' I said, shooting up from the table. 'If that nosy old bag next door had a life, you wouldn't even be here. It was a malicious call and it has absolutely no grounding whatsoever. She doesn't have her own kids and she doesn't seem to understand that kids scream when they're young. If she did have them, she'd get it.'

There was a horrible silence after my rant. I wanted to push the defensive words back down my throat, pull myself together again. But it was too late. If Peter had been here, he would have told me off. He would say I was over-sensitive and too ready to fight back at the smallest criticism. But the police officers' insinuations weren't small, they were huge. They cut deep into my fears of what I was truly capable of in those desperate moments with Rosie. Their intrusive probing questions sent lightning strikes of panic through my whole being.

I took the J-cloth from the sink and rubbed a smear of butter from the edge of the table.

There were other questions, seemingly hundreds of them, until my mouth was parched and my head aching. Finally, PC Connolly pulled the plug.

'Okay, Mrs Bradley. I think we have everything we need for now. What time will your husband be getting home?'

I sighed and pressed my fingertips into my forehead. 'Any moment now.'

'Okay, good. Okay, we'll be in touch over the next couple of days,' she said, pushing her small arms into her huge coat.

'About what?' I said, throwing the cloth in the sink.

'Just to confirm we've made the visit and that everything seems in order,' PC Connolly explained.

'Oh good,' I said, letting out a huge breath and a little nervous laugh.

I felt an overwhelming desire to hug her, relieved that they had not seen into my mind to witness my imaginary hand striking my child to stop the screaming. Instead they had seen the woman who would never, ever intentionally hurt Rosie, even in those desperate moments; they had seen the better part of my nature, where I had danced with Noah to Luther Vandross; they had decided that everything was in order.

My obvious relief elicited a small smile on PC Connolly's face. 'And we'll be notifying Social Services about our visit.'

I crossed my arms over my chest. 'Why ever would you need to tell Social Services?'

'It's standard procedure, Mrs Bradley.'

Pursing my lips, I answered with a clipped, uptight, 'Right, okay,' holding back a show of panic.

Once they had gone, I shook my head in disbelief, unsteady on my feet, unable to sit down. I blew out a few deep breaths, and then worried I might faint. The stress felt dangerous for the baby. I sat down with my head between my legs and stayed there for who knows how long.

'What are you doing, Mum?' Rosie said, standing right in front of me side by side with Noah.

'Have the police gone now?' Noah said, running around the kitchen shouting, 'Nee-nor, nee-nor.'

'Yes, they've gone. Calm down, Noah. I'll make a pot of tea. Noah, you can watch telly now.'

'Can I too?' Rosie asked.

'I just want a quick word.'

Rosie groaned.

Ignoring her, I filled the kettle and flicked it on. 'So, what did PC Connolly ask you?'

'Not much. Just about what happened and stuff.' She picked at the bandage on her hand.

'Is it still sore?'

'It's okay.'

'So you told her about how it happened, yes?' I was trying to sound light-hearted, to tease it out of her as though we were having a gossip about something.

She shrugged.

I placed the milky cup in front of her and inspected her face for something that would give me a hint about how she felt.

'Are you okay? It was probably a bit scary talking to a real-life policeman, wasn't it?'

She put her fingertip into the tea and started swirling it around and then licking it, goading me, knowing I hated her doing this. I resisted telling her off.

'Police *woman*,' she said.

I took in a deep breath and counted to ten in my head.

'It didn't worry you at all, talking to her?'

'She was nice.'

'Fine. Good. I just wanted to check you're okay.'

'Can I go watch telly now?'

After our ordeal, I decided that I might need to flop in front of the television too. I craved their bodies next to mine, secure and safe in my arms.

'On one condition...'

'What?' Rosie sulked.

'That you watch a Wildlife on Four with me.'

She beamed. 'That's a deal.'


We both snuggled up next to Noah and listened to the soothing cawing and buzzing of the hot savannah as we watched a leopard cub gently paw his mother's face in play and affection. The cub's mother licked him briefly, looked around her, and licked her baby again.

'... possibly the injury that the cub has sustained in the attack might be fatal.'

'Is he hurt, Mummy?'

'I think he might be.'

'Don't worry. His mummy will look after him,' Noah said confidently.

I kept my fingers crossed, hoping the poor little cub would get better.

There was a close-up of its bloody leg.

I gasped. 'Maybe we should watch another show?'

'No, no! I want to see if he's okay.'

Knowing Rosie would worry all night if she didn't find out what had happened to the cub, we continued watching.

The leopard mother tugged at the scruff of the cub's neck, trying to drag him through the grass. It was clear the cub's back legs were paralysed as they flopped lifelessly behind him. I looked at Rosie, whose face was slack with horror.

'Poor cub,' she murmured, close to tears.

'Five hours later,' flashed up on screen. I braced myself.

Sheltered under a bush, the leopard mother is tearing meat from a carcass. There is a close up shot of a severed cub paw.

'Oh God,' I said, fumbling around for the remote control, 'LA LA LA!' I cried, trying to shout over the narration while dodging in front of them and covering their eyes. The narrator continued in rueful, soft-spoken tones, 'Perhaps in a mercy killing, knowing her cub would suffer, the mother eats her own young.'

'Mummy, what's happening?' Rosie was recoiling from the screen with the cushion over her head.

Noah darted around me, 'I want to see! I want to see!'

Abandoning the frantic search for the remote, I stood in front of the screen and switched it off by the mains. 'Phew! Gosh! That was a bit traumatic, wasn't it?' I laughed, trying make light of it.

Rosie's eyes were stripped with fear as she emerged from the blanket. 'Did the little cub die?'

'I'm afraid so.' And the rest, I thought.

'His mummy ATE HIM!' Noah screamed gleefully.

Rosie shouted back at him and hit him, 'Shut up, Noah! No, she didn't. She would never ever do that.'

'She HIT ME!' he wailed, cradling his arm.

I couldn't believe I had made this day worse, with the best of intentions, but I was relieved that we were in the television den at the back of the house where the noise was less likely to carry to Mira's pricked ears. The one small window in the room faced the garage belonging to our other neighbour, the quiet widower Mr Elliot, who owned the bookshop on the high street.

'Enough of that you two. No hitting, Rosie. Noah, of course she didn't eat him,' I said, rolling my eyes at Rosie.

Rosie smiled, 'It's okay Mummy. I know why she killed him. Because he was in pain and she knew the other animals would get him if she didn't and then she ate him because she was hungry. It's survival.'

'That's right. You're a smart cookie, aren't you?'

Our eye contact lingered, her blue eyes telling me she loved me, as mine told her the same, a mutual apology maybe.

And somehow that brief moment between us was enough to remind me of both the lightness and depth of our bond, the highs and lows, the tears and the laughter.

'No more tantrums now, Rosie.'

'Let's not talk about it ever, ever, ever,' Rosie cried burying her head in my tummy.

'Okay, that's a deal.' I liked the idea that we could wipe bad things from our memories that easily.

After a day from hell, after the worst of us, we could still have the best. A private, impenetrable moment between mother and daughter. We had bounced back from an intense fight and I felt connected to her deeply.

I had been restless, knowing Peter would be home soon. When he finally arrived, he weaved into the kitchen, clearly drunk.

'What's going on in here then? Cooking me a curry, eh?' he slurred.

I continued emptying all of the spice jars out of the larder cupboard, creating groups for each letter of the alphabet, and he stumbled as he took off his biking shoes. His eyelids were heavy. The smell of stale sweat mixed with the dried spices turned my stomach.

'Where have you been?'

'At Jim's?' he said. He washed his hands in the sink, losing balance as he pushed the soap pump.

'You said you'd be home by two.'

'I sent you a text.'

'I don't even know where my phone is right now.'

I shoved the allspice jar and the anise jar into the left-hand corner of the top rack.

'Ooops,' he sniggered. 'Vics was there. She made Pimms. Our swansong to summer! We sat on the terrace wrapped in blankets. We missed you.'

'I can't believe you were two doors down all this time.'

How different our day could have been. I pictured Rosie running through the garden with Beth, lost in an imaginary game, whizzing back and forth through the hedges between her camp and Beth's. And me, with my best friend, who would be jangling her bangles and laughing her head off as she poured more Pimms into my glass, telling me to seize the day, to relax and enjoy life as much as she did.

'Sorry.' He handed me the arrowroot jar as though it was a peace offering.

'Did you happen to see a couple of police cars flying round the close today by any chance?' I asked angrily.

'Trouble in the 'hood, was there?' He opened the fridge and pulled out a bottle of wine.

I took it from him and put it back in the fridge. 'I think you'd better have some coffee. You're going to need to sober up for this.'

I handed him a coffee pod.

'Sounds ominous,' he said, taking it and dropping it three times before slotting it into the machine.

'Those police cars were at *our* house.'

The noise of the coffee machine was so loud, it drowned out what I had said.

'The police did what?'

'The police cars were at our house. Mira called the police on us.'

Even before he had a sip of coffee, the lax, drunken muscles of his face tightened. He sat down on the stool at the island and shot back his espresso.

'Say that again, Gemma.'

'Mira called the police and two officers came round and basically accused me of abusing Rosie.'

'You're having me on.'

'If only.'

'Tell me exactly what happened,' he said, almost aggressively.

The spice jars slowly filled up the racks as I methodically took him through every detail, missing nothing out. Peter's face became progressively graver.

At the end, I waited for him to react. I was expecting outrage and incredulity.

'You should have changed your shirt,' he said.

My mouth gaped open. 'What?'

'The blood would have made it look much worse.'

My hands hung suspended in the air in front of me, palms open, as I stared at him gormlessly almost, at a loss. 'But, Peter, I didn't do anything wrong.'

'I know that.'

'A guilty person changes their bloody clothes,' I said, disbelief catching my throat.

'Is Rosie okay now?'

'She clammed up completely when I tried to ask her about what she said to PC Connolly.' My stomach lurched at the thought.

'Probably because she's still traumatised.'

'Likewise.' I rolled my eyes, feeling misunderstood and undervalued.

He shook his head back and forth before he responded. 'The police are trained to make everyone feel like a criminal, aren't they? It doesn't mean they think you are.'

'I promise you they were really quite reassuring by the end,' I said, biting my lip, wondering why I couldn't mention that Social Services were to be notified.

'And they can't change their minds?'

'Jesus, Peter. You're really freaking me out.'

I imagined the two officers chatting about me on their drive back to the station, analysing and reassessing their information; at their computers, tapping out a report for Social Services.

Peter jumped off the stool and wrapped his arms around me. 'Sorry. I'm so sorry. I didn't mean to. What an ordeal.'

Over his shoulder I noticed the cumin pot was the wrong side of the cardamon seeds. I shrugged him off and switched the jars round. 'If that Mira woman is watching us, what will she do next time Rosie has a tantrum?'

'Rosie cannot have another tantrum,' Peter stated firmly.

'Right, yes, it's that simple.'

A twitch of a smile appeared on Peter's face. 'A cream egg?'

'Don't even joke,' I smiled, relieved he was coming round.

Both of us looked over at the kitchen window to Mira's house and a nasty spread of hatred rolled through my body.

'Why does Rosie put herself through it?' Peter asked desperately. 'It can't be any fun for her.'

'And it's only ever directed at me.'

'You're her safe haven, I suppose.'

How ironic, I thought, when I was possibly the one person most likely to retaliate. Perhaps this was what she was aiming for, to push me and push me and push me, to check that my love was truly unconditional, to make sure I loved her enough to take the battering. It scared me to think that she needed to test me so radically, that she suspected a weakness in me.

Peter moved away and pulled his fingers across his scalp. When he turned around, there wasn't a hint of the joke left in his expression. He looked as unsettled as I felt, and he opened his mouth long before he spoke.

'Where does she get it from?' he said under his breath, staring at me like a man about to be hit by a train.

I took a step back from him as though he was now capable of hitting me.

'What difference does that make?' I hissed back.

He turned away from me and bent over the kitchen work surface with his head in his hands.

I left him there, escaping to the study and pushing the door shut, leaning my forehead into it, the pressure on my skull causing a pleasant circle of pain.

Distraction became urgent. I sat at the computer. A slick of sweat cooled my face and my fingers trembled as I typed in the password for my work emails. I needed to silence the lingering implication on Peter's lips.

# CHAPTER FOURTEEN

Enclosed in her small, green dining room, Mira shuffled her chair tightly in, until her belly was up against the edge of the table and her back was straight. The only sound was the flick-flack of photographs through her fingers. The motion reminded her of sifting through piles of autumn leaves as a child to find the best, biggest and brightest leaf.

While Barry slept upstairs, she discarded one snapshot after the other, her mind stuck in the unpleasant groove of a day that she had wanted to forget.

PC Yorke and PC Connolly had left hours ago. They had asked many questions. At first she had felt important, and then empty. She had wanted to talk to Barry before he went to bed but the words never came out. She had wanted to ask him if she had been mistaken. She didn't feel confident about any of it anymore, and she was fretting about the role Deidre had played. Her sister had always been the strong-minded, unwavering one of the two of them. While Mira shilly-shallied over which biscuit to choose from an assortment box, Deidre would snatch the one she wanted without hesitation. There seemed to Mira to be so many considerations and uncertainties and options in an average day; she found it hard to get through without prevaricating over something or other. If Deidre hadn't been there, would Mira have actually made that call?

Before Deidre had squeezed herself back into her car to return home – most definitely over the limit after three gin and tonics

– she had praised Mira for 'doing the right thing' and she had reminded her of all the little babies who had died because people turned a blind eye. Nevertheless, 'the right thing' was beginning to feel like a grey area. Was it too late to take it back? Would it be worth calling PC Connolly again, and talking through her doubts? She couldn't imagine police people looking kindly on doubts.

Uneasiness hung in the air around her. The Bradleys' house next door, which had for so many years sat benignly next to theirs, seemed now to have an iniquitous glow. Every time she thought about Gemma, her stomach jumped into her throat.

By interfering, she had thrown everything off balance.

Her involvement did not sit well in her heart. Mira was sifting urgently through the photographs for answers. There was a score to settle in her past. She knew, logically, that there was no connection between her own childhood and Rosie's. Rosie's was privileged and elitist and cosseted. Rosie was unaware that private schools, like New Hall Preparatory, only educated 7 per cent of the country, and she would definitely be unaware that 93 per cent of the country did not call toilets 'loos'. Whereas Mira's childhood had been normal. She had been educated at the local state comprehensive, whose pupils thought the children at the private school down the road were a 'bunch of knob-ends'. And she had a mother who called a toilet a toilet, and cleaned it herself, by the way. They had been brought up in different worlds. But at the same time she knew there was a deep-seated tug from the core of her that drew her to Rosie. The protective urge was fierce, as though she had known Rosie in previous lives. Before Rosie had moved in, Mira had thought Chloe, with her long locks of rusty red hair, was unique, especially beautiful. When Chloe had sent her goodbye note in the blue plastic bucket, Mira had cried.

The muted colours of the faded Kodak moments in front of her were becoming like pieces of a jigsaw, where the bigger picture on the front of the box was forever mutating into another scene.

The emerging picture scared Mira, but she was too curious to stop looking now. Her memory was on rewind, hurtling towards her younger self again, to see that girl whose wide eyes had been as vulnerable as Rosie's once upon a time.

The cream cardboard of the first page of the album was still blank. She was forever indecisive.

There was silence next door now as she opened the next envelope of photographs, sticky as though fresh from the developers.

The first photograph in the pack was a collision on her senses. The curled edges of a nightmare lay in her fingers. Craig Baxter. The pulse at her throat throbbed. His smooth forehead, his overgrown crest of black hair, the turned-up upper lip, feminine, contrasting with his muscled forearm that wrapped around Deidre's neck. This, Mira had hidden under her mattress all those years ago. Every night, she had reached for it, snapped on her torch, and gazed at him in the circle of light.

The dining room grew hotter. There was a crease across his middle where Mira remembered folding the photograph in half to hide it properly. She studied Craig's features, hungry for a morsel. His limbs, slouched onto the beige leather couch, the length of them, the bulk of his thighs, the broad shoulders. A packet of cigarettes rolled up into one sleeve; keys to his car in one hand, the other behind his head; one eyebrow raised towards the camera. At twenty-two, he had been a real man, with a job, a Ford Grenada with two exhausts, and money in his leather wallet. But her sister had him.

There was an ache in her belly as her eyes rolled over his body under the white T-shirt. The cotton had smelt of the smoke which had billowed from the barbeque that day. When the wind changed direction, they had shuffled their chairs round the small patio, like none of them had legs. Craig closer to Mira each time, their thighs almost touching. She had locked her legs together, stared down at her bare feet, at the flecks of rain disappearing into the warm patio slabs. Aware of his hands so close to her body, she sipped at her soda pop too frequently.

'Mira, get the kebabs going, will you?' Her mother's voice, her back to them, eyes in the back of her head.

Everything had belonged to Deidre, even their mother's love. Mira had been angry, and, in the light of Craig's attention, entitled to get something of her own. Craig's attention was revelatory.

In the end, she couldn't resist his continual advances, the stolen moments, the comforting grip of his hot hand holding hers under the table. The slow steps, to drag out their time together, the fluttering in her stomach. Her shoulder socket pulling as he led her by the hand, the path underneath her feet becoming soft, the smell of the damp leaves, the noise of other school friends passing by so near, unaware of their presence a few feet away. The feel of his lips on hers, mingled with the musty reek of her uniform. She sprayed perfume on her neck and in between her legs in the toilets before meeting him. Thursdays after school became a regular date. Her self-consciousness, the thrill, the greedy joy in his blue eyes, flicking from her chest to meet her gaze as he unbuttoned her school shirt. Mira swooned at the memory. The euphoria of that weekly tryst came back to her as if it was yesterday. After their fumble in the woods, they would walk and talk, like a normal boyfriend and girlfriend, or maybe even like a brother and sister. Nobody questioned them; he was Deidre's boyfriend.

'I've got to stop off at the newsagents to get more milk. Mum went mad at me when there wasn't any this morning.'

'Your mum blamed you for that?' he asked incredulously, ruffling the tip of his quiff lightly. Mira admired the flattering angle of his face, as he dipped his chin, pouted a little, like a model.

'Yeah, course. They blame me for everything.'

'I saw Deidre knock that milk over with my own eyes.' At last, there was someone to bear witness. He might not have spoken up for Mira at the time, but he had registered her mother's bias.

Craig was rooting for the underdog, but hadn't quite found his voice yet; like her, she supposed.

'I'm used to it.' This wasn't true. Mira never got used to it. Every injustice carved a sharp groove onto her heart.

'You should stand up for yourself.'

'No point,' she shrugged.

He picked a strand of her waist-length hair, and twirled it in his fingers, a habit of his that sent waves of pleasure through her. When he did this, she mapped her future out with him: her place lying next to him in his bed, the shiny tiles of his flat that she would clean for him, the meals she would prepare for two. The fantasy had kept her going, helped her to get up and out to school in the mornings.

Before Craig, Mira had been in the background, blending in, efficient without a fuss. She had kept it simple, let the days roll by, pottered along unnoticed.

They never made reference to the mammoth nature of their betrayal. Their kissing and fondling existed in a moral vacuum, exempt from any possible consequences, desire burning out any guilt. Mira learned that cheating could take place in a special mental compartment. Her judgement and outrage at others who cheated was as solid as ever. Her own situation was different. Every cheater wants to justify their cheating, to diminish their wrongdoing, and Mira was no different. At fourteen years old, she was naive about the cost of that denial. However much she hated her sister, she had never consciously set out to hurt her.

Now, in her stuffy dining room, all grown up, she contemplated a life with Craig, whom she had loved, and wondered how life could have been if it had not gone so spectacularly wrong.

Mira heard the door behind her open. Barry stood behind her, hair ruffled, in his stripy pyjama bottoms and T-shirt.

'What are you doing still up?'

'Couldn't sleep.'

He sat down on the chair next to her, glancing briefly at the table of photographs.

Mira lugged the album across the table to show Barry. 'It's lovely, isn't it?'

'Are you feeling all right about all that stuff today?'

'The police said they're dealing with it, so that's that.' The embarrassment of her overreaction pinched and plucked at her cheeks.

He let out a breath, as though relieved. 'As long as you're okay.'

'Rosie's being looked out for now.'

'Good. I'm back off to bed.' He kissed her on the forehead.

Tears stung her eyes. She had a sliding feeling, as though she was slipping into the shadows, again peripheral and insignificant, a nuisance. She bit her lip and her eye caught a photograph of herself standing in the infamous brown-flowered dress, when it was too big for her. Almost belligerently, she stuck it down slap-bang in the middle of the first page of the album, a little wonky. She would be the star of this album. She could own her own story. Perhaps she was sick of being in the background, of questioning her decisions, of questioning her very existence. It was time to put herself at the very centre of her own life. And if that meant upsetting a few people along the way, then so be it.

Strangely, the very decision to be proactive, to stick that first photograph down, diminished the angst she felt about Rosie, and it helped her to find some peace that day, and finally some sleepiness too.

# CHAPTER FIFTEEN

*TOP SECRET*

*Dear Mummy,*

*Noah told me he wanted to put the policemens and policewomans – SOOOO CUTE – in the Worry Box at school. I laughed at him and I told him how to say it properly without the extra sssss. But I think I do too. Not actually put them inside, like DUH! they wouldn't fit, but put my thoughts about them inside. I have never put anything in the Worry Box. I bet Noah hasn't either. I think the teachers would guess it was my writing and then call me into Mr Roderick's office to tell me off for being a liar-liar pants of fire or something and I would want to kick Mr Roderick in the nuts (that's what Max in Year 4 says every time he gets told off, which is A LOT).*

*If I did put it in the worry box then this is what I would write.*

*INVISIBLE INK ALERT: I almost hit Mrs E (can't spell it or say it) with my silver shoe. Was she the one who called the police? I did NOT tell PC Conerly that you slammed the door on my wrist. I know you are worried that I did. You would be really, really, really, really, really, really cross if I had told her. Like this :(((((( . But you always tell me to tell the truth. You say you'll be very disappointed in me if I don't tell you the truth. BLAH BLAH BLAH. See? Sometimes mummies are wrong. Sorry you got told off, mummy.*

*Why am I always such a peanut brain? Why peanut? Why not pine nut brain or a pumpkin seed brain or a raisin brain. Answers on a postcard!*

*Love,*

*Rosie xx*

*P.S. Will they come back?*

# CHAPTER SIXTEEN

My brain was packed full of worry. I barely had any space left to focus on small decisions. As soon as I brushed my teeth, I questioned whether I had or not. I stared into my drawer for my pyjamas before realising I was looking in the wrong drawer. I read my book in bed but I didn't take in a word of it.

Unable to sleep once I had turned the light off, I climbed out of bed and crept in to see Rosie.

Her duvet was bunched up around her head. I pulled the duvet away, down over her splayed limbs and saw that her pink electronic diary lay across her open hand. The door of the diary was open. When I gently removed it from her, she frowned in her sleep.

I studied her features. They were neat while mine seemed untamed. Her nose, long and straight, like Peter's, her black hair, as thick as a tree trunk in a ponytail, while mine disappeared to nothing. Her pale skin would freckle in the sun, while mine burnt. The muscles on her calves were stronger, shapelier than the spindles I had inherited from my mother. Rosie looked nothing like me. Had anyone else noticed?

I closed the pink plastic door shut on her secret scribblings, disciplined enough not to peek, in spite of my curiosity, and placed it by her bed. All of our secrets safely under wraps.

'Rich and the kids are out on a ride. They'll be back in a min,' my sister said, plonking the meat on her over-cluttered surfaces and clattering around the copper pots and pans hanging up to bring down the largest boiling pot and two colanders, one plastic and one metal. Jackie pushed some old bills and colouring books from one end of the kitchen table to the other to make room for the colanders. Her kitchen was as haphazard and charming as mine was tidy and sterile.

'Do you know how to use this?' Jackie quipped when she handed me the peeler.

'Of course I do. I use it to peel the carrots for my power shake every morning,' I joshed.

'Ha ha.'

Armed with a potato peeler each, the Aga warming our backs, we sat at the table with the colanders in our laps and peeled. I relished in the mundane task, realising how little time I made for cooking, or for my sister, for that matter.

'How was Rosie this morning?'

'Bit quiet. Bit too nice.'

'When Stella is feeling guilty about something, she compliments me on my hair,' Jackie said, raising an eyebrow.

I laughed.

'I don't know what you're laughing at?' Jackie grinned, flicking a straggle behind her back.

She was thin and dark, like me, but her thinness was more muscular, her arms had defined sinews visible under her skin, and her hair was permanently windswept, like my hair on a very bad day. She probably used washing-up liquid to wash it. Her pale skin was ruddy in circles on her cheeks and deeply lined around the eyes and across her forehead. She was older than me by two years, but most people would probably guess ten. Her concern about this was at zero. Unless it was horses she was grooming, she didn't care about appearances. The eldest of her four children, Stella, learnt to French plait her own hair at five years old.

'And how are you?' she asked.

'I'm not sure. I read a story online last night that was about this woman whose kids were taken away from her when her husband accused her of hitting them even though he was the nutter, not her.'

'It does happen,' Jackie replied, without looking up from her potato.

'And once she got into the system, she couldn't get out of it. She lost both her children. And her family and friends turned against her.'

Jackie's hands stopped peeling for a second before she answered. 'If you start reading stuff online, you'll only freak yourself out.'

'But what about Social Services?'

'If they do get in touch, you have nothing to hide. It'll be fine.'

But there was something niggling me, at the back of my mind, telling me it wasn't fine, and I certainly didn't want Jackie to think it was fine. None of it felt fine.

'You reckon?'

'Stop worrying. That woman next door has obviously got major issues.'

'But Rosie does scream a lot,' I said, quietly.

'All kids scream.'

'What if Mira calls the police every time she does?'

'You can't live like you're stepping on eggshells.'

'What do I do then? I can't gag Rosie.'

Jackie paused, wiped a strand of hair from her eyes with the back of her hand and looked at me.

'Do you ever think about going part-time?'

It was like a nasty little kick in the shin.

'Do you really think her tantrums are about that?'

'What do you think?'

'I think she tantrums because she's a pain in the arse.'

'Keep your voice down, Gem,' she said, even though she knew Rosie and Noah were well out of earshot, playing on the swings outside with Peter.

'I give her everything any child could dream of and she throws it back in my face.'

'I know she's hard work.'

'Hmmm,' I said, doubtfully. 'But you think I neglect her.'

'Neglect her? Oh come on, Gemma, don't put words in my mouth. I know how much you love Rosie, and so does Peter, and Mum. Don't go getting all paranoid about us, of all people.' Jackie was shaking her head at me.

'You'd be paranoid too if you had the police asking you about whether you abuse your kids.'

Jackie placed her hand on mine, and spoke gently, 'Let's forget about it.'

A curl of isolation wrapped itself around my head like a dense mist, separating me from Jackie. There was so much she didn't know. Everything she said would fall short of what I needed from her.

'You would support me though, wouldn't you, if it came to it?'

'Now you're sounding crazy.' And Jackie stood up and walked out into the garden. She had never liked the confrontation I would endlessly push for.

I saw her through the window. My regret fought with my anger. I knew I should go out there to say sorry. But if I admitted to being in the wrong, she would automatically be in the right, and the child in me couldn't handle that.

Mum's arrival was a welcome interruption.

'What's going on, you two?'

Before I had a chance to reply, Jackie flung the backdoor open and stepped back into the kitchen.

'Look, Gemma, none of us is getting it right, okay? I am an absolutely crap mother most of the time. I barely manage to bath them once a week, and I always let them play outside when they should be doing their homework, and I feed them pasta pesto too often, and, seriously, I could go on and on, but the thing is, you know all this because I talk about how crap I am all the time.

The difference is, you never do. You never ever admit to making mistakes. You're always telling us how perfect everything is.'

Mum's eyes batted furiously as she looked from Jackie to me. In old photographs, Mum's eyes were as bright as buttons. Now they had a milky film, as though the sadness and disappointments of life had brought diaphanous curtains across her vision to shield her. 'Sorry, Jacs,' I said, and hung my head. My heart contracted with shame. My sister never raised her voice to me. 'I didn't mean to take it out on you.'

Jackie dropped her hands from her hips, stepped into my arms and hugged me tightly.

'Sometimes it's okay just to ask for help.'

'I'm the worst sister ever. And the worst mother ever,' I moaned.

'No, no, you're an amazing mother, and don't for a second forget it.'

We stood stuck to each other until mother piped up.

'Plainly, *I* haven't done a very good job though. You're a pair of basket cases,' she said, and all three of us fell about laughing.

'You're right. You totally fucked us up,' Jackie said, kissing Mum on the cheek.

'Hi Mum.' I kissed her other cheek. 'It's okay, I blame the hormones,' I joked, holding both hands over my stomach, trying to warm it, to soothe it somehow, to counteract the surge of stress hormones. If its exposure to high levels of cortisol was anything to go by, the poor little mite was going to be crazier than all of us put together.

Peter came back in, with dirty trousers from the mud pit that surrounded the swings. 'What's all this hugging about?'

'Sorry, you have to be a crap mum to get a hug. But you can have a cup of tea,' Mum said, waving a teabag in his direction.

'What about being a crap dad? If you don't hug me, it's discrimination.' And he hugged Mum, who stiffened a little at such an open display of affection.

'Speaking of crap dads, either of you called him recently?'
Mum asked.

Jackie and I glanced at each other and grimaced.

'Girls, seriously,' Mum reprimanded.

'I called him after Jill's funeral,' Jacs offered up sheepishly.

'That godforsaken village he lives in is ten miles from a village
shop and he's all alone now. You really should call him.'

'He was coping all right when I last spoke to him.'

'You know, he might surprise you, he might be able to offer
some good advice,' Mum said.

'Don't you *dare* tell him about the police, Mum,' I begged,
knowing Mum spoke to him weekly.

'There's no shame in it, darling. You know, I spoke to John
last night and apparently something like this happened to Immy's
friend, a few years back...' Mum began.

'Did you tell John, too?' I cried.

'It's only *John*.'

She told John everything. John and Sarah, and their daughter
Imogen, had lived in the next-door house to us on the Victorian
terrace we had grown up in. John and Sarah were the parents Jacs
and I wished we had. I minded less that she had told John.

'Go on, what happened,' Jacs said, bringing us back to the
point.

'Well, apparently, Social Services called to arrange an appointment and then they came around to her house to interview her,
and they interviewed the son at school.'

'Why were they suspicious in the first place?' I asked, my
heartbeat quickening at the mention of Social Services.

'It was a mum at school who made the allegation. She accused
her of neglect.'

'And they were completely innocent?'

'Completely, apparently. It turned out the child had some
allergy or something, which explained how skinny she was. They

dropped the case in a couple of weeks. But Imogen remembers her friend went through hell. They spoke to their doctor and the child's teachers, and all sorts.'

There was silence. Possibly, we were all thinking the same. I knew what I was thinking: no smoke without fire. When someone points a finger, you are naturally left wondering why. If it isn't true, why accuse them in the first place? I recognised the hypocrisy of my suspicions. It was an insight into how other mothers might feel about me if it got out.

'It won't come to all that. As I've said, you've got nothing to hide,' Jackie restated reassuringly.

Some of us have more to hide than others, I thought. I knew that my sister would never have had the urge to hit her children and I knew how shocked she would be if I told her that it came to me when Rosie was in a tantrum. I had never seen Jackie raise her voice to any of her four near-feral children. They wouldn't know a boundary if it smacked them in the face and I had often judged her for it.

I stood to clear the empty cups of tea. 'More tea, anyone?'

Jackie stood up. 'Peter, come out to the paddocks with me and say hello to Still Standing. She's doing so well.'

'Love to,' he said, and they both disappeared outside.

I was left alone with Mum, who helped me put the mugs in the dishwasher.

'I was wondering, darling, if it might be a good idea for you to have a day out with Rosie this week.'

'Actually, I was thinking of booking a surprise trip for all of us to Disneyland Paris, or something, as a bit of a treat.'

'No, I meant, just you and Rosie. Something simple.'

'Oh. Yes. That might be a good idea.' Dread twisted in my stomach. I felt actual fear of a whole day alone with her.

'Are you very busy at work at the moment?'

The potential promotion, which I had kept secret for now, loomed largely in my mind. 'No more than usual,' I said.

'You know, I realised last time I looked after them that you arrive home terribly late at night.'

Here we go again, I thought. Jacs and Mum had obviously been talking. To save a row, I decided to ignore her, as though she hadn't spoken at all. It was the way my mother and I had always operated.

'Maybe I'll take her into London to see a show,' I suggested.

My mother seemed happy to drop it too. '*A Midsummer Night's Dream* is on at the Barbican.'

I tried not to laugh. 'I was thinking more like a musical.'

'She's very bright. You don't need to dumb it down,' Mum sniffed.

When I was young, my mother would slam the door shut to the sitting room if Jacs and I watched a soap opera on the television instead of a documentary. 'I'll have a look at what's on,' I said, trying to placate her.

'It'll be lovely, darling, whatever you do,' my mother said.

I wished I shared her optimism. Online later that night, the pressure to choose the right show sent me into paroxysms of indecision. The bigger shows were booked out, the smaller ones were not special enough, some were too grown-up, some too babyish. It was like choosing a party dress for her all over again, but worse. I was bound to get it wrong. After two hours of research, prevaricating hopelessly, I bought two tickets for a musical production performed by a circus troupe from Paris. And I crossed my fingers.

# CHAPTER SEVENTEEN

Rosie was standing there under a film of drizzle in her red-and-white striped nightdress, slap bang in the middle of Mira's driveway, staring up at their house. Her black hair was slick and shiny, a neat strip in front of each shoulder, as though it had been combed one-hundred and two times.

Mira, who had been about to pull her own nightdress off to get dressed for work, leapt to the side of the window out of sight.

'Barry,' Mira whispered. 'Look, Rosie's out there.'

He poked his head over his newspapers and peered out of the window.

'Whatever is she doing?' He looked at his watch. 'It's seven in the morning.'

Mira looked on at her, reluctant to go out to her, worried about what the child had to say. It was a chance to study her face. She was pretty, in a pale and interesting way, not unlike Gemma Bradley in terms of colouring, Mira thought. But that was where the similarity ended. Rosie's features were refined and in proportion, like Peter's quiet, self-contained handsomeness, while her mother's features were attractive, but less settled somehow, less refined – thicker brows, wider smile. More like a child's than Rosie's, Mira thought.

'I'd better go see what she wants,' Mira said, pulling her dressing gown down from the hook on the back of the door.

When she opened her door, Rosie scarpered, disappearing as though she had never been there.

Mira stood with her back leaning into the door, like it were a barricade, long enough to hear Gemma's car crunch out around the roundabout and out of the cul-de-sac.

Had Rosie been coming to ask for help? A sense of responsibility for her burrowed its way into her soul. Whatever was going on next door, Mira was inextricably involved now. Rosie had come to her house for a reason. If Mira didn't respond, she would be letting her down.

Most days, Rosie and Noah came home through the back gate at around four o'clock. Their nanny would arrive at their house at about a quarter to four. There were after-school clubs – which Mira could find out the times for if she watched carefully – but essentially, there would be a ten-minute slot when Rosie would be alone, with Noah of course, walking across the recreational ground from the back gate of their school. If Mira intercepted their journey, Rosie would be able to talk to her freely without her mother's input. It would provide Rosie with some time at least for her to communicate with a trusted grown-up. There was no crime in bumping into someone randomly was there?

'Did you speak to her?' Barry said, coming down the stairs dressed in his gardening scruffs.

Mira moved away from the door. 'She ran off before I got the chance.'

'What an odd bod.'

'Children who are going through a lot at home often do strange things.'

Barry stopped midway through tucking his shirt in. 'Are you okay, love?'

'Oh, for goodness sake, of course I am. Stop asking me all the time,' Mira snapped.

Once Mira had thought of this plan to help Rosie, she became quite set on it. Throughout her normal Monday at school – hearing the children read, clearing up the learning tools, writing accident reports, monitoring dinner – she was clock-watching. She was reminded of how she used to clock-watch at school throughout double Biology on Thursday afternoons, when every minute felt like a lifetime before she could escape to meet Craig. The clock face above the blackboard had had a white face and black numbers and the second hand was red, moving forward in slow motion.

She looked up to a similar clock in the Year Two classroom. It was five past three, and twenty seconds. Twenty-one, twenty-two, twenty-three, she counted, almost willing the clock to take her back in time.

The children had been walked out into the playground for pick-up and it was quiet at last. She felt inside her skirt pocket for the little square photograph nestled there. Before leaving the house that morning, she had peeked into the dining room to check everything was in order for her work on the album later. The photograph of Craig had been lying there on the top of the pile. It had struck her that it was a bit like leaving a text message from your lover on your phone display for your husband to read. Barry hadn't known about her involvement with Craig, and she didn't want him to find out now. So, she had pocketed it.

Occasionally, its corner pricked her thigh through the material of her skirt as she moved about, reuniting named coats and shoes to their corresponding pegs, slowly clearing the space. Every now and again, she would slip her fingers into her skirt pocket to feel for the photograph. Working her fingertips across the smooth surface, sliding them across the edges, imagining his face was a comfort to her, like flicking through worry beads. The image of Craig in his white T-shirt was crystallised in her memory.

'You feeling okay?' came a voice from outside of her head. Patricia's voice.

Mira realised she was sitting down on the low gym bench with a trainer resting in her lap.

'Oh, sorry, I felt a bit light-headed. I'm fine now,' Mira lied, unable to explain why she had stopped to sit, why the dreams of the past had taken over her like a temporary blindness of the present.

'You sure? You look like you've seen a ghost.'

'It's the pong of this, probably!' Mira joked, stuffing the trainer into her gym bag.

'Off you pop home, Mrs Entwistle!' Patricia said.

By a quarter to four, Mira was parking up in her drive. A few minutes later, the Bradleys' nanny's blue hatchback whizzed around the roundabout.

Mira changed quickly into an old tracksuit and trainers.

Her route to the recreational ground was more convoluted than it would have been from the Bradleys' back garden. This fact had always irked her. The houses on the close with access to the grounds via their back gates were considered more desirable than the houses without access. An estimated fifty thousand pounds was added to the value of those privileged few on the other side of the road. It was a microcosm of the social divide in their town. Those on the west side seemed to drive bigger cars, tended to send their children to the same private school and shopped in Waitrose over Tesco.

Mira had to walk to the top of the close onto the main road, walk a few hundred yards down the B road (which lacked a pavement), round the corner into the small gate on the other side, through a small car park and finally onto the large expanse of green at the brow of the town's hill. The views beyond the tennis courts and the playground encompassed thickets of trees over rolling hills dotted by beautiful large Arts and Crafts houses that she imagined belonged to millionaires. The view reminded Mira of the fairytale *The House with the Golden Windows*, where the little girl in her simple house dreamt of living in the house she could see across the valley whose windows shone gold. When the little girl finally made the trip to visit the house she had coveted, she realised the windows were broken and dirty. Looking back over the valley to her small house, she was amazed to see that the windows of her own home were shining golden as the sun reflected upon them, and she understood that her home was where she had always been happy and loved.

There were no golden windows on the millionaires' houses today. The sky was a suspended ceiling of grey.

Mira began to run for a few paces along the lines of the football pitches, and then stopped to walk, and then began to run again, her lungs shouting at her to stop this unfamiliar activity, shocked by how unfit she had become.

A handful of children emerged from the chicken-wired back gate of New Hall Prep, inadequately secured by a keypad with the pass code 1066 known widely to all.

By the time she spotted the familiar little figures of Rosie and Noah in their brown and yellow tartan uniforms, she was red in the face and her breasts ached from all the bouncing up and down.

Catching her breath, she power walked over to the corner of the football pitch where she estimated their journeys would converge naturally.

'Hello, you two!' she puffed, slowing down to fall into step with them.

Noah replied a mumbled 'hello' while kicking his football in front of him. Rosie didn't reply at all and sped up, which Mira thought was rather rude. Her behaviour reflected how poorly their parents had taught them manners, Mira thought petulantly.

Mira jogged to keep up with Rosie's quickened pace. 'Good day at school?'

'Uh huh.' Rosie tugged her school rucksack further onto her shoulder and checked behind her for her brother. 'Come on, Noah.'

They turned left out of the recreational ground through a discreet hole in the hedge and ducked into a gloomy walkway. The bough of branches overhead stole the light and the oak-panelled fences that lined the mulch path seemed to push nature away with ugly, uniformed force. A little shiver ran down Mira's spine, which she put down to the drop of temperature. Estimating that they were three back gates away from the Bradleys' garden, she got straight to the point. 'Was everything okay this morning, love?'

'Uh huh,' Rosie replied.

'If you want to come in for a cup of tea and a piece of cake, just knock on the door or send a message in the blue bucket, any time, all right? My door is always open.'

'No, it's okay!' Rosie cried, breaking into a run. 'Come on Noah!' she yelled behind her. Noah charged past Mira, almost knocking her over.

Mira understood that their parents had fed them their fear. She would try again tomorrow, and the next day, and onwards, so that they knew that she was there for them, and that she was on their side.

# CHAPTER EIGHTEEN

*TOP SECRET*

*Dear Mummy,*
    *INVISIBLE INK ALERT: Noah swore on our whole family's lives that he would never EVER, EVER tell you that we talked to Mrs E (I do not know how to spell her weird name). If you found out what I did, you would kill me. I promise I didn't do it on purpose. I was curious, like Alice in Alice in Wonderland going into a hole. (Curious is a word I used in my composition at school and I got a gold star for it).*

*This is how it WENT DOWN:*
    *I went outside to get my school bag from the car (CHECK). SUDDENLY I saw the hole in the hedge that Noah uses to get his football (CHECK). Then SUDDENLY I was in her garden (CHECK) and then SUDDENLY I saw Mrs E in her bedroom window (DOUBLE CHECK).*
    *In Noah's Charles Dickens pop-up book Pip in Great Expectations is very brave when he visits Miss Haversham. She looks scary in the picture with a pointy nose and grey hair but she is nice really. Mrs E has grey hair too but it is short and sticks up at the front. I am not brave at all. Noah would say I am a big fat poo-head for not telling that police*

*woman that you are a lovely mummy and that you didn't mean to hurt my wrist.*

*Daddy says butt-head and wee-wee brain to make Noah laugh. When he thinks I am not listening he says shit a lot, like ALL THE TIME. I bet he would call that police woman MRS SHIT-HEAD.*

*Love you,*
*Rosie.*
*xx*

*P.S. When I go round to Mrs E's house I hope she will have Mr Kipling battinburger cake. YUM YUM IN MY TUM.*

# CHAPTER NINETEEN

Peter breathed slowly and heavily over my shoulder as we read:

**PRIVATE AND CONFIDENTIAL**
*South East Assessment Hub*
*Silway Centre*
*Greyswood*
*GU52 92L*

*Dear Mrs Bradley,*

*RE: Police response visit to 4 Virginia Close, 16 October 2016*

*I am writing to inform you that Social Services have been notified about the above incident that followed a concerned call from your neighbour. PC Connolly and PC Yorke made an assessment, after speaking to you and your children at the above address, concluding that there was no immediate cause for concern.*
*To ensure you feel appropriately supported, you can contact me at Children's Services on the above number with regards to your child/ren.*

*Yours sincerely,*
**Miranda Slater**
**Social Worker South East Assessment Team**

In an oddly disconnected moment, I inspected the outside of the envelope for signs that would give away its sender, like an ink stamp or a sticker, worried the postman would have guessed at its contents.

The gossip mill of a small town could be toxic. I imagined the mothers at school finding out. After all the years Rosie had been at that same school, I wasn't friendly with any of them, except Vics. I liked them when I joined them for pub drinks at the end of each term, but I often came away paranoid that they judged me for my absence at the school gates. They seemed to know so much more than me about the ins and outs of school politics. Some of them were so involved in their children's school careers they should have been on salaries. There were times when I had to repress the compulsion to tell them that my dedication to my children was as authentic and loving as theirs, just exposed differently. I was certain that I would be on Prozac or permanently drunk if I had stayed as a full-time mother. What would they make of this letter? No doubt, it would light up their school pick-up chatter.

The faded blue borough council stamp was the only clue to its contents. It could have been about council tax or the electoral role or any number of things. The fact that it wasn't thudded in my gut.

'What does this mean?' Peter said.

The base of my spine ached with its new load and I rubbed there, pressing the stress away.

The memory of PC Connolly's parting words resurfaced. 'It's *standard procedure*, apparently,' I informed Peter, anger rattling through my voice.

'Is it? They didn't say anything about getting social workers involved, did they?'

'I told you, PC Connolly specifically said there'd be no further action.'

I skimmed to the bottom of the letter to the name at the bottom. This Miranda Slater woman can fuck right off with her offer of help, I thought.

'Maybe they searched their files at the station and found records of your stint in Holloway?'

I couldn't laugh. I re-read the letter and it riled me further. 'Appropriately supported? Jesus. I don't feel very supported when two police officers turn up on my door accusing me of abusing my children. I feel totally *un*supported.'

Peter gulped back his wine like water.

'A hangover isn't going to help anything,' I snapped.

'Don't use this to have a go at me.' Peter took the letter from me. 'Let me read it again.'

I moved over to the window, peering out through hedge to the Entwistles' house.

'The thought of having to call a social worker makes my blood boil, seriously, don't you think it's insulting?'

'I don't know. I don't know anything about this kind of thing. Can we ignore it?'

The flimsy inanimate letter in front of us seemed to be alive, radiating trouble.

'I don't need their help.'

'Will it look bad if we don't get in contact?'

'Who cares?' I snatched up the letter and crumpled it into a ball and threw it in the bin.

Peter and I looked at the bin for what seemed like a long minute, before he said, 'That was a bit rash.'

We both burst out laughing.

'A bit hasty, maybe,' I snickered.

Gingerly, I picked it out and smoothed it onto the table.

Peter chuckled, peeling off an old piece of grated carrot. 'And you didn't even put it in the recycling.'

I searched his smiling eyes for that reassuring connection between us. It was there, but I also spotted my anxiety reflected back at me.

Our mirth subsided.

I folded the grubby sheet back into its envelope. 'I'll call her and tell her politely that we don't need any help.'

The smile fell completely from both of our faces after I said it. In the space of a few seconds, Peter looked like he hadn't slept or eaten in a hundred years, as though the laughter had wrung him dry of every tiny last bit of optimism.

He rubbed his face and sighed, 'What are we doing so wrong?'

'What am *I* doing so wrong, you mean?'

'I didn't say that.'

'Mum and Jacs think I don't spend enough time with her. Like it's an attention thing.'

He looked almost hopeful again. 'Do you think they have a point?'

'You and I both made the decision to have a joint income, Peter.'

'I'm not blaming you.'

'It seems like it.'

'We're on the same side.'

'Sorry.' I rubbed my fingers at my hairline, hearing the scratch through my skull. I didn't want to be obstructive.

'D'you think we should make some lifestyle changes?'

'Like what?'

'We could sell the house? Reduce our overheads?'

'I don't know,' I moaned, feeling my brain hurting.

Peter looked around him. 'I love this house.'

'The kids would be devastated. And Rosie might get worse.' But I didn't say what would sound selfish and un-motherly, that I loved my job, that I didn't want to stay at home filling the hours before pick-up with tennis lessons and coffee mornings.

'But at least Mira wouldn't be listening next door.' Peter shot a filthy look in the direction of Mira's house.

'That is not a good reason to move.' However much I detested her being so close, I was not going to run away from the life we had worked so hard to create.

Peter poured more wine and cleared his throat. 'Maybe this social worker woman might be able to recommend someone to talk to?'

'What kind of someone?'

'A counsellor or something.'

'No,' I barked, sounding like my mother. My heart was beating in my eardrums.

'Don't fly off the handle, okay? You always bloody fly off the handle,' he snapped with a rare flash of anger.

I breathed in, as though sucking back an unexploded grenade. 'I don't like the idea of strangers knowing our business.'

He flashed his palms at me, surrendering, 'Fine.' He stood up, knocking the stool over, leaving it and weaving out.

I wrapped my arms around my middle, and imagined the tiny curl of a baby there. Perhaps when it was born, Rosie would realise that the world didn't revolve around her, that her tantrums wouldn't get her anywhere. I might consider asking her to help me transform the spare room into the nursery. If she engaged with a project, she might forget about her own dramas for a change.

In the meantime, if she had a tantrum again, I would put her in the television den, where the noise would bounce off Mr Elliot's garage wall. We could fix a lock onto the door, take down the oil painting and cover the dangerous edges to keep her safe in there while she screamed it out. Or give her a cream egg. Anything to keep the police and the Social Services away.

Deep down though, I hoped it wouldn't come to that. I hoped she had been scared by the police visit as much as we had and I hoped that our day out in London would heal us, temporarily at least.

# CHAPTER TWENTY

*Dear Mummy,*

*INVISIBLE INK ALERT: I bet you a gazillion Monopoly pounds that Mrs E will come up to me and Noah on the rec tomorrow again. She comes every day. I don't talk to her. I just run away with Noah. She told me not to be shy. On Monday I won't be shy. I'm going to tell her that you are AWESOME and LOVELY and that I love you so so so so so much.*

*Love you (again),*
*Rosie.*

*P.S. We are going to LONDON tomorrow!!!!! BIG THUMBS UP EMOJI. You are the best.*

# CHAPTER TWENTY-ONE

Rosie pointed out of her side of the car window. 'There's Mrs E.'

When Mira spotted us, she stopped, parked her shopping basket on the camber and waved. Rosie waved back.

Resisting the urge to slap Rosie's hand down, I sped on down the hill towards the station. Through the rear-view mirror, I could see Mira turn to watch us go. Had she really expected me to stop for a little chat?

As soon as Rosie and I were standing on the train platform, hand in hand, I stopped seething about Mira and I felt a surge of eagerness and delight at the prospect of sitting in the auditorium with Rosie to watch the musical show, which my mother would think terribly lowbrow, a fact that added to my glee.

We found two table seats on the carriage and sat down opposite each other with two hot chocolates in paper cups.

I looked at her and saw how grown-up she was. Her white shirt was buttoned up to the neck, like the girls in the fashion magazines, and the necklace Peter and I had given her for Christmas rested on her collar. I was starry-eyed with pride. Without the stresses and distractions of daily life, I understood how I had lost sight of how fast she was growing up. I couldn't believe we had never been to London together before, just the two of us.

'Tell me about school. What's the latest?'

I had wanted to know about her friends. Or teachers. Or books she was reading.

'I got thirty out of thirty in my spelling test, and a silver medal for the times table competition.'

Knowing she had wanted a gold medal, I mustered up some enthusiasm to say, 'Well done, darling! That is wonderful.'

'I only didn't get gold because stupid Edmund distracted me. He says girls aren't good at maths.' She rolled her eyes to the heavens.

'That's annoying of Edmund. Was he told off?' I said, possibly too aggressively, fighting the desire to get my phone out and email the school about this irritating Edmund who ruined Rosie's chances of a gold medal.

'Mum, don't you *dare* talk to the teachers.' Her blue eyes flashed.

'I won't, but it isn't very good that he got away with that.'

'He didn't!' she cried. 'This is why I never tell you stuff. You just stress me out and then cause a fuss at school and then it is just so embarrassing!'

Oh God, I thought, reel it in, calm down, put your own shit aside, Gemma. I talked myself down from my default competitive mode.

I imagined a tantrum in this full train carriage. She didn't often have tantrums in public, suggesting she had more control over herself than we gave her credit for. But she did have them. Her last public display of fury had been in the summer of this year. We had been enjoying a game of rounders on the recreational ground in the glittering sunshine. Before the game, Rosie had been edgy and moody. Rounders had been an idea to snap her out of it. When Noah had hit the ball into the hedges, Rosie had ordered him to get it for her, and I had reminded her that as a fielder it was her job to get the ball while Noah ran. She refused. I became insistent. She had thrown herself down onto the grass and rolled around, wailing in that high-pitched way. Her screams had echoed around the grounds. Dog walkers frowned, children stopped on their scooters to stare, mothers with prams stole sideways glances, families on their picnic rugs chewed on their sandwiches pretending it wasn't happening, until I dragged her home by the arm, feeling rumpled, aggravated and humiliated.

The train carriage was relatively quiet. I imagined her losing her temper; the day ruined before it had started. Strangers had little tolerance for noisy children, and even less tolerance for bad parents.

I would do everything to make every second of her day happy today. If it came to it, I had her iPod in my handbag for emergencies.

'Sorry, sorry. I didn't mean to stress you out. I absolutely promise not to talk to the teachers. You are an absolute superstar for getting silver.'

Rosie dropped her chin onto the palm of her hand and slumped towards the window, her mouth down-turned, her eyes barely registering the landscape that shot by outside the window.

I was panicking. How could I bring her back? When she descended into this kind of a mood, it could be impossible to get her out of it. Her eyelids would hood and her shoulders would round and her answers would become monosyllabic.

Then she said, 'The new boy, Ben, is really cool, you know. He is literally like the funniest boy I have ever met.'

'Oh, yeah? Is he handsome too?'

'Muuuum!' She rolled her eyes and looked around her self-consciously. 'I didn't mean in that way,' she said, but I could see she was blushing.

She was back. Her small smile was like finding a gemstone in mud. If I could keep a cool head, there would be no reason for her to tantrum.

'What does he say that's funny?'

'He just is. Like Daddy when he says, "Answers on a postcard", Ben says, like, "Talk to the hand."' Rosie giggled, blushing more.

'That's quite funny,' I chuckled, enjoying her amusement.

And she began to talk more about this boy, Ben, and how he had asked every pretty girl in the class out except her, which his friend said was because he liked her best. She talked ten to the dozen; a long-winded, wonderful, barely intelligible story about how Charlotte and the other girls in her class were vying for his attention. Her eyes lit up and her hands gesticulated wildly and she overused the slang 'I was, like...' and 'awesome', which I studiously ignored. I assumed the whole carriage was listening and watching her with awe, impressed and charmed by this funny and enthusiastic child, so full of life and intelligence, and I listened hard to the details so that I could respond well.

'What did Charlotte do when Noah laughed at your joke?'

'Oh, she didn't talk to me for the rest of the day.' She crossed her arms over her chest.

'Is everything okay between you and Charlotte?'

'Yes, Mum! I know you don't like her but she's so, so, so nice, you know.'

'Are you sure?'

'I just can't believe you don't believe me,' she cried, defensively.

Again, the knife edge.

'I really do believe you. I think Charlotte can be very lovely when she tries. I'm only responding to what you were telling me. It's not very nice to ignore someone for a whole day.'

'That was just one day. The rest of the time she is my best, best friend.'

'Good. I'm glad you two get on so well.'

'We do,' she said, staring out of the window again.

We didn't talk very much more for the rest of the journey. Plainly, she was still hurt by my scepticism about Charlotte. I didn't push it this time. It had been a breakthrough to hear her talk about the social dynamics in her class, and the boy scandals. Slowly, slowly I would try to win her trust again over the day.

Today was going to be a turning point. Miranda Slater's patronising letter – all crumpled and stained – would gather dust, that much I knew.

There was a buzz outside the theatre as we queued to get in. I bought her candyfloss and a souvenir key-ring. I clutched her hand to keep her safe in the throng of the theatre audience. Despite the many decades I had grown up and lived in London, I was nervous in the city with her. She was a country girl, ill-equipped to negotiate the pace of city crowds.

During the musical I stole glances at her face: gripped, enthralled, absorbed. After the performance, we had shared a huge ice cream at Fortnum and Masons.

In the taxi on the way back to the train station, she snuggled up to me.

'I think we should do this again soon, don't you?' I enfolded her in my arms.

The enticing lights of a city nightlife outside of the taxi window was a world I had no desire to be a part of while I had my daughter nestled next to me.

'That was literally the best day of my whole life,' she said. My stomach flipped over with surprise and love.


The train station was peppered with drunks and rowdy groups of revellers, and that same sense of insecurity came back to me about Rosie's safety.

'Keep up with me darling,' I said, pulling her arm. 'Come on, or we'll miss the eight o'clock.'

'Can I get a magazine?'

'No, no, darling, we don't have time.'

'Please, Mum, I can get it with my own money?'

Feeling the creep of tiredness, I relented, knowing it would give me some time to read the newspaper if she was occupied.

'Okay, quickly, we only have ten minutes.'

Just before we got to the checkout, she said, 'Actually, Mum, I think I want the *National Geographic* one instead.'

'Go on, then, quickly.'

I watched her go while I kept our place in the queue. She disappeared into the aisle where the children's magazines were shelved. The seconds were ticking by towards eight. I let a suited man go in front of me.

And then a couple more minutes went by. I left the queue, my heart began to flutter out of rhythm as I made my way to the magazine aisle, expecting to see her knelt down, sifting through the bottom shelf, indecisive. The aisle was empty. I ran to the end, looking left and right frantically, right along the soft drinks section, left along the bestseller shelves. She was nowhere to be seen. My pulse throbbed in my throat and my head spun.

'Rosie!' I screeched. Strangers stared at me with a mixture of concern and suspicion.

'Rosie! *Rosie!* I ran outside. 'I've lost my daughter!' I cried helplessly as I scanned the criss-cross of humans.

I ran back into the shop, and rushed towards an official person in purple uniform and described Rosie to him.

'I didn't see anyone.' He rubbed at his a fuzzy moustache and looked at me blankly.

'What do I do? Who do I talk to?'

'Err.' He looked to his equally gormless colleague.

'I could check in the storeroom?'

'What? Oh Jesus, what the hell would she be doing in the storeroom?' I shouted, losing my composure. I ran out of the shop.

The various signs dotted around the train station blurred as I looked for an official person to talk to.

The information desk was at the other end of the station. By the time I got there, I was panting and I breathlessly bombarded the young woman with my garbled description of Rosie. Immediately she was on the tannoy. An echoey, electronic voice ricocheted around the station.

The wait was almost unendurable. A few minutes later, the crowds pushed out little Rosie. She ran towards me smiling, holding two magazines in the air.

'I lost you, Mummy!' she cried. A young woman in a purple uniform waved her away.

Relief didn't register immediately.

'Where the hell have you been?' I yelled, gripping her shoulders.

Her face crumpled, 'The girl in the shop got me another one from the cupboard. It's for Charlotte.' The pages of two *National Geographic Kids* magazines flopped open from her fingers.

'Never ever, ever leave me like that again. Do you hear?' I shouted, shaking my finger right up to her nose. A woman passing us frowned at me.

'But you said...'

'I didn't say you could go wandering off without telling me, did I? You silly, *silly* girl!' I was overreacting. She had been out of my sight for seven minutes. She was back safe. Let it go, I thought.

'I'm sorry, Mum,' she said, tears rolling down her cheeks.

'Oh, Rosie,' I said, squeezing her too tightly to me. 'It's okay now,' I said. 'It's over. You're okay. Sorry I got cross. I was just in a panic.'

During the journey, the mood between us was forced. I was feeling low, although I was trying hard to hide it. I willed the train to go faster.

On the cold and foggy walk from the platform to the car park, I held her hand, which was floppy in mine.

'Can I have my iPod?' she asked as she belted herself into her seat at the back. Usually she would sit up at the front with me.

'No, darling.'

'Please?'

'No, you can't.'

'Why not?'

'It's only five minutes until we're home.'

'So?'

'So, you don't need to play a game.'

'I promise to switch it off as soon as we're home.'

'What's the point?'

'Please,' she pleaded, edgy, antagonistic.

Like a dog about to fight, I bristled. 'No.'

My nerves were frayed. The effort of our day came down on me like a ton of bricks. The surface of our moods had been glassy smooth, but our ongoing troubles lay deeper, churning underneath like a riptide beneath our smiles.

I turned the ignition.

'Don't start the car!' she screeched. 'Don't start the car!'

'Drop it. The answer is no!' I barked.

'Please. I just want five minutes. That's all. What's the big deal?'

I was entrenched. There was nothing she could say to change my mind. 'Don't ruin the lovely day we've had together.'

'I'm not! I just want to play a game. That's all.'

I clutched the wheel to quell the intense resentment that was worming like a parasite through my flesh. I couldn't concede defeat. 'No. And don't ask me again.'

'You're so stupid!' she screamed at the top of her lungs.

In an aggressive, unsafe manoeuvre, I swerved into a small driveway and slammed on the breaks. The car behind me beeped angrily. I didn't care. My hands shook as I scrabbled frantically in my handbag for her iPod and I chucked it at her.

'There you go! There you go, you little brat! I hope it's worth it.'

'Ow! It hit my leg.'

'I try my best. I really do. I try my best to give you everything you want and it still isn't good enough, is it? Why are you being like this to me? Why? *Why?*' I ranted, hitting the steering wheel with one hand over and over again. I hated her. I hated myself. I hated us. There were no tears, just hot-faced loathing.

'You look funny,' she laughed.

It took all of my willpower to hold back the venom, to methodically push the handbrake down and pull the car out of the lay-by, to continue home.

'Do you *want* to upset me? Is that it?' I whined, a lump of desperation in my throat. I clicked on the indicator into Virginia Close and the feelings of inadequacy and regret clawed at my insides.

'I don't *care.*'

'You are *insatiable.* I give and give and give and nothing is ever good enough.'

'La, la, la, la, shut up, shut up, shut up,' she sang from the back.

Anger flooded my bloodstream. In a split second, a mindless, animalistic ferocity took me over. Flipping, I rasped in a deep guttural booming voice, hurting my throat, 'Go on then! You carry on like that and I'll never take you on a day out ever, ever again!'

'I don't want to anyway. I wish I had a different mummy,' she yelled, her voice nearer to my ear.

A surge of raw, reciprocal hatred rose up from my gut. My wrath knocked away barriers of intellect or reasoning. I stopped thinking, stopped feeling, stopped pretending, stopped holding back. Uninhibited malevolence shot through my clenched teeth, 'That's lucky then, because I'm *not* your real mummy!'

There was a hefty, savage silence.

My whole body quivered with shock and I grabbed at my throat with one hand as if strangling away the foul words that had already escaped, the car wobbled.

'Don't say that,' she said quietly.

I pulled up outside our gates by the roundabout, too stunned to speak again, too cowardly to turn back to look at her. I wished I had struck her instead. It would have been a lesser blow.

Neither of us moved to get out; an excruciating purgatory.

What had I done? How long I had kept the secret, how successfully, and now the spirits of that secret were howling around my head as though I had opened a chest of demons.

Eleven years ago, the hot flushes, the mood swings, the night sweats and the irregular periods hadn't been considered abnormal symptoms of coming off the pill. When my periods had stopped completely, the doctor with the ear hair and untrimmed eyebrows had delivered his news, informing me of my diminished ovarian reserve and FSH count of over fifteen, informing me that I would never be able to conceive my own child.

'There we go then,' I had said to him across his wide desk.

'It's a lot to take in,' the doctor had said, glancing over at the box of tissues on the mantle as though someone had died.

I had held my breath, holding in the desire to shout at this tweed-suited old man, irritated by his sad smile. *Why was he sad, when I wasn't?* I had thought.

The memory was paralysing. Why had I not been sad? My hands were glued to the steering wheel.

Rosie's deathly whisper punctured my eardrum. 'It's not true is it, Mummy?'

Powering my reluctant limbs into action, I climbed out of the car and round to open her door. The ghastliness of her whitened face was as dreadful as anything I had ever witnessed before in my life.

'Of course it's not true. I was just angry.' I bent in to scoop her out of the car, just as I had when she was a baby, her face upturned to mine, the mass of me oppressive. Me, the vile mother. She, the frightened child.

'You promise?' she asked, her wide eyes rimmed red in horror.

'It's not true! Of course I'm your real mummy,' I stuttered, the half-truth breaking my heart.

I lifted her up, and her legs encircled me, the weight of her almost bringing me to my knees.

Rosie's chest heaved against my body in quiet sobs. 'Why did you say it then?' she asked, sounding utterly baffled.

'I was just angry. So, so angry. You know when you're angry you say things you don't mean? Like when you say "I hate you, Mummy", do you mean that when you say it?'

'No, of course not!' she cried.

'And listen,' I said, burying my head into her neck. Her hair smelled the same as it had from the first ever moment I had held her. 'I should not have shouted at you like that. It was totally wrong and I am truly, truly sorry. Nobody should ever shout at you like that, whatever you might or might not have done. Do you understand?'

'Yes,' she nodded gravely, adding, 'And I'm sorry for screaming, too.' And she broke down again. The poor child would have no choice but to believe me. I was all she had.

# CHAPTER TWENTY-TWO

*TOP SECRET*

*I HATE YOU. I HATE YOU. I HATE YOU. I HATE YOU. HATE. HATE. HATE. HATE. HATE. HATE. I'LL LEARN YOU A LESSON FOREVER. I DON'T CARE THAT YOU SAID SORRY. I WISH IT WAS TRUE. I HATE YOU MORE THAN THE WHOLE UNIVERSE.*

# CHAPTER TWENTY-THREE

'Don't eat this, will you?' Mira said to Barry.

'Why are you keeping it?'

'Just in case.'

'In case of what?'

'In case we fancy it.'

'You hate Battenberg cake.'

Mira couldn't look at Barry. She knew he would be blinking wildly through his thick lens.

'You're not up to something are you, Mira?'

'What could I possibly be up to?'

'I don't know, love.' Barry kissed his wife on the top of her head as she read the newspaper.

'Bye,' she said, adding, 'Don't forget my glue-dots and the hoover bags.'

'They won't have any glue-dots in the hardware store.'

'Go to the newsagents then.'

He left without responding. Mira knew he was unimpressed when she spoke to him that way. She didn't really care. She wanted him out of the house so that she could get ready into her running kit.

Initially, she had been offended by Rosie's rebuff, but in the four days this week that Rosie had run from her Mira had rationalised it. It was a hard thing for a child to admit that their mother might be hurting them. It wasn't a rejection of Mira, per se, it was a natural reaction. Rosie was bound to be defensive, and Noah was just a silly little boy who followed his big sister without thinking for himself. Interesting, too, that neither of them had told their parents of how they 'bumped into Mrs Entwistle' every day.

So, Mira regarded her afternoon task as another part of her routine. She'd get there in the end – if there was somewhere to get to – and today might be that day.

They weren't out of school until five o'clock on Thursdays. She regarded the other children's outfits and chatter and random cartwheels, and she guessed the afterschool club had been gymnastics. In a world full of vulgarity and ugly sights, this vision of innocence was always a delight.

She noticed that the majority of children released from this club were girls. Noah would surely feel out of place. Mira thought it was rather strange that this strapping six-year-old boy would do gymnastics, and assumed Gemma used it as childcare rather than a response to his burning desire to do handstands. From her experience at Woodlands, this was typical of this sort of mother.

Rosie and Noah were last out. Their rucksacks bounced on their backs as they ran out of the gate. How pretty Rosie was, she reflected, surprised by this rise of affection for her.

As Mira jogged towards the point where they would meet, at the corner of the rugby pitch, she noticed that her breathing was less laboured when she said hello. It made her smile to herself, that the by-product of her do-gooding was added fitness. What goes around, comes around, she thought.

'Come on Rosie, let's go,' Noah said quietly, frowning at Mira.

Rosie's arm was being pulled by Noah, but her body didn't follow, and Noah jerked back as though on elastic.

Mira stopped jogging and fell into step with them. 'How was your day at school?'

Rosie looked up to Mira briefly. There were black rings around her eyes and her expression seemed guarded and suspicious. There was a change in her, Mira sensed.

'Not good?'

'School was fine,' she said, almost shouting it, and then she hung her head. She twirled a section of her hair at her scalp, twisting it into a knot.

'I wouldn't do that, pet. You'll only have to brush it one hundred and *one* times at bed,' Mira said. Mira's paternal grand-mother would say this to her when she and Deidre visited her in Wales once a year.

'I don't ever brush my hair at bed time. I do it in the morning.'

'*You* don't do it. *Mummy* does it for you,' Noah jibed.

'Shut up,' she snapped back, elbowing him.

'You should do it yourself. You're quite old enough. It makes all the difference in the morning. One hundred brushes at bedtime. One hundred brushes in the morning.'

'You've got short hair.'

'I do now. But when I was younger I had long hair down to my waist.'

'Mummy won't let me grow it any longer.'

'That's a shame,' Mira said, although she knew that having waist-length hair was impractical for children, and the only reason she had been allowed to have it long when she was young was because her mother couldn't be bothered to take her to the hairdressers.

'My mum is *super* mean,' she said, glancing up to Mira, check-ing for a reaction.

'Is she?'

'She's not mean,' Noah cried.

'Why did the police come round then?' Rosie asked.

Noah shrugged, but his little face was filled with fear.

Rosie jutted her head forward at her little brother and pulled her hand free of his. 'She isn't mean to *you*,' she spat.

Mira sucked in her breath. Something had definitely happened. Not that Mira had heard any screaming since the weekend.

'How about some Battenberg cake at mine?' Mira asked, looking from Noah to Rosie, her heart racing in anticipation of Rosie's reply.

'No!' Noah cried and ran off.

'Yes, okay,' Rosie said casually, and she took Mira's hand.

The child's touch sent goosebumps rippling up her arms.

'I'll just have to tell Harriet that I'm going over to Beth's at number two,' Rosie said.

'What a sensible little girl you are,' Mira said.

Rosie tugged her hand free, crossed her arms and hunched her shoulders as she walked. 'But you can't come into my house,' she said.

'Of course,' Mira said. 'I'll meet you round at mine then in five minutes.'

'Okay,' she said and charged off through the hedge.


The cellophane on the cake shone on the table like a slab of gold. Mira didn't want to unwrap it yet in case Rosie changed her mind. She wondered if Rosie's nanny had believed Rosie's lie.

Although the thought of Rosie lying sat uncomfortably with Mira – who believed herself to be an honest soul and encouraged it in others – she felt the end justified the means. A ribbon of thrill wormed through her insides at the prospect of Rosie opening up to her and confessing something that would confirm her suspicions.

The stripes of the tea cosy matched the pastels of the cake. With the smart plates, forks and tea cups laid out neatly, the table was a pleasing sight. The only niggle was whether it was right to serve tea in the kitchen, or whether the dining room would have been more appropriate. The piles of photographs were suddenly a potential embarrassment to her, and she jumped up to make sure the door was tightly closed. She had made slow progress with her album this week.

It was half past four. Barry would be back in an hour and a half, roughly. It still gave her time. Not that it mattered hugely if he found Rosie at his kitchen table. He liked children. He wouldn't scare her. And Mira could tell him a little white lie about how their little tea party had come about.

The doorbell rang and Mira jumped up, smoothed her skirt and answered the door. Never could she have imagined being so nervous about a child coming to tea.

'Hello, dear, come in,' she said, and she led Rosie, straight-backed and arms crossed over her chest, into the kitchen.

Mira poured the tea and sliced the cake. Neither of them talking. For some reason, it didn't feel awkward for Mira.

Within minutes of Rosie sitting down, she had wolfed down a whole slice of Battenberg.

'Can I have another slice,' Rosie asked.

'Sure,' Mira said casually.

She would delay the second slice of cake.

'So, how was your weekend? You and your mum went somewhere special together did you?'

'How did you know that?' Rosie asked.

'I saw you in the car remember? Your mum seemed to be in a bit of a hurry.'

'We went to London to see a show.'

'How splendid. It must have been nice to have a day out with mum.'

'Mummy loves musicals.'

'What were your favourite bits?'

'I loved the bit where he does that amazing acrobat show.'

'Acrobats? Well I never. That sounds marvellous.'

'It was awesome!' she cried. Her eyes were dead behind the stage smile.

'You're a very lucky girl to get to go up to London and see a show.'

Rosie's eyes narrowed. 'Can I have more cake now?'

'In a minute, Rosie,' Mira said, sternly, deciding to get straight to the point. Mira didn't believe in this wishy-washy protocol that the teachers at school believed in, where you had to let the child take the lead, wait for them to say something or ask them to draw a bleeding picture. Nonsense, Mira thought. She knew that the very nature of abuse encouraged secrecy in a child.

'Is there something you want to tell me, pet?'

'No?'

'I know you're a smart little girl and I know that your mum would not like you coming round here, which makes me wonder why you did.'

'I wanted some cake.'

'Did you and your mum have another fight?'

Rosie's gaze was fixed on the cake in front of her.

'I think that maybe you did.'

'Mummy is very clever, you know.'

'Yes?'

'She, like, runs this massive company and she can even fire people.'

'That sounds very impressive.'

'Yes, it is.'

'She must be very busy.'

'Yes, really busy, like a VIP.'

'It must be exhausting being so very clever and important all the time.'

'I don't know.'

'Is that why she gets so cross?'

'I don't know.'

'Has she ever hurt you, pet?'

Rosie stayed silent.

'You can tell me you know. I am on your side.'

Rosie stared at Mira. 'Why?'

'Maybe because my mum wasn't very nice to me when I was little and I know how it feels.'

'Why wasn't she nice to you?'

'I don't really know.' Mira couldn't tell a ten-year-old the reasons.

'What did she do?'

'She slapped me once,' Mira said, surprising herself with the confession, while also maintaining a safe disconnectedness from it.

Rosie sucked in her breath and gaped at Mira. 'Did it hurt?'

'My lip bled, just here,' Mira said, dabbing at the left-hand corner of her mouth, as though it was bleeding again after all these years.

'Ouchy,' Rosie said, sucking in her breath and staring at Mira's lip as though she saw blood too.

Mira swooped in with the question she had been waiting to ask. 'Do you ever bleed when your mummy hits you?'

There was a beat of silence.

'Yes, I really bleed and it hurts so much and makes me cry. That's why you can hear me screaming all the time.' Her face took on a sickly translucence and her blue eyes blinked madly at Mira.

Mira felt like she had swallowed a beautiful butterfly. The information Rosie had delivered fluttered in her stomach, but having wanted it so much she felt sad to have trapped it.

'I'm so sorry, pet,' Mira whispered, slumping down, feeling the weight of the child's words on her shoulders. The bitter sting of her own mother's slap came to her again.

'I think I'd better go home now,' Rosie said, and she stood up and walked out of the house, going the wrong way first, into the living room, and then correcting herself and heading away.

Unable to rally herself out of what felt like a stupor, Mira watched her go.

Then Mira called out to the door, which slammed open against the wall in a gust of wind. 'Don't you want that second piece of cake, love?'

It took gargantuan effort to rise from her chair to clear up tea.

After the kitchen was spotless, she shut herself away in the dining room. Her head was swimmy with self-doubt as she mulled over Rosie's confession. A hotness grew across her left cheek.

She rubbed at it, letting it collapse into the heel of her hand, propping her head up while she absent-mindedly sought out each and every photograph of Craig from the pile. It was like plucking currants out of a bun. She wasn't completely present in her task; her mind was elsewhere, on Rosie. She was thinking about what the poor child had divulged, about the responsibility that lay on her shoulders.

Having counted fourteen snap shots altogether, she turned them through her fingers, which were sticky. Sticky but cold. The photograph that rested momentarily on top of the pile was of Craig in blue jeans standing just inside the front door of her childhood home. Deidre had taken so many random shots of him back then, like some kind of obsessed super-fan.

Mira had a flash of his lanky figure in that same doorway. She was back inside that house again, staring at him, unable to believe he was there on the doorstep.

With one sweaty hand on the glass, she had held it open for him.

'Deidre about?' Craig had asked, tugging at his quiff.

'She's at work,' she had answered pointlessly, knowing he knew this.

He had sauntered in anyway, his broad shoulders curled inwards.

'I could murder a cup of coffee.'

The clatter of his car keys on the kitchen table. Instant coffee with a splash of milk and two sugars. A cigarette from the glass.

Chat about his day. Even chat about Deidre. Important to keep up the pretence.

'I was just doing my homework.' The words sounded babyish, and she regretted reminding him of the age gap.

'Oh yeah?' He flicked his ash and with his other hand he picked at a spot on his forehead.

'I'm watching a film. I have to write an essay on TV adaptations. Want to watch it?'

He raised an eyebrow and smiled. 'Back in my day, we never watched TV for homework.'

Mira took him through to the living room, where she had drawn the curtains, a pink dusk cast over the room.

The black and white still of *Pride and Prejudice* was paused on Laurence Olivier's face, imperious and disdainful, as though he was real and could see through to them. If Mira hadn't liked him so much in the film, she would have stuck two fingers up at him for judging her.

Craig sat down right next to her on the couch, thigh to thigh, and reached over her for the can of coke she had half-drunk. The intimacy of this gesture made her head spin.

'Go on, then, let's watch it.'

She pressed play.

Having thought he would laugh at the way the actors talked or the poor quality of the grainy black-and-white, he sat still and quiet. She stole a look at him. He was rapt, elbows on knees, a wrinkle in his brow.

She was trying to concentrate on taking notes in her file, but his breathing, his smell, the darkened room, the romance of the film, his profile near hers were too distracting.

There was no way she was going to get her notes done with him here, so she lay back into the sofa, contented enough to know that she could watch the film again later when everyone was in bed.

He lay back next to her, wriggling his arm through under her neck, pulling her into the crook of his armpit. It felt like luxury, lying there with him.

In these moments, Craig seemed to give her permission to unpack herself.

She had learnt how to put herself away, how to create a façade that was so far away from who she was inside. She was accustomed to being disagreed with, competed with, shouted at and controlled, knowing that she could survive all these ignominies if she made sure she didn't react to them. Until Craig, she had begun to doubt the relevance of her voice in life, doubted its value, lost perspective on her basic needs. Craig's attentions had reawakened her.

'Deidre'd never watch a weird film like this.'

'We can turn it off?'

'Nah, I like it.'

What he didn't know was that Deidre and their mother were due back early that evening, after a Trade Union meeting about equal pay. With each minute that went by, she wanted to tell him, but couldn't bring herself to spoil the moment. He would think they had over two hours before they would clatter through the front door. In reality, they only had about half an hour. There was time to tell him, to draw away from his body, to act normal. There was time.

And then his hands reached between her legs and normal was forgotten. Although the desire was there, she wished he would slow down. He unzipped his jeans and shoved them down hurriedly. She tensed up, tried to close her legs. He gently prized them apart, not looking into her face, just down there, focused, shaking with desire.

'This is my first time,' she whispered, pushing him away with a lack of conviction. Part of her wanted it to happen, part of her didn't. She knew they were now stepping over a line. Kissing and touching were one thing, underage sex was another.

'Have you got any...?' She was too shy to say the word 'condom' out loud.

'It's okay,' he said, kissing her on the mouth briefly before pushing himself inside her.

The stretching and ripping sensations ruined any enjoyment. She recognized this coming-of-age moment, and how different her expectations had been. While he grunted and gyrated on top of her, lost in his own pleasure, she winced with pain, astonished that she was actually losing her virginity. She imagined how she had wanted it to be: candles and kissing for hours in bed with him, without the burden of secrecy, free of Deidre and her mother forever. She let the image go, accepting that her life would never turn out to be quite as lovely as her dreams had been.

Equally, she had never thought that life could turn out to be quite as hellish as her nightmares.

The act had lasted about ten minutes. After which, they had wriggled back into their clothes. The film was back on. She was nestled into him again, thinking that she should have just stayed there all along, worrying about the wetness down there, unsure whether it was from his body or from hers. She was sore, throbbing and stinging. But also glowing from a sense of achievement.

Her mother and sister's arrival had happened very quickly.

Possibly they had dozed off. There was no time to pull apart. Deidre was standing in front of them, over them, seconds after the lounge door was opened. 'What the fuck?' Deidre said, under her breath.

The pink curtains were ripped back by Mira's mother. The grey light from outside settling onto the sad scene.

Craig shoved Mira away. 'She came onto me. You know what she's like,' Craig said.

He leapt up and scampered away, Deidre charging after him, leaving Mira lying crumpled into the corner of the sofa, her arm covering her burning face. The shouting between Deidre and Craig continued outside.

Mira's mother stood by the window where she had drawn the curtains. She was silhouetted. A grey lumpy mass.

Mira uncurled herself, her heart racing, her body cold. She ran to the door, to get up to her bedroom where she could hide her shame away. Then her mother made a sudden movement, darting in front of her, stopping the door with her foot, trapping Mira.

The front door banged. Deidre stamped upstairs. Craig's car hurtled and screeched out of the driveway.

When Mira first felt her mother's slap, she hadn't realised what the pain in her lip was or where it had come from. Then she saw her mother massaging the palm of her right hand with her thumb. Mira had tasted the blood seeping onto her gums. She looked into her mother's eyes. With the light from the windows now illuminating her face, Mira could see the mottled pallor of her mother's skin. Her eye sockets sunken, her breath reeking of cigarettes. Mira read years of confusion and regret in her eyes; unless she had been seeing her own confusion and regret reflected back at her. Whatever her mother was thinking or feeling in the moment, it wasn't hatred. For the first time, both Mira and her mother were fused, with something that felt like misplaced recognition. A smile had formed on Mira's lips, designed to acknowledge some kind of love, or connection to her mother, at least. Her mother's slap. The only time in their life that her mother had touched her physically with violence. The engagement of sweaty hand to face almost flattering. Years of disinterest brought into focus; one moment of attention and truth, so sharp and specific.

'Get out of my house,' her mother said.

There was no smile on her mother's face. But there were no tears in Mira's eyes. She felt nothing. Mira had not been frightened to leave home. She was fifteen years old but she felt older. She caught a bus straight to Craig's flat. He had opened his door wearing only a pair of tracksuit pants, and looked to the floor, snorting, as though at a private joke.

'Shit, this is all I need.' He had pressed the heel of his hand into his forehead.

But strangely, Mira didn't sense the unkindness.

'I'll go.'

'Don't be daft,' he sighed, standing aside to let her in.

His flat was pokey and over-heated with magnolia-painted woodchip walls and curtains at the windows that reminded Mira of hospitals. The steady flow of traffic from the main road out of town rumbled through the double glazing.

'Your sister's a fucking nutcase.' He had pressed the volume down on the television with the remote control and then pulled on a T-shirt that had been slung over the back of a chair.

They had perched on the edge of his nylon sofa opposite his television, a football game flickering away on mute.

'Mum slapped me,' she had said, touching her split lip.

Their eyeballs had followed the little red and white footballers running around the pitch.

'Did Deidre go mental at you?'

'She stayed in her room.'

'I feel bad for her, if I'm honest.'

'D'you still love her?'

He had taken a swig of beer before he answered. 'Nah.'

A strong urge to slap him had come over her, just as her mother had slapped her an hour before.

She hadn't, of course. To be allowed to camp out there with him, she had to play nice. She would have done anything to put off going back home.

At this point, there was still hope. Hope. Pain. In her lip, in her shoulder, hunched in her jaw. Where was she?

A low ceiling, green walls, the carpet on her cheek, a table leg in front of her face. She was under the dining room table, her knees up to her chest, with the fourteen photographs of Craig bent in half in her smarting right hand. The edges were cutting into her skin. Although there was nobody to see her like this, she was ashamed of herself. A grown woman curled under the table like a dog. How had she not remembered moving from the chair to the floor? Had she been sleeping?

On all fours, she crawled out from the table through the chairs' legs and stood up. The prints were like razorblades. She had to get rid of them. It might be the only way to stop the trundle of memories rolling over her hard-won sanity.

She checked her watch. Barry would be home any minute. She nipped out of the back door and down to the bottom of the garden.

The smell of the compost heap made her gag. Her knees were wet through. She pressed the photographs deep into the stinking pile. The unwanted reminders of him would be gone tomorrow when the bonfire was lit. She imagined the edges of his face curl and melt, burst into flames and end as black satin cinders that would blow away in the wind and leave her be.

When she took PC Yorke's card out of the cubbyhole in the bureau, she turned it over and over. Her fingers smeared the card in soil. She stared at the filth smudged across the embossed writing, obscuring the numbers. She spat on it to clean it away, and dialled. She had to save that little girl.

'Save who?' Barry said. He had glue dots in his hand. 'Are you all right, love?'

Oh God, Mira thought, had she said those words out loud?

'Hello, PC Yorke speaking,' she heard in her other ear.

She hung up. She couldn't do it. She couldn't say it. If she said it out loud, with Barry listening, it would be real, and Mira wasn't ready for it to be real yet.

# CHAPTER TWENTY-FOUR

The hill up from the station had seemed steeper than ever. It was later than usual. After a meeting over-running and a delayed train, it had been a long Thursday; longer still due to four nights without sleep. It was the fifth night since I had vomited up and swallowed back down my long-held secret, and I feared life would never return to normal again. *Because I'm not your real mummy. I'm not your real mummy. I'm not your real mummy,* echoed round and round in my head. Every time I thought of Rosie's face afterwards, my chest constricted, and every minute of every day holding back the truth from her felt like trying to drag a rollercoaster back from the brink of a monumental drop.

I forced myself through the front door.

Harriet unpacked the dishwasher as she listed the afternoon's events.

'Noah finally got his handwriting pen,' Harriet said with a motherly pride.

'About time,' I said, just to cancel out her misplaced satisfaction.

'And Rosie popped round to see Beth.'

'Was that in the diary?' I glanced over to the whiteboard schedule, knowing I would not see a play date with Beth written down.

'It was a last-minute thing. But I think they must have raided the sweet jar because she was a little hyperactive when she got back.'

'They should have that sweet jar under lock and key when Rosie goes round,' I said light-heartedly.

But paranoia set in like a ticking time bomb. Why had she been hyper? Had Vics seen a change in Rosie? Had they talked? Had Rosie told Vics about what I'd had said? Rosie's visit to see Beth should not have been particularly noteworthy on any other week. It was home from home for Rosie over at 2 Virginia Close. Surely Vics would have called me straight away if she had been worried. Unless Rosie had sworn her to secrecy?

I went up to kiss them goodnight.

Noah was already asleep.

Rosie had her teddy tucked under her chin and her book close to her face.

My assessment of Rosie began: the rings under her eyes were as black as night and she wouldn't look up from her book.

*I was not her real mummy.*

'Night, Rosie.' I kissed her on the forehead.

*I was not her real mummy.*

She flashed me a fake smile and returned to her page. 'Night Mum.'

*I was not her real mummy.*

'Good day at school?'

'Fine.'

'Love you,' I said and I blew a kiss to her from the door.

*How would I ever tell her?*

'Night.'

Worries about the rings under her eyes consumed me all evening. Peter was as subdued as I was. Since I had told him what I had said to Rosie in the heat of the moment, he had seemed distant and disconnected. We didn't talk properly and we made the unusual decision to eat supper in front of the television.

Before bed, I read through my emails in preparation for tomorrow.

When I finally sank into my pillow, my eyes blinked into the dark.

A memory of Rosie and me driving together last autumn came to me. We were alone, just the two of us, possibly on the way to a play date or a party. As we wound through the countryside, Rosie had jumped up in her seat excitedly and pointed, 'Look, Mummy, oh wow, did you see that?' Expecting something extraordinary or outlandish, I asked her what she had seen. She was full of wonder. 'The wind blew into that big tree and there were hundreds of shiny leaves raining down like sparkles. Oh, it was beautiful, Mummy,' she had sighed.

Whenever I saw trees shedding leaves in autumn, I thought of Rosie's face lit up and how she had seen sparkles.

I would suggest a walk this weekend through the woods. The trees were bare at this time of year, but the leaves were still thick on the ground.

I had to sleep now.

My legs were twitching, restless. While my eyes were tired, my body had other ideas. It wanted to keep me awake, knew I needed to think.

It became torturous to lie in the dark with my thoughts churning through my head. I struggled on, replaying my argument with Rosie on a loop, eyes dry as I blinked into the dark.

Peter whispered, 'Gemma.'

'What's up?' I mumbled, pretending to be sleepy.

Peter turned over to face me, 'Are you awake?'

'I am now.'

'I can't sleep.'

'I've got a busy day tomorrow,' I yawned, turning away from him. I couldn't bear the thought of talking to him about Rosie and our row. He had been so angry with me when I had confessed to the monumental slip-up.

He was silent. His breathing heavy.

'Can I just ask you something?'

'Go on then.'

I lay on my back and waited. There was silence for quite a few minutes before he formed the question.

'What if we told Rosie the truth properly?'

'No.' My tongue felt thick in my mouth.

'Fuck,' he said, sitting up and bending over his knees as though he was about to throw up.

'I know I really screwed up, but we just have to ride it out. She'll settle when she realises nothing's changed.'

Peter brought his body next to mine. 'Remember how you used to read stories to your bump?'

'She loves books now, doesn't she,' I replied quietly, grateful to him for reassuring me when I hadn't asked for it. I turned to face him with my knees pulled up to my chest under the duvet.

'And you breastfed her and nurtured her and loved her all these years, all of her life. You are all she has ever known. How much more real can a mother be?'

The answer to that question was too blatantly obvious to say out loud without undoing all of his kind-hearted words.

'Sometimes I wish I knew what Kaarina had been like as a child,' I said simply.

After three months of searching through donors' files, having gained access codes to numerous clinics' websites, we had found Kaarina Doubek, the dark-haired, blue-eyed 24-year-old medical student from the Czech Republic who wanted the 5000-euro fee for a solo cycling trip across Morocco and a deposit for a flat, whose grandparents on both sides had lived into their nineties, whose hobby was jazz piano, but who admitted to being a terrible cook and very lax about tidying her bedroom. After which she had included about ten exclamation marks and a smiley face. I had liked how open and funny she had been, while many donors barely got beyond their measurements and flattering photographs.

Peter turned onto his back. 'Does it matter where she gets it from?'

'You seemed to think so the other day.'

'I was just over-worrying.'

'But now Rosie's older... I don't know... certain traits of hers, I've started wondering... you know?'

'Her intelligence and wit come from me obviously,' he quipped, clearly trying to keep it light, frightened of what we were opening up.

'On paper, Kaarina was very smart. And so is Rosie.'

'And we've always believed it's more about nurture than nature.'

'I don't know anymore,' I admitted.

Peter's face was shrouded in the darkness of the room. If the moonlight had reached him, I wondered what I would have seen.

Kaarina had not been Peter's first choice. He had been in favour of a very beautiful six-foot-tall mathematician with a passion for flower arranging and blonde hair, similar to Peter's.

His main gripe with Kaarina Doubek was that she had opted not to meet the donor recipient or the child in the future. I knew this was not going to be a problem for me. If we were not going to tell our baby that he or she was not genetically mine, then we would never need to meet Kaarina.

After some arguing, we had eventually rejected the mathematician based on her size-eight shoe size, and both of us had fallen about laughing and then had rampant sex, releasing the tension of our search.

'Well, Rosie's temper definitely comes from you,' he snorted now.

'It's easier for you,' I shot back sharply, proving his point.

'Believe me, none of this is easy for me.'

'Do you remember that photograph of Kaarina in her file?'

'No,' he sighed.

'The one of her when she was a teenager?'

'I think so.'

'Rosie looks just like her in that photo.'

'I've forgotten what she looked like.'

'Come on, Peter!'

'You shouldn't have asked me to burn everything if you wanted me to remember what she looked like.'

I shuddered. I longed to see the photograph of Kaarina again now, to see into her eyes again, into her soul maybe. In my head, her face had morphed into an angry grimace, just like Rosie's when she was having a tantrum.

'Rosie and Noah look more and more different by the day.'

Peter pushed himself up and put his hands behind his head. 'Do you think we would've told Rosie sooner if Noah hadn't have come along?'

I stared at the moon shadows on the wall. 'Who knows.'

'We should have sued that bloody doctor.'

I thought of Dr Drummond's box of tissues on the mantle and his sad smile.

'You know Pattie and John Ambrose?'

'From New Hall?'

'They had four unsuccessful rounds of IVF and then got pregnant naturally with Toby after they'd given up all hope. There's no rhyme or reason to it sometimes.'

'No wonder they're broke.'

'They're blessed. We were blessed.'

'And we got lots of brand new linen out of it,' Peter retorted. Always a joke from Peter. But I didn't feel like laughing.

'We needed those new sheets.'

'You spent three grand we didn't have on Egyptian cotton.'

'When Dad legged it with Jill, Mum painted all the bathrooms pink.'

'I got off lightly then.'

'I was just giving you a three-grand taster of all the bills to come,' I laughed half-heartedly, referring unnecessarily to the expense of the IVF treatment and egg donation for Rosie's conception.

The thought of the high price of that clear-out gave me palpitations, just as it had when I had handed my credit card over to the shop assistant, only an hour after the unsparing consultation with Dr Drummond. I did not want to think about that shopping binge, or that linen cupboard. I did not want to think about how I had wanted to drench every old sheet I ripped out from the cupboard in my tears, but how I was unable to find even one tear to grieve for the child Dr Drummond had told me I would never have.

'Making Noah was loads cheaper, that's for sure,' Peter snickered, snuggling closer.

'We should go to that hotel again some day,' I said whimsically, thinking about how we had held hands along the windswept beach, and how there had been writing in the sand marking the year 2010, as though marking Noah's beginnings.

It had been on our first weekend away without Rosie, who had been four years old and on a sleepover with Granny Helen. We had walked for miles along the cliffs, soaked in a steam bath, eaten a five-course supper, ripped each other's clothes off drunkenly on the four-poster bed and then fallen asleep too tired to have sex. It had been the next morning that we had made a new baby out of the healthy eggs I had not known were there.

'As for Number Three, he was practically free,' he laughed, placing his hand on my growing belly. The vision of a drained bottle of red and empty containers of curry sprang into my mind. We had not planned on a third. I was not ready for a third.

I crossed Peter's two fingers over. 'Let's hope this one's an easy baby,' I said.

'He?'

'Did I say he?'

'I think so.'

'Wishful thinking.'

'Don't you want a baby girl?' he asked, surprised.

'Boys are easier.'

'I know Rosie's hard work, honestly, I really understand, but we'd never change her.'

'Of course not,' I replied. A chill ran up my spine. 'But being her mum is so hard sometimes, Peter.'

'I know, I know,' he soothed. Finally the jokes had run out.

'Sorry,' I said, pulling myself away from him. 'I'll be back in a minute, I'm just going to check on her.'

I crept into Rosie's bedroom. My heart seized up. The sight of her curled up at the bottom of her bed – dysfunctional even in sleep – was captivating; the frowsy smell of her bedclothes reminding me of how grown-up she was becoming. I feared the speed of her growing limbs as I brought the duvet back over her body, wanting to protect her from the chill of the night forever, wanting to protect her from all of life's dangers, knowing this was impossible.

I was taken back to her tenth birthday a few months before. We had given her a pair of clumpy black boots that she had wanted, even though it was the height of summer. She had tried them on with her nightie, squealing with delight. Her long, skinny legs had stuck out of them and I thought she looked like a fashion model. Briefly, time had flashed forward to give me a glimpse of what she would look like as a teenager, and how beautiful she would be.

To celebrate, we had given her the choice of either having tea and cake with a few of her school friends, like Beth, or going out as a family to a pizza restaurant. She had chosen the pizza restaurant with us, which had delighted Peter and me.

Sitting opposite her in the restaurant as she sipped at her fizzy drink and talked about the book she had been reading would go down as one of the happiest times of my life. Strange, that such a small, prosaic ten minutes in a nondescript chain restaurant could have provided such intense joy. The ten years of nurture and love – and drudgery – seemed to culminate in this beautifully simple moment. I was sharing a relatively grown-up chat with my daughter – whom I might never have been able to conceive – about books. Pride had throbbed through me like a heartbeat, and I had wondered whether my feelings had the power to push light out from my skin.

When the alarm went, it was still dark. I woke up with a sinking feeling, remembering the conversation Peter and I had had the night before. I hadn't been able to explain how I really felt, as though there was a mountain of the unsaid between us.

I couldn't face getting out of bed to make the early train for my meeting.

One of the aphorisms that I had written on a neon pink Post-it and stuck to my computer at work read: *Failure will never overtake me if my determination to succeed is strong enough!* When it came to Rosie, failure was overtaking me, flooding me. With all the determination in the world, I was not succeeding.

To divert my thoughts, to relocate the idea that I was quite capable of standing on my own two feet, I tried to decide which suit I would wear today. The blue or the grey? It was ten to five, which gave me five minutes before I had to get out of bed.

Then the door to the bedroom opened. I expected to see Peter and I was surprised to see Rosie, instead.

'Darling, you're awake. Is everything okay? It's too early to get up.'

'I wanted a cuddle before you go to work.'

'Oh poppet, come here,' I said, raising the duvet so that she could climb in.

She snuggled into my arm and I kissed her hair.

'Is everything okay?'

'Yes.'

'You sure? You didn't have a bad dream or anything?'

'Nope.' She looked up at me, her blue eyes blinking.

'Beautiful girl,' I said, kissing her nose.

Her smile warmed me like sun on skin after a long winter. I drank in her affection, never wanted it to end. I remembered that Rosie had only been a few hours old, swaddled in my arms on the hospital bed, when I first realised quite how hard the cover-up would become. Jacs had cooed that Rosie's 'thick dark hair' was just like mine. I had nodded and agreed, but inside I had been angry with her for her naivety; envied her for sharing her genes with her conventional baby.

'Don't let daddy forget to put your gym kit in your bag. Your T-shirt is drying in the laundry room.'

'Okay.'

'And I've laid out your pinafore on your chair.'

'But I want to wear my skirt today.'

'But the pinafore's smarter.'

Every morning I would tug and tuck and smooth and preen Rosie until she looked box-fresh perfect. It was hard for me to turn off that setting, to let Peter take charge.

'Okay.'

'And remember to take your water bottle. The blue one, okay? The red one leaks.'

'Yes, yes. We can, like literally, remember stuff even when you're not here you know, Mum.'

'I can like *literally* not believe that,' I teased.

'Daddy lets us have chocolate spread for breakfast when you're not here.'

I raised an eyebrow. 'Don't ever joke about that.'

'It's okay. I like muesli better anyway. It's Noah who likes the chocolate spread.'

'You're such a good girl,' I said, winking at her, playing into her good-girl routine, although it did make me proud to know she now liked the organic muesli I had insisted she ate every morning.

She blinked wildly at me. 'I want to be able to wink. Charlotte can wink and she's been trying to teach me but it's totally *impossible*. I even tried Sellotape on one eye. Can *you* teach me?'

My heart leapt into my mouth. I remembered Kaarina's jaunty profile description. She, too, had been unable to wink. At the time, it had been an irrelevant and jokey detail, adding charm to her profile. Now – in my sensitive, paranoid state – it became a large neon sign that encapsulated the genetic mystery of Rosie.

'Grandma Helen always told me that real ladies don't wink or whistle. Don't learn bad habits from me,' I replied, a little too sharply.

'Sorry.'

To salvage the moment, I said, 'How was Beth yesterday? Did you have fun?'

'She was fine,' she mumbled, and then she suddenly wriggled out of my arms.

'Where are you going?'

She yawned. 'I'm going back to bed. I'm tired.'

'Oh, okay. You sure it was okay with Beth yesterday?'

She walked out as though she was deaf and I heard her bedroom door click closed.

# CHAPTER TWENTY-FIVE

*TOP SECRET*

*Dear Mummy,*
*MY HEAD FEELS LIKE A BIG HOT AIR BALLOON FILLED WITH FIRE.*
*If you talk to Vics about Beth, I'm DEAD.*

*Which lie shall I tell?*
   *a) That I was stolen by aliens for an hour?*
   *b) That I was kidnapped by a man in a white van?*
   *c) That I snuck down to the sweet shop instead of going to Beth's?*
   *INVISIBLE INK ALERT: d) Definitely not that I went to Mrs E's for cake.*

*I think c) is my best.*

*INVISIBLE INK ALERT: I don't know why I said that to Mrs E. I was very angry with you – you said you say things you don't mean when you're angry, so, like, whoops, I did! When you said you weren't my mummy it felt just like a slap on my face. I don't know why I keep looking at your face now and trying to find bits of it that are like mine. I think I have your hair. I love my hair. I hope it doesn't get all frizzy like yours when I am old. When I look at daddy, it's easy. I have his nose and mouth and face.*

*Don't get too cross about c) and eating too many sweets. It's a lie remember?! ;).*

*Usually I say, I love you. But I don't really feel like it. So I'll say, I might love you tomorrow.*

*From,*
*Rosie*

*P.S. I love you (I'm writing this bit today just in case I forget tomorrow).*

# CHAPTER TWENTY-SIX

Finally, Barry was gone.

PC Yorke's phone rang and rang. As Mira waited, she picked at a semi-circle of dirt under her fingernail.

'Hello, PC Yorke speaking.'

'Hello PC Yorke, it's Mira Entwistle from Virginia Close. I wanted to talk to you about little Rosie Bradley.'

PC Yorke had listened quietly. After she had finished, his chit-chatty tone of before had disappeared. He turned officious and cold with her, as though Mira had been the one to hit Rosie. PC Yorke had then told her that a response team would be called out to speak to her about what had happened.

'But I have to go to work.'

'I'll send them over to Woodlands,' he said, knowing exactly where she worked. He had been a boy at Woodlands Primary himself, fifteen odd years ago when she had first started at the school as a dinner monitor.

When she hung up, she was a little annoyed that he hadn't at least given her any credit for getting the information out of Rosie. Goodness me, she thought, if I'd left it to that whippersnapper PC Yorke – who had eaten with his mouth open at school – Rosie might have continued to suffer alone!

In between each poof of a pillow, she glanced out of the bedroom window into the Bradleys' garden.

She wondered how long it would take the police to call Gemma after they had interviewed her at Woodlands.

When the safety of a child was at stake, the response would have to be swift, Mira knew this much.

She worried that Rosie would be cross with her for breaking her confidence and upsetting her mummy. However ironic, this troubled Mira greatly.

There was something about her newfound attachment to this girl that had shifted her attention away from her charges at Woodlands Primary, away from her little Alice with the lisp, shouty red-headed George and Olivia who wet her pants every day. Having doted on them from the moment they had started in Year Two, she didn't feel engaged with them in the same way. None of them seemed to be as compelling as Rosie.

This didn't sit well with her. She knew she was letting them down in small ways every day. Like when she smelt the dry urine on Olivia at the end of Monday, realising that she had failed to spot the accident. And on Tuesday George had been given a red warning card by Sally – *Mrs* Edwards to the Year Twos – for hitting Humphrey. This would not have happened if Mira had recognised the escalation of George's shouting and intervened in the altercation sooner.

Today she would try to work harder for her Year Twos, she thought, before remembering that the police response team would interrupt them.

Her stomach crunched, sending her hurtling for the toilet.

She needed something to take her mind off things and so she allowed herself a cup of tea before work and settled herself at the dining room table. She didn't have to be at school until nine-thirty that morning.

As she sifted, she noted that there weren't any photographs of her much beyond 1983, the year she had turned sixteen. The older photographs with their square white borders were plentiful. The snaps from her early teenage years were larger matt prints, but there were fewer of them. By her mid-teen years, there were only a handful of larger, glossier prints.

Not that there were that many of Deidre either, not until the later years, when there was a flurry of her with her husband, Doug, and then when she was pregnant, and then with her son, Harry, when he was a baby.

Mira found a brown envelope to store these ones away. These were not going to make the album.

As she popped them into the envelope, one by one, she stopped at the one with Harry sitting on Deidre's lap. Before putting it in, she noticed that Harry was chewing a baby-blue toy rabbit.

The room began to spin with a whoosh of love.

She pressed the photograph into her chest as though hugging it. She rocked back and forth on the chair as she held it to her, steeling herself before she peeled it away from her body to look again at the blue rabbit.

So that she didn't pass out, she rested her forehead onto the table. The wooden edge dug a line across her skull; she pressed harder, a pleasing pain. She closed her eyes and pushed the chair back, bending over further until her head was between her knees. Something plastic in her fingers. Not a photograph any more. A stick. White and long. A blue line. No, a blue cross. A faded blue cross. She was on a toilet, in a bathroom with black and white tiles. Craig's voice came to her.

'Let me see those instructions,' Craig had said, grabbing them from where Mira had left them at her feet by the toilet.

Her head was between her knees. She couldn't look at him.

The instructions crackled in his hands.

She noticed how his big toe curled up from the floor tiles as he read. It was twice the width of his second toe. It was square and hairy and she didn't like it. Would her baby have his toes? she thought, before laughing.

'What's so funny?' He scrunched up the instructions and chucked them at her head playfully.

She couldn't stop the giggling. 'Nothing.'

'You're such a weird kid,' he smirked, beginning to laugh too.

'Sorry,' she snorted, before pulling up her pants and flushing the toilet.

He blocked her way to the sink, pulling her hips into his. The warmth of his skin on her breasts distracted her from the blue cross.

His hand moved down her long hair, over her right breast and down to where it met the top of her knickers. He slipped his hands into the front, and he groaned, under his breath, 'What I want to do to you now is called statutory rape.'

She let her head roll back, yielding to him and he lifted her onto the sink, pushing her knickers aside.

'We could go away somewhere together,' Mira murmured.

He panted, 'Yeah, yeah,' and he pushed inside her.

How she loved him. She loved him. She loved him so much. 'I love you,' escaped from her lips

His movements slowed. She felt a softening of him inside her. He pulled out.

'Shit, Mira,' he mumbled, and he left her there on the side of the sink. Unsupported by him, she slipped off. Her ankle gave way and twisted slightly.

In the adjoining bedroom, she had to hobble past him and around his bed to the pine chest, where she had a small drawer for her clothes. She had only meant to stay a few nights, and seven weeks later she was still there.

She clipped her bra around her waist. Her reflection in the mirror showed only her torso. She was headless. Her stomach protruded over her pants, her swollen, sore breasts drooped. What a miracle that Craig had desired that ugly lump, she thought.

Perching on the edge of the bed self-consciously, she pulled her white school socks on, feeling her waistband dig into her belly, and wondered where they would squeeze the cot in this small room.

'Get off will you?' he said.

The black and red duvet was pulled from under her.

He shook it out violently before laying it down, whacking at it and smoothing it flat. 'NHS'll give you one for free, you know.'

'Give me what?'

'You know. A whatsit.' He mimed sticking an imaginary something up between his legs.

'Oh.'

'You'll have to tell the doc you shagged some spotty fifteen-year-old git though or I'll be locked up.'

Her ankle throbbed. She thought about pain. She was brave about pain. The pain of childbirth was considered unbearable by even the most hardy of women. She'd cope.

'You okay?' he had asked as he crafted his quiff with gelled palms.

'Yup.'

She turned away from him and took her hairbrush from the drawer.

One. Two. Three. Four. Five. She counted in her head, brushing from the widow's peak at the front and continuing right down to the ends. Seven, eight, nine, ten.

Craig said something else to her, she thought, but she hadn't heard him. Twenty-five, twenty-six, twenty-seven. Her arm had begun to ache at forty. Craig stamped out of the room. Forty-nine, fifty, fifty-one. She counted in time to his heavy footsteps, which shook the floor under her feet. Eighty-eight, eighty-nine, ninety, ninety-one, ninety-two. Her hair was silky smooth. One hundred. Her mind was calm again.

Dropping the photograph, Mira ran her fingers through her cropped grey hair: wiry and stiff and requiring no brushing, but just as thick as it had been back then. What would she look like with it long now? She had spent her adult life with it short. Thirty-four years ago, she had asked the hairdresser to cut it off. It had been an angry, almost violent self-destruction – a symbolic act – and she wondered whether she should be bothered by the fact that her haircut, all of her adult life, had been a visible representation of that one bad moment in her history. She thought of growing it out. Her image and others' view of her would be radically altered if she wore long hair again. It was an amusing thought, to open up that side of herself again after so many years of hiding her. It was out of the question, obviously. But amusing all the same.

Cutting into her playful thoughts of swishing her thick hair around her shoulders, came Craig's vile words again. 'The NHS'll do it for free, you know.' He hadn't even been able to say the word 'abortion'.

She went upstairs to find a hairbrush. The only one she could find was in Barry's shoe rack. One, two, three. She brushed from the widow's peak and down through her imaginary tresses. Ten, eleven, twelve. Once she got to one hundred, she was calmed all over again, just as she had been at fifteen years old standing in Craig's bedroom.

When Mira arrived at school, little Olivia in Year Two pointed at her and cried, 'You're all dirty, Mrs Entwistle!' Streaks of black shoe polish were smeared down the front of her T-shirt, over her breasts and right down to the top edge of her skirt, like black shadows of her former self.

# CHAPTER TWENTY-SEVEN

'Hello Vics?'

'Hello? Hello?'

'Sorry, reception's bad.' I shouted, 'I'm on the platform.'

'Gem!' Vics cried. 'What are you doing on a platform at this time? Are you skiving?'

I laughed, and then wanted to cry. All morning at work I had been distracted and unable to concentrate, preoccupied by Rosie. Repeatedly, I had played back Rosie's strange mood change when I had asked her about Beth. What with the unsettling events of the week, I couldn't help worrying that it was connected.

'Sort of. I wanted to pick Rosie up from school today.'

'You're venturing into the vipers' nest of New Hall Prep playground?'

'I'm feeling a bit out of the loop.'

'You're a braver woman than I.'

'I know. I must be coming down with something,' I laughed, weakly.

'Fancy coming round for a cuppa afterwards?'

'Yes please,' I sighed, comforted by that thought. 'I'd love that.'

'It's been too long. We're three doors down and I haven't seen you in three weeks. How does that even happen?'

'Sorry.'

'We got Peter very drunk the other week.'

I almost said sorry again, and then realised I wasn't to blame for that at least.

'That's okay. He probably needed the release.'

'Everything all right?'

'Yes, fine.' I stared at my reflection in the carriage window, which distorted me, wiggling my edges and narrowing my head as though it were in a vice.

'You don't sound fine.' I imagined Vics' tanned forehead form two deep wrinkles in between her eyebrows, and thought with fondness about how, when she was about to listen to something of importance, she would flick the two sides of her brittle blonde bob in a deft movement behind each ear.

'I'll fill you in later. Are you sure it's all right to have Rosie again?'

'Again?'

'Yesterday afternoon?'

'I didn't have Rosie yesterday.'

My throat constricted. 'What?'

'Beth goes riding on Thursdays, remember?'

'But Rosie told Harriet she'd gone round to see Beth yesterday afternoon after school.'

'Nope. Impossible I'm afraid.'

'So where did Rosie go then?'

Vics' silver bracelets jangled. 'I'm sure there's some logical explanation. Maybe Harriet got it wrong?'

'Yes, yes, I'm sure,' I replied, knowing Harriet never got things wrong.

Aside from an aberration from Harriet, I couldn't think of any logical explanation for why Rosie would lie. There had never been a hole in her schedule that I couldn't account for, that I couldn't fill with the life I had planned for her. I had a pressing, nauseating desire to get home to her to find out exactly where she had been; but my stomach churned at the thought of what I would uncover.

# CHAPTER TWENTY-EIGHT

The police response team, consisting of the one officer, PC Raynor, had arrived at Woodlands Primary after lunch, later than expected. Even so, Mira had not had time to clean her blouse or change into something borrowed.

While the officer was speaking to her in that hot little side room next to Patricia's office, she worried that the strange black stripes of shoe polish would give the wrong impression entirely and deem her quite the most unreliable witness they had ever spoken to. She *cursed* her memories! Those photographs were poison on her brain.

'What will happen to Gemma Bradley?' Mira asked, after she and the officer had been through the details of Rosie's confession.

'In the light of your information, I think we would need to speak to Rosie first.' The young police officer's stomach was popping out of his uniform at the front and his youthful, cheerful cheeks, redder with every minute in the room, belied the purpose of his visit.

'Rosie will say what I've said.'

He pulled up his trousers from his belt. 'We'll keep you informed.'

'What is likely to happen to her?'

PC Raynor stood square on two feet, as though about to recite a poem. 'The Child Protection Officers will speak to Mum and then speak to Rosie at school and decide what action to take, based on whether they consider Mum's actions to be lawful chastisement, where no further action will be taken.'

'No further action. I see. So, it's okay to bloody your ten-year-old's lip, is it?' Mira asked, vexed.

He looked at Mira – a brief glance down at her smeared blouse – scratched his cheek and calmly replied. 'But, at a guess, based on the information you've provided, and depending on what the little girl says when they speak to her, they might well deem it assault.'

Mira pressed her fingers into her lips. 'Could Gemma be arrested for that?'

'Yes. That is a possible outcome.' PC Raynor cleared his throat.

The shock of it. The thought of it. Mira had expected that the Social Services would get involved, at the most. She had not expected this.

'So I did the right thing, then,' Mira said quickly, before PC Raynor could spot the doubt shooting through her expression.

'We'll be in touch,' PC Raynor said, nodding officiously and holding the door open for Mira.

The hit of cold air from the corridor was like breath from an oxygen mask. She felt high on it.

In a daze, she sauntered back to the classroom, and imagined what it would have been like if her mother had been arrested for that slap all those years ago. Even considering everything she and her mother had been through, she would not have wanted that.

# CHAPTER TWENTY-NINE

The 14.02 train was a completely different experience to the rush-hour trains I usually caught. There were dozens of free seats to choose from, and I could even put my bag on the seat next to me.

Directly in front of where I chose to sit was a woman on her own reading a detective novel, two rows down there was a business man with a laptop, and across from him, an older man in a blue anorak with his hands in his lap.

I spread my newspaper across the pull-down table, scolded my mouth on my tea and urged the train to move like the wind.

As I watched the cityscape morph into green trees, I thought more about Rosie's lost hour. Perhaps she had been collecting conkers on the recreational ground, perhaps she'd been hiding in her den at the bottom of the garden, perhaps she had simply wanted some time to herself away from Harriet and Noah. And who could blame her?

There had to be an innocent explanation, and then again there was that familiar gnawing worry that she was slipping from me. Not physically, like in the train station, but emotionally. I tried to put the never-ending analysis aside for a moment to console myself that Rosie's age – double figures, ten years old – was a hormonal time. She was in the emerging adolescence phase, where a girl's body hints at puberty and her moods darken, where she craves independence and starts the fight for separation, while still too immature to be able to cope alone. The tussle was there inside her already; but the power fights seemed frighteningly premature. I dreaded it as a precursor for what was to come. There were signs of trouble ahead that I could ignore at my own peril.

Twenty minutes or so away from my stop, I heard an unintelligible announcement on the tannoy and noticed that we had been at the same station platform for longer than we should have been. I asked the lady in front of me what the guard had announced.

'Might be stuck here for a while.'

'How frustrating,' I said, feeling the delay as a personal attack.

School pick-up time was an hour away; I felt impatient and twitchy, eager to surprise Rosie at the school gates.

More than that, the stationary train seemed to have portent, a message in its refusal to carry me where I wanted to go.

The newspaper lost its appeal and I turned on my phone to call Harriet to ask her to be home, on standby, just in case.

'No problem, Gemma,' she replied, efficient and loyal as ever. 'Anyway, Rosie promised to show me a special acrobatics routine she'd been practising today and I'd hate to miss that!' she laughed.

I knew Harriet meant well, that she was showing me how dedicated she was to my children, proving to me that she was a nanny of excellence, which she was. But envy spread through me. She was referring to fun times with my daughter that I was not part of. And again, if this train didn't move soon, she would be the first one to hug my daughter after school. I felt wretched for all the hours Harriet had spent with her that I had missed. And even worse, I knew that I hadn't been psychologically capable of spending all those hours with Rosie performing those repetitive, thankless, relentless tasks of motherhood.

'One more thing, Harriet. Rosie definitely said she was going to Beth's yesterday afternoon, didn't she? And not some other friend?'

'Yes, she definitely said Beth. Why?'

'No reason.' Another phone call came through. 'Sorry, Harriet, I have to get this, it could be work,' I said.

'Hello?'

Above my head, yellow letters moved across the information board with no information.

'Hello, is this Mrs Bradley?'

'Yes, speaking?'

'Hello, this is DC Miles from Child Protection at Greyswood Police. Are you in a convenient place to speak?'

'Child protection?'

I noticed the old man in the anorak look up from his phone.

'Sorry, could you hold on for a second?' I asked.

I stood up, leaving my seat to move to the corridor where I wouldn't be overheard.

'Hello?'

'Yes, sorry to alarm you, Mrs Bradley, but we've had a call from one of your neighbours that we're duty bound to follow up on and I'm afraid we're going to need to speak to your daughter at school today.'

My mind blanked.

'Hello, Mrs Bradley?'

I managed to make words come from my throat. 'Sorry, we must have gone through a tunnel.' I stared out at the platform, watching a man bite into a large Cornish pasty. 'Could you repeat what you said?'

DC Miles repeated what she had said. Her words spun around my head and I tried to order them into a sentence that made sense.

'Are you telling me we have to go through all this again?'

'I understand that when the response officers visited your home on October sixteenth no further action was taken, is that correct?'

'What has Mira said this time?'

'We are not at liberty to give you details at this time.'

'Does my husband know about this?'

'We have been unable to reach your husband.'

I imagined his indignation.

'Mira must have a vendetta against me.'

'You understand that we have to follow-up on all referrals.'

'I don't give you permission to speak to Rosie at school without me there.'

'I'm afraid, the allegation concerns you, so, myself and a social worker will be speaking to Rosie alone or with one of the teachers depending on what Rosie feels most comfortable with.'

This stranger had just called Rosie by her name. She didn't know Rosie. How dare she call her Rosie?

'I don't give you permission to speak to her at all.'

'Please let me reassure you that we'll make her feel as comfortable as possible. We'll just have a quiet word with her before she pops off home. It won't take longer than fifteen minutes or so.'

'No. This is not going to happen.'

Two young teenagers in school uniform pushed open the door from the platform. I thought of little Rosie being interviewed alone with her tartan skirt pulled over her knees, about how scared she would be.

'I understand this must be very worrying for you, Mrs Bradley, but we only have your daughter's safety in mind.'

'That's what PC Connolly said when she barged into our home the other week. But what about all the stress you are causing for Rosie? If you care so much about her, how can you put her through all this?'

'With regards to the allegations that have been made, to be honest, we don't need your permission to speak to your daughter,' DC Miles said. She spoke softly, as though tired, her power cumbersome.

I knocked my head back, as though knocking back a shot, and blinked up at the ceiling of the train to stop the gathering tears. I was not going to be weak. I was going to fight this all the way.

'This is outrageous.' I kicked at the train door with my foot, feeling the pain shoot up my leg and into my teeth.

'We will be in touch shortly.'

'You know my husband and I'll be making a formal complaint after this is all over. You are making a terrible mistake and after you speak to my daughter, you'll realise that.'

'As I said, we will be in touch, Mrs Bradley.'

DC Miles hung up.

My hands were shaking violently. They were barely coordinated enough to grip my phone.

My handbag and my newspaper were on the seat as I had left them.

The two teenagers who had jostled past me had joined our carriage. They whispered and giggled at the far end.

When the man in the blue anorak glanced up at me again, I guessed he would see a change in me.

The world and everyone in it felt like an enemy. I gathered up my belongings and went out into the corridor again to call Peter.

As I listened to Peter's ring tone repeat, I remembered he would be out on site today.

Giving up, I called the school. I was matter-of-fact with Clare the receptionist. 'There'll be a couple of police officers coming in to talk to Rosie after school today and I just wanted to confirm that this has been cleared by me,' I said.

When I hung up, I put my palms to my cheeks and felt the hotness.

Humiliation pushed through my body right into my fingertips, hot under my nail beds.

*Please train, move*, I thought, *please start moving. I need to get to my daughter. I need to protect her. Please, if there is a God up there, please help me.*

The tannoy fired up again, the response to my pleas ignored: 'Due to an electrical fault on the train, please could all passengers move off the 14.02 train to Hazelway and wait on the platform for further information. We are sorry for the inconvenience caused to your journey.'

I wanted to scream. Who could I talk to about the delay? Might there be a guard who could shed some light, get things moving? Might there be a complaints line for me to call? Was there a manager I could shout at?

I piled off the train with the rest of the passengers, who began to sigh and text.

The guard I found to complain to ignored me as if I was invisible. The message board delivered no news in response to my insistence that it should. The other passengers stared blankly at my gesticulations and 'can you believe this?' eye-rolling. The complaints line put me on hold until I gave up. The rail website flashed me a red exclamation mark. It dawned on me – more slowly than it had on many of the other passengers seemingly – that there was nothing I could do.

I leant against a cold wall and I stared across the tracks, at nothing in particular, deciding that perhaps this delay was fate. My heart thumped; the rumble of a panic attack. The bustle of an over-packed train platform was like a buffer, like the padding on the walls of a cell, protecting me from myself. What would I be doing at Rosie's school? Shouting at everyone, pacing outside the door? Exacerbating the situation? And if I was at home? Would I be cleaning and organising? Using the time to get started on the nursery? Pacing some more? Smashing Mira's windows? Wherever I was in the world, I was utterly powerless until they had finished talking to her. The tension of the wait for the train stretched every minute into some unbearable endurance test. I focussed with tunnel vision on staying sane, on keeping it together, so that I could get home to Rosie in one piece. She needed me and I berated myself for not being there.

# CHAPTER THIRTY

Mira put two pieces of bread in the toaster. She didn't notice the smell of burning until it was too late and Barry's arm shot around her and pressed the release button. Two blackened slices popped out.

'Whoops. I forgot to turn it down after the potato farls last night,' Mira said.

'Mind on other things?'

'The foxes got in last night,' she said bitterly. 'Hancock's gone.'

Barry sighed heavily. 'I'll fix the coop, again.'

'They come in through the Bradleys garden you know.'

'You don't know that.'

'I do, it's that gap at the bottom of their hedge. They come in through the woods.'

'Do you want me to fence it up?'

Fearful it would stop Rosie coming in too, she quickly stamped on that idea. 'No, no. You're right. They'd come in somehow anyway.'

'The less we have to do with that lot next door now the better, I say.'

'You'd have been happy to leave Rosie to suffer, I suppose, would you?' she muttered tetchily. The toast burnt her fingers as she removed it from the toaster.

Barry opened the window that backed onto the Bradleys' hedge to let the smoke out. 'I never liked that you were messed up in their business, that's the truth.'

Aggressively, Mira scraped at the charcoal layer. Black speckles sprayed over the work surface until she was left with four brittle broken pieces of toast. They were still edible. She was not going to waste two fresh slices from the loaf.

'If Gemma's arrested, it'll prove I was right.'

'That'd be a terrible shame, love,' he tutted.

'Can't take it back now, can I?' she asked doubtfully.

Barry continued crunching loudly on his burnt toast. A few of the black crumbs had made it onto his lips. She watched them suspended there as he chewed. They made him look foolish.

And then he said, 'My dad used to chuck books at my head when I got my spellings wrong. Every word. Clunk.' He mock-hit the side of his own head, and scrunched up his nose, twice, which shifted his glasses up and down, like he was pressing the arms behind his ears for comic effect. He was not laughing. This facial twitch of his was becoming more frequent, like a nervous tick. Mira felt guilty about sniping at him. She wanted to tell him how cruel his father had been.

'Times have changed,' she said instead.

Barry poured his tea from his cup into his saucer and back again to cool it. He hadn't done this in a while. Ironically, it was something his father had done when he was alive.

'It can't be hot, it's been sitting there ten minutes,' Mira said.

Barry took a small sip, and then gulped the tea down as though it was water. 'Rosie is a strange child, I'll say that for her.'

This offended Mira. He didn't seem to understand how connected she felt to Rosie now. Rosie's disclosure had made her feel special, as though Rosie had trusted her, chosen her above everyone else to confide in.

'Gemma's the problem, not Rosie.'

'So you keep saying, love.'

'Don't be fooled by her nice appearance.'

'Appearances make no difference to me.'

A pang of doubt shot through her. 'You really think I did the wrong thing?' she asked meekly.

'Don't you worry. Any decent citizen would have done as you have,' he stated flatly.

'Thanks,' she sighed, relieved.

She took a napkin and wiped away the burnt bits from his lips. 'Rosie will thank me one day,' Mira said.

# CHAPTER THIRTY-ONE

Minutes after I had boarded a new train, finally, after over an hour of fraught waiting, DC Miles' number flashed up on the screen.

'Hello DC Miles,' I said, haughtily, waiting for the grovelling apology.

I stopped in the cyclists' carriage, letting the throng pass me into the Quiet Zone of this new train.

'Hello Mrs Bradley. Are you home yet?'

'My train has been delayed but I'm on my way now.'

'Well, okay, we've spoken to Rosie,' she paused, 'and because of what she's said, we want to do a video interview right away.'

'What has she done to her?' I demanded, immediately assuming that Rosie had implicated Mira. Is that where she had been yesterday? With Mira? Was that really possible? My heart began to race. It was all happening too fast. I couldn't keep up.

'Rosie's told me some things that I'm concerned about and we need to get a bit more information from her.'

'Why can't you tell me what she's said?' My stomach was turning over and over with fear.

'Again, I'm very sorry, but because it concerns you, that isn't possible.'

I froze. 'What do you mean it concerns me?'

'As I said, we can't give you more information at this time.'

What did Rosie say? She must have got muddled and said something wrong by mistake. 'She can't go through this without me. You have to wait until I get home. I need to see her. She needs me.'

'Your nanny is here and has kindly offered to take her to the interview room and then return her home and wait for your husband's return.'

'But I haven't been able to get hold of Peter!' I cried desperately.

'Harriet has offered to stay with her as long as necessary and wanted me to tell you that Noah is staying at his friend's house tonight.'

Something inside me collapsed.

'Oh my God. It's going to be horrible for her. Oh my God.' I clamped my hand over my mouth. I didn't want this woman to hear my distress.

A young cyclist began to stare. My focal point became his blue eyes, as though he and I were friends, as though his steady attention might provide some stability.

DC Miles voice spoke to me from some faraway place, 'Are you okay, Mrs Bradley? Are you with anyone right now? I feel it is important you get hold of someone who can support you, is that possible? To call someone? A friend or a family member?'

'Oh my God. I don't know. Oh my God. I feel a bit faint. I just can't believe that I'm stuck here like this.'

The cyclist disappeared into the next carriage.

'Please focus. I think it is important that you call someone. Can you think of someone to call?'

The electric doors beeped open and the cyclist returned with a plastic glass of water. I wanted to hug him for his kindness. My grateful smile was probably more like a grimace as I took the cup from him. The cool water soothed me.

'Yes, I'll call Peter. I'll call Peter. He'll know what to do. I'll call Peter.'

Peter answered straight away in his clipped I'm-an-important-property-consultant tone of voice. 'Hello. How can I help?'

'Peter, you're not going to believe it...' I stopped to expand my chest as far as it would go to find enough air to talk. There didn't seem to be enough air.

'Gemma?'

'Sorry, I'm finding it difficult to breathe.'

'What's happened, Gemma? Is the baby okay?'

'Yes... It's not that...'

I tried to recount DC Miles' information to Peter, but I was barely coherent. He asked me again and again to go back and fill in the gaps before he finally understood what was happening.

The train pulled into the next station. The cyclist lifted his bike out of the carriage. I smiled at him, wishing he could have stayed with me.

'It's okay,' Peter said. 'I'm at the Surbiton site today so I can get home quickly. I'll get hold of Harriet and meet her at this interview room place and bring Rosie home.'

'Mira must've accused me of something terrible, I just know it.'

'Well if she has, then Rosie will put them straight, won't she?'

'What if she gets confused and says something she doesn't mean?' *What if she tells them she can see rage in my eyes? What if she's the one who senses my notional hand raised and poised to strike? What if she is calling out to them for help?*

'You're getting ahead of yourself.'

'Peter, I'm not feeling too good and there's nowhere to sit.'

'You're pregnant, Gemma, you need to find somewhere to sit.'

'Yes, no, I don't know. The train is full.' I slumped down to the floor and rested my head on my knees. 'I'm okay now. Honestly. I'm okay.'

'Darling, you're almost home. Get a cab from the station, promise?'

'Promise.'

'We'll sort this out. I love you. See you at home. I love you,' he repeated.

'Love you too,' I said vaguely, wondering if I said it before or after I had hung up.

When I returned home forty-five minutes later, Peter and Rosie were not there.

Like a lost old lady who has been told to wait until her relatives rescue her, I sat in silence, with my handbag on my lap, willing them to come clattering through the door, desperate for my phone to ring with news of their imminent arrival.

I didn't hear the knock, but somehow I was at the door.

I didn't open it, but somehow it was open.

'Hello, my name is DC Miles, we spoke on the phone? And this is DC Bennett. Myself and my colleague need to come in if that's okay.'

The sight of them angered me.

'Where's Rosie?' I barked.

'Can we come in please?'

'Where's Peter?'

I was livid. I looked out, beyond them to the gates, now closing us in.

'It would be better if you let us in, Mrs Bradley.'

Rather than allowing them entry, I reeled back from them, but the effect was the same, and the two police officers entered my home in their thick black vests.

'I demand to know where my daughter is.'

'Rosie is safe. Can we ask you who else is in the house?' DC Miles said, glancing upstairs furtively.

'Nobody's here. Not that it's any of your business who's in my own house.'

'Calm down, Mrs Bradley,' DC Bennett said.

'Sorry, but this is not a convenient time I'm afraid,' I said, feeling anything but sorry. I needed them to leave, right now. I urgently wanted to stop it before it became a reality, because the reality would be too disturbing to live through. But they continued to stand there, in my house.

'Okay, Mrs Bradley – the time is 17.35 p.m.' DC Miles looked at her watch and then at her colleague and then at me, speaking factually and unemotionally, as though reading through a shopping list, she continued, 'Having spoken to your daughter, we are arresting you on suspicion of assault causing actual bodily harm to your daughter. The justification of this arrest is to allow for a prompt and effective investigation and to prevent physical injury to a person. You do not have to say anything but it may harm your defence if you do not mention when questioned anything which you may rely on later in court. Anything that you do say may be recorded and given as evidence in court.'

Shell-shocked and uncomprehending, I tried to process what she had just said but my thoughts flatlined. I held my breath as though letting it out would kill me.

'Are you serious?' My knees began to give way.

DC Miles steadied me. 'Are you okay? Your husband said you're expecting, is that right?'

'No, yes, I mean, yes. Nine weeks. Nobody knows at work yet,' I said, pointlessly.

'I know this is probably a big shock.'

'No, no, this can't be happening. I can't believe it's happening,' I said, shaking my head at her, my eyes wide, my mouth open, a dryness on my tongue.

'We're going to need to take you down to the station now,' DC Bennett said.

DC Miles stepped towards me. 'Do you think you need a glass of water or something before we go?'

'I think I do,' I said through chattering teeth, bizarrely grateful to her, as I had been to the cyclist. A detached, dangling thought entered my mind when I looked at her: I decided that she was too pretty to be a real police officer. Her chocolate-brown fringe was enviably shiny and her curled eyelashes widened her green eyes. She wasn't real. This was a dream. None of this was real.

'Which way is the kitchen, Gemma?'

'Here, this way,' I said, pointing and letting her lead me to the sink, where I glugged at a mug of water, tasting old tea.

She rubbed at my back. 'Are you feeling better? Do you think you're ready for us to go now?'

'It's all been a terrible mistake. I never meant to hurt her wrist.'

'Okay, don't talk to us about it now because we'll be interviewing you down at the station and that'll give us an opportunity for you to give us your side of the story, okay?'

'Can I have some more?' I wasn't ready to go down to a police station. I would never be ready. Was there enough water in the tap to delay me forever?

'Rosie must've explained something wrong,' I continued.

'As I say, it's best you save this for down at the station, okay?'

'Okay,' I nodded, like a child.

'Do you think you're ready to come with us in the car now?'

'Okay, I think so,' I nodded again, looking to this woman as though she would guide me to normality, back to safety again.

The police car was unmarked, a nondescript blue, but once inside, in the backseat, I felt marked. As DC Miles drove me away, I wanted to lie down across the seats to hide away in shame. Would Mira be waiting at her window, nodding in approval as we passed her five-bar gate, tutting at me as we drove away from the cul-de-sac, away from my home, the home that I had chosen to keep my children safe and secure. How ironic. Noah and Rosie, whom I longed for now. They would be utterly confused. I was their sun and their moon. I felt my heart was being yanked out of my chest.

I slumped down and covered my face as well as I could by leaning into my left hand, away from the window on my side.

'Are you all right back there?' DC Miles asked.

'Fine,' I replied. I was so far from all right it was as though I had left the body of the woman she was asking. Thoughts jumbled, charging and crashing in different directions. Rage towards Mira bloomed in black clouds through my mind, dissipated only by helpless confusion and fear. Was this really happening? Even as it was happening, it wasn't possible.

Why hadn't Peter called? Peter would be on my side. He knew me. We knew each other so well, too well. After sixteen years of being with him, I could predict most of his moves, most of his reactions. On Sundays at the White Horse, he would always order the same half pint of bitter to start and choose the same newspapers if they were free, and curse under his breath if they weren't. He knew my habits just as well. He knew I would always order a double shot in my latte at the end of my meal, and that I would talk too quietly for him to hear, just in case there was a mother at school at the next table, and en route home, he knew that I would always comment on the beauty of the rolling hills, and remind the children of how lucky they were to live here. He *knew* me. Surely he would not believe I was capable of assaulting Rosie.

When I had shut her wrist in the door, I might have been cross but it had been an accident. When I left her in her room while I danced with Noah, I was separating myself, as all the parenting books told me to do, to protect her. I couldn't have predicted the broken glass. How could I be in this police car, now driving past the clock tower on the high street, having been arrested? It was beyond comprehension.

A tight feeling began to build in my chest as I sucked in every particle of air I could find, but the sweet taste of the air-freshener that bobbed from the mirror made me want to gag. I was about to be led into a police station as a child abuser; it took my breath away. I had no frame of reference.

As we drove cautiously through the high street, I tried to recall those intense fights with Rosie, in anticipation of questions, but the details wouldn't come. I could have been calmer with her, wound her up less, I don't know. My memory was messy and more about feeling than detail, like watching a screen-burst of our rage. The autumn wreath bouncing on the carpet, her fingers shooting through the door that I slammed; the teeth marks on Noah's arm, her shoulders squeezed by my hands; the beat to a disco track, the blood on her palm. In the eyes of a stranger, cruelty and carelessness and neglect could have fuelled each scenario. I dreaded the police officers scrutinising me, forcing me to relive the shameful details. Laid out on the table, it would look bad. More so, they might have ways of tricking me into revealing more than I should, more of what my mind had put me through in those stressful minutes, more about what I had felt capable of doing to her. The legal parameters of domestic assault were a mystery to me, but I knew I had been wrong to think those things. I might not have actually hit her, but I had certainly wanted to.

# CHAPTER THIRTY-TWO

*TOP SECRET*

*Dear Mummy,*

*Daddy said I was allowed to take my diary to Vics'
house. Beth is asleep. She makes a funny noise when she
breathes. I'm glad it's not too quiet though. I am scared
when it is. I'm so scared anyway. I don't think I will be
able to sleep all night and my pillow is wet from all my
crying. I am worried you will never come back. I know
that Daddy says you have gone to a police station but I
keep imagining that you have gone into the dark, dark
woods where there are serpents and dragons to kill you
and then what would I do without you? Daddy said you
were going to be asked some questions just like the police
asked me. The pretty police officer was really nice. She
smiled a lot. She will be nice to you too, Mummy. The
other woman Miranda Slay-something was a bit weird.
She was a social worker and she had big teeth and a long
grey ponytail that she kept stroking like it was her snake
pet. She creeped me out. Also I don't think grown-ups
should have pink dangly pens like hers. I like your smart
black pen that you use for your work and I want to have
one when I am grown-up. I hope you don't have to talk
to snake-lady.*

*Daddy says you will be home later. Sometimes Daddy
says stuff just to make me feel better and then it makes me*

*sadder because I know he is lying. You never lie to me. I think that is really cool. I want you to come home, mummy. Please, please come home. I'm sure you can hear me.*

*INVISIBLE INK ALERT: I want so badly to say how sorry I am. When the police wanted to talk to me again on the flowery sofa in that weird house that was not like a real house that Harriet took me to with that big weird window mirror I was too scared to tell them that my imagination was getting very big and it felt like I was writing a composition at school that I couldn't stop writing and it ran away with me like the dog with the spoon. I feel bad because I broke the one rule that they said was the only rule in the room. (I wondered what other rule they had in the upstairs room of the house and I thought about all those different rules in all the different rooms in the world and my eyes went cross-eyed – only in my head. If I really went cross-eyed I would look like a weirdo). Then they asked me what the difference between telling a lie and telling the truth was. The story went like this: If someone stole my pencil case at school and then told me they hadn't stolen it even though I knew they had, was this a lie or the truth? .... DUH! DUH! DAH! Even Noah could answer that dumb question.*

*It's just I wasn't really lying, mummy, I promise you. Mrs E said some stuff about her mummy slapping her and there being blood on her lip then I kind of imagined you slapped me like it was a film and then I thought I could taste the blood and see the red dripping down my lips and I was so angry with you for saying that thing about not being my real mummy that it was like the anger was boiling up inside me and the story just came out and it kind of became like real and it got stuck in my head and I couldn't get it out until it was really real, real. Now I am imagining it again and I am thinking that maybe it was real. Was it real mummy? The blood was crimson. Crimson is the word that the writer used in that book you read me about those wolves when they died in the white snow and I remembered it and thought about the crimson blood dripping down and down onto my white school shirt, white like the snow. Get it? When I told the police about that white shirt and the crimson blood (but I said red instead of crimson and I did not tell them about the wolves) I thought they looked a bit worried like they were watching the same scary film that was in my head and I felt flutters in my stomach and I didn't want them to stop listening to me so I went on about it a bit.*

*My fingers ache from all this writing. My teacher says I should be a tortoise not a hare when I write, but I feel like a hare scrambling through the woods to watch you be killed by dragons. How would I save you in my story? If I told the truth to Daddy he would hate me and I think Daddy is the only one who really loves me in the whole world. I will always love you more than you love me, but I think Daddy loves me more than I love him or maybe just the same. I love you more than anyone. If I told that pretty police lady that I lied she might send me to prison and I would get so told off and I don't want anyone to be angry with me anymore. I want everyone to be happy and I want to be a good girl so that you love me more than I love you, so that I can love you even more than that, and then you will want to be my real mummy ALL THE TIME even when you are cross with me. Mrs E was so nice – not a Mrs Shithead at all – and I think she will understand. I think I want to ask her what to do. She won't tell me off for lying. I wonder if*

*I can creep out of Vics' house like a tortoise and go to Mrs E's house to ask her?*

*I'm going to save you from the dragons. You watch.*

*Love,*
*Rosie*

*PS I am only a bit scared of the dark. If I see a fox with shiny eyes I am going to hiss at it like a snake and it will run away.*

# CHAPTER THIRTY-THREE

She was knocking on the door. Mira knew it was Rosie.

Next door, the child's beautiful home had been evacuated, as though it, too, like Gemma, was a danger to the children, in spite of its velvets and silks. It loomed empty and imposing. No lights. No chatter. No screams.

Mira herself had once knocked on a door in the middle of the night. A red door.

Cold and shivering. Knock, knock. Shuddering. Freezing. The night had closed in on her from behind. The door had been the last obstacle. Behind which there would be safety, if not love.

Bang, bang, bang. 'Mum! Deidre! Please! It's me!'

No reply.

On the night bus on the way there, a blue sign had instructed passengers to give up their seat for pregnant women. Mira wasn't a woman, she was a girl. Did this make a difference, she had thought? It didn't matter on a night bus in suburbia. It was empty. Strip-lit but sheltered at least. She couldn't relate to The Thing – and that was what she saw it as at that stage, a Thing – inside her that would give her a huge belly like in the blue sign.

Again, at the door, she had called for them. 'Mum! Deidre! Mum! Let me in!'

As she had pounded her fists, she wanted to be back on the bus, where a little bit of hope had still been alive, where she had imagined her mother and sister would forgive her for what she had done with Craig. Denial was better than this rejection; being on the bus was better than being shut out, with a home but homeless, at fifteen years old and pregnant.

Had her mother lain still in her bed listening? Had Deidre sat by the window watching? Had Craig tossed and turned on the bed that they had shared? Had he felt bad for sending a pregnant fifteen-year-old girl away? Had any of them felt bad?

Mira lay still in her bed. She felt bad. Rosie would be cold, too. Goosebumps would be prickling her skin, her breath would be gauzy, her feet would be damp.

She imagined how a ten-year-old might sneak out of the house after lights out. It would be easy. If her father and friends were still awake, she would most likely have to escape through a back door. Mira imagined Peter Bradley's face covered by his hands as his friends consoled him, talking in circles, weary with worry about Rosie and the damage Gemma had inflicted, while Rosie quietly slipped away unnoticed. It was not easy for Mira to know she had been the cause of this. But if Barry had hurt her baby, she would have wanted to know and she would have killed him for it.

The yellow dot of Barry's earplugs, lodged safely in place, reassured Mira that Rosie's knocks would not be heard.

She climbed out of bed and down the stairs, grabbing her coat and torch on the way.

Rosie was frowning at the door, her arms crossed over her towelling pink robe, her sheepskin slippers, wet at the tips.

'Sssh, come this way,' Mira whispered with her finger to her lips. She led Rosie around the side of the house, past the chickens, right to the bottom of their long garden where her potting shed sat, near the compost heap.

The padlock to the door was stiff and rusty, and it took a few tries to unlock it. The lightbulb hung at the centre of the shed, illuminating the pine shelves of tins and pots and tools and casting a dull light on Rosie. Mira was shocked to see how her skin was as white as the mist and her eye sockets as black as her hair.

'Sit yourself down there,' Mira said, pointing at the metal stool, bracing herself for the child's tirade. But Rosie sat as timid as a mouse.

'I've an old kettle in here and some malt drink. Fancy some?'

Rosie nodded. 'Granny Helen has that.'

'Does she make it for you when you go and stay?'

The plastic kettle rushed, steaming up the small window above the workbench. Mira brushed some old soil away, wondering how long it would take for Rosie to say what was on her mind, reminding herself of the sweet peas she wanted to pot for Rosie. She thought it would be good for the child to do some gardening, and if she potted sweet peas, Rosie could add them to the charming collection that Gemma and Peter's gardener tended to so beautifully on their south-facing wall.

'We don't really stay at Granny Helen's for sleepovers we just go for tea or lunch or something.'

'Is she nearby then?'

'She's in London.' Her teeth were chattering as she spoke.

'That's a long way to go for tea.'

'Mum says she is best in limited doses.'

'Ha. Families are a bit like that. Everyone goes their separate ways when they're grown-up. It's hard to imagine that at your age.'

'I don't ever want to move out of home.'

'You think that now, and then suddenly you'll be dying to get out.' Mira stirred the two tin cups of malt drink.

'I won't.'

Strange, Mira thought, that a child clings to a dysfunctional home. Strange that Mira had longed to see her mother's face again after the period away from her at Craig's house. Even her wrath was preferable to no mother at all.

That closed door had been an injury. The fear that she would never again talk to her mother had brought her to her knees on the doorstep, where she had curled up all night, with her bag clutched to her middle, until her mother had finally let her in.

'How's your mum doing?' Mira asked pointlessly. The silences were awkward. They reminded Mira of how wrong it was to have Rosie here when she should be tucked up in bed.

'I don't know,' Rosie murmured, barely audible. She hung her head. When Mira passed her the hot drink, Rosie's big eyes were shot through with veins, and Mira's guilt spiked, knowing she had been responsible for separating this girl from her mother.

'It's going to be very hard for your mummy but it has been very hard for you too, hasn't it?'

Rosie's little hand let the cup slip slightly and the drink sloshed a little onto her dressing gown.

'Careful love,' Mira said, straightening the mug, feeling how cold Rosie's fingers were around the warm metal.

Mira waited for Rosie's understandable anger towards her, and felt ready to withstand it, knowing her motivations for breaking her trust and telling the police had been true.

'It's all my fault,' Rosie said finally.

Mira was taken aback.

'How so?'

'When I cut my hand on the picture I told that first police lady that Mummy shouted at me all the time and so today they came back to my school to ask me more questions and then I told them some stuff about what we had talked about when I had cake with you and now Mummy is in big trouble.' Her chin dimpled and her eyes blinked rapidly.

'You were a good girl for telling them the truth.'

Rosie took a sip of her drink, sniffing and then wiping away a tear. 'But what if I didn't tell them the truth?'

'Of course you did, pet,' Mira said, her heart breaking for Rosie. She supposed a period of denial was inevitable after opening up for the first time. It was apparently common for many abused children. She had read about it in the newspapers.

'You *don't understand*, Mu—' she stopped, a flash of much-needed pink on her cheeks, and continued with more measure in her voice. 'You don't understand, it's just I got into this big story in my head and I started to imagine all these horrible things because I was so angry with Mummy.'

'Of course you were angry with your mummy.'

Rosie was looking up at Mira with her eyes wider than ever, her drink growing a milky film. 'What would the police do if I told them it was all a big, fat lie?'

Mira felt suddenly cross. 'For goodness sake. Has your mother frightened you that much?'

'Mummy gets really, really cross when I lie.'

'Lying is very naughty indeed and everyone will be very cross with you if you lie. Very cross indeed. The police will take you into a cold dark room and lock you up if you lie.'

Mira had to exaggerate or else she feared Rosie would take back what she had confessed. It was natural for Rosie to believe that pushing it all back inside again was easier than facing up to the truth about her mother.

Mira had learnt the hard way on that front. Having been let back home, she had existed in a fug of lies and cover-ups and secrets in those early days of her pregnancy. Looking back, if she had given her mother and her sister time to adjust to the idea of a baby in the house, maybe everything would have been different.

'They'd really lock me up?' The cup slipped from Rosie's hand completely, clattering onto the floor. Rosie stared fearfully up at Mira as though she would strike her and leapt up from the stool to stand behind it, away from Mira and the mess.

'Don't you worry,' Mira said kneeling next to her, patting at the hot liquid that soaked into Rosie's thighs. 'Accidents happen. Nothing to worry about. Gosh, you're a nervy little thing, aren't you, pet? We'd call you Rosie Rabbit-in-the-Headlights at forest school.'

Rosie stood very still as Mira cleaned her up and then said, steadily, decisively, 'I think I need to go back now. Thank you very much for my drink.'

Mira, still on her knees with the cloth soaking her lap, twisted around to Rosie who was now at the shed door. 'Don't you want me to walk you back?'

'No thank you very much.'

'Don't forget, Rosie Rabbit, lying is a sin!'

Rosie stepped out into the night and closed the door carefully behind her.

Yes, Rosie Rabbit, lying was a sin. And sins were punished. Mira remembered that God had taught her this lesson by abandoning her in her hour of need, and she wondered if she had ever really recovered.

Mira's kneecaps were grinding into the gritty floor but instead of standing, she collapsed over her thighs and cried for the sins of Gemma Bradley and she cried for Rosie, but not for herself. The past was in the past. She would not allow self-pity when there were human beings so close to home who were suffering much greater agonies than she had.

# CHAPTER THIRTY-FOUR

'Time of arrest?'

'17.35.'

'Offence?'

'Assault of a child causing actual bodily harm,' DC Miles replied to the man behind the counter – the Duty Sergeant, I'd been told. He ran his eyes across me from behind his modern rectangle glasses, taking in details of my appearance with professional speed.

He tapped into his computer as he spoke. 'Based on what the officers have told me I will be detaining you here in the station, okay?'

'Okay.' My lips quivered. I bit the side of my mouth. DC Miles disappeared into the back room and I felt that much more lost without her there.

'Any drugs or alcohol in your system in the last twenty-four hours?'

'No.'

'Sorry, what was that?'

I tried to put some energy into my voice. 'No.'

'Any medication or medical conditions we need to know about?'

'I'm pregnant?' I said, wondering if that was relevant, hoping it might mean he was kinder to me. 'Nine weeks.'

He tapped that in.

Nine weeks pregnant and I was under arrest. How had this happened to me?

'Occupation?' he said.

'Head of Human Resources at CitiFirm.'

Before typing it in, he flicked one of the spikes of hair fanning across his forehead as though it had itched him all of sudden.

'You have a right to speak to an independent solicitor that's free of charge. And that can be in person or on the telephone.'

'Do I need one?' I tried to ask, before realising my voice box wasn't working properly again. After clearing my throat, I said, croakily but loudly enough to be heard, 'I think I know someone.' There was only one solicitor I would call, amongst the dozens that I'd worked with over the years.

'You'll have an opportunity to call them before we take you down to one of the detention cells, okay?'

A cell. I was going to be put in a cell.

'I can't believe this is happening,' I said, shaking my head back and forth, biting my lip and pressing my fingers into my forehead, one escaped tear leaking from my right eye. I sucked in my breath and looked at the ceiling. I was not going to cry.

The custody sergeant looked at me, and then at DC Bennett, who had been standing quietly beside me, and scratched under his hair again, 'It won't be too bad, we'll get you interviewed as soon as we can, okay? Would you like a tea or coffee now?'

I felt pathetic. 'Sorry, it's the hormones. A tea would be good, thank you. Thank you very much.'

DC Bennett took over. 'Okay then, Gemma, could you empty your pockets for me please?'

In a daze, I placed each of my possessions onto the high counter. The chewing gum, the lucky stone that Noah had given me, the velvet button, the tube of lip balm. I looked at them lying there, thinking about how personal they were to me, these small little pieces of my life. Didn't they in themselves prove that I loved my children? The chewing gum and lip balm were generic pocket-things, but the others were not. Noah had given me the grey pebble when we had been walking on the beach. He had asked me to keep in it in my pocket forever. And so I had, until now. And the little black velvet button belonged to Rosie's Scottish china doll. It was a jolt to be taken back to that evening a few weeks ago, when I had found the button, when everything had been simpler. Peter and I had been going out to meet Jim and Vics at the local pub for some supper, but we had been delayed by a frantic search for the lost button. I had found it down the side of the sofa, which had delighted Rosie. The babysitter had offered to sew it on that evening, but it had seemed important that I do it myself, so I had popped it into my coat pocket, this same coat pocket. And look, it was still there, not sewn onto the doll's blouse and now in a plastic bag at a police station.

'And the handbag, please,' DC Bennett said.

'Wallet. Sunglasses. House keys. Car keys. IPad...'. DC Bennett listed the contents, placing them into a clear plastic bag while his colleague behind the counter typed the items into his computer.

The soft leather of my wallet, the discreet designer logo on the edge of my sunglasses, my silver key ring with my initials engraved onto the heart, the branding of my car on my car-clicker, the snakeskin cover to my touchpad, all of which I had worked so hard to buy, seemed gaudy and out of place here. How little they meant, how unhelpful and useless these over-priced little badges of success were to me now, how worthless.

'Sign here and then you can call your solicitor, okay?'

After I had signed the small black pad, another officer led me to a small room that smelt of dusty telephone books even though there had probably not been a telephone book in there for decades. The officer's Sikh turban created a surreal silhouette through the frosted glass of the door and reminded me of when Rosie had very politely asked our brick layer why he was wearing Mummy's Indian scarf on his head, and how in response he had unravelled it and shown her his long hair. The look of amazement on her face made me smile even now and reminded me of how inquisitive and confident she was, and for a second, took me out of hell.

The plastic receiver was sticky. I knew the Letwin Assosciates' telephone number off by heart. Philippa could surely help me. I liked her, having needed her countless times for legal wrangling over contractual issues. Strangely, I had only met her in person once before at a Christmas party. She'd had an immaculate grey bob and a short, lined forehead that gave her a permanently determined expression, and she had repeatedly sucked on an electric cigarette, holding it to her red lips with her heavily ringed fingers. The real smell of cigarette smoke had lingered in the air for a long while after she had walked away.

'Letwin Associates, how may I direct your call?'

'Could I speak to Philippa Letwin please?'

'Who's calling, please?'

'Gemma Bradley, from CitiFirm.'

I was put on hold for a few minutes while Beethoven's 5th Symphony played into my ear; how appropriately doom-laden.

'Someone asking for too much money again?' Philippa croaked with her husky smokers' voice.

This was how she always greeted me on the telephone.

'I'm afraid it's not work related.'

'Don't tell me, you're getting a divorce,' she sighed, and then breathed in, probably from her e-cigarette.

'I wish it was that simple.'

'Spit it out then woman.' I heard her tapping into her computer.

'I've been arrested.'

As though her attention had snapped into place, her voice sounded less muffled.

'You know I'm not often surprised in this job, but now you've got me. What for?'

'They say I've assaulted my daughter, but I didn't do it. In fact, I'm not even sure what it is that I've meant to have done.'

I was sounding brave, but I felt anything but. There was something about speaking to Philippa Letwin that gave me some false courage, and reminded me of how to conduct myself professionally in a stressful situation.

There wasn't a moment's hesitation before she said, 'How can I help?'

'I know before you turned corporate, your background was in criminal, wasn't it?'

'I wish I'd never moved on.'

'D'you think you'd know someone who might come down and get me out of here?'

'I'll do it.'

'I can't ask you to do that.'

'You didn't. I offered.'

My professionalism disappeared and the urge to cry again pushed at my throat. 'Thank you, Philippa. Thank you.'

'Give Lucy your details and I'll be there as soon as I can. They'll have twenty-four hours to charge or bail.'

I didn't really want to engage with what this meant for me, still hoping that I would be out of here in a couple of hours and back at work tomorrow as though nothing had happened. I knew I could ask her everything when I saw her. 'And Philippa, don't mention anything to anyone, will you?'

'Client privilege, Bradley.'

The Custody Sergeant took me back to the custody desk. 'Take a seat, we'll be with you shortly.'

Wiping a scratchy grey tissue under my nose, resolutely not at my eyes, I sat down on one of the three plastic-moulded chairs. Immediately I was handed tea in a plastic cup which scolded my mouth, and within five minutes I was being led by DC Bennett down corridors that reminded me of halls of residence at university, but interjected by barred gate doors and CCTV cameras and ominous warning signs.

Beeps and clanging and thuds echoed around me, but there was no screeching or weird, scary people as I had seen on television, simply a series of police officers passing us, briefly looking me up and down, too busy to concentrate on me.

I could smell the reek of vomit and disinfectant before DC Bennett even opened the cell door.

'If you could take your shoes off and just leave them here please. Do you want a blanket or anything?'

'No, thank you,' I said, thinking about how horrible the blanket would be and how many others might have had it before me.

As I bent down I noticed a pair of laced high boots two doors down and wondered who was behind that locked door.

'I know it's not the nicest room in the world.'

'How long will I be in here for?'

'When your solicitor gets here, we'll come get you, okay?'

I stood in the middle of the room and he slammed the heavy metal door closed.

The white walls shot up around me, the smell from the low metal toilet in the doorless cubicle soured my tastebuds. Everything was too unfamiliar to take in, and I stood paralysed in the middle of the room, transfixed by the shadows moving behind the warped glass of the grid window above the plank bed. I was catatonic with fear. My attention was drawn to this natural light, outside of which was freedom, and I wanted to stand on the bed to peer out to feel connected to the outside world somehow, but I felt self-conscious of every move I made. The CCTV camera, in the left-hand corner above the cell door, flashed its tiny red light. I sat down on the low bed with my knees pulled up to my forehead, my face buried in the lock of my arms, hiding from my surroundings.

By the time the little small square window slid open, I was shivering violently.

'You're going to speak to your solicitor now, okay?'

Bleary-eyed, I slowly unpeeled, one vertebra at a time, to sit straight. My back was stiff and my sitting bones were numb as I stood from the bench. I must have been in the same hunched position for over an hour, too frightened and forlorn to move an inch from the spot.

By the time I was sitting in front of Philippa Letwin's red lips, her perfume and cigarettes stinging my eyes, I was in a stupor, barely managing to articulate a sentence to answer her questions. Her teeth were yellow as she talked.

'I've spoken to the DS and basically your daughter has accused you of slapping her face causing a bloody lip. Can you talk me through this from your point of view?'

Rosie's accusation didn't register properly at first.

'Slapped her? Are you serious? I've never slapped her? Why would the police make that up?'

'The police didn't come up with that, Rosie did.'

'No, no, she wouldn't say that when it never happened.'

'Apparently Rosie can't specify exactly when it happened, which is good for you.'

'It didn't happen at all.'

'She told the police that when you came back from work, you were in a "grumpy" mood and you slapped her because she hadn't finished her homework.'

I wanted to laugh with relief, knowing for certain that I didn't do it, feeling confident I could persuade anyone of this. 'I have never slapped Rosie in my life. Surely they can't believe I would.'

'Have you had any other dealings with the police or Social Services before this recent spat with the neighbour?'

'No, never. The first time was two weeks ago as I told you.'

And then came the question that shocked me out of my momentary relief.

'Can you think of a reason *why* Rosie would lie then?'

My mouth was dry, I gulped repeatedly before I spoke. 'I have no idea.'

I could pull one reason out from the recesses of my mind. I felt nauseous and an uncomfortable feeling crept under my skin. 'She must have got confused or something. The police must have twisted her words.'

'Have you heard of TED?'

'Who's Ted?'

'Tell me. Explain to me. Describe to me. That's how the police question a child witness. In a recorded interview if they tried to lead the child into an answer to suit their own narrative, it would be inadmissible in court.'

'There must be ways of getting stuff out of kids.'

'But why would they bother? Believe me, they don't have time. So I'm going to ask you to think about why she might have lied.'

'She must be angry with me about something.'

'Get her not to be, because you know, if she takes it back, the case'll be dropped like that,' she said, snapping her fingers in the air like she could conjure a magic trick.

'When can I talk to Peter?'

'When you're home.'

Home. There's no place like home, I thought, echoing Dorothy's whimsical words after the storm. I felt my feet encased by ruby red slippers, as red as Philippa's lips, and imagined Rosie's envy of them. A haze obscured my vision and I felt the violent shuddering take over my body again. My poor, unborn baby would be feeding on toxic adrenalin.

To calm myself down, I focussed my mind on Rosie's face, her beautiful blue eyes filled with regret and concern.

A few months back, when I had been out at the supermarket one weekend, Peter had texted me a photograph of Rosie that was meant to act as an amusing begging plea for sweets for movie night. The dark circles that ringed her eyes and the exaggerated desperation in her expression spoke more to me of pain than of fun. I had pretended to be won over, but the image of her face had stayed with me for days. She had looked unhappy, and I wondered now if such unhappiness – undiagnosed, brushed under the carpet – could lead to a lie, a big lie, a lie based on a depth of feeling I had no handle on. It was hard to examine the possibility that the decision we had made to withhold information from her about her maternal donor was festering in her subconscious. However tormenting her tantrums were, and however much I knew I needed to fix them, part of me had hoped that they were some form of cathartic release, an exposure of her frustrations, not the repression of something more hateful or sinister, something that she felt deep down, an unexplained something, something that would lead to an innate confusion about her core identity.

As I pictured that face of hers, my whole being seemed to ache, and I wondered whether I was separate from her at all, whether there was an almost other-worldly communication between us, as though our emotional worlds were interlaced. We seeped into one another; our pain was intertwined, never more so than when we fought. And as I sat in this small, stuffy room, powerless, completely powerless to help her, I felt this more keenly than ever. If she was hurting, I was feeling it. Her pain had become mine. This was love. This was punishment. A just punishment, perhaps, for my own lies.

'In the meantime, you'd better get it together for this interview,' Philippa patted my hand.

I squeezed her fingers as though she were my mother, panic charging through me, 'What if they don't believe me?'

'Then you'll be in deep shit,' she said, squeezing my hand back.

*

Back in the isolation of the cell, bent into the same position as before, the torture of revisiting my fight with Rosie, when I had unleashed my secret, began to churn like a rumination. *I am not your real mummy, I am not your real mummy, I am not your real mummy.* There was no peace in my repetitive, tormenting analysis of how and why and why and how. All I knew was that the shame of what I had said in a moment of anger wrapped itself around my face like a plastic wrap.

DC Miles unwrapped the cellophane from a CD and placed it in the black machine that sat on the desk between us.

'Have you ever been interviewed before?' DC Miles said, smiling. Her teeth were so white I imagined diamonds embedded in them.

Next to DC Miles, DC Bennett flicked open his black book and wrote onto the top of a clean page but remained silent as DC Miles continued.

'No,' I replied.

The double shot of espresso that Philippa had forced me to drink beforehand had sharpened my mind and I felt a little more clear-headed.

'So you've never been arrested?'

'No, no.'

She tapped onto the touch screen of the machine. Next to me I could hear Philippa's gravelly breathing as she rolled her pen up and down the notebook that rested on her lap.

'This interview is being recorded and may be used in evidence if this case is brought to trial. It is 19.32 on November the second 2017. Present here is myself, DC Miles, my colleague, DC Bennett, and then Mrs Gemma Bradley and her solicitor, Miss Philippa Letwin.'

DC Miles opened her purple A4 notebook onto her lap and leant back in her seat, and looked me straight in the eye.

'You've been arrested for the offence of assault causing bodily harm to your daughter. You do not have to say anything. But it may harm your defence if you do not mention now something which you later rely on in court. Anything you do say may be given in evidence. Okay,' she paused, 'my first question is, are you responsible for slapping your daughter causing her lip to bleed?'

'No, I have never slapped her. Never in my life.'

'Can you tell us why your daughter would have said that?'

'Honestly, I don't know. I can't understand it.'

DC Miles looked over at DC Bennett, and DC Bennett pursed his pointy wet lips.

'She said the left corner of her lip was bleeding and that she "was crying with pain",' DC Miles said, reading from her notebook.

'I don't know why she said that. She can be quite a drama queen.'

'What do you mean by a drama queen?'

'I mean she gets a bit over dramatic about stuff sometimes and works herself up. She has a really vivid imagination.'

'Do you ever get angry with her about not doing her homework?'

'If she's messing around, I can get cross, yes.'

Philippa cleared her throat. 'When you say "cross", what do you do when you're cross with Rosie?'

'I shout at her,' I said, dropping my gaze to my lap where I saw how my fingers picked at the skin around my thumb.

'And when you shout at her and you feel that cross, do you want to do anything else to her.'

Philippa spoke up. 'It's not relevant what she "wants" to do. Please could you stick to questions relating to the charge?'

'I'm just trying to understand how you feel in that moment when Rosie hasn't done her homework.'

'I get frustrated with her, of course.'

'And angry? Or "cross" as you put it?'

'All mothers get angry, don't they?'

She paused her questioning as she read from her purple notebook and smoothed her chocolate brown fringe down with both hands.

'And on the sixteenth of October, you were visited by PC Connolly and PC Yorke, is that correct?'

'Yes.'

'Tell me what happened that day.'

'Rosie had a massive tantrum and she threw a teddy at the picture, which must've fallen off the wall, and when I went in, the glass was smashed everywhere.'

'How did she cut her hand?'

'She was trying to tidy up the glass.'

'Why didn't you do that for her?'

'By the time I had got in there she had already started picking it up.'

'Why wouldn't she ask you to do it? Doesn't she know the dangers of cut glass?'

'I would have thought she'd have known, yes,' I admitted, crushed by the thought of Rosie sitting there amongst the cut glass.

'Might she have been scared of telling you?'

'I don't know.'

'Might she have been scared of your reaction?'

'I suppose she might've thought I'd tell her off, yes.'

'How would you have punished her, by hitting her?'

'No. I have told you, I would never ever hit Rosie.' I was beginning to feel a little disorientated.

'Why was Rosie having a tantrum that day, Gemma?'

'I sent her to her room because she bit Noah on the arm.'

'Does Rosie often have violent reactions to situations?'

'She can get quite physical with me sometimes.' I was hit hard by the vision of her circling me and screeching, and kicking, and how much she seemed to hate me.

'In what way?'

'When she tantrums she hits me and pulls at my clothes and stuff like that.'

'That must be really hard to take.'

I gulped, trying to swallow a lump in my throat. 'Yes, it is.'

'So hard that you want to hit her back?'

'No. No. I do not hit her back.' I shook my head, imploringly. No, no, no.

'Do you ever feel like you are going to snap when she is having a tantrum?'

'I do shout at her,' I said, quietly, unsure of myself.

'How do you think she feels when you shout at her?'

Shrugging, I conceded, 'Upset, I suppose.'

'And scared?'

'That's a horrible thought, but yes, probably scared too.'

'Do you scare her to get control of her?'

'No! I never want to scare her, it just comes out like that.'

'I suppose you never want to hurt her either, but it just comes out like that.'

'No. That's not true. That is twisting what I said.'

Philippa leant forward, 'Those questions are leading. She has made it clear she has never hit Rosie.'

DC Miles consulted her notes again, smoothed her fringe. The silence seemed to last forever.

'Your next-door neighbour Mrs Mira Entwistle told us that she had been round to your house a few days before the incident on October sixteenth, and noticed that Rosie had hurt her wrist.'

'Yes, she got it trapped in the door.'

'Tell us how it got trapped in the door.'

'She and Noah were playing and he slammed it on her hand.'

'And if we were to speak to Noah, he would remember this would he?'

I looked to Philippa and then held my head in my hands. 'Sorry, I don't know why I said that, I was the one who slammed her hand in the door by accident. I swear it was a mistake.'

'So why did you just tell us that Noah did it?'

I started feeling the room's heat. Sweat stung the torn-at flesh around my thumbnail.

'I don't know, I really don't know. I would never hurt her on purpose. I was trying to keep her away from me because she was screaming at me and flailing around and I didn't know how to control her and so I stormed out of the bedroom and pulled the door shut, but just as I closed it she put her hand through it.'

'When you don't know how to control her, do you think a quick slap might be the answer, to shock her out of it? I mean I would understand it if you felt that way. It can be frustrating when they scream and I imagine you feel pretty desperate.'

'I feel desperate, yes, I feel so desperate, but I don't want to slap her.'

'Okay, right, let's go right back to 2007, when you took Rosie to A & E for a fracture of the right ulna.' DC Miles pointed to her right forearm.

My mind flicked back through the years, through the many A & E incidents, back to the Whittington Hospital where we had taken Rosie when she was about eighteen months old. She had woken in the middle of the night screaming, and I had instinctively known she was in pain, though I hadn't been able to place where in her body.

'Yes, Rosie broke her arm.' I looked to Philippa. I couldn't understand how they knew about that.

'How did it break?'

'We're not sure.'

Philippa shifted in her seat.

'Two police officers came to speak to you about this, didn't they?'

My heart skipped a beat. 'Well, yes, they talked to us at the hospital briefly, but the doctor said it was standard when a baby breaks something. We think she got her arm stuck in the bars of her cot. Is this really relevant?'

I looked to Philippa, whose expression remained unreadable. I began talking again, letting the words tumble out by way of explanation.

'Peter had thought I was being melodramatic, and kept saying she'd had a bad dream or colic or something, but I knew she was in serious pain and when the X-rays showed a fracture, I felt vindicated.'

'You felt vindicated when you found out your daughter had broken her arm?'

'I was devastated for her, obviously, but relieved, quite honestly. I had imagined all sorts of other grim things that she might have had. Her screams were so piercing.'

That night in A & E came back to me in full colour. It had been the most worrying of my life, as they had subjected my baby Rosie to test after test, before finally finding her broken arm. Privately, I had harboured fresh concerns about Kaarina Doubek's medical records, fretting that she had lied or that the donor clinic had covered up a genetic condition that we were about to discover in Rosie. The police had been the least of our worries. Their attitude to us had been friendly, casual even, their presence barely registering as I had cradled Rosie. Afterwards, we thought nothing of them. I had had no idea it would have been placed on a police report and filed on my records somewhere.

'Do you see that there seems to be a pattern here? Rosie hurts herself and your explanations are...' she paused, looked to DC Bennett, and said, 'a bit rubbish, quite frankly.'

'When you mention all these things, it sounds bad, I know it does, but seriously, they are totally unrelated, you have to believe me,' I pleaded, feeling acutely anxious now. I ripped a bit of skin off my thumb and sucked at it, tasting the metal, imagining the red absorbing into my tongue and how it might spread through my body, colouring my thoughts.

'Do you lie often, Gemma?'

'I don't lie. I am not *lying*.'

'So, if you're not lying, that means your daughter is a liar?'

DC Miles' eyes seemed to have turned from green to red. Blinking it away, I clung to the edge of my chair and breathed deeply, trying to grip onto reality.

'No, my daughter is not a liar.'

'So she's not lying then? You did slap her?'

'I think she's got mixed up or something and told you something that isn't true. I don't know why she'd do this, I don't know why, honestly.'

At a desperate loss, I pushed my fingers into my hair and then worried the blood from my thumbnail was smeared onto my temple. I began wiping the side of my face with my fingers, and checking for the blood on my fingers.

'Sorry, do I have blood on my face?' I said, showing the left side of my face to Philippa.

'No, Gemma, you don't.'

'My thumb was bleeding and I was worried it...' I trailed off as I noticed how DC Miles and DC Bennett were looking at me. DC Bennett bent into his notebook and scribbled something down.

'Are you sure you're not the one getting mixed up?' DC Miles asked.

I couldn't answer her question.

'You understand why it seems strange to us that we have three unexplained incidents where your daughter has been hurt in your care?'

I felt cold to the bones and my muscles began to quiver. Every scratch of pen was deafening, every creak of a chair raked across my hearing like torture.

'I don't know,' I rasped, barely audible.

'Are you okay, Gemma? Do you need a glass of water or something?' DC Miles asked.

I shook my head. 'I don't know why she's lying about this.'

'Would you say you had a close relationship with Rosie?'

'I love her so much.'

The blue walls of the room seemed to wrap around me, like a much-needed comfort blanket.

'Yes, of course you do, Gemma. But sometimes things can get out of hand, can't they?'

'Sometimes I think she hates me.'

'Why would she hate you?' DC Miles' voice was soft and sympathetic.

'I don't know. I really don't know.'

'Tell us why, Gemma.'

'I seem to spend my life feeling guilty about her.'

'What do you feel guilty about?'

'Not being good enough. Ever.' I felt the tears rising.

'Look, being a mother is tough, I understand that, we can get you and Rosie the help you need.'

Her patronising tone agitated me. 'I don't need any help,' I stated indignantly.

'There is no shame in it, if it makes things better. But we have to talk about what happened first.'

'I have told you what happened.'

Philippa spoke up, as though sensing my irritation brewing. 'I think that Gemma has been very cooperative and told you everything she can.'

DC Miles sighed. 'Yes, okay. We'll wrap things up for now. Gemma, I understand today must have been very stressful for you as the implications are huge and I'm concerned about that.'

Her words hit me with a jolt. I resented her patronising tone and the 'huge implications' she referred to. I knew DC Miles was not concerned one iota. One by one DC Miles had pushed my buttons, the last of which was the jackpot: fury shot straight out of my mouth, 'Does it really concern you?'

The mood of the room changed. She sat up straighter, and looked over at DC Bennett, whose hand had stopped writing abruptly.

'Yes, it does concern me, Gemma.' DC Miles smiled, calmly blinking her curly eyelashes at me. 'I have a duty of care to make sure you're okay and you do seem very upset.'

'Of course I'm upset, because all of this is completely ridiculous. I haven't done anything wrong and you're acting as though you don't believe me.'

'It is not our job to sit here and judge anyone, Gemma, we are just trying to establish what happened so that we keep your daughter safe, do you understand?'

'But she is safe! Or she was, until you lot barged in,' I yelled, completely losing my temper.

DC Miles held my gaze triumphantly, and then closed her notebook.

'Okay, I think we have what we need for now. Before I finish this interview, is there anything else you would like to say?'

'No,' I said, unrepentant. They were trying to break me down into some gibbering wreck and I was not going to be broken.

'Thank you everyone. The interview is now terminated and I'm turning off the tape. The time is 20.16 on November second.'

As she turned it off, my defiance turned itself off too.

Awkward and sullied, I stood up with the officers.

I wanted to switch the machine back on and have a rerun so that I could do it better next time. I couldn't face going back to that cell again. I needed so badly to go home, to see Peter's loving face, to feel his arms around me, to hear him tell me it's all going to be okay.

*

As I was led back to my cell, a piercing screech rang through the corridor. It was getting louder and louder. Two cell doors down, three officers held down a young woman as she yelled and struggled and kicked out. She was wearing the same fashionable black lace-up boots that I had seen placed just where she writhed now.

'Fuck you, you fucking motherfuckers! I haven't done fucking nothing and you're locking me up in that fucking hole again, get your hands off me you fucking perverts!' she screamed, her face red and contorted, her bobbed brown hair sticking to her face, which was wet with tears or sweat or both.

'What you looking at you stuck-up bitch? Eh? Wanna cop a feel too, you fucking lesbian whore!'

'She's in weekly, that one. Can't stay off the booze,' DC Bennett said, looking on sympathetically. 'Sometimes I think she wants to end up in here.'

I didn't know how to respond, but as I looked on at the woman, half-fascinated, half-terrified, I recognised her anger. In my restrained and educated way, I had done the same in that interview room. I had lost my cool and destroyed any hope I might have had of getting DC Miles on my side. Everything I had been striving to achieve – the perfect children, the perfect family, the perfect home, the carefully calculated work-life balance – might as well have been smashed to pieces, because in that one vital second under pressure, I couldn't hold my temper, just like this raving banshee couldn't right in front of my eyes.

DC Bennett slammed the cell door.

My desire to rant and rave and kick was growing, billowing. It took Herculean effort to hold it down. It growled and boiled in my body until the tension to hold it there was unmanageable, as though the smallest provocation could unleash it. I was almost grateful to be locked away in the cell.

The woman's wailing echoed through the metal door. I wondered what had prodded at her anger that night, what lay deeper, what had built up over the years to come bursting out in such a fury on the officers that night. The sound of her terrible anger became mine; this anger that I felt now, that I was trying so hard to control, to suffocate, to keep away from a naked flame. I felt the surge of a self-pitying, tearful frustration, like a lifetime of repressed rage, rise up through my body and I slapped the wall with both hands as if I was trying to shove it over. The shockwaves shot up my arm and stung my palms and I did it again, and again, until my hands were hot and red and painful. It wasn't like me, to have done that. I wondered at the police officers watching me on their screens, imagining them laughing at me, this middle-class woman, with her tailored navy trouser-suit, slapping at the wall, but it made me feel better to let it go, to feel the pent up tension in my body ebb away.

I sat slumped on the floor, impotent, numb. However much I might have pounded on and scraped at these walls, they would remain intact, while my skin would be torn to shreds.

Tucked under my armpits, my hands throbbed. A flash of Rosie's contorted face mid-tantrum came into my mind. I couldn't summon the teenage photograph of Kaarina Doubek, whose face had housed all my fears about Rosie's ill-temper. I saw only my own anger reflected back at me.

In spite of Philippa Letwin's repeated reassurance that I would be released on bail shortly, I couldn't help feeling that I would never be set free.

# CHAPTER THIRTY-FIVE

Mira's eyes snapped open in the dark. The crunch of car tyres pulling up on the cul-de-sac had woken her from a brief, uncomfortable sleep.

She felt damp. The hardness of the slimy, mossy slats radiated through her hip and her shoulder.

She blinked away the drowsiness, trying to place where she was. On seeing the view of the back of the Bradleys' house, her heart jumped. She was curled up on the floor of the Bradleys' gazebo at the bottom of their garden. Then she heard the mechanical slide of the gates open and the crunch of footsteps on the Bradleys' gravel. Frantically, she scrambled up and crawled on her hands and knees back through the hedge.

The light was on in the potting shed.

After Rosie had left, Mira had not gone back to bed. Instead, she had found the hole in the hedge where the Bradley children crawled to retrieve their balls or skitter across to Victoria and Jim and whatshername's at number two and she had clambered through it to the Bradleys' garden to check that Rosie was not curled up on the doorstep. Mira wanted to keep a vigilant eye on the house, to be on the look-out for Rosie, making sure Rosie knew she always had someone to turn to, that she would never have to sleep on a doorstep as Mira had done.

She put the light out in the potting shed. The yeasty smell of Rosie's spilt drink was still present. Mira's heart melted at the thought of the little girl's nervy disposition. She wanted to be her guardian angel, just as she had wanted to be for her own baby. The drips of condensation on the window where the kettle had boiled shimmered in the moonlight. The rivulets morphed into steam on a shop window, somewhere in her past. She felt the damp heat of the bustling chippy on a cold winter's evening. The waft of vinegar and salt filled her head, taking her back.

She had counted out five one-pound notes into her mother's hand.

'What d'you want?'

'Cod and chips and a deep-fried Mars.'

'You sure that's a good idea, chubby buttons?' her mother had said, and she went to poke at Mira's middle. Mira leapt back, knowing her mother's fingers would press through the flesh to hit the taut drum of her pregnant stomach.

'All right, chill out, love, I was only kidding,' her mother responded, looking hurt more than angry.

'I've got period pains, that's all,' Mira said.

They had sat on the bench as they waited for their order. Her mother recommended she take some of her heavy-duty painkillers when they got home. This had been a kindness Mira wasn't used to. When Deidre wasn't there, she let her guard down a little. It must have been exhausting for her mother to keep up the stonewalling routine, most probably long after her anger had died away. Mira guessed that her mother had known all along that Craig was the real villain of the piece. But it was almost worse when her mother was nice to her.

Mira moved her hand to a small smooth bald patch on the back of her skull, underneath all her hair where she had twisted and tugged. She enjoyed the snag of pain when a few strands came free into her fingers.

Back in the car, the vinegar from the fish and chips stung the ulcer in Mira's mouth and the indigestion pushed up her throat.

She had had enough. The months of hiding her bump had sapped all of her energy, but no amount of putting off telling her mother was slowing down the changes in her body. Soon, it would be impossible to hide it.

There had never been a moment of doubt that she would keep the baby, but everything she had read about in the pregnancy books in the library were as different from her own experience as she could imagine. She hadn't had a scan or a doctor's appointment or even a chat about baby names. She had conspicuously bought tampons every month, which she threw away, bought two baggy navy jumpers from the charity shop to wear to school, eaten for three instead of two to hide the bump under fat, rolled her socks down to conceal her swollen ankles, turned down all invites to the parties her friends were going to.

All the way home from the fish and chip shop, blood had roared in her ears, drowning out the car radio. She was never going to feel ready, but she couldn't hold it in any longer.

They parked up outside the house.

'Mum, wait a seccy.'

'Yes?' Her mother replied irritably, her hand poised on the car door handle.

'I've got something to tell you.' The words were more like a wretch.

'If you're going to tell me that you failed your Geography mock, I know. The teacher called me.'

Momentarily side-tracked, Mira said, 'What? Mr Dilcot called you? What did he say?'

'He said your marks were crap and he didn't understand why. He said you'd fail your O levels if you carried on like this.'

'Why didn't you say anything to me?'

'I didn't want to upset you, you know, after everything you've been through with Craig and everything,' she explained, looking away. 'Come on, these'll get cold.'

Mira was touched. She wanted her mother's show of affection to last. This could have been the perfect diversion, to back out of her decision to tell her. Or, this could be the perfect time to tell her, while she was in a good mood.

'Mum, you know how I've got really overweight and everything?'

'Yes?'

'Did you ever wonder why?'

'I guess you're depressed about that shit-bag dumping you.'

'Nope.'

Her mother's hand fell from the handle and she turned to face the passenger seat where Mira sat, the veil of denial had dropped clean off her eyeballs as they ogled Mira's stomach.

'You're not.'

'I'm twenty-six weeks.'

'Christ!' Her mother glared at her for a second, speechless, and then leapt out of the car and slammed her door. 'No, no, no, no, no, NO.'

Mira stayed put inside the car. 'Yes,' Mira mumbled to herself.

Her mother charged round the front of the bonnet to her side and motioned at her to wind down the window.

'I'm not having a baby in my house, get it?'

'But where else would I go?'

'I don't want to be a bloody grandma!' she yelled, stamping to the front door.

Mira noticed how her mother's hands trembled as she struggled to put the key in the lock. It was the first time Mira had considered how much stress this would put on her mother and she felt she had been heartless to tell her about her pregnancy.

Too scared to go in the house, Mira rolled up the window and ate her fish and chips and Mars Bar in the car. The hot food had steamed up the glass, where she had finger-traced a stick figure with a big round belly, within which she drew a heart. It had made her smile. Mira was warmed by the food and the little life radiating from her womb. But the heat became scolding.

Her hand jerked back from the potting shed window. The steam from the kettle that she must have clicked on by mistake burnt her wrist. She cradled it. Tears fell onto the back of her hand. She yearned for Barry and ran across the garden into the house.

Before she returned to bed, she found the brown envelope in the dining room and picked out the photograph of the baby-blue rabbit. Tearing it away from the rest of the picture, she curled her fingers around it and climbed the stairs. With it tucked in her palm, she snuggled into Barry, drawing heat from his body until she felt a little less empty inside.

# CHAPTER THIRTY-SIX

The curtains in the children's rooms were open and their beds empty. It was as though the soul of our home had left with them. The silence scared me.

I went straight upstairs to the bathroom for a shower. The smell of urine hung off my clothes. The sweat – that now reeked of that recent fear – was cold and wet in the lining of my suit jacket as I shrugged it off. In the mirror, before the steam from the water obscured my face, I saw my ghostly, unkempt appearance. My thick eyebrows would usually enhance my eyes, bringing out the blue, but instead they hooded them, and my lips were cracked where they would usually be plump. If I had forced a smile like Audrey Hepburn's, they would bleed.

Just as I opened the shower door, I heard something outside the bathroom and I grabbed a towel to cover myself. Blood rushed through my head, my heart was in my mouth.

'Hello?' I called out, unable to hide the trepidation in my voice. 'Gemma?'

I dropped my head in my hands and cried out with relief. 'Peter! Oh my God!'

When he opened the bathroom door, it was as though it was the first time I had ever laid eyes on him, as though I fell in love with him all over again. There he was, his face scrunched from sleep and his body musty in his boxers as I held him to me.

'You're here!'

'Of course I'm here.'

'I didn't think you'd see my text. I thought it was too late.'

'I couldn't sleep until I heard from you.'

I laughed and I saw tears well up in his eyes as he watched me laugh.

'Can you believe this is happening?'

'No, I literally can't. Rosie won't talk to me. She's clammed up completely. The only information I know is what DC Miles told me.' He was shaking his head, bemused, searching my equally distraught face for answers I couldn't give.

'She's lying.'

'Of course she's lying.'

'Did she really not say anything about it to you?'

'Totally stonewalled me, and everyone else. In fact, she was mute all evening. She wouldn't even open her mouth to ask for the most basic things.'

'Does she understand what she's done?'

'She can't have meant to lie. She must have got her words twisted or got carried away or something.'

'Maybe'. I thought back to my own interview, and how pushy DC Miles had been, and how confused I had become, but remembered Philippa Letwin's information about TED: Tell me, Explain to me, Describe to me. The police were not allowed to lead a child. But I was not in the mood to spell this out to Peter. Rosie could wrap Peter around her little finger, she was his princess, the apple of his eye, there was no way Gemma could broach with Peter the idea that this whole nightmare might have been predicated on malice or spite or revenge.

'When Rosie's home, we'll talk to her together.'

'What if she changes her statement and the police think I've forced her to?'

When I thought of talking to Rosie, I couldn't disassociate her from the police, as though they were in cahoots and I was their shared enemy.

'Kids must lie to the police all the time, they must be used to it.'

'I can't believe she said all those awful things about me,' I said, feeling the tears push at my tired, dry eyes. For the first time that day, in the face of Peter's unquestioning loyalty, I became the victim when before I had been the accused. There was acute relief in this, but there was horror in it too: to play the victim, I had to believe that my own daughter had turned against me.

'Are you okay?' He stepped closer, took my arms and flipped them over, as though checking them for damage, and ran his hands slowly, gently over our baby inside me, and finally checked behind each ear. I laughed, 'What are you doing?'

'Making sure you're intact.'

'Can you believe I've been locked up in a *cell*, Peter? And they took my fingerprints and everything.'

'Oh Gemma.' He took my hands in his and kissed my palms, which still felt raw. I winced. He stopped kissing them and brought them right up to his face.

'These look sore. What did they do to you?'

I pulled them back to me and looked at the thread-thin lines of broken skin.

'Nothing. I tripped.'

'How did you trip?'

'I broke my fall up the steps on the way in, that's all. It's doesn't matter. I'm fine. Honestly, I fine.'

If the police had seen the footage of me on CCTV in the cell, they might not have identified the meek victim I was portraying in front of my husband now. It was simpler to be the victim, to ignore the bad decisions that might have brought me here. I didn't want to confront the fact that the past might finally be catching up with me.

He moved closer to me and kissed my lips and then ran his finger along the cracked skin. 'Have a shower and come downstairs. I'll make you some toast and tea.'

I ran my eyes across Peter's gentle features, wondering if I could tell him about the fear and anger that had overwhelmed me in that cell; contemplating how my true feelings would sound to him. I felt a pain in my heart, like a tear, when I realised it might be dangerous to say too much to this man, my husband, with whom I had been through so much.

Before the recorded interview with DC Miles, it wouldn't have occurred to me to imagine a scenario when anyone – let alone Peter – would have to choose, when any kind of rift would be great enough to pull us apart, but I was changed. My world was to be divided between those who believed me, and those who doubted me. I would be on the look-out for signs in everyone close to me.

I could never forget that Rosie was his flesh and blood.

Cynicism and distrust had entered this new world of mine, and it sent bolts of loneliness ricocheting through me.

My body was wrapped up in a snuggly dressing gown and my skin had that after-shower clean feeling. The physical smells and sensations of the cell were sloughed off. The toast and the tea were warming me inside.

'Is there really nothing this Philippa woman can do?' Peter asked, buttering more toast than we could ever eat.

'I don't think so.'

'So you're really saying that this social worker woman will have the power to stop you being alone with your own children?'

Peter was lagging behind. My shock had been and gone. After I had been released from the station on bail, Philippa had taken me for a coffee at a coffee shop next door to the police station. She explained what could pan out for us as a family over the next few weeks: safeguarding plans, surprise social worker visits, intrusive questioning, police statements garnered from family and friends, doctors' examinations, doctors' reports, medical histories, teachers' reports, multi-agency meetings, and so on. Our lives were to be exposed to strangers in gruesome detail. Much of it I wasn't able to take it in. And there was nothing I could do about any of it anyway, unless Rosie changed her story. The CPS hearing, set on 4 December 2017, four weeks away, was a future I couldn't fathom.

'Yes, it's called a safeguarding plan.'

'I don't understand how it's going to work,' Peter said.

'Basically, you'll have to police me.' My cheeks burned with fresh humiliation.

'I can't do that.'

'You'll have to. If I am caught alone with them, I'll be in deeper shit than I already am.'

'But how will they know?'

'Social Services make surprise visits apparently, and they'll ask the kids and we can't ask the kids to lie.'

The irony of that statement hung in the air between us, but both of us let it go. Plainly we weren't ready to talk about Rosie again. The logistics of a safeguarding plan was easier somehow. There were clear parameters to work with.

'And that crazy maniac next door will be watching us like a hawk,' I added, glaring out through the kitchen window.

'What about when I work late? Or have to go on conferences? I mean, I have three scheduled over three weekends between now and Christmas.'

'I don't know,' I said, feeling like I didn't know anything anymore. 'Harriet can't do weekends because of college.'

'And seriously, how often do I get home earlier than nine? Once a week at the most? Can Harriet stay later than eight?'

The reality of the situation seemed to be hitting him like a series of bullets.

'No. She has a bar job. That's why she never babysits for us.'

'What about the mornings? I leave at seven!'

'Harriet can't do the mornings either. She has to be in college at nine.'

'I won't even be able to nip out for bike rides at the weekend or meet Jim for an afternoon pint.'

'Welcome to a woman's world.'

'Women don't like bike rides or beer.'

'Ha bloody ha.' But I smiled. Peter could always get a smile out of me, even in the worst situations.

'It's just the principle of it that pisses me off.'

'Tell me about it,' I cried, reminding him of who the victim was.

'Sorry. I know it's worse for you.'

I deflated. 'No. The whole thing is horrendous for all of us.' A fresh wave of anger rose in me. I pushed it down. There was going to be no more hitting walls.

'What if they stay with your sister until this is all over?'

'She's too far from school.'

'What about an au pair?'

'We can't have someone new here while this is going on.'

'Well what the hell are we going to do then?' he yelled, throwing his hands in the air.

'I honestly don't know. I can't ask Mum, she's always got way too much on.'

Peter stuck his hands in the air again. 'That's it! You can ask Helen. That would solve all our problems.'

'I said I *can't* ask Mum. She'd have to give up work.'

'She'd have to take a break for a month, not even. That's not even half of one term. I'm sure the students would survive without her.'

'Would *she* survive without *them*?'

'Aren't her grandchildren more important?'

I shook my head. 'It's too much to ask. We went through all this before we hired Harriet.'

'Maybe she wants an excuse to slow things down a bit. She never stops complaining about the bloody place.'

'Don't be fooled by that old routine. She's spent thirty years complaining about it, it doesn't mean anything. There's no way we can ask her to give it up.'

'God, Gemma, you are *exasperating*. We can't do this on our own. You have to ask her.'

'I'm too tired to think about this now, way too tired. I can't even face the thought of telling her, let alone asking such a massive favour.'

'She's your mother and she loves you.'

'We'll see how much when I speak to her.'

I picked up the second piece of toast and then put it back on the plate. The thought of eating it made my stomach turn.

He reached to the top of the cupboard where he kept the whisky.

'How's about a hot toddy to cheer us up?'

'God, yes, a virgin one for me. I'll light the fire next door.'

I knelt at the wood-burner in the sitting room, enjoying the humbling simplicity of the process of crumpling the newspaper and fanning the kindling.

Peter joined me with two mugs. 'Want me to do it?'

'Why do men always think they can light fire better than women?'

'I don't know about other women, but if your track record is anything to go by...'

I didn't give him the satisfaction of laughing, but I was inside. It was true. I rarely got a fire going the first time.

The flames were tentative, slowly melting the paper with blue heat. Patiently and gently, I blew on the flame until one stick of kindling burst into flames. 'There you go, see?' Maybe it was patience I lacked.

I stretched out on the sofa, with my feet at the end near the fire, and my mug resting on my chest, the aroma of hot lemon and honey filling my head, the fire warming my socks. Peter's position mirrored mine on the opposite sofa.

We both stared into the flames as they leapt about angrily.

'At the station there was this crazy woman ranting and raving and she called me a stuck-up bitch.'

'Charming.'

'She was really pretty,' I continued, like this was relevant. 'She had these really trendy boots on. If you saw her on the street, you'd think she was as normal as anything.'

'What was she in there for?'

'She'd headbutted a bouncer outside a pub.'

'Nice.'

'She probably was nice, without the booze.'

'Headbutting someone is pretty defining.'

'Haven't you ever felt like headbutting someone?'

He snorted, 'No!' then added, 'I probably have, actually.'

'I have too.'

'But neither of us have ever done it,' Peter said.

'That's maybe just luck.'

'Or good sense.'

'But we're not always sensible, not always, not every second of the day.'

'Speak for yourself,' he said in a manly sensible voice, clearing his throat.

'Seriously though, one moment of madness and that'd be it, your life would be over. It would undo everything good that you had ever done.'

'She's lucky she wasn't in for manslaughter.'

'I'm not saying it was okay what she did, I'm just saying that maybe after a lifetime of shit, she just snapped.'

'It would have to have been a hell of a lot of shit.'

'What if her dad beat her up, or her mum even? What if she'd grown up with violence?'

'A lot of people come from the most grim backgrounds and still don't go headbutting people just because they've had a few too many shandies.'

'It's not an excuse, I'm just saying it might be her story,' I said, propping myself up a little on a cushion. 'It's so easy to judge. None of us know who we really are until we're tested or how we would behave under the wrong circumstances.'

'I feel guilty now. I want to give the girl a hug.'

I inspected my hands. They burned as though they were two balls of fire, and my wrists were beginning to ache.

'Part of me is not sure any of it was real.'

'Imagine what Rosie went through.'

'Now that makes me want to headbutt DC Miles,' I said.

He snorted through a sip of whisky. '*There's* that Campbell-woman spirit I know and love,' he laughed, reaching far over the coffee table to squeeze my shoulder.

'Superwomen. All of us,' I said flatly, with a flash of my palms slamming the wall.

'Wait till your mum hears about this. She'll be campaigning with her students outside the police station holding placards with "Rough Justice for Gemma" on them.'

I felt the swell of a belly laugh form in my stomach but it didn't quite make it out. 'Stop it. I wouldn't put it past her.'

'It's funny with your mum, she looks out with the fairies most of the time, but it's staggering how scary she can be.'

'All those ailments though.'

'Mother of God, her handbag is like a pharmaceutical's factory.'

We turned our heads to smile at each other and then looked back to the fire. I took a sip of my drink.

'And there's you, who won't even take a paracetamol for a headache.'

'I'm not like her at all,' I stated firmly.

'You're more like her than your sister is.'

'So you're saying I *am* like her?'

'You and your mum are both quite determined when you want to be.'

'So is Jacs,' I said, flipping my argument, suddenly defensive of my mother's spirit. 'She's as stubborn as an ox, just like Mum. Remember woodshedgate?'

I laughed out loud at the memory of Jackie and Richard's argument over their woodshed. Richard had promised he would build it – it was pretty vital considering they heated their house with a log burner – but he was notoriously lazy and hated asking tradesmen to do the job he knew he could do himself. Months had passed as their log pile on the driveway had become soggier by the day, until Jackie had taken the job on.

'I've never seen Rich so put out,' I laughed.

There was a lull as we listened to a log slipping in the fire. A moment of insecurity.

'Who needs men, eh?' Peter added.

'We want you more than need you, darlings,' I grinned, holding up my mug to cheers him.

He sent me a small melancholy smile back, 'At least I'm wanted.'

'Mum taught us to stand on our own two feet. That's a good thing this day and age,' I said defensively.

'God forbid you might ever need anyone, Gemma.' There was an edge in his voice that went beyond the mild joshing.

'What happened to liking the Campbell-woman spirit?'

'It has its moments.'

'Give me an example of a bad moment.'

'I'm not stupid. You're tricking me into an argument.'

'Promise I won't get annoyed. Cross my heart, hope to die.'

'I can't think of anything specific.'

'Go on. Try.'

'I'm not sure this is wise.'

'I'm not going to start headbutting you if that's what you're scared of.'

'Okay. When you had to go for that interview for the promotion a couple of years ago, you didn't confide in me and tell me you were shitting yourself or even that you wanted the job, you just got grumpier by the day and then the night before you suddenly made Rosie throw out all her plastic toys.'

'She didn't play with them anymore!'

'Except one.'

'That bloody diary of hers. I'd be reading it now if she hadn't taken it with her.'

'How do you know she has?'

'She never sleeps over anywhere without it.'

'The only plastic toy you let her keep is now her most treasured possession.'

I sighed, smarting at the criticism in spite of promising not to.

'I wish I'd never asked now,' I sulked. 'I don't know how to explain it. When I'm stressed I see mess in places I never did before.'

'Spoken like a true pro.'

'There's nothing wrong with keeping things organised if it helps me think stuff through, is there?'

'But you shut everyone else out, including the kids.'

'Do I?'

'A bit.'

'I never thought of it that way.'

I had never thought of my self-sufficiency as anything but the one good trait that I had inherited from Mum. How discombobulating it was to think otherwise.

'I suppose when I think back to how amazing Mum was when I was young and when I think of how lucky I am in comparison, I just think I don't have anything to complain about.'

'Everyone has *something* to complain about.'

'Mum was a proper trooper though,' I said absently, but as I said it I had a flash of Mum's dark bedroom after my father had left her, left us, with the curtains drawn and a glass of water in my hand. I had wanted her for something – I couldn't remember what – and had known it was impossible to ask her for anything when the curtains were drawn on her migraines. I had wanted her but couldn't have her, and I learnt to find a way to get on by myself.

'It might be good for her to be here with all of us,' I said, trying to find justification for the arrangement, ways she could gain from it, to dismiss how unconditional and selfless her move here would be if she accepted.

'I really believe it would be, you know,' Peter said.

'I'll try her tomorrow,' I agreed, unable to imagine asking her for such a colossal kindness. It was not supposed to be a test of how much she loved me, or her grandchildren. But now faced with the task of asking her, I knew it would become exactly that.

# CHAPTER THIRTY-SEVEN

*TOP SECRET*

*Dear Mummy,*

*It's the middle of the night. Spooookkkkeeeeee. I can't sleep. Dad told us you will get out of prison tomorrow and we can go home. Mega happy-face. A hundred happy faces. We have to go riding tomorrow first. Mega sad face. Horses are a bit scary and big. Why do we have to go riding? Becky's riding shoes stink.*

*I feel a bit mega, mega bad about you going to real prison. I hope you didn't have to eat sprouts in there. I can't wait to give you a big sorry hug. Question: Would you eat sprouts if the police gave you one hundred fluffy neon pencil cases? The police could get those for you. They can do anything. They even put children in prison, don't they?*

*INVISIBLE INK ALERT: Mrs E is nice. She doesn't want me to go to prison to eat sprouts ever, ever, ever. Not even for ONE THOUSAND MILLION FLUFFY NEON PENCIL CASES. I have to keep my secret that's why I can't talk even one word about anything to daddy. If I did, I would have to lie to him and I can never lie to daddy. He is cleverer than me and he'd find a super-spy way of getting me to talk.*

*When you are out of prison, don't worry, everything will turn back to normal. I won't lie anymore and you won't shout any more. Okay, whoops! Normal is the totally opposite. You'll shout like a loony and I'll lie my head off. YEEEEEEAAAAAH. I HEART NORMAL. I am so happy you are not in prison anymore.*

*Sorry again, sorry again and again. I'm so sorry, I'm saying sorry from Sorryville,*

*Rosie*

*P.S. At home after we have hugged and made it up together, you can't be cross with me anymore. That's the rule, remember. OR ELSE... (Just kidding).*

# CHAPTER THIRTY-EIGHT

I had called my mother hundreds of times before, but I had never done it with sticky hands and a fluttery stomach. As I clutched my phone, I watched the trees at the bottom of the garden bend over to the right, as though pointing out to sea, to an escape route maybe.

'Hi Mum.'

'*Darling*, how are you and the bump?'

'Fine, fine. How are you, first?' I asked, procrastinating, gauging her mood.

'Oh you know, only the usual,' she sighed.

'How are your wrists?'

'Sore, and that stupid doctor told me I had to stop using the computer.'

'Might a rest be a good idea?' I asked hopefully.

'My students email me about everything these days, it would be quite impossible.' She had such a gentle, girly voice, it was easy to forget the ferocity in the subtext. There was no point persuading her further, even if it meant she'd have to have both hands amputated.

'We're all so reliant on the bloody things.'

'Computers or hands?' she chuckled.

'They're fused these days, aren't they?'

My mother chuckled again. 'So, how are my grandchildren doing?'

'Well, actually, that's what I'm calling about.'

My heart raced. I couldn't believe what I was about to tell her. I couldn't believe I was about to ask her to give up her life for us. It wasn't a fair request, none of it was fair.

'We've had a bit of a nightmare,' I began.

I clearly and succinctly pushed out the bare facts of my arrest, with minimal emotion and dollops of positivity. My mother was silent all the way through. 'But it's going to be fine,' I finished off, wondering if my mother was still on the other end.

There was a long silence.

'Mum, are you still there?'

'Plainly, those police officers have misinterpreted something Rosie said.'

'Yes,' I agreed, knowing this was the only bearable way of looking at it. 'But unless she changes her statement, which, to be honest, is still possible, the police will want to investigate her allegations further and so we're going to have to run with it.'

*Run with it?* Like it was a strategy meeting.

'Will it be dropped if she changes her statement?'

'Yes, immediately apparently.'

'And there I was complaining about my wrists.'

'Your wrists are just as important.'

'Nonsense. What's this lawyer like?'

'Very good I think.'

'What does he suggest you do now?'

'Well, that's the thing, *she* says that we have to be as compliant as possible.'

'Which means?'

'It means I might not be allowed to be alone with the kids, and Peter and I were thinking...'

'That's preposterous,' she interrupted before spluttering out a series of swear words under her breath.

'It's part of some kind of safeguarding plan, just while they carry out what they call a closing strategy investigation. A social

worker will be coming round,' I said, floored by the reality once
again. My hands began sweating. My cheeks flushed.

'A *social worker?*' she cried.

'Yes, obviously, if there's a safeguarding plan.'

'Well, I don't know anything about this kind of thing,' she
said, smugly, the better parent. I drew in a calming breath and
continued.

'As soon as Monday, apparently, to draw up some agreement
or something.'

'And you say this Philippa woman is good, yes?'

I sighed and rubbed my temple, 'Yes, Mum. She helps me out
all the time at work. I really like her.'

'She's not an *employment solicitor* is she?' Mum said, as though
this might be the lowest form of life.

'She trained in criminal law.'

'You'll need a really good one, you do realise that, don't you
darling.'

I rolled my eyes to the heavens. 'Yes, I do realise.'

'You know what can happen if those social worker types start
nosing around don't you?'

Instantly, my womb seized up around my baby and I felt like
groaning as the nausea rolled through me. 'Of course I bloody
well know.'

'And it won't be just Rosie, it will be all three.'

I wanted to shout at her SHUT UP, SHUT UP, SHUT UP!
Don't say it, Mum. Don't even think it. I felt feint, almost giddy
with fear.

'Over my dead body.'

'Don't say things like that.'

'Rosie will take it back, I'm sure of it.'

'But, still, I really think you need the best lawyer you can find,
why don't I put you in touch with my guy?'

'Philippa is an outstanding solicitor.'

'But this isn't something you can get wrong.'

'Mum, leave it okay? It's my choice not yours,' I snapped.

She sniffed and rustled something, 'Okay, if you think she's good, but if you change your mind, just say the word.' She sounded hurt, as though my rejection of her advice was a stab in the eye.

I lost the will to follow through with it. I doubted there was any point.

'Sorry, I didn't mean to snap.'

'That's okay. You're under a lot of strain,' she said quietly. I imagined her dabbing her eye like an actress in a silent film.

'Look, I'll call you later, okay?'

'I wanted to help, that's all,' she added.

Having been poised to bottle it and hang up, I knew I could not now. 'Actually, that's why I was calling,' I said, going through the motions of the request pointlessly. 'If Rosie does stick to her statement, we'll need someone to live-in here to help with childcare and everything. Just until the fourth. Well, you know, if the fourth even becomes a thing...'

At least I could tell Peter I tried, but there was no way my mother was going to say yes. We couldn't even get through a telephone conversation without sniping at each other.

'And you thought of me?' Her voice quivered.

'Well, yes, of course we did,' I said irritably, knowing her ego would enjoy the flattery.

'David wouldn't like it,' she said, sounding gleeful. Ever since my mother had joined the university as a lecturer, she had talked endlessly about David, the dean of the university. Peter was convinced she was in love with David. Whether this was true or not, one thing was certain, she absolutely loved aggravating him.

'Of course.'

'And Ming Ho and Anya really are at crucial turning points right now.'

'I can imagine.' I looked out to the trees, which had bounced back to upright. I zoned out of my mother's predictable excuses. I didn't blame her, I just didn't like listening to it.

'And I'd have to get John to look after Minxy.'

'Yes, I know. It was too much to ask,' I sighed, waiting to hear more reasons why it was impossible. I felt a flash of regret and then anger towards Peter for putting me in this position. I should never have asked her.

'What hours would you need someone?'

'To cover Peter from seven in the morning until drop-off time – the kids are out of the door at 8.15 – then someone needs to be home, here, when they come in at four – unless they have after school clubs when its later. And then I get in at six-ish, mostly, and Peter at nine-ish. We also need cover at the weekends. Peter's got three conferences coming up.'

'What about Harriet?'

'Peter and I thought it would be best to give her paid leave until it's all over.'

There was a long pause. 'Mum, are you still there?'

'You know, I would feel quite terrible about letting my post-grads down, but it isn't beyond the wit of man to find a substitute to take over my course for a few weeks. In fact, I have a retired lecturer friend who'd love the work.'

'Really?'

I was fully aware of what a serious abdication of responsibility it would be for her to abandon a course midway through the term.

'Yes, darling. Until you know what's happening,' she said.

I sucked my breath in, inhaling deeply, a rush of gratefulness making me unsteady on my feet.

'Are you sure? We'll probably argue all the time...' I flapped my fingers at my eyes, to stop the tears.

'This is a family emergency,' she choked, and cleared her throat. 'The bigger problem will be getting rid of me.'

'We'll throw you out, don't worry,' I smiled, imagining I might want to live with her forever I was so grateful. 'Thank you, Mum. Thank you so much, you are a total life saver. I can't even describe how relieved I am.'

'Let me know what the social worker says and if it all goes ahead as that solicitor woman predicts, I'll pack a few things and get down to you on Monday. I'll collect the rest of my stuff when I pop back in the week.'

I thought of Rosie's return home later, the dread of it brewed in the pit of my stomach. But with my mum arriving soon, I knew I could cope. Until Mum had said yes, I hadn't realised quite how much I had needed her.

Now that the call to Mum was out of the way, I had a whole Saturday to myself, with nothing to do. The quiet in the house was eerie. Many other weekends, I had longed for time away from ferrying the children around to clubs and parties. Weirdly, I craved the mad rush to football club with Noah, the damp pitch-side conversations, the hectic drive to Rosie's tap class, and then the arguments over homework.

I decided on a long bath. My body felt lighter in the water and I marvelled at my popped-out stomach. My baby was cradled safely in there for now. I talked to it of all the plans we would make once this nightmare was over, and I talked about how much it would love its big brother and sister. I promised I would make everything right. I promised with all of my heart. Then I closed my eyes and rested my hands there, using the powers of touch and thought to send a message of my true love and devotion.

Soothed after my bath, I read the newspapers over breakfast, but I missed the hugs from Noah and the chats in the car about books with Rosie. When Peter and I decided to go for a roast at the local pub, I missed the spilt apple juice and the fidgeting and the interrupting that would infuriate me so much. I missed them. I missed them even more given the circumstances of our separation.

I couldn't imagine what it was going to be like to see Rosie. I was nervous about how she would react to me. A whole lifetime had been lived since I had seen her last. My concerns about her were bad on a good day, but now they were on a whole new scale. The worry had grown exponentially with every twist and turn of the last twenty-four hours.

In the hour before they arrived, Peter had taken a nap, but I felt too jittery to catch up on the sleep I'd missed. I ended up watching bad television as a distraction, which, thankfully, seemed to host a world of troubled, disaffected people with much bigger problems than mine.

Noah had banged on the door and shouted through the letterbox, 'MUMMY! It's us! LET US IN. LET US IN!'

I raced upstairs to wake Peter and then raced down again to open the door.

Noah's head bulldozed into my middle, sending a cramp right through my womb that made my eyes water. Over his head I saw Rosie. I smiled at her, probably with an edge of sadness, and she looked away and bolted past us, up the stairs and slammed the door of her bedroom.

'That went well,' Vics said, stepping forward and hugging me while Noah was still clutching my legs.

'Hi Vics.' I squeezed her tightly, holding my chin on her shoulder, smelling the familiar scent of orange-blossom in her hair and hearing her bracelets jangle.

'I rode on HENRY, Mummy!' Noah cried, breaking us apart. His mud-splattered glowing face was a picture of health and fresh air.

'And who's Henry, my darling?' I asked, bending down to his level, feeling torn by how gripped I was by his beauty and excitement and how my mind wandered up the stairs to Rosie shut away in her room.

'He's the Shire,' Vics explained.

'He's massive, Mummy, seriously he's so massive and I was so high up from the ground.'

'Goodness me, were you scared?'

'No!'

'Good boy,' I said, and then wondered why this should be praised. Fear was a normal reaction to sitting on top of a seventeen-hand beast like Henry at six years old.

'I'll get the kettle on, go on up to Rosie,' Vics said. 'Come on Mischief, let's get you a biscuit.'

Vics took Noah's hand and I was free to go to Rosie, reluctantly.

I knocked on her door first.

There was no response.

I opened it. 'Rosie?'

'Go away,' she mumbled from under her stripy pink pillow. Her red wellington boots had left a patch of mud and straw on the end of her duvet. However difficult it was for me to leave the mess, I did.

'Come on,' I said, sitting down on the bed next to her. 'Come here for a cuddle.'

'No.'

I was willing to sit there all day and all night if that is what it took.

Quite a few minutes later, she burst out from under the pillow and collapsed into my lap, clasping her arms around me.

She smelt of bonfire smoke and horsebox.

I had a million questions for her and none of them were appropriate for this moment. If I'd had a wish, it would have been, of course, that she would tell me why she had lied, that she would promise to tell DC Miles the truth. She had the power to put an end to this hell as quickly as she had started it, while I could forge the beginning of a new phase of understanding between us. If I could get to the bottom of why she had been so angry with me, then we would have a hope. And in that moment I had a lot of hope, and huge amounts of faith in her, in us. We had four weeks.

'How was Rising Star?'

My jumper muffled her reply. 'I cantered.'

'Wow. That's incredible. Good girl. Well done, darling.'

She squeezed the breath out of me and I held her tight to me. 'Oh Rosie, you must have had the most horrible day yesterday.'

There didn't need to be any pretence between us. In however many ways I might have failed her, she knew I didn't slap her. She knew I knew. And she now knew that I still loved her, in spite of the lies she had told. That was what unconditional love was like between a mother and a daughter. My mother had once told me that even if I had murdered someone, she would still love me. And I had believed her.

She wept, and whimpered, heaving great sighs between the sobs, and I held her to me close. 'Sorry Mummy, I'm so sorry,' she murmured, exhausted.

Peter emerged from around the door. 'You okay?' his expression said, and I nodded my head at him, and shooed him away.

As she cried, I knew that none of my recriminations could be worse than the ones she would be telling herself. Her contrition was all-encompassing. It would all be over soon, I thought.

'Do you want to come downstairs for a bit?'

'I'm just going to write in my diary,' she said, sitting up, looking me in the eye for the first time, hangdog eyes, pitiful sadness.

'That's a good idea,' I said, cupping her tear-stained face and kissing her on the forehead. 'And you know, any time you're ready, you can tell me or another grown-up, like Daddy, or Grandma Helen, or anyone, all about why you said all that to DC Miles, okay?'

Rosie's expression turned instantly sour. 'There's nothing to tell,' she snapped.

'Okay, okay,' I said, instantly regretting how soon I had broached it. 'As I say, whenever you're ready.'

And I retreated out of her bedroom, feeling uneasy, and slowly made my way down to Vics, who was sitting at the kitchen island staring out of the window, with her heavily ringed fingers encircling a mug of tea.

She jumped when she saw me. 'Sorry, in a daze. How is she?'

'All cried out.'

*'You took a whole lot of loving for a handful of nothing,'* Vics sang inappropriately, screwing up her eyes, her hands at her heart.

I laughed, relieved that I still could, having felt wrung out by Rosie's outpouring.

'Does anyone still listen to Alison Moyer?'

Her eyes sprang open and sparkled at me, like darts of light on a choppy sea, outshining her garden-tan crinkles. Vics had a high-reaching, freckled forehead that lent her an air of wisdom and somehow belied the less serious bright white-blonde hair and unfashionable blue eyeliner that she wore every day, rain or shine.

'I have her CD in my car,' she cried defensively, handing me a steaming cup of tea, bangles clanking.

'You would. You're mega uncool, as Rosie would say.'

'I'm retro-cool, darling,' Vics grinned, then she tucked her hair behind her ears, getting down to business. 'How is she?'

Paranoia singed at the edges of me, like the burning edges of a piece of paper. I felt ashamed of what had happened, and wondered if it had changed how Vics viewed me, if it had left a trace of suspicion in her mind. 'She's writing in her diary.'

'I bet you want to read that.'

'I wonder whether I might have to.'

'Did you manage to get anything out of her?'

I wanted to ask Vics if she believed Rosie, but I was too scared. If there had been even the vaguest of hesitations, I would have been crushed. Vics would be honest and sometimes I didn't need it.

'I thought I'd wait a bit.'

'Does she know how serious it could get?'

'That's a good question actually. I wonder if she does.'

It hadn't occurred to me that Rosie would, of course, not fully understand the consequences of her lie, and the processes involved following my arrest, and what it could lead to.

'I think it might be wise to tell her.'

'I don't want to scare her.'

'It's a tough one.'

'Does Beth have a diary?'

'Beth? Have you ever met your godchild?'

'I wish Madam up there was as chilled out as her.' I pointed up in the direction of Rosie's bedroom and rolled my eyes. Childishly, I was trying to garner some solidarity from Vics, some acknowledgement that Rosie was a nightmare and that I was the victim.

'If she takes it back, will the case be immediately dropped?'

'Yup.'

'Probably best to be gentle with her rather than force it out of her.'

'Obviously,' I said defensively.

'Sorry, I know you wouldn't *force* her.'

I smiled knowingly. 'No, you don't know. You think I'm too hard on her, everyone does, admit it.' I light-heartedly raised my eyebrows over my cup of tea, pretending that I could take whatever she might throw at me, but I was braced, expecting it might cut right through me.

'I'd say you're strict, about manners and things like that. They're always so well turned-out.'

I looked right into her bright eyes, inspecting her for signs of shiftiness, wondering if she thought I was so strict I might actually hit Rosie.

'Maybe I shouldn't care so much.'

'It's good to care. Look at Beth! Poor thing goes to school with birds' nests in her hair and toothpaste down her cardigan.'

I imagined a typical morning before school. If Rosie looked messy, I worried the teachers and other parents would judge me for being a bad mother, slovenly or neglectful. While Noah could bowl about making mistakes all over the shop, with filthy hands, knotty hair and unfinished homework, and I would be endeared, not enraged.

'Peter accused me of being a control freak like Mum last night.'

'You? Who rearranges my herbal teabags in alphabetical order? Can't be talking about the same woman,' Gemma laughed.

'God, I'm a nightmare,' I said, and dropped my head in my hands. 'No wonder Rosie goes mental on me sometimes.'

'Come on Gemma, I'm just kidding.'

'But you're not, though, are you?'

My impossible standards, my impossible need to control every aspect of her life, down to every last granule of sugar she consumed, every hair out of place, every toy she played with, every thread of her clothes and every second of the routine I had imposed on her (however remotely). 'Eat with your mouth closed!'. 'Sit up straight!'. 'Stop picking your scab!'. 'Brush your teeth!'. 'Do your homework!'. 'No! Do it better!'. 'No, you can't have another biscuit!'. 'No, you can't have any biscuits at all!'. 'Stop running in the kitchen!'. 'Finish your broccoli!'. 'Stop playing with those beads!'. 'Stop breathing!'. 'Stop living!'. I watched her like a hawk when I was there, and grilled Harriet or Peter for a minute-by-minute download of the moments when I wasn't.

When she was around me, I wondered if she felt that she was trapped in a cell, utterly powerless. It was no wonder she wanted to pound me with her fists, just as I had pounded at the walls.

'Of course I'm joking,' Vics insisted, looking hurt and surprised by my forcefulness.

'I realise everyone thinks I'm too strict with her but I'd never hurt her,' I said, my voice breaking a little. I dug my nails into my palm.

Vics put her hand on arm. 'I've never doubted that for a second.'

I let out a little gasp, and pressed at my lips to hold it back. 'Thanks, Vics. Sorry.'

The paranoia ebbed away, replaced by the truer knowledge that Vics was on my side.

'I'll give them breakfast or tea any time you need me too. You have to try to look after yourself.' She glanced anxiously at my stomach.

I shrank away inside, desperately self-conscious of my new neediness and vulnerability, degraded by the forthcoming restrictions on my parenting. Everything had to change rapidly, literally overnight, and instinctively I baulked at the reordering, while knowing I had no choice.

'It's okay, Peter's going to go in late this week if necessary, although Mum should be here by Monday. We're not really sure when the social worker is coming round though. I think it's more likely to be in the afternoon on Monday or Tuesday.'

'Have you told Harriet yet?'

'No. I'm going to tell her tonight. I'm dreading it. I think I'm just going to say we've had a personal family crisis.'

'Which is true.'

'Yes,' I laughed, 'I suppose it is.'

# CHAPTER THIRTY-NINE

*TOP SECRET*

*Dear Mummy,*
*ALERT! EVERYTHING IN INVISIBLE INK!*
*YOU ARE SO CRITICAL. I actually said sorry and you*
*really actually just didn't listen. You never listen to a word*
*I say. You want to force me to tell you. I can't say the words*
*out loud to you about what I said to the police lady because*
*it will sound so, so, so bad, and you will think I am such*
*a horrible girl and you will think I am horrible and mean*
*and you will tell your friends, like you always do, and my*
*cheeks will burn off my head with embarrassment and you*
*will get cross and say I am not your real mummy again and*
*I will KILL MYSELF. YES, I WILL LITERALLY KILL*
*MYSELF. Please don't ever ask me to tell you about it. Please*
*don't, Mummy, I beg you.*

*Rosie*

*P.S. I have nothing else to say.*

# CHAPTER FORTY

It was school pick-up time. Mira put on her jogging tracksuit. Before she left for the recreational ground, she popped a couple of chocolate biscuits into her pocket and wrote *Gone to get milk!* on a Post-it that she stuck onto the kettle for Barry. She removed the unopened carton of full fat from the fridge door and brought it with her.

Before she turned right into the main road, she ducked down and stuck the milk into the hedge on the corner of number seven.

On the recreational ground, her heart was going to burst in her chest. Whether it was the running or the anticipation of seeing Rosie again, she didn't know.

The second lap up the pitch gave her a view of the wire back gate of New Hall Prep. She watched for signs of children. There were a few parents milling about chatting.

When the children started to pour out, Mira slowed down, almost jogging on the spot.

Just as she saw Rosie's washed-out little face bound through the gates with her black mane of hair swinging, an older lady stepped towards her with her arms outstretched. Rosie flew into this woman's arms. It was like a knife in Mira's back. She felt winded, paralysed. Noah emerged and charged at this woman with similar gusto.

As this unit of three walked towards her in the dusky winter gloom, the woman bent a little to hear what Rosie was chatting about. Mira inspected her for family resemblance. She was not tall and broad like Rosie, she was slight, like Gemma, with shoulder-length crispy dark hair that stuck out from underneath an eccentric velvet hat. Her bone structure was pronounced, almost beautiful, but her eyes – a milky blue – sank a little too far into her small bird-like head, as though they were shrinking away from life, warily, frightened of what might jump out at her. Mira decided that a woman who was so frail and timid must have led a sheltered life. She didn't like the look of her one bit. And when she saw her boney hand clasp Rosie's, Mira felt a wildness come over her, and she winced, the wind sharp on her gums.

But she recognised a more powerful enemy when she saw one, and she retreated out of the grounds, her disappointment acute. While the police investigation was underway, Mira had been determined to be the back-up Rosie might need to see her through such uncertainty – and potentially Gemma's volatility – but plainly someone else had stepped into the breach, possibly as part of the safeguarding plan DC Miles had mentioned to her on their follow-up visit.

Never one to mope, Mira set about thinking of other ways to get in touch with Rosie. By the time she had made it home, the plan was there, as easy as pie.

'Hey love,' Barry said, with his head in the fridge. 'Cuppa?'

'I could murder one.'

'I thought you'd given up on that jogging business.'

Mira had forgotten about her tracksuit. 'I just wanted to be comfy.'

'Got the milk?'

'What?' she asked, remembering that the milk was in the hedge at the bottom of the close. In her agitated state earlier she had run past number seven, quite forgetting the ruse.

'Didn't you go out to get milk?'

'Oh, I left it in the car.'

Before she had a chance to run out, Barry piped up. 'Didn't you walk?'

Mira wished he would just shut up. 'I just left it there while I checked on the chickens.'

Her breathing was ragged when she returned, having run all the way there and back.

'You took your time.'

Drops of tea on the floor marked Barry's journey from the kettle to the bin. Two mugs sat steaming on the side, waiting for their blasted milk.

'For Pete's sake, Barry, sometimes I think you let the bags drip on purpose to annoy me,' she puffed, pushing Barry's legs away from the under-the-sink cupboard where the floor cloth lived.

'By the looks of you, you need to get out jogging more often.'

She wiped the droplets away with more rigour than was necessary. 'Why do you say that?'

'The car's only a few feet away from the front door and you're huffing and puffing like you've run a marathon.'

'I put the bins out,' Mira lied, telling herself to remember to do it later when he was snoozing in front of the television. It was too dark now to see out, so he wouldn't notice.

Barry handed her a cup of tea and his eyebrows raised up above his bottle-top glasses. 'Everything okay, love?'

'It feels like the Spanish bloody Inquisition round here,' Mira huffed, grabbing the mug and leaving him standing in the kitchen. She called over her shoulder. 'I've just got to write a thank you note to little Sam for making me that collage.'

'Right you are. I'll put the casserole in.' He seemed placated.

The bureau drawer was a little stiff and the card with the robin on the front smelt musty. She worried that a girl like Rosie, with so many privileges, would laugh at the card. The other option was the embossed writing paper, but that seemed too formal. The robin card was more suitable for a ten-year-old.

She thought hard about what she was going to say before she put pen to paper.

> *Dear Rosie-Rabbit,*
>> *I hope you got back home safely the other night.*
>> *I'll be in the shed potting my sweet peas tomorrow afternoon after school if you would like to squeeze through the hedge for a slice of Battenberg and a mug of hot chocolate.*
>> *Needless to say, it might be best to keep this note at school. We both know why!*
>
> *Love from your friend,*
> *Mrs E.*
>
> *P.S. Use the blue bucket to reply! It's on your side!*

The next day, Mira left the house early to make a detour to the front gates of New Hall Preparatory. The wrought-iron gates and the long winding drive reminded Mira of Manderley in *Rebecca*.

The Edwardian building was an old manor house, but inside there was that familiar cabbage and smelly-feet tang in the air common to all schools, regardless of how elitist the institution strived to be. However, Mira had to admit that the potpourri and new blue carpets were certainly additions Woodlands could do with in their front hall.

'Could you please pass this on to Rosie Bradley in Thistles, Year Five, if possible?' Mira said, pushing the card through the hatch. 'I'm her next-door neighbour and she dropped it on the drive. Thought it might be important.'

'Of course, how kind, thank you. I'll put it in her cubby hole,' the receptionist said, taking the innocuous-looking little card from her.

'Thanks ever so,' Mira trilled as she left, trying to mimic the pretentious ways of her sister Deidre.

She drove back down the drive and out through the wrought-iron gates thinking that there weren't any gates posh enough or high enough to hide Rosie away from her, however hard Gemma Bradley tried. At ten years old, Rosie had her own mind. At fifteen years old, Mira had not had her own mind. Mira's mother's smoke had blown into her quiet mind. The smoke was forever billowing from her mouth, filling the kitchen. Mira spluttered, coughing up the smoke, experiencing again the atmosphere of that kitchen. Willingly, this time, she strained to recall the details as a memory unfurled.

The radio had been turned off for once. There had been a sound of a car door slam. Her mother had jumped up. 'Quickly, repeat your story one more time.'

Mira had replied dutifully, sulkily, 'I did it with this boy at a party when I was drunk and then he left. He was at a different school and I don't know who he is.'

Her mother's intransigence had worn her down. The long, angry lectures. The stomping about. The irritable tone with the doctors. The tutting while on hold to Social Services. The kicking of the bin that stuck.

If Mira spoke up, she was shouted down. If she cried, she was blanked. It didn't matter what she did or said, there was no getting through to her mother. If Mira kept this baby, she would be chucked out. Simple. Non-negotiable. Conversation over. Fuck you, you little whore.

'Now the reasons you want to give it up.'

The silver bottle top was goopy. Mira smelt it. Her stomach heaved, but the milk was not sour.

'I don't want the baby. I can't cope. I've stopped eating. I want to kill myself.' Mira reeled off the reasons as she plonked herself at the kitchen table and poured milk into her mother's mug of tea and some into her evening bowl of cereal.

The drill. Mira knew it well.

Mira pressed her fingers around the doorstep-cold milk bottle until they were numb at the tips. She imagined the numbness spreading malevolently through her whole body; the creep to non-existence.

Smoke clung to the social worker's greasy parting of hair. The fumes of old cigarettes were fresh from her mouth with every question. The questions had been brief. The answers fell out of Mira's despondent mouth. Her mother's lumpy behind was wedged into the corner bend of the worktop as she let her daughter tell convenient lies.

Ten minutes was all it took. Adoption had been agreed. The social worker was about to leave.

'Always my little ball of trouble, weren't you love, right from word go,' her mother had added, smug with the achievement of the afternoon, rolling her eyes at the social worker who was packing up her things.

Another cigarette was lit at her mother's lips. The tip burning brightly into Mira's eyes, the second-hand smoke inhaled, down, down, deep down into her womb where the baby's tiny lungs were forming.

Mira's hand was around the milk bottle, squeezing it, her eyes were on her mother's cigarette, the bottle was levitating above the table, light in her hand, lighter and lighter as it floated above her head, and moved through the air towards her mother, who ducked, holding her hand to her face, the bottle smashing into her knees; soaking, stinking, sour shock.

Triumph and disbelief danced behind her mother's hysteria. The social worker's long, greasy day had come alive. The baby's fate was sealed.

# CHAPTER FORTY-ONE

Rosie sloped down to breakfast, rubbing her eyes, coming in for a cuddle, just as she always had. I tried to act naturally while I bustled around – filling their water-bottles and wrapping their cucumber snacks in foil – while I formulated sentences in my head, working out the best way of telling them about the changes to their afternoon routine, the changes to their lives.

I lent my elbows into the breakfast bar opposite them.

'Guess what, guys?' I said, cheery and full of enthusiasm.

They both continued eating their cereal.

'Daddy's going to be taking you into school again today.'

They both grinned through mouthfuls.

'*And* Grandma Helen's picking you up.'

'Again! But why can't we go by ourselves like normal?' Rosie cried.

'What about Harriet?' Noah asked, as if she might feel left out.

'Grandma Helen doesn't like Harriet, you know,' Rosie interjected.

'That's not true. They're just different,' I said.

Noah piped up, through a mouthful, 'It's true, Mummy, she told me she thinks she is a huber-less.'

Trust Mum, I laughed to myself, to be competitive with Harriet by bad-mouthing her to the children.

'Humourless, not a huber-less, you idiot,' Rosie jeered.

'Don't be mean, Rosie,' I snapped, before remembering our new circumstances. 'We knew what he meant. And don't worry, Harriet is going to take a little holiday for a few weeks and Grandma Helen is going to stay with us for a while.'

Rosie stopped shovelling cereal into her mouth for a split second and eyed me suspiciously. 'Why?' Rosie asked.

'Does there need to be a reason?'

I was working on a 'need-to-know' basis. There was too much for them to take in for now.

'Last days Harriet sent us a postcard when she went on holiday,' Noah said.

'Yes, last summer. But I'm not sure you'll get a postcard this time, she might have a lot of college work to do.'

'But we didn't get to say goodbye!' Rosie cried.

'Don't worry, she said she'd pop in this week to see you.'

'And Grandma Helen is looking after us when you and daddy are at work?'

'Yes, and to help me,' I added, wondering if they would notice that my mother was to become my shadow, and Rosie's covert protector for the other side.

'That's good,' Rosie said, smiling and continuing to eat her breakfast.

'And,' I said, pausing, to keep their attention, 'there'll be another visitor this afternoon.'

Rosie scraped her bowl and the sound of silver spoon on porcelain screamed through the kitchen. 'Who?'

'Well, because of everything that's happened,' I began, glancing over at Rosie, 'a lady is coming over to have a chat with us, just to make sure we're all okay.'

'What lady?'

'She's a social worker.'

Rosie's spoon clattered into her bowl. 'Like in *Tracy Beaker*?'

'Not exactly like in *Tracy Beaker*,' I said, thinking, yes, exactly like in *Tracy Beaker*.

'What's a social worker?' Noah said.

'They take children away from their mummies,' Rosie said, pushing her chair back from the table, ready to bolt.

Noah's eyes widened.

'No, no, stop it Rosie, you're scaring Noah, they don't do that.'

'Are you saying that Jacqueline Wilson is a liar?'

'*Tracy Beaker* is fiction, darling, you know that,' I said, evading the very good point she was making.

Rosie stood up.

'Rosie, sit down. A social worker's job,' I said authoritatively, 'is to make sure children are safe.'

'But we *are* safe!' Rosie cried.

'Yes, but they don't know that, so we have to tell them that you are.'

'I'll tell them I'm safe,' Noah said proudly.

'Yes, darling, of course.'

'Me too,' Rosie said, her bottom lip wobbling. 'I really will this time.'

The 'this time' sent a shiver down my spine.

'Of course you will,' I said, hugging her, feeling a frisson of hope.

After they had left for school, I headed straight up to Rosie's bedroom. Her diary was not in its usual place in the drawer of her desk by her bed. I looked under her duvet, in her sock and pants drawer, under things, on top of things, in the toy boxes, in the nooks of her cupboards, in rucksacks, behind her books, everywhere. It was nowhere. She had taken it to school. She didn't trust me. She had been right not to.

Before Miranda Slater was due, Peter, my mother and I tried to continue a normal routine as much as possible, but as soon as the children were out of the room, we fell stony silent with nerves.

When the doorbell rang, my mother said, 'You know where to find me.' And she moved regally up to the spare room, as though she was quite above such an insult of a Social Services visit.

While Peter waited in the kitchen, both Rosie and Noah hovered behind me as I opened the door. I could hardly breathe I was so worked up.

The children were exceptionally polite, shaking her hand, with brief, timid eye contact.

'You two can go upstairs and play your games if you like, just while I talk to Mrs Slater.'

I was skittish and over keen to please and I barely made eye contact or registered any detail of her appearance or mannerisms in those first ten minutes, seeing only the generic features of an unfamiliar human being, for whom I had to project the image of our perfect family life. All of my concentration was taken up with this main objective.

When she had called me earlier in the day to warn us of her visit, she had been matter-of-fact in her tone. To her, her visit to our home was business as usual.

While I made a pot of tea, and fanned some digestives onto a plate, she had brought out her notebook and asked Peter and I some basic, seemingly innocuous questions – for example, whether Rosie dressed herself or whether she had any medical conditions – and then she explained the safeguarding agreement that they would draw up and sign. Once we agreed to this – although I was secretly hoping that it would be obsolete quite soon – she had suggested she talk to Rosie alone and 'look around your home, if that's all right by you.'

Downstairs, filled with apprehension, and clinging to the possibility that Rosie would confess, I had boiled the kettle to make another cup of tea for Miranda Slater, who liked two sugars.

Peter and I did not dare talk to each other. He pretended to read the newspaper while I cleaned the already clean kitchen. Both of us must have been thinking the same. What would Rosie say? Would she put me in the clear? Was this nightmare about to be over?

After about ten minutes of quiet, we could hear Miranda Slater moving about the house, stamping across rooms, opening and closing doors, cupboards and drawers.

The spare room was too far away for us to hear any exchange with my mother or Noah.

When she returned downstairs I half expected her to hold up a dirty pair of knickers and place them in a plastic bag for evidence of my slovenly nature.

I had a terrible urge to laugh. I bit hard on the side of my mouth and tried to compose my features into a suitable expression for the gravity of the situation.

'Everything all right?'

Somewhere inside me, I could probably locate the fear that had been rampaging through my mind and body all through the dark sleep-deprived night, but now it was nowhere to be found.

'Yes, thank you,' Miranda Slater replied, sweetening her smile.

Peter closed his newspaper.

'I'm just going to have a quick peek,' she said, opening our fridge. I imagined her judging me for all the expensive supermarket ready-mades stacked up in there.

After making some notes, Miranda Slater settled down opposite Peter and I at the kitchen table.

For the first time, I took in her appearance. She had a large face, with skin mottled like hamburger meat and an oddly incongruous sleek grey ponytail, a mane beautifully brushed. She wrote on paper locked into in a pink file that was covered in what looked like a child's sparkly stickers. Her pen was topped with a hat of homemade ribbons and beads that bobbed about as she bent over to mark her pages and her ponytail dangled onto her notes. She breathed with her mouth open, her two front teeth jutting out.

I waited for her to tell me what Rosie had said, to inform us that they would be taking the new information to DC Miles, and that they would be closing the case.

When she looked up at us finally, her insincere, ever so slightly bored smile fixed itself onto her face and she continued with the questions she had begun before taking Rosie upstairs.

'You were saying, Gemma, that you go out on day trips as a family?'

I was incredulous. Where was the information about Rosie's changed story? Peter and I shared glances. Perhaps she had to complete the forms to tidy up the bureaucracy before they discussed dropping the case?

I answered diligently, trying to hide my frustration.

'Yes, on holidays we do loads of day trips – like last year when we went to the Matisse chapel in Venice, and when we went to Barcelona for a couple of days, the children loved the Gaudi buildings.'

Miranda Slater cocked her head to the side, as though she was expecting so much more of me. I didn't know if we should simply ask her what Rosie had said to her, or if that might sound pushy and intrusive.

'And at home? At the weekends? What kind of stuff do you do?'

'Um,' I began to feel a little panicky, like seeing an exam paper question I couldn't answer, and I looked to the fridge schedule for help. 'The children do Saturday clubs until about two, and then we have swim club at the leisure centre. And on Sundays, Noah has rugby, and I go for my run in the morning while Peter takes them for a bike ride and then we have lunch at one at the White Horse.'

'The best roast beef in the country!' Peter bellowed. At which Miranda Slater almost grimaced.

'And then we're home in the afternoon when the kids can watch a film.'

'That sounds very organised.'

'Oh, and they have birthday parties to go to sometimes.'

'And we do see friends,' Peter added.

The only people who dragged us kicking and screaming out of our weekend routine, were Jim and Vics. When I thought of Vics and how she laughed at me for my love of order, the urge to giggle came over me again, at the absurdity of my rules. I wrung my hands. 'Yes.'

'And Gemma, do you and Rosie have any days out, just the two of you?'

'We went out for the day just the other week.'

'That sounds nice.' She smiled. 'Do you do that often?'

'It's an area I could definitely work on,' I replied, trawling my brain for an example of a frivolous, happy time with Rosie. I drew a blank.

'Okay...' she said, marking into her page. 'So, Gemma, tell me a bit about Rosie.'

'Well, I know she's a handful, and she's said all these awful things to the police, which we just can't understand, but she's got this incredible spirit and determination and she's so funny and great fun to be with,' I burbled. I felt passionate about Rosie, charged with motherly pride.

'When you say she is a "handful", tell me more about that.'

'We do have a few issues with her tantrums, but I really feel we are working on them and they're not happening as often these days, are they Peter?'

He shook his head, 'No, not really,' he replied, with an infuriating lack of conviction.

'How often would you say they happen?'

Peter and I answered together. Peter said, 'Two or three times a week?' and I answered, 'Once or twice a month.'

Miranda Slater looked up from her file and raised her eyebrows. She stretched her lips into a smile for us, 'Which is it?'

'Well, it is roughly once, and sometimes twice, a week, depending on how tired she gets at school.'

'Yes,' Peter agreed.

'I just don't want you to think that things are worse than they are,' I added.

Peter squeezed my knee. He would have known that the probing was frightening me. I was under no obligation to tell Miranda Slater about Rosie's beginnings in Prague, but I was petrified that she would prize it out of me. There was no way that this woman, this stranger, was going to know a secret that my own mother didn't know. Anyway, I couldn't trust her to keep it, however much she might try to reassure us about boundaries and trust.

She nodded slowly, with a half-smile that I couldn't interpret as she wrote in her notes; concentrating hard, pressing down with her biro, her writing rounded and childish.

'How is she at school?'

'She always has glowing reports,' Peter said.

'The teachers say she is very motivated and well behaved.'

'Good, good,' Miranda Slater said, grinning and nodding at us. 'That's good.' Seemingly we had just won some brownie points.

In response to her nodding, Peter nodded like a dope. It seemed impossible to be ourselves in front of this woman.

'Peter, in your opinion, your job is secure?' She was nodding again before he had even answered.

'Yes. Well, as secure as any job is these days.'

'Indeed,' she said, rounding her letters on the page carefully. I could not see what she was writing, but she was pressing so hard I was surprised her biro didn't break through the paper.

'And your salary is what?'

Peter shifted in his seat. 'Is this really relevant?'

'We need to build a picture of your family's emotional and financial stability, Peter, is that all right?' The ponytail was flicked behind her back and her unfortunate toothy smile broadened again.

I spoke for him. 'Peter earns £50K and I earn £100K.'

She wrote the figures down, seemingly unmoved by the enormousness of the joint income, and uninterested in who earned more than whom.

'Would you say you had any money problems?'

I guffawed. Miranda Slater's smile miraculously disappeared, and she tilted her head to the side slightly. 'You *do* have money problems?'

'No, no, we don't,' I said soberly.

I listened out for the children who had probably found my mother. Usually, they would be fighting and telling on each other by now, but they were being especially well behaved with Grandma Helen.

'And your monthly outgoings are manageable?'

'Mostly, I suppose they are,' I replied.

'Do you have any debts?'

'We have credit cards, but nothing else,' I said.

Peter stood up and began pacing around the kitchen.

'Would you say you suffered from any stress or anxiety about money?'

'No,' I said, feeling stressed and anxious about Peter's reaction to her questions about money. 'We know what comes in and what goes out.'

Predictably, she nodded and smiled for what seemed like a long time, and then wrote in her report.

'And who looks after Rosie and Noah when you're at work?'

'We have a nanny – Harriet Stock – who comes in the afternoons.'

'Do your kids get on with her?'

'They adore her. She is an absolute godsend,' Peter gushed, sitting down again, as though this was the kind of question he could tolerate, while my skin crawled with the implications.

'But mum's coming to live with us now, so we've given her paid leave for now, just while...' I trailed off, not knowing how to say it out loud.

'I see. That's good, good, so your mother is coming to stay,' she said, writing more. 'So, she'll cover the hours Peter's at work, is that right?'

'Yes,' I said, through gritted teeth. She spoke of this as if it was an acceptable infringement of my freedom.

'How many nannies have they had since they were born?'

The question riled me. Here we go. Here comes her judgement.

'Harriet has been with us for three years.'

'And before that?'

'Before Harriet, we had Nicky, who was with us when we moved here.'

'Mmmm... uh huh... okay... So, why did Nicky leave?'

'She moved back to Australia.'

'And you'd say the children bonded well with her?'

'Yes. She's a primary school teacher now.' In truth, Rosie had screamed for half an hour every day before Nicky arrived.

'And before Nicky did you have anyone?'

I looked to Peter, a veiled warning shot before my white lie. 'In London, we had Jola, who helped us out until we moved out here.'

What I didn't mention was that sandwiched in between Nicky and Jola, we had employed two more – one Filipino lady, who we soon discovered was stone deaf, and one Czech woman who fell pregnant and implied it was Peter's – but I wasn't ready to admit to those two mammoth mistakes.

'So you went back to work when the children were how old?'

My mouth felt dry. 'Rosie was six weeks old. With Noah, I took three months.'

I waited for a look of disgust from Miranda Slater, but she kept her head buried as she wrote this information down.

I wondered if she had children of her own, and how long she had taken off work. 'How was that?'

'What?'

'What was it like going back to work after having Baby?'

'Which baby?' I was being facetious, but I couldn't help myself. 'Tell me about Rosie first.'

'I had a good support network.'

'Uh huh... Hmmm... Any family members help out?'

'Mum sometimes, but she had a lot on at work.'

'But she's not so busy now?'

'She's decided to take a sabbatical, of sorts.'

'Okay, right... Hmmm... Yes... But you say she wasn't supportive when Rosie was a baby, is that right?'

'I didn't say she wasn't supportive, I said she was busy. She helped out when she could.'

She nodded slowly before she spoke. 'Did you suffer from post-natal depression after either of their births?'

I had been waiting for this question. It was the one I had worried about most in the middle of the night.

'No,' I said, sipping my tea, unable to look her in the eye.

After Rosie's birth, I had barely coped. I remember pacing around with her, crying, while she cried. The soreness and tenderness in my body made everything more difficult, like I was doing the hardest thing I had ever done in my life while injured and ill. Deep down, I feared we had done the wrong thing in fighting so hard to have her. When the health visitor had come round with the 'Is Mum Depressed?' survey, I had lied on the form. I was transported back to our dark kitchen in London, where I had read the form that the health visitor had slid in front of me. Each tick that I had made – through bleary eyes – had been a lie: '5 – Do you have suicidal thoughts?' No, tick. I was scared to tick the boxes that might reveal the true depths of my despair, and shock, and the sense of profound inadequacy. Maybe some women are not meant to be mothers, I had thought at the time. Maybe my body had been telling me something during those gruelling years of being prodded and punctured by fertility doctors.

A sense of impotence engulfed me. My ineptitude as a mother was being brought to the table – the truncated maternity leave, the flow of nannies, the lack of mummy-and-me time, Rosie's tantrums, the big lie, the arrest. What terrible endorsements of my parenting. Gone was the urge to laugh. I suddenly wanted to give up, present Miranda Slater with my wrists. Apathy, or worse maybe, numbness, stopped me battling. How could I possibly convince this woman that I was a good mother, when I knew that I wasn't? Could I admit to this? Would this be conceding defeat? Would this mean I would certainly face prosecution?

*'Yes, Your Honor, I love my children but I have a strong aversion to being a mother, guilty as charged.' The crash of the gavel. 'I sentence you to life imprisonment for fucking up your kid!' Arguably, two life sentences.*

As though Peter had sensed this in me, he spoke up, out of turn, 'She is a wonderful mother. All of this is absolutely ludicrous. I can't actually believe we are sitting here having to justify our decisions just because of some terrible misunderstanding. Didn't Rosie tell you up there? That she got confused?' he asked.

'I'm afraid I can't pass on what she tells me.'

'Well, I'm telling you now, Gemma would never have slapped her. Honestly, if you knew her, you'd know she was incapable of it.'

Tears that would not fall blurred my vision. If I had looked at Peter, I would have broken down.

There was silence for a while.

'You understand, Peter, that we are here to make sure that your children are safe,' she said.

'Yes, yes, the system,' he said, dropping his hands into his lap.

And then she turned to me. 'How do you *feel* about being a mother, Gemma?'

The question was like an electric shock, and I swiped an errant tear.

I remembered looking at Rosie when she was lying in her cot, her fists in little cotton mittens to stop her scratching her face with her miniscule nails, wishing she would sleep for a little bit longer, wishing I didn't have to wake her for her feed. I did not like breast feeding her. Her hard gums on my nipple; a violation almost. Every suck gave me an unpleasant shudder. I kept these feelings to myself, ashamed of them, knowing I would sound wrongly-wired if I admitted it to anyone. A week before I returned to work, I weaned her onto the bottle. It was revelatory. I think I loved Rosie a little bit more as she gazed up at me, her lips locked around the plastic teat. I was liberated, hopeful again. The bottle helped me to feel a little bit more like me.

'I don't know how I feel about being a mother.' I hesitated, knowing how I should have answered her but worn down by all these questions, worn down. Who was 'me'? I would never be the Gemma I was before I gave birth. Gemma the mother was in her place. Rosie had needed me to be defeated and to relinquish control of that pre-baby 'me'. Her needs were designed to consume me absolutely. It shouldn't have been too much to ask. I had failed her. And I would probably fail the next one.

'I suppose sometimes I feel like the worst mother in the whole universe,' I said, pressing hard into the centre of my chest, as if pressing at the place where all my tension was held.

Peter gaped at me, outraged, as though I had just stopped dead in the middle of a running race I had been winning.

But Miranda Slater gave me her first genuine smile. It was a sad smile, actually, and there was recognition in her eyes, from woman to woman, from mother to mother possibly.

'I guess that was a really hard thing to say out loud,' Miranda Slater said gently.

I pressed my fingers into my eye sockets. It was my turn to nod excessively.

# CHAPTER FORTY-TWO

Rosie's cheeks were stuffed full of a whole slice of cake when she spoke. A hornbeam hedge leaf stuck out of the top of her head and little bits of pink-and-yellow sponge darted from her mouth. The sight of her made Mira want to laugh out loud but the girl looked sincere, and so Mira turned back to her green plant pots and pushed the sweet-pea seeds into the soft soil as she listened.

'I just wanted to tell you it's all fine now.'

'That sounds lovely, Rosie Rabbit. I'm so glad for you,' Mira nodded, knowing that she would not have snuck through the hedge to see her if everything had been fine. Mira placed a steaming cup of hot chocolate in front of Rosie.

'Mummy and Grandma Helen both picked me up from school and Mummy gave me a set of neon pens that I always wanted.'

'Where does your mummy think you are now?'

'Making dens.'

'She won't check?'

'I told her that grown-ups aren't allowed past the gazebo.'

'And Noah?'

'That's *easy*. I paid him five pounds to stay away from me.'

'Very resourceful,' Mira grinned.

'Guess what?'

'What?'

'Grandma Helen is living with us! It's so cool.'

'How long is she going to live there, petal?'

'Not sure.'

Mira remembered that bird-like woman and felt cross. The plastic green pot cracked in her hand. The two slits of the split pinched her skin. She sucked her palm and glanced over her shoulder at Rosie, whose confident smile had dropped off her face momentarily.

'Are you okay?'

'Now, now, chin up. No need to look like the cat's just died. How about you help me plant some of these, eh?'

They stood side-by-side as Mira showed Rosie how to fill the pots and press the seeds deep into the cool, damp soil. They worked silently. Rosie was the first to speak up.

'This lady with weird stick-out teeth came round to our house.'

'It's what's on the inside that counts.'

'But I don't know what's in her insides?'

Mira chuckled. 'Who was she?'

'She was a social worker.'

Mira knocked over three potted plants with her elbow as she turned to Rosie. 'Did she ask you lots of horrible questions?'

Rosie stared at the spilt soil. 'Not lots.'

'Tell me one.'

'She asked me what my favourite subject was and I told her it was maths.'

'Maths?'

'It's not *really* my favourite.'

'Oh?'

'I like art and forest school best.'

'So why did you say maths, you big banana?'

Rosie giggled. 'Because she was being nosey.'

'She's just doing her job, pet.'

They fell silent as they continued their potting. And then Rosie spoke up again.

'You know how your mummy slapped you?'

'Yes, petal.'

'Were you telling the truth?'

Mira felt her blood run cold with fury. Rosie's hot chocolate was on the edge of the workbench. Mira nudged it and the hot liquid cascaded down Rosie's blue duffel coat and onto her red wellingtons.

Rosie squealed. 'Hot, hot, hot!' she cried, hopping up and down and shaking out one wellington.

'Dear me, how careless of me, eh?'

Mira bent down and brushed Rosie's coat with a cloth, and Rosie lost her balance slightly. Mira stopped being so rough, remembering how little Rosie was, and how vulnerable. Softening, she looked at her, and buttoned up one of the toggles. 'Never mind, my little Rosie Rabbit,' she said gently. 'D'you think your mummy'll notice your dirty coat?'

'I don't *care* if she does. She'll just blame me for it. She blames me for *everything*.'

'Has she been blaming you for everything that's happened recently?'

'Not really but only because Granny Helen is here.'

Mira nodded gravely. 'Off you pop then. Better not be gone too long.'

'I don't want to go home.'

'Take a couple of pots of these and say your school gave them to you.'

'Thanks,' she sulked, like they were poor consolation.

'And why don't you send me a note in the blue bucket to tell me how you're getting along?'

Her face lit up. 'That's a good idea!' Then she balanced the pots into the crook of her arm, freeing a hand. 'Can I take two more pieces of cake so I can give Noah one?'

'Of course,' Mira said, slicing two pieces and wrapping it in a napkin. 'Next time you come, you can have two cups of hot chocolate to make up for it and we'll check on our little seedlings, okay?'

'Bye,' Rosie said, hugging Mira goodbye as if it was the most natural thing in the world. Mira's heart shattered into a thousand pieces.

'Bye, petal,' she called back, her voice breaking a little.

Mira clutched the side to stay upright as Rosie scampered out, her pockets stuffed full.

How Mira had hungered for her own child's arms to hold her as Rosie's had, to share secrets together, to heal their troubles, to fight, to make up, to feel their little rosebud lips on her cheek, to see their shiny eyes light up when they spoke of happy things, to inhale that edible, intoxicating smell of newness and innocence, sugar and mud.

Rosie's departure left Mira with a grotesque yearning in her chest.

Abandoning her sweet peas, she hurried back into the house and straight into the dining room.

Her fingers worked through the photographs as nimbly as a tea picker's: happy photographs into happy piles, sad photographs stuffed into brown envelopes.

The album would be filled with a dreamy past, the rewriting of her history; it would tell stories of cordiality and smiles and contentment. All the dismal memories had to be expunged, replaced by the bigger picture of childhood bliss. It was better to see the good rather than dwell on the bad.

She heard the front door bang. Barry was home.

'Hi, love! I'm in here!' she called out.

Barry came in to see her.

'Shall I run your bath for you, love?'

'Thanks, I won't be a minute.'

'When d'you think you'll finish it?' Barry said, leaning into the doorway, watching her adept plucking and sifting.

'Really soon now,' Mira said. She would not be able to explain to Barry how or why she had found her way with it finally. She had been too busy trying to remember the past, to seek the truth, when what she really needed to do was to forget.

Then her fingers made contact with a photograph she had long forgotten about.

Bang. BANG. The door to her teenage bedroom had been shoved open. Click. The doorway flashed, and flashed again. Mira had pulled her dressing gown from the floor, to cover at least her belly, if not her bra and pants. It was too late. Deidre had got what she wanted.

'Those stretch marks are so gross,' Deidre had jeered. 'It's like you've got a giant alien baby scratching at your insides.' The camera flashed again, leaving globs of red and green swimming before Mira's eyes. Violated. Resigned. She had dressed for school, knowing she would have more to contend with there.

Her school friends had reacted to her pregnancy with the predictable mix of quiet, suspicious awe and nasty snickering. She had not been popular before her pregnancy; now the mean girls had a tangible reason to dislike her. There was one girl who had been friendly. But she smelt of urine and Mira didn't like her. Mira didn't need friends. She had her baby. When she was in break time or bored in lessons, she spoke to it, quietly. They had a bond only she could understand. She remembers thinking that the rest of the girls in her class were immature, and she told them so often enough to keep them away.

Mira pressed the photograph to her chest, where her heart thumped through to her fingertips.

She felt Barry's presence behind her.

'What's that one?' he said, peering over her shoulder.

'Nothing.'

'Come on, let's see it, hand it over, is it an embarrassing one?' he teased.

Mira scowled. 'Stop it.'

Not getting the hint, he tugged at the corner of the photograph. 'I bet you look drop dead gorgeous.'

It was unlikely he would identify the teenager with long, pretty hair and a pregnant belly, but she couldn't risk it.

'If you dare touch me again, I'll scream until I'm sick.'

Barry reeled back, and Mira was also aghast by her reaction, mortified by its childishness.

'I'll call down when the bath's run. I've booked the March Hare for seven.' The quietness of his delivery spoke volumes about how wounded he was.

The door clicked closed. She was not in the mood for their Friday-night date at the pub to celebrate their twentieth-fifth wedding anniversary. A pint and a pie were what Barry had wanted to mark the occasion. All she wanted was to immerse herself in the album until she had finished ridding it of all unhappiness.

As she sat opposite Barry on the small round table by the roaring fire, they avoided mentioning their fight. He was a little withdrawn, but the traditions of their anniversary played out like clockwork. She sipped fizzy wine. He supped a pint. They ate chicken pie and chips and reminisced about their small registry-office wedding on the edge of town, followed by a jolly knees-up at a pub similar to the one they sat in now.

While she smiled and pretended to be taken back to the charming moments of their wedding day twenty-five years ago, all she could remember was her guilt. How fraudulent she had been in that ivory suit, how sick she had felt when she promised to be true to him in her vows, how much she had been shamed by Jesus Christ's face looking down on her from his cross. She had not been true to Barry. She had married him on false pretences and she had prayed to God the Almighty to forgive her for wanting to hide her sins from the man she loved. She hoped that this new start, this handsome marriage, could help her to move on from her failures, from her shabby past, from the unendurable agony of letting her firstborn go.

The memory of her baby had to be lost and forgotten about; undisclosed, therefore unreal.

'Here's to the next twenty-five,' she said, holding up her flute.

Twenty-five years of marriage had not been long enough to forget. She was still a fraud. Time had not been a healer. But that was her cross to bear. The guilt, the secret, the white lies were part of her life, just as breathing was. Barry was the only good thing to have ever happened to her and she had been willing to make personal moral sacrifices to keep him.

He clinked her glass and pushed his spectacles – whose lenses had darkened in the bright pub – up his nose. 'Blimey, in twenty-five years, we'll be seventy-five.'

'Can always rely on you for a cheery thought.'

'You don't think we'll get lonely in our old age, do you?'

'As long as I go first, I'll be fine,' she grinned.

'I'll bump you off then before I'm about to croak.'

'Good plan. There's nobody else who'll miss me.'

They looked deep into each other's eyes for one long-held moment, acknowledging their bond.

'It's a shame we're not closer to your Deidre's Harry. Being around the young 'uns keeps us young, so they say, or not as sad about getting older, I wouldn't wonder.'

'Goodness gracious, I'm grateful we're not closer to Harry. He's the kind of child who puts you off children.'

But Mira knew what he meant. He was referring to their own childlessness. He would always test her on their anniversary, just to check that nothing had changed.

When Barry shared his Eeyore-morose fears or philosophies on life, Mira enjoyed the power she held to snap him out of it.

'I don't regret a thing about us, Barry,' she said, putting both her feet on top of his boots as though she was a child about to dance on his feet.

'I know. Me neither,' he said, beaming. 'We're a good team, just the two of us.'

Last year, and on the many years before it, this similar conversation had left Mira feeling warm and comfortable. She had never wanted another child, and had been thankful that Barry had been unwavering on the subject. Their agreeable match had given her all the nurturing and fulfilment she needed. This year, however, her mind darted straight to Rosie. Her sweet, new little confidante, who made her feel like singing and dancing when she was with her, and ever so young again.

She couldn't wait for the morning to check for the blue bucket. She hoped that the little accident with the hot chocolate hadn't scared her away.

# CHAPTER FORTY-THREE

*TOP SECRET*

*Dear Mummy,*

*I had the most embarrassing day ever. The doctor told me to stand there in front of her with my pants and vest on and then she looked all over my legs and arms and my TUMMY and asked me why I had that bruise on my arm. What a dumb doctor. How could I remember when I got that bruise? The nurse took a photo of it, like she's going to put it on Instagram. My arm! Imagine? BORING.*

*We are doing parables at school this week. It is really hard but I have made up a brilliant one – smiley face emoji – that I'm going to do for homework. It is about a girl who lies. I'm only going to show Granny Helen. Not you.*

*Uh oh, I think I can hear her coming upstairs. She always checks on me when she goes to bed. She goes to bed so early. If she is a grown-up why is she going to bed so early? It's so annoying. Better go.*

*Rosie*
*P.S. No time.*

# CHAPTER FORTY-FOUR

'Hi, everyone!' I cried, dumping my bag on the floor, kissing Rosie and Noah on the head as they were bent over their homework.

'Hi,' they mumbled.

'Hi, darling, you're early,' my mother said, the only one to raise her head from the homework sheets strewn across the kitchen table. 'Good day?'

'The usual,' I sighed.

How could I describe to my mother how hard the week had been since my arrest. The swiftness of the changes to our family life had been hard to grasp. The adjustments felt like a whirlwind that I was caught up in, rather than an ordered plan.

The noises and bustle of life outside home had become almost unbearable. While I tolerated work, signed contracts, held conferences, I longed to be back home, cocooned with my mother, who had settled into our life with surprising grace and pragmatism – she had always been good in crises.

I continued hoping that something would shift soon, that Rosie would break down, but she hadn't and we were stuck in a surreal holding pattern, loitering above reality. Each day, like another bead on a string that was tied to the dreaded fourth of December.

Endlessly, I second-guessed what was going on behind the scenes of that police station, what picture DC Miles was building of our family from the outside-in, from information gathered from a series of professionals whom we barely knew. There was Dr

Peed – whose name had never failed to make us giggle – whom we saw twice a year when the children had a verruca or tonsillitis. Mrs Brewer, Rosie's form teacher, whom we met once a term for ten minutes to discuss her excellent grades. Miranda Slater, who had probably disliked me on sight.

I only ventured out locally if I absolutely had to, driving whenever possible, with my hood up or sunglasses on, hoping I wouldn't bump into anyone; I'd had a bad experience on the high street at the beginning of the week.

It had been Tuesday evening and I had been nipping in and out of the chemist for some iron pills, when I spotted Charlotte's mother coming out of the beautician's two doors down. She sported a coat with a real-fur lined hood, which made me feel cross with her way before I remembered why I wanted – needed – to avoid her. Unfortunately, it had been too late. Our eyes had met. There had been no time to duck into a shop or change direction. I slowed down, and instantly my face flushed and my mouth dried. I put a chewing gum in my mouth, ready for the inevitable.

She walked straight past me. It was more devastating than any awkward small talk could ever have been. However much I tried to persuade myself that she might have been rude for all sorts of other personal reasons, I suspected that the rumour was out already. It never took long.

One of the teaching assistants at New Hall Prep, who had two children at the school, might have been the weak link between school protocol and parent gossip; or the school receptionist's sister might clean Charlotte's house; or the duty officer at the police station might be sleeping with the school receptionist's sister. Who knew how one indiscreet moment could lead to wildfire. 'Don't tell anyone, but...'

My adrenalin levels had spiked and my downcast mood was momentarily flung aside as I concocted creative retorts to embarrass her with in the playground and heartfelt emails to make her feel bad. Deep down, I knew it was futile to engage with the woman on any level. She was not renowned for her incisiveness and she had been looking for a reason to snub me ever since Charlotte's first fight with Rosie, which she blamed Rosie for, of course. Nevertheless, I now wished we could go back to how it had been before between us, when I would politely endure her inane, barbed chatter, and have a laugh with Peter about it afterwards.

'Cuppa?' I asked Mum.

'I'll do it,' she said, rising from the chair, which I gratefully sat down on.

'So, what've you got tonight, you two?'

Neither of them answered me.

'Hello? What homework do you have?'

'Place value,' Noah said, arcing his pencil along a number line.

Rosie ignored me completely. 'Granny Helen, will you read my fable through?'

'A fable?' I said, trying to ignore the fact that she was ignoring me. 'That sounds interesting. Can I read it?'

I stood up and moved behind Rosie's chair to peer over her shoulder. Rosie covered her work with her hand and said, 'I want Granny Helen to read it.'

'I'll get supper on,' I replied, hurt, but trying to hide it.

'It's okay, darling, I've promised them my special tuna bake.'

'Right, everything is in order, seemingly.'

I felt rejected, superfluous. It had been awkward getting out of work early, but at least there had been the sense from Lisa that I would be missed.

Since Sunday, when Rosie had clung to me and sobbed herself inside out, I had tried hard to be nice, too hard. Our hugs had lingered, but they were laced with the unsaid. Our conversations had included laughter, but the content was inconsequential. When I kissed her goodnight, she had pulled the duvet around her ears as though protecting them from anything I had to say.

In only a few days, both children had begun to ask Granny Helen to knot their ties, to fill their water-bottles, to help with their homework, to put more ketchup on their sausage buns. The three of them had created a functioning self-sufficient unit that I didn't feel part of. I was out of place and phony – mechanically patient and upbeat with the children – and I couldn't wait for the next morning when I could escape from scrutiny, from the self-consciousness around Rosie, and back to work.

However, while they were busy and engaged, happily ignoring me, I thought of Rosie's diary. Her school bag was at her feet. I picked it up.

'Got your PE kit in here?' I asked, half expecting her to grab the bag from me.

'Think so,' she replied, letting me look.

Her trainers and gym kit were scrumpled up at the bottom. The diary was not in there.

'I'm off to have a bath.'

My heart sped as I slowly climbed the stairs.

I crept into her room. And there was her diary lying on her bed, available and ominous.

As soon as I held it, light in my hands, I remembered that it was locked with a code. I typed in as many birthdays and number combinations as I could think of. It refused to open. I could hear Noah's voice getting louder as he approached the stairs, and then Rosie's. Just one more guess. And another. Their feet were on the stairs. I dropped the diary and nipped out of the room.

Peter was my only safe haven. When he came home that night, late, after the children were in bed, I craved some time alone with him, away from my mother. I missed our suppers together, just the two of us, where we indulged in an analysis of the days we'd had, where I felt we put the world to rights, where he calmed me with his gentle spirit. Now, if we wanted to talk about anything intimate, we had to snatch conversations when my mother was out of the room, when she was fetching something or talking to a friend on her mobile.

'I think they prefer Mum to me,' I laughed, chucking some red peppers into the pan.

'Don't be silly.'

He stood behind me and rather half-heartedly slipped his arms around my waist, pecking me on the neck. As much I wanted to enjoy his affection, and respond accordingly, I couldn't. I felt my shoulders rise. Getting the message, he let go and poured a large wine glass of red, right up to the brim.

'I wish Rosie had opened up to you yesterday,' I said cautiously.

Peter had been subdued on the day he had taken Rosie out of school for the medical examination. He had not been allowed into the consultant's room with her. I had been desperate for details from him.

'I told you, it didn't feel right to ask her,' he said defensively.

'I know, so you said.'

'What's that supposed to mean?'

'It wasn't meant to mean anything.'

He slammed the fridge door closed. 'You know when she came out of that consultant's room, her little hands were freezing cold. She'd been standing half-naked in front of a strange doctor who must've asked her weird questions and made her feel bloody awful, and so, to be frank, the only thing she needed was a hug and a hot chocolate.'

'Sorry.'

I backed off. Deep down, we knew everything was too precarious for an all-out row.

'When I spoke to Philippa...' I began.

He interrupted, 'You spoke to Philippa Letwin? Why didn't you say?'

'I'm saying now.'

'What did she say?'

'Nothing much. She said we might have to go to some kind of safeguarding meeting with the police and Miranda Slater.'

'Really, when?'

'Not sure. But she warned me that if we put any pressure on Rosie it could majorly backfire.'

'That's what I was trying to tell you.'

'I know. That's why I told you what she said. I was agreeing with you.'

'Oh, right, okay. Sorry.'

'Sorry too,' I said, abandoning the stir fry and turning to him. We both chuckled – it wasn't the first time we had bickered over an issue that we both agreed on – and then we hugged. My cheek rested on his shoulder.

Peter pulled away enough to look down at my bump. 'When's your next scan?'

I counted up five months from September on my fingers. 'January.'

'But everything feels okay in there?'

'Very. I never forget he's there, but I haven't been giving him as much thought as I should.'

'I'm not surprised with everything that's going on.'

'Apparently, third babies are universally neglected.'

'Poor bugger doesn't stand a chance.' Peter grinned, kissing me on the lips.

When my mother came in, we pulled apart physically, but all through supper his hug stayed with me. We were both on the same side. I guessed he was as terrified of talking to Rosie as I was. Neither of us knew how to handle her, and maybe we never had.

\*

I knocked on the spare room door.

'Hello?' my mother said from behind it.

'Mum? Can I come in?'

'Come in, of course, darling.'

She was propped up in bed reading a tatty paperback.

'Everything okay?'

'Not really.'

She placed her novel down on the eiderdown, and patted a spot next to her.

I lay down with my feet crossed at the ankles. My head sank back into the down pillows and I wished I could drift away on them into the clouds.

Tiny forget-me-nots dotted the walls. Flowery wallpaper was unfashionable, but I had chosen it because the pattern had reminded me of the curtains I had in my bedroom when I was growing up, which my mother had let me choose. If the baby turned out to be a girl, maybe I would keep this wallpaper after all, I thought. I enjoyed thinking ahead, to the baby coming home, as though I could skip the bad bit in between.

'She's asleep finally,' I sighed heavily.

'You know, I catch her writing her diary when I go up to bed.'

'I am so sick of telling her off about that. I keep telling her she has loads of time before lights out to write in it.' I was too tired to be cross about another of Rosie's infractions.

'She settles down after I've been in.'

'I wish I could read it.'

'I've tried to.'

'Mum! You haven't!'

Mum looked shamefaced. 'That bloody code. But look at this.' She brought Rosie's school literacy exercise book out of her side table.

'Why have you got this?'

'I wanted to have a read of her compositions.' She leafed through to the last page. 'Here, this is the one she wrote this afternoon.'

I took the exercise book and deciphered Rosie's scrawling handwriting.

*<u>MY FABLE by Rosie Bradley</u>*
*<u>The Deer in the Snow-globe.</u>*

*Once there was a little girl called Serena who had a wonderful collection of pretty snow-globes that she kept by her bed. She stared at them when she went to sleep. Her favourite snow-globe was really pretty. It had snowy mountains inside. The little girl with plaits was skidding down the mountains on her sled and there was a tiny, cute deer with white spots on his back. Serena would dream about turning into the little girl on the sled because in real life she really enjoyed whizzing down on sleds with the snow spitting in her face. It was the best in the world. One night, the snow-globe suddenly lit-up and shone brightly into Serena's sparkly blue eyes. Amazingly, the tiny deer began to talk! He said, 'Hello Serena. I'm called Brambles. If you tell your mummy a lie, I'll let you ride on the sled down these mountains.' He was a very naughty deer but Serena really wanted to go on the sled. The next day, Serena told her mummy that she had cleaned her teeth but she really had not cleaned her teeth. She even wet the toothbrush to pretend. Her mother believed her! At night, Serena stared at the pretty snow-globe. Then Brambles said, 'Hello Serena. You can go on the sled now.' Then Brambles tapped his hoof twice and Serena was suddenly inside the snow-globe. The snow was not cold. It was soft. She went on the sled hundreds of times until she was really tired. 'Can I go home now?'*

*Serena said. 'No, you can't ever go home,' Brambles said.*
*'But why?' Serena said. 'You lied so now you have to live*
*here for the rest of your life,' Brambles said.*

*Serena banged on the inside of the globe. She was trapped*
*forever. She could see her humungous, cosy bed from the*
*tiny mountain. She cried a lot because she was really sad*
*and missed her mummy. She wished she had never told her*
*mummy a lie.*

*The End.*

Goosebumps had run across my skin as I had read it. It had
transported me into her sweet, innocent mind.

'No wonder she didn't want me to read it.'

'But she wanted *me* to read it.' My mother put her hand on
her chest melodramatically.

'Do you think it's a cry for help?'

'I think it's an opening for me to talk to her.'

'Yes,' I said, rereading the end. 'It's a bit like a confession.'

'A rather charming one, don't you think?'

'A little derivative...' I replied, churlishly, unable to admit to
the delight I had felt while reading it. The image of the cell walls
shot up around me again, the doubt on the faces of DC Miles
in the interview room came back to me in glorious, puppet-like
horror. I was not quite ready to eulogise about Rosie's talents with
my mother yet.

'You can't say that. You're supposed to be hopelessly biased,'
Mum chided, snatching the textbook. She placed her glasses on
to read it. 'Some of my students don't have as much imagination.'

'Anyway, let's hope it provides a good segue.'

'I'll try tomorrow over homework. I'll send Noah off somewhere.'

'Peter went into the station to give his statement yesterday.'

'Yes, he told me.'

'They even called Vics the other day.'

She smoothed her hands across the velvet eiderdown. 'I'm sure Vics had a glowing report for them.'

I imagined how easily the police created doubt, even in my own mind about my own actions.

'They'll be talking to the school at some point too.'

'The whole thing is simply ghastly,' she cried, ripping off her glasses and slamming the textbook closed, as if the school's involvement was the final straw. 'I'm at the gates with those women and I'm telling you, they get hysterical about a missing sock after PE, just imagine, *imagine*, what they'll be like if they get wind of this, and if it does get out, if it hasn't already, mind, you know who'll be affected most?'

'Rosie.'

'She needs to understand how serious this could become.'

'Don't go in heavy-handed with her tomorrow, Mum.'

She shook her head and looked to the ceiling. 'No, no, I won't, don't worry.'

'It'll be counterproductive,' I insisted.

'I'll be the model of diplomacy.'

I bit my lip, knowing that diplomacy and my mother were not best friends.

She picked up her book and reached over and kissed my cheek. 'You can sleep here if you like but I will be reading for a while so I'll be keeping the light on.'

I dragged my weary body off her bed and kissed her on the cheek. 'Night, Mum. Thanks.'

'And tell that madam to put that diary away.'

'I'm sure she's asleep now. It's almost eleven.'

Before brushing my teeth and washing my face for bed, I stopped to listen at Rosie's bedroom door. I could tell from a rustle of her duvet and a self-conscious cough that she was awake.

I stormed into her room and ripped back the duvet, suddenly livid.

'Right, enough is enough. It's time to put that away. And if I catch you with it after lights out again, I'll confiscate it.'

I was sick of her bad behaviour, I was sick of being messed around. Peter and I had been pussyfooting around her like a pair of timid mice. Mum was right. It was time she faced the reality of what she'd done.

'No,' Rosie cried, closing it and lying on top of it.

'Give it to me, now.'

'No. It's mine.'

'I'm telling you, give it to me, NOW.'

'I'll tell Granny Helen that you're shouting at me again.'

'Granny Helen thinks you should go to sleep!' I bellowed, furious at the suggestion that she and my mother had complained about me behind my back.

'La, la, la, la!' she sang.

'I won't tell you again, Rosie. Give it to me.'

'LA, LA, LA, LA!' she sang, putting her hands over her ears.

'I WON'T TELL YOU AGAIN.' The rage was uncontrollable, it had taken over me. I was at its mercy, cowering in the background as it tunnelled through me. I lunged at her, and pushed her body away from her diary, trying to roll her over. I was going to get that diary if it was the last thing I did. Rosie pushed me away, slapping at the top of my head, screaming at me wildly. And then she bit my arm. I yelped and shoved her off the diary, and she threw her arms in the air and span dramatically over towards the wall, which the back of her skull thudded against.

Her scream was ear-splitting. My hands shook in shock, my blood coursed with terror.

My mother was at my side, 'What the hell is going on in here?' Her face was contorted as she bent down to Rosie. 'Are you okay, darling?' Rosie crawled into her grandmother's arms.

'Mummy pushed me! It hurts so much!' she wailed, cradling the back of her head with one arm, clutching her locked-again diary in the other, crying in distress.

Peter appeared behind me. I wasn't sure how long he had been there or what he had witnessed in that half-lit room.

He murmured, 'What did you do?'

'She *drives me to it*!' I yelled, louder than her screaming, right into his face, beyond caring, losing the last shred of my composure, letting ten years of frustration out in five terrible words.

His expression hardened as he moved past me. 'Excuse me. Helen, sorry, can I have a look? Let's see your head, darling,' he said gently, clicking on her lamp. Her yelping subsided as he inspected her skull through her hair. 'There's a bit of a bump,' he said.

I had to get out. I had to leave them. There was too much feeling pressing to get out. My own screams for help were imprisoned in my body. I thought I would go mad. There was nowhere for it to go. How it could ever be discharged? Who was I? I was a danger to myself, I was a danger to Rosie.

I ran around the house, collecting my handbag, shoving on my shoes, finding my car-keys, and outside, into the damp night air, into the car, locking myself in; my key jerked around the ignition, my hands trembled so violently I couldn't get it into the slot.

There was a loud rap on the window and I jumped out of my skin, dropping the keys into the foot-well.

'Open the door,' my mother shouted, knocking repeatedly.

I unlocked the passenger door, which she opened and held on to, preventing me from moving the car.

'Where are you going?'

'I don't know, I just need to get away,' I cried, scrabbling at my feet to find the key. 'Can you shut the door?'

'Look, I know it's tough right now but you can't run away.'

I found the key and fired up the engine. 'You don't know bloody anything, Mum! *Close* the *door*!'

'I think I do know a few things after bringing up you and Jackie on my own, thank you very much.'

I clutched at the steering wheel with both hands as though I was careering over a cliff, and screeched, 'Oh yes, sorry, it was so much bloody harder for you! How could I possibly forget how hard it was for you and how bloody brilliantly you coped? I'm so sorry that I am such a *pathetic disappointment.*'

My mother stood stock-still, and glared at me. 'Self-pity doesn't suit you.'

'Yes. Silly me. I must maintain a cool fucking head at all times, just like you. But how could I possibly compete with the Master of Self-control?'

Tight-lipped, she replied, 'This is not about me. This is about you and Rosie.'

'You don't know *anything* about me and Rosie.'

'I know you're both Campbell women and Campbell women don't give up on each other.'

'Right, yes, the Campbell woman,' I sniped, tasting the acid of my sarcasm on my tongue. 'That's the thing – I've been meaning to tell you for, what, how long now?' I paused, with my finger to my lip facetiously, my heartbeat thundering in my ears. 'Um, ten years now, that she *isn't* a Campbell *at all*. She's a Doubek. Her real mother is Kaarina Doubek, from the Czech Republic, height, 5'9", shoe size 6, with a love of bike riding and piano playing.'

My mother spluttered, as though blood flooded her throat, and she instantly slammed the car door, shutting me away, shutting away what I had just told her. For a split second we stared at each other through the window, locked in mutual disbelief and horror. Her hands were clasped around her middle, her milky blue eyes unblinking, shrinking even further back into her head, stunned by my revelation. I revved the engine, opened the electric gates of my home with my natty little clicker and backed out at a speed almost careless enough to clip the gates. As I three-point-turned on the roundabout, I glimpsed my mother standing there on the drive in her dressing gown. But I rejected her vulnerability, just as she had rejected mine. If she was such a fearless, spirited Campbell woman, she could cope with Rosie. I was done.

# CHAPTER FORTY-FIVE

*TOP SECRET*

*DEAR GEMMA,*
   *WHO IS CATREENA DOOBECK? WHY IS SHE*
*MY MOTHER?*
   *I HATE HER AND I HATE YOU. I HOPE YOU*
*NEVER COME BACK.*

*ROSIE*

# CHAPTER FORTY-SIX

I was driving off, free. A lightness gathered in my chest. As I got to the end of the road, with the choice to turn left or right, I didn't know which to take.

A car beeped behind me. I made a knee-jerk decision and swerved left, almost colliding with an oncoming car. I began driving down the B road out of town, towards a village whose pub had an open fire and good wine. I couldn't go in there alone. I might bump into someone I knew: a mother from New Hall Prep who would tell the other mothers that I was a child-abusing wino, and a pregnant one at that.

Headlights flashed past me, disorientating me. I clung to the wheel, with my body bent forward, trying to be especially careful. The idea of hitting a cyclist or a pedestrian was even more of a worry than usual, as though there might be a better time than tonight to run someone over.

I thought of Rosie's head clunking into the wall, and worried about concussion. Had it been hard enough? I didn't think so, I didn't remember so. Her scream suggested otherwise, but I knew how piercing her scream could sound when she didn't get the shoes she wanted. I thought of Noah, fast asleep, and then worried he would wake up and need me. I knew my mother would comfort him, in her no-nonsense way, and I knew Peter would make him laugh so that he forgot why he was sad.

There was a garage coming up. I indicated and pulled in. The lights in the shop were bright and welcoming. It was pitiful that I was grateful for them.

Having wandered down the sweets aisle, picking out a large packet of chewy mints, I made my way over to the counter to pay, and then spotted the locked cigarette cupboard.

'Could I please have a packet of Marlboro Lights?' I asked boldly. My cheeks flushed. It had been over ten years since I had bought a packet of cigarettes and I felt as though I was asking for a bag of crack-cocaine.

'We only have Marlboro Menthol,' the young woman said, unfazed.

'That's fine, and a lighter please.' I wondered if she could tell I was pregnant.

As I waited for my bankcard to go through, I noticed a special-offer gift box of a mini bottle of Baileys and chocolates to go with it. It was the perfect size for one. I wanted to buy it but I couldn't face the humiliation of asking for it. Instead, I nipped to the back of the shop and I chose a bottle of cheap Merlot with a screw cap so that I wouldn't have to buy a corkscrew.

Back on the dark windy roads again, I picked my brains for ideas of where to pull over. The lay-bys were too dark, some with lone cars sitting there. Or an anonymous residential street in town, until I remembered that there was no such thing as anonymity in a small town. On every single road, I knew at least one someone, or one someone's friend. I longed for London and considered driving up there. The less radical idea was a pub car park. If I spotted anyone, I could jump in quickly and drive away.

The Swann Inn was the closest. I pulled into the corner of the car park, right at the back. Hidden behind the bonnet of the car, I sat on the waterproof rug that I kept in the boot, took a swig from the bottle of wine and lit my first cigarette in ten years. It was bliss. I groaned in pleasure. And apologised to my unborn baby. One wouldn't hurt.

The dizziness reminded me of my first ever cigarette when I was thirteen years old in a fast-food restaurant with my best friend. I remembered how naughty and reckless I had felt, just as I felt now, and I was sad that my adulthood had been completely devoid of such fatalism. Everything had become about 'doing the right thing', about controlling the outcome.

With each drag, the anger dissolved, as though it had been bolstering me, helping me cope. As it slipped away, I felt small and weak and unworthy. I wanted to hold Rosie in my arms, feel her warm softness, to kiss her better, to feel her love, her forgiveness. In spite of Rosie's behaviour, what an idiot I had been to stomp into her bedroom like that. Unknowingly, I had been a walking pressure cooker: one little tap and all the heat had come out at once.

And now my mother knew everything.

Despair crept in through the cracks of my coping strategies, and then a deluge of melancholy engulfed me. The battle to keep my head above water was all at once completely unmanageable. I had been gripping onto the routine, the rules, the sameness, for what? What had it brought me? I had been charging around in a permanent state of exhaustion, juggling work and fridge schedules, clocking in and out of the children's lives, while they didn't get a say in any of it. All in the name of providing the best for them. But what was The Best? A child who hated me? A husband who drank too much? A family whose members passed each other like ships in the night? For what? For a better house that drained our bank account, for brilliant careers that left us too tired to have sex, for a bigger car that killed the environment, for a smarter school that rewired anxiety into their young minds.

I was holding a mirror up to The Best and its reflection was ugly.

How much room was there left for spontaneity, light-heart-edness, romance, boredom, generosity, for hours whiled away fruitlessly, thoughtfully, with books flicked through, newspapers discarded, laughter and games and chatter and innocence.

Didn't I only have one life? Didn't the children have only one childhood? Did I really want to live it like this? Was I mad?

My stomach flip-flopped. I lit another cigarette – two wouldn't hurt. I loathed to end my short snatch of rebellion and contemplation (who would have thought the two went together?).

The journey home was quieter. I thought of my mother. She would be smarting from a decade in the dark, a decade of ignorance, a decade of seeking out resemblances in her granddaughter, finding pride in supposed inherited traits, seeing the line of her genes follow down into another generation of Campbell Women. Her inability to wink was an odd quirk, which was traceable only to Kaarina's genes, and seemed to highlight so much else that we didn't know about her heredity. The apocryphal Campbell family stories of rare talents or unusual features from great-aunts and great, great grandparents did not apply. Rosie had been an unwitting fraud. And my mother would have to relearn her relationship with her in the light of their new, less biological, connection to one another. If she had always known, there would have been no trauma of finding out. She would have accepted it without hesitation. Just as Rosie would have. The thought was spine-chilling.

When I slipped back in, sheepishly, I found the front of the house silent. My mother and Peter were in the sitting room by the fire.

It was too hot in there. There was a sharp tang of alcohol in the air.

They looked up casually as though I was the missing guest they had been expecting.

My mother was in the blue-velvet wing-backed chair to the right, and Peter was on the sofa next to her. I was unable to look either of them in the eye, scared stiff of what I would see. Perched on the edge of the sofa opposite Peter, I was like a schoolgirl in a head teacher's office.

I straightened the coffee-table book in perfect line with the book underneath it, neither of which I had ever made the time to read.

'How was Rosie's head?'

'I gave her some paracetamol. She's fast asleep.'

'Go on, tell me how awful I am.'

'I'm sure it was an accident,' my mother stated firmly.

'You don't sound so sure.'

'Gemma, don't,' Peter said.

My mother's wan face was turned at Peter's as if they were embroiled in a torturous love affair.

'Don't what?'

'Get narky,' my mother said, rattling the ice in her tumbler before taking a sip.

'I'm too tired for all this,' I said standing up.

My mother slammed her glass on the side table. 'Sit down.'

I slumped back into the sofa, sliding my eyes back and forth across the picture rail that we had fixed in there, exactly ten inches from the ceiling.

Sitting forward, I said, 'If we'd told you about Prague, we would've had to tell everyone.'

'I'm not worried about what I was or wasn't told, I'm worried about what Rosie knows.'

I glared at Peter, assuming he had persuaded my mother that it was best for Rosie to know the truth, after all these years, as though either of them could possibly understand it from my point of view. 'So it's two against one, is it?'

'Stop being so childish,' my mother snapped.

'I've never felt right about telling her and I still don't. Especially now. Sorry,' I sighed, sulkily, sounding very un-sorry.

My mother sat up straighter, and closed her eyes for longer than a blink.

'You did the right thing.'

I was flummoxed, and I looked to Peter and back at my mother. 'Really?'

'Yes, darling. You did it for her own good.'

I was then embarrassed by her support, unused to it. I didn't know what to do with myself or what to say. My throat crunched with un-cried tears. Ten years of holding it back, ten years of unnecessary guilt.

'I did it for my own good too,' I said, my voice wobbling.

My mother came around the table and knelt by me, squeezing my knees with her hands. 'You've been so strong.'

'I don't know though, Mum, I don't know. Look at us now.'

Had I? Was it strength or weakness? Certainly, my mother's support would make it easier to continue as we were.

My mother returned to her armchair. 'Well, Peter and I were talking about this. If she found out so close to the hearing, it'd be destabilising, actually, you know, potentially disastrous. Is there any chance, any chance at all that she could have overheard anything at any point?'

'She didn't need to overhear, I pretty much told her.'

'Peter said you reassured her it wasn't true.'

Turning to Peter, I asked him, 'You still think she believed me?'

'Yes,' he replied simply, brushing a hand through his hair. I so wanted to believe it.

'I have an idea,' my mother said, sitting forward. 'Do you have any old photos of when you were pregnant with her?'

'You think that would reassure her?'

'Might be worth a try. You and Jackie used to love looking at yourselves in baby photographs,' she grinned.

'Did we?'

'You were so sweet.'

We beamed at each other, mother and daughter, rebooting the love.

'We've got those lovely ones that you took in the south of France by the lavender fields, Peter, remember?'

'The last holiday we ever enjoyed,' Peter joked whimsically.

'One thing though, does she know what an egg donor is?' my mother asked.

'Of course not,' I guffawed. 'She's only ten.'

'They're frighteningly well informed these days,' my mother added.

'There is no way she'd jump to that conclusion. I think the photograph idea is brilliant.'

'She'll see where she *really* comes from,' Peter said, smiling shyly at me.

My mother held her glass up to me, and announced proudly, 'Indeed. She's a Campbell girl all right.'

I swallowed away a fountain of tears. 'Yes, she is, isn't she?'

'And a Bradley, thank you very much,' Peter added.

'You're probably in there somewhere,' my mother laughed, rolling her eyes at him.

Relief and elation made me giddy for a few moments, until I thought of my sister.

'What about Jackie?'

'We can't tell her too. It's too risky,' my mother said.

'But she'll be so hurt.'

'How can she be if she never finds out?'

'Right, yes, I suppose,' I muttered, feeling uneasy, my sense of shame reinforced.

For the rest of the evening, I tried very hard to maintain a buoyant mood. All three of us did. We upheld the pretence of being a normal family, although we probably sensed that normal was a thing of the past.

I wondered whether there was a part of me that had wanted my mother to challenge our decision. Her surprising and unquestioning acquiescence and her desire to keep the truth hidden away had prodded at a ball of shame, lodged somewhere deep inside me that I hadn't known was there. I was taken right back to the doctor's box of tissues on the mantle, to my inability to cry, to the strange embarrassment I had felt about being infertile, about being imperfect, about being desperate. The memory of those messy, disturbing feelings overwhelmed me. I wanted to crawl into bed and pull the duvet over my head and sleep like the dead.

I looked at my watch. My jaw clicked as I yawned.

'I've got to be up in four hours for an early meeting.'

Tomorrow, I would be slinking out of the house before everyone woke up.

# CHAPTER FORTY-SEVEN

*URGENT*
*Dear Mrs E (I can't spell it, sorry)*
    *Can I come to your shed please? Please bring some*
*chocolate biscuits.*

*Love,*
*Rosie.*
*P.S. I really like the dark chocolate digestives.*

Mira had found Rosie's note in the blue bucket just before she left for work. The lined notepaper had almost broken apart in her fingers, suggesting it had been in the damp air all night. Mira had sent back a mini-gingerbread man wrapped with a reply:

*Dear Rosie,*
    *Do please come over any time after four thirty today.*
*Eat his toes off first!*

*Love Mrs E.*

The blue bucket had flung itself about on the dank line as though the gingerbread man was on a rough sea, which had made Mira giggle. It reminded her of how much joy she had felt when Rosie had first moved in and delivered her *I'm called Rosie and I'm 3* note, which she had kept in a drawer with all her other cards from her children at Woodland's.

Having returned the latest blue bucket message, Mira had been distracted all day at school, counting down the minutes until she could leave.

At four o'clock she raced to the supermarket to buy the biscuits, and then to the garden centre for some seeds, which she took straight to the shed.

With two pairs of socks on to keep her toes warm, and the radio to keep her company, she shook out the soil into green trays ready for her cabbage and leek seeds.

There had been no time or date on the note from Rosie, but she suspected she meant after school sometime today. Or maybe after dark. Either way, Mira planned to wait in the shed all night if she had to.

It had been about a quarter past five when Rosie had burst in on her.

'Did you get the biscuits?' Rosie said, out of breath. Her ponytail skewed to one side, a sore rough patch edging her bottom lip.

Mira gave her the packet of biscuits.

'I'm really hungry,' she said, picking at the packet frantically, checking behind her at the door, her breathing ragged.

'Give them back to me, Rosie,' Mira said sternly.

Rosie stopped fidgeting, and handed them over.

'Sit down and calm down.'

She sat down, but her teeth bit at her bottom lip and her eyes darted behind her frequently.

'Nobody followed you here did they?'

'No, definitely not,' she said earnestly.

Mira gave her a biscuit. Rosie nibbled it around the edge with quick mouse-like bites. 'I've' – nibble – 'got' – nibble – 'to get' – nibble, nibble – 'get back in ten minutes.'

Mira was bitterly disappointed. She had hoped for some more time with Rosie.

'Your note said *urgent*. Is something the matter?'

'It's so urgent I can't even tell you.' She was leaning forward, gesticulating at Mira, waving the half-chewed biscuit above her head.

'You know you can trust me.'

'Cross your heart, hope to die, stick a cupcake in your eye?'

Mira tried not to laugh at this reworking of the phrase. 'Yes, cross my heart.'

'I think I'm adopted,' Rosie blurted out, stuffing the rest of the biscuit into her mouth and taking another.

Mira wiped her mouth, tasting metallic earth, soil across her lips. She stared bug-eyed at Rosie, who she had never thought looked like her mother. Her whole body flushed with heat.

At first Mira couldn't hear any sound coming out of her mouth, so she cleared her throat. 'Why do you think that?' But it had come out too loudly.

Rosie's chin dimpled and her face crumpled. 'I heard her say that Catrina Doo-doo Shitface or something mega weird was my *real* mummy,' she cried, her face mottling red and white. The bad language was like needles in Mira's eardrums.

'Are you certain?'

Rosie spoke through sobs. 'I opened my window in my bedroom to tell Mummy not to go in the car but then Granny Helen came out and they argued and I heard it.'

Mira knew she should go to Rosie, to hug her, but she was rooted to the spot, looking on at the child as though she were a stranger or an apparition.

'When did this all happen?'

'Last night.'

'Didn't you ask them about it today?'

'Mummy had a work meeting and I was too scared to ask Daddy or Granny Helen.'

'Why were you scared to ask your daddy?'

'I'm worried that my daddy isn't my real daddy either,' she cried, heaving out her tears, her little shoulders rounded, her arms wrapped across her stomach as if it ached.

'Shut up,' Mira snapped.

Rosie held her breath, stunned by Mira's outburst, but her face fell apart again and quieter tears rolled, one after the other, down her cheeks. 'I thought you were nice,' she sniffed.

'I am nice, but you don't want Mummy or Daddy to hear us, do you?' Mira knew that nobody could hear them. The shed was too far from the house.

Rosie's expression darkened. 'Why don't you call them Peter and Gemma?'

Mira didn't like her melodramatics and she turned to her soil trays and ripped open a seed packet.

'It's not such a bad thing to be adopted, is it?'

'What? Are you kidding me?' Rosie shrieked.

Mira's jaw tightened. 'You've got a roof over your head and food on the table, haven't you? It's not so bad.'

'How can you say that? It would be the worst thing in the whole world!'

'It depends who your birth parents are, doesn't it? They might be murderers and rapists.'

Rosie looked petrified. 'What are rapists?'

'Horrible, horrible people.'

'If they're horrible then that means I'm probably all horrible too, just like them.'

'Don't be silly, you're not all horrible.'

'Mummy thinks I am.'

'Your *mummy* is the horrible one.'

'Don't say that! I want her to be my real mummy!' Rosie sobbed, her face paler with each juddering breath.

Mira raised her voice, 'Your real mummy is the mummy who gives birth to you, and don't you forget it.' Black spots were swimming before her eyes and headiness weakened her knees. 'Your real mummy loves you *so much*.' Mira groaned, dropping to her knees, holding the side of the workbench with both hands as she let her head hang between her arms.

She breathed, short and sharp, in and out, holding on to the bench. Her mind blanked, and short-circuited to the past. She was in labour, holding onto a metal hospital bed, hanging her head, holding the plastic mask to her face, delirious with the pain. The stretching and cramping was more like a ripping of flesh; a torture wrack rigged to her womb, twisting the handle, pulling her insides apart, until she thought she might die. Never could she have imagined such agony, such a possession. She moaned as the contraction began and, as it built to its excruciating heights, she roared like an animal.

'Push, Mira, push, that's it. I can see Baby's head, good, that's it, push... And again, good girl, push,' the midwife insisted.

And then similar to a black-out, the final push, where she left her body behind to break through barriers of pain into the unimaginable new world of motherhood.

But where was her baby? Where did he go? He was there on her chest, warm and mucky, ice-blue skin, dry lips parted for a nipple, black shining eyes searching for hers. Where has he gone? He was there a minute ago. He was there.

'Where is he?' she cried, patting her chest, straightening upright on her knees.

'Are you okay, Mrs E?'

'Where is my baby?'

'What baby?'

A little girl was standing next to her. Wide-eyed, tear-stained. She grabbed the girl around her head, feeling the warmth of her young cheek on her chest.

'Are you okay?' the girl repeated.

'I'm fine. I'm fine,' Mira panted, coming to, releasing the past, enduring a surge of love for the baby she had lost. She clung to Rosie as though she was he.

Rosie pushed Mira's arms away. 'You're squeezing me to death.'

'Sorry, pet,' Mira said, suddenly revolted by her, the imposter who was not her baby. 'Off you trot. Mrs E's got a bit of seeding to do. Off you trot,' Mira said, shooing Rosie out.

# CHAPTER FORTY-EIGHT

We were lying next to each other staring at the ceiling. The radio alarm clock was muttering away in the background. Neither of us had had a wink of sleep. Rosie had woken up twice in the night after complaining of a headache.

'You're still worried?'

'Don't be daft.'

'As I keep saying, I really don't think she hit it hard enough.'

'You're sure.'

'Yes, honestly.' But I was feeling jaded, infected by his worry and I began to doubt myself. 'But if she's still got a headache this morning, we should probably get it looked at.'

The second time Rosie had woken, at about two in the morning, I had talked Peter down from taking her to A & E, guessing that her wakefulness had been emotional rather than physical.

When I had come in from work yesterday evening, having missed her on the morning after our big blow-up, she had been grumpy and tearful over her maths homework – not surprisingly – and, rightly or wrongly, I had not talked to her about our row and my exit, unable to bear a face-off. I had known it was the wimp's way out to pretend nothing had happened, but I had been in a volatile mood too. After very little sleep, I was too tired for Rosie's hysteria.

'Symptoms of concussion can appear days after the accident, you know.'

'Yes, so you've said a hundred times.'

'I didn't see what happened clearly enough.'

'All I wanted was the diary and she just wouldn't move off it...' I stopped. Did he really want me to go through it again?

'Don't worry about it.'

'Peter, I really think she's fine. It's more likely she was anxious after our fight. I should have talked to her last night. I was just too bloody knackered.'

'Maybe book an appointment anyway.'

I thought of Miranda Slater and DC Miles.

'It will look bad if she goes to the doctor's.'

Peter frowned at me. 'I don't bloody well care.'

'Of course. I didn't mean...' I trailed off, realising how awful that had sounded.

'Hmmm,' he mumbled, climbing out of bed.

Without uttering another word to me, Peter dressed and left the bedroom. His bad mood unsettled me profoundly. If Peter wasn't on my side, who would be? I had a palpitation, a precursor to all-out, blinding panic. Peter was the only one who understood me and loved me and defended me and put up with me. And we were having another baby together. I couldn't survive all this without his support.

Stiff with self-loathing, I lay in bed until I heard my mother next door, turning on taps in her bathroom, which usually meant she would go straight in to wake up Noah and Rosie.

I wanted to see Rosie first.

'Rosie?' I whispered, sitting on her bed. 'Rosie? Time to wake up, poppet.'

A smile appeared on her face. Her eyes fluttered open and the scowl appeared instantly. The duvet was yanked from under me to cover her head.

'Can we talk?'

No reply.

'How's your head?'

Again, nothing.

'Rosie, do you want to take the morning off school today? I'll call and tell them you've got a doctor's appointment or something.'

'You're going to *lie?*' she mumbled from under the duvet.

'Well if your head doesn't feel any better we're going to have to go anyway. So it's not really a lie.'

'A little white lie.'

'For now, yes.'

'I don't want to go to the doctor's.'

'Either way it'd be nice to stay at home for a bit, wouldn't it?'

'Why?' she asked suspiciously.

'I thought we could cosy up with a hot choccy. Just me and you.'

I imagined Miranda Slater peering in through the window, spying us alone together during school hours, and calling the police.

'But you have to go to work like *always.*'

'I'll tell Lisa I'm working from home.'

'Another *lie.*'

'It's up to you,' I sighed, standing up. Her uniform skirt was crumpled on the floor. While I waited for her answer, I picked it up, plucked off the odd leaf, and placed it back neatly into the drawer. Her tights were muddied at the knees. I wished she would change into her scruffy clothes when she was den-building, but I would not be saying anything about it this morning. I stuffed them in the laundry basket.

She piped up finally. 'Hot chocolate's got *sugar* in it *by the way.*'

'I know. It doesn't matter.'

I stuck a few loose pencils into her pen-pot, feigning nonchalance.

'Can I have frothy-coffee milk in it too?'

'Sure.' I smiled, rescued. 'After Daddy and Noah are gone we'll get it on the go. You can stay in your jammies if you like.'

*

Downstairs, I frothed the milk in our coffee machine and heated up two chocolate croissants from the freezer.

Upstairs, my mother remained in the house, in her room 'reading', just in case Miranda Slater paid us a surprise visit.

I laid the table for two and sat down with the photograph album under my drumming fingers.

The album cover was embossed with silver: *2006–2009. The Baby Years: Rosie and Noah Bradley*. At great expense, I had hired a company to collate all of our photographs from our computers to make hard copy albums. It was like looking through the book of a life perfectly lived. There weren't any unfortunate photographs of post-pregnancy tummies or of broken cots in bad holiday rentals or of pooey nappies around ankles or of double-chinned snoozers in the sun. All of those rejects were on a memory stick somewhere long lost.

When Rosie came in, I jumped up. Her ponytail from last night was still in her hair, scrunched round by one ear and her pyjama top was back-to-front. I noticed the raw skin under her bottom lip and resisted the urge to get some balm. No nagging or picking or neatening allowed, I told myself sternly. Anyway, her cheeks were bright as though she had slept much better than Peter and me.

'My head doesn't hurt any more,' she said, sitting down. 'I don't need to go to the doctor.'

'Oh phew, good, I'm so glad it's better,' I said, kissing where she had hit it. 'I'm so sorry, so, so sorry,' I added, knowing how inadequate my apology was, wishing with every fibre of my being that I could take back our fight. The guilt was sliding around inside me like a black serpent.

She let me hug her, but she didn't reciprocate. 'That's okay.'

When I brought out a chocolate lollipop stir-in from the treat jar, she gasped, 'Am I allowed one of those?'

'Yup.' I placed the lollipop and a mug of frothy milk in front of her.

'What's that?' she asked, pointing at the album as she stirred the lollipop into her milk.

'I want to show you some photos.'

She frowned, looking like Peter had earlier. 'Of what?'

'Me, when I had you in my tummy.'

Her whole face lit up. 'You have photographs of me in your tummy?'

'Yes, of course I do, darling.' I reached for her hand and held it. 'You've seen them before. When you were little.'

'I don't remember.'

'Can I see?'

'Don't you want to finish your drink?'

She pushed it aside. 'It's too hot. Can I please see now?'

So I opened the album. As I flicked through briefly, I wished I could show Rosie some of the reject photographs. The funny anecdotes that went with them would make her laugh. As it was, I only had the glossed-over version of our past together, which seemed suddenly woefully simplistic.

Nevertheless, I started from the beginning, which was what this was all about.

'That's you in there,' I said, pointing to my stomach in a series of four cheesy soft-focus photographs. I wore a white cotton maternity dress and a floppy hat and I stood in front of a field of vibrant purple.

Rosie brought her face up really close to the page. 'How do I know it's me?'

'What do you mean? Because I'm telling you it's you, silly. See? June 2006.' I pointed at the black italics underneath. 'You were born a month later.'

I tried to turn the page, but Rosie stopped me. She seemed fascinated by the photographs.

'Where's Daddy?'

'He was taking the photos.'

There was a long pause.

'So who's Katrina Doobik then?'

It was like a thump in my head. 'What?'

'You told Granny Helen that she was my real mummy.'

'You misheard,' I said, my stomach lurching, my head spinning off my shoulders.

'No... I didn't...' she stuttered, her lips beginning to quiver.

'Yes, you did.'

'But...'

My mother's words rang in my ears. If she found out now, three weeks before the hearing, it would be catastrophic. Our family would meltdown. It was essential to maintain the equilibrium. The tightly run unit would only survive if I stuck to the script. Rosie had to fall into line.

'That's final. You misheard, and that's that. Okay? Look I'm showing you evidence and you still don't believe me.'

'YOU'RE A LIAR!' she screamed and she tore out the page of the album. 'That's probably a fake or something. Look it's all blurry and weird like you you've smudged paint on it or something.' And she screwed it into a ball and chucked it at my head.

I stood up, incensed by what she had done.

'*YOU'RE* the *little liar*, young lady. Who the hell do you think you are?'

'Who *cares*?'

'Don't speak to me like that!'

'Shut up!'

'How dare you? It is unacceptable to—'

'Shut UP!'

'If you carry on like this I'll—'

'SHUT UP!'

'What are you trying to do to me?' I howled, rising from the table.

Rosie repeated 'shut up', 'shut up', 'shut up', again and again and again like a mantra that had the power to eat into my sanity.

'STOP IT!'

'Shut up, shut up, shut up, shut up, shut up, shut up, shut up,' she screeched. I needed to leave the room but she pulled at me and yanked at my jumper until it cracked at the seams.

'I said STOP THAT!'

And then my mother appeared at the door. Her small face was stern, her milky blue eyes fearful.

'What's going on in here?'

'Mummy's a LIAR!' Rosie screeched and wailed, and clasped my arm, yanking it with all her might, her head pressing into my ribs.

'DON'T TOUCH ME!' I was trying to pull my arm away from her, but she was gripping on too tightly, an alien creature suckered to me, sapping my life force. Violence swarmed my brain. I imagined my hand rise above her head and coming down on her, anything to make her stop.

To Mum I begged, 'I can't cope, Mum, I can't cope. Get her away from me.'

'Rosie, come here darling.' She moved towards her, as though moving towards a wild animal whom she wanted to befriend and tame. Prizing her off me, she held her hand and drew her back, protecting me from her, protecting her from me.

'Look what she's done!' I brandished the destroyed photographs at my mother. My hands were quivering, more terrified of what I could have done than what Rosie had actually done.

'Okay, calm down, Gemma.'

'Me, calm down? Are you fucking kidding me? She's the one who needs to calm down!'

I bent down low and pointed right into Rosie's face. 'D'you realise that Mummy could go to prison because of your lies to DC Miles? And do you know what'll happen? You won't be able to live with me ever again. Is that what you want? Really? *Really?*'

'That's ENOUGH, Gemma,' my mother hollered.

Rosie cowered behind my mother. 'My head hurts,' she sobbed, holding the back of her head.

And more quietly, my mother added, 'You're frightening her.'

I was dumbstruck, tranquilized. My skin turned to gooseflesh. Taking a step back, I thought of what might have happened if my mother hadn't walked in.

I straightened up. 'I have to get ready for work,' I said mechanically, walking away, leaving behind the totemic union of my mother and Rosie.

As I went upstairs, I caught a snippet of their conversation. 'But Granny Helen, I thought I was one of those *adopted* children.'

My mother laughed. 'Goodness gracious, you've got an active imagination, my darling. Come on, let's...'

But I switched off from them, closed my ears, took myself upstairs where I dressed and made my face up and left the house without saying goodbye.


I asked Peter to meet me in London after work, as we used to do often before the children.

The restaurant had been a nostalgic choice of mine. Peter and I had shared many candlelit dinners there in the past. For this reason, it might have been a bad choice. Possibly too romantic for the purpose. Then again, maybe that's exactly why I chose it. If Peter didn't like what I was going to say, he would be too self-conscious to cause a fuss, and he was too much of a gentleman to walk out and leave me there.

To be honest, I wasn't even sure how he would greet me.

I was already seated at the table when he arrived, and as soon as I saw him I had a pang of regret about what I had planned.

Sixteen years ago, when he had walked into the cinema foyer to meet me on a blind date, his elegant features had rendered me weak at the knees. Before we had met that first time, Jacs had told me two facts about him: he grew up in the countryside and he had been in the year below Richard at their primary school. Knowing these two facts, I made two snap judgements: he wore green wax jackets like Richard and he was emotionally stunted – like Richard. A photograph of him in a fashionable black pea coat standing next to a very beautiful brunette in shiny red heels, who I had been told was his ex-girlfriend, smashed at least one of those assumptions to pieces, which I replaced with another: I wasn't pretty enough for him. But the doubts had melted away from the moment he shook my hand and said, 'Gosh, you're much lovelier in the flesh,' with a familiarity – but not a hint of suaveness – that suggested he had known me all my life. He later admitted that it had simply tumbled out of his mouth when he saw me, but that it had ruined the whole movie for him, throughout which he had worried he had come on too strong and put me off before we'd even started.

Sixteen years on, I loved him even more than I had at first sight. I knew him better now, but my instincts about him had been right. He had turned out to be just as kind and trustworthy as I had suspected he was, if not more. When he kissed me under the streetlight, when our souls met, he became mine, as much as I became his, and I dreamed that it would always be that way.

Until this morning – when he'd barely been able to look me in the eye – I had been confident our feelings were as unshakeable as they had been back then.

I wanted one last shot to prove to him that anyone would buckle under the pressure Rosie put me under. He was the only one who had seen her in action, at her worst. Even a living saint would struggle to stay composed. However ashamed I was of what had happened, I needed him to stick by me, to believe in me, to know in his heart of hearts that I would never willingly hurt her. If he believed in me, then I could believe in myself.

The waiter led Peter to our table. We held each other's gaze as he wove through the tables, just as we had when I walked down the aisle towards him, the rest of the room blurring into nothingness.

We were shy with one another, more so than on that first date.

'You were so angry with me this morning.'

'No,' he said, shaking out his napkin onto his lap before we had ordered.

'The photo album idea backfired rather spectacularly.'

'I know, I spoke to Helen.'

'Mum called you?'

'I called the house to check on you.'

'Oh,' I said, feeling the shame burning away the words I wanted to say. I wanted to tell him my side of the story, explain how foul Rosie had been, how intransigent, what a brat, how she'd ruined our photo album.

'What are we going to do?' he asked.

I laughed without smiling. At least he still believed in me enough to ask me for solutions.

'That's why I wanted to meet you here,' I said, leaning forward on my elbows, trying to be confident about this particular solution. 'I think it's best I take myself out of the equation for a bit and spend a few days in London.'

'Where will you stay?' There was a hint of panic in his voice.

'At Mum's.'

'Have you asked her?'

'She won't mind.'

'It's quite drastic.'

'Honestly, I can't be around Rosie right now, Peter. Surely you see it's getting out of hand?'

'Have you spoken to Philippa Letwin about it?'

'She says we have to do what's right for the family as a whole.'

'How do we know what that is?'

'As long as we put the children first.'

I wanted him to say that they needed their mother; that I was the one they needed first and foremost. I held my breath, hoping to hear it.

'It'll be a clean break from all the fighting I suppose.'

My heart sank. Yes, a clean break. Nice and clean. Just how we liked it.

I sighed. 'Philippa said the courts won't look on the move unfavourably at least. If it comes to it.'

'Will it come to it?'

'That depends on Rosie.'

We paused. A never-ending reel of worry to unravel every time I thought of what could happen to me, to the baby, to us, if she didn't change her statement. The unutterable public humiliation of standing in a Magistrate's Court on 4 December pleading not guilty to the prosecutor's charges of child abuse; the financial ruin of the legal fees if it went to the Crown Court; and, of course, prison. All of these horror stories flickered through my mind, obscuring the most terrifying of them all: losing Rosie and Noah and the baby. That was literally unimaginable.

As though reading my mind, Peter moved on. 'Your mum has been amazing with her.'

'Who'd have thought?'

'I was staggered by how well she took it all.'

'Yes,' I said vaguely, unsure.

'We can't make any decisions about what we tell Rosie now anyhow,' he said.

'When I'm back home we'll talk about it.'

I had a panicky flash of never going back home, of weeks away from them. They were everything to me and I was walking away from them, for who knows how long. For their own good, I told myself. I suddenly understood how suicidal women justified driving into a lake to leave their children orphans. If you truly believed they were better off without you, then what else was there to do?

'Look after Noah, won't you? He's getting lost in all this.'

Peter grasped on to my forearms across the linen tablecloth, as though pinning me down. 'I'll miss you.' Tears shone from his eyelashes, framing bloodshot eyes. He looked as frightened as I felt.

'I'll miss you too,' I whispered, recharged by the strength of his hands on my wrists, wondering if I'd care if the whole world crumbled around us, as long as I still had Peter and the children. 'I'm so sorry.'

'You can get help, you know.'

'With what?'

'There are groups you can go to.'

I whipped back my arms from under his and wrung my fingers under the table. I wanted to tie them in knots to stem the fury. I couldn't believe it. Ten years of sharing the burden of Rosie, gone. All my hope drained away.

'It was an accident,' I hissed.

His eyes had deadened, dried as though never wet, and he looked to the waiter to order the bill.

'Helen said she's still got a bad headache.'

'That's rubbish. She told me it had gone this morning,' I scoffed.

Peter looked at me coldly. 'I have to get back.'

'But we haven't eaten?'

'I said I'd take her to the after-hours doctor if she wasn't better.'

There was no way I could tell him not to worry about Rosie. It would seem callous or irresponsible.

'Call me to let me know how she is,' I conceded.

He dropped forty pounds cash on the table and he left me there, alone. For the first time in our marriage.

Just as a drunken kiss or a punch to a stranger's jaw had the power to destroy lives overnight, my incautious, despairing shove of Rosie had injured her and destroyed us. The terrible thing, the worst thing, was that I could do nothing to take back that split-second switch to rage. Every second since was too late. I didn't know how I would live with the guilt.

# CHAPTER FORTY-NINE

*Dear Rosie Rabbit,*

*I would like to say sorry for my funny turn the other day. You were very caring and brave.*

*I spoke of my baby boy, who has been a big secret in my life. You are the only soul in the world who knows (apart from my family of course). Not even my dear darling Barry knows. If I told him, he would think I was a terrible person.*

*On 7 May 1982, when I was only fifteen years old – not that much older than you! – I gave birth to a beautiful baby boy whom I had to give up for adoption. He would be 34 years old now. There is not a day that goes by when I don't think of him. Sometimes I wonder if I see him on the street or in the supermarket! Imagine that!*

*I try ever so hard to be strong about it, but when his birthdays come up or when something reminds me of him, I am afraid I go to pieces. You see, I was forced to sign the papers by my mother. I thought I would die from heartbreak. I certainly never imagined how I could go on living. It is hard to describe how wild I went when the two ladies took him away from me in the hospital when he was only fifteen days old. There has never been a more devastating moment. I didn't even care what the nurses and doctors thought of me! It was like having my heart and soul ripped from my chest and honestly, my dear Rosie, I think I still have that hole where my heart was. If I didn't hear it beating, I don't think I would know for sure it was still there. They say time is a healer. What a load of codswallop!*

*He was poorly when he was born. I always wondered whether it was his way of staying with me a little bit longer in the hospital. He needed his mummy's milk, you see. I still remember every tiny detail of his face because I used to stare at him when he was feeding from me. He had a rather large nose – a bit like mine! – and thick glossy black hair – a bit like his useless father (who was terribly vain about his hair)! His mouth had a dip in the middle, which lined up symmetrically with the deep groove in his chin. I imagine he is a handsome fellow now. But I would say that, wouldn't I? Every parent is a little biased about their children.*

*So, it's not surprising I can be a little strange sometimes. Please forgive me for scaring you. I feel very well again now. And maybe I can show you some photographs of me when I was pregnant, to make you laugh! I was not a pretty sight, let me tell you.*

*Please don't be sad when you read of my loss. About sixteen years ago, he would have turned eighteen years old, which means he could have contacted me if he wished. I spent his eighteenth year hiding the post from Barry to check for a letter from him, but I gave up in the end. Deep down, I have always known that he is probably too happy to bother with me.*

*Please do come by to see me again soon. I very much hope things are easier at home for you.*

*With much love,*
*Mrs E (I won't spell it. I like Mrs E!)*

\*

Mira folded up the letter and slid it carefully into an envelope and wrote *Rosie Bradley* neatly on the front. To Mira, it was like a delicate relic that even the slightest smear or crinkle could destroy or sully. The weather had been dry over night, but she would find a plastic sandwich bag to wrap it in to prevent the damp from the garden getting to it, and a few sweeties for luck. It was likely Rosie would check the blue bucket straight after school.

For now, she left it in the centre of the bureau and she went upstairs to find her watch for work. The stairs seemed to leave her more breathless than usual. Writing about her son had taken everything out of her, but it had given her a thrill, as though the hope that they would be reunited one day was nearer somehow. As though sixteen years of his silence had not passed.

She heard the front door open.

'What have you forgotten?' she called down to Barry.

'Just those bills with our address on! I need them to collect my rake from the post office!'

'Okay, love,' she called back casually, and then with a start, remembered where the bills were kept. She charged downstairs, sick to the stomach with fear. If he saw the letter on the bureau addressed to Rosie, Mira didn't know how she would explain.

When she arrived at the bureau, she found that Barry was already holding the opened letter in his hand. His eyes behind his darkened lens suggested he had managed to read enough to know everything.

The shame of looking at him was like hot pokers thrust into her eye sockets.

Mira snatched the letter, turned on her heels and skittered out of the house to rapidly wheel the bucket and letter over to Rosie before Barry caught up with her. It was important she explained her behaviour to Rosie, or she risked losing her too. Barry was not going to get in the way of that.

*

Every second of her day at school was torture. She tried to keep herself upright.

She was irritable with the children, especially the ones who had forgotten their PE kit, and snappy with Patricia, who seemed to be blaming her for the fact that the children didn't know the words to their Christmas songs, even though it wasn't yet December.

At least the pettiness of her school day distracted her from the rift that had split open her home life. Every time she thought of it, she caught her breath. It was unfathomable that Barry now knew about her baby boy, whom she had managed to keep secret for all of their marriage. She couldn't truly believe it had happened. So she soldiered on, the severed connection between body and mind allowing her to function on a low-level, emergency-only setting.

Barry wasn't at home when she got back from work. Weary from the pretence of being normal, she plodded up the stairs, desperate to soak in her bath. Thankfully, Barry was bound to be late back from Boscarny House, where the lady of the house would not let him go until every thread of grass and every leaf was where it should be.

But just as her tired limbs were enveloped in the silky warmth of the bath, Barry came into the bathroom, carrying two glasses of red wine and a bowl of cheese puffs, her favourite, on a tray. Aside from everything that he had learnt about her today, he was thoughtful enough to bring her what she needed most: routine, comfort, and a little luxury to remind her that life would carry on. He was telling her that nothing had to change.

He didn't say anything. He simply sat in the wicker chair. Next door, all was quiet.

They both sipped their wine in the tense, loaded silence. Part of her now wanted Rosie's screams to fill the emptiness.

She said finally, 'It was the right thing to do to give him up.'

Little ripples of water were spreading in circles from her heart.

'Of course it was, love.'

'I gave him a better life.'

'You were fifteen years old,' he murmured, shaking his head slowly back and forth.

'He was the only man I ever slept with. Until you.'

'Man?'

'Boy,' Mira corrected. She couldn't tell him everything, not everything. There were some secrets that were worth taking to the grave.

'Does he know?'

'He didn't want anything to do with it.'

'That's probably a blessing.'

'He'll have a proper father who loves him now.'

'And a mother,' Barry added.

Mira swallowed hard, but she could not bring herself to talk of another 'proper' mother. She was his mother.

'I put my name on the register but he never got in contact, so that's that.'

Barry reached for some crisps and stuffed a large handful into his mouth from his palm.

'So he must be happy,' Mira added.

'And you're happy too,' Barry stated, as though he needed it to be so.

Mira hesitated. 'Sometimes I look at a man's features on the street or in cars or in the supermarket and wonder if it could be him.'

'Your paths would never cross.'

'How do you know?'

'That stuff only happens in films.'

'Life is stranger than the films sometimes.'

'Anyhow, it wouldn't matter either way.'

'But what if I want to see him?' she said quietly.

Barry crashed his glass down on the basin side. 'That's not your right!'

Her mouth fell open. Wide-eyed, she said calmly, 'Careful, that's our wedding crystal.'

'He has his own life and you have yours and don't you forget it,' Barry said, pointing his finger aggressively.

Over twenty-five years of marriage and she had never seen him lose his temper. It was shocking, riling even. How dare he?

'His life came from my body. He *is* my life.'

'How can you say that?' Barry yelled, standing up. 'I'm your life!'

The bath water fell stony cold. There was something frightening in Barry's eyes and she wanted to get out of the bath, get out of his confined space, but she did not want to be vulnerable and naked in front of him. She did not want him to sneer at her used-up belly, which had once held that baby boy.

'Keep your voice down,' Mira said, glancing over at the window, fearful that the Bradleys would hear. The irony of that.

'This is my house, I can shout all I like!' He was taut with anger, rooted to the spot with it. Mira imagined a wind blowing, turning him to stone. His finger pointed at her in accusation.

Mira held her nose and sank down into the bathwater, covering her head, holding her breath. She would stay there until he was gone. One, two, three, four, she counted. Thirty-three, thirty-four.

A deadened flow of Barry's ranting reached her from the outside.

Then silence. She couldn't hold her breath much longer, but she would. Sixty-one, sixty-two. If she died here, she didn't care. It was pleasant to be away from it all. It was easier; though she wondered how she could anchor her head under when her instinct would be to gasp for air. She imagined Barry's merciful fingers as a bracelet around her neck, pinning her to the bottom.

Then two arms shot down into the water and pulled her body out. She spluttered into Barry's chest, her body soaking his jumper. 'Mira, my Mira, oh my love, don't do that, I'm sorry, I'm so sorry,' he sobbed.

'Let's never talk about it again,' Mira said, cold flesh in his arms.

'Never, never,' he agreed, kissing her head.

# CHAPTER FIFTY

*Dear Mrs E,*

*Thank you very much for your letter. I feel very sad for you. When my dwarf rabbit ran away from us I cried all night. He was black with a white ear. Mummy hated him. She probably killed him. She hates everything that I like best. I think she has finally got sick of me now. She even moved to London because she hurt my head. When Daddy took me to the doctor he wanted me to tell him all about when Mummy slapped me. It was really difficult. What I had said to Miss Miles was more like a story and it is hard to remember a story I made up from like ages and ages ago. It was like three weeks ago. I make up gazillions of stories every day in my head. Do you think it is hard to remember stuff too? Please could you help me to remember what I said to Miss Miles?*

*Don't be sad about your baby. Unicorns are magic and if they know you are sad they will bring your baby to you on a rainbow. But Granny Helen thinks I have an active imagination because she told me that I was not one of those adopted children.*

*Please can I come to see you if you are there?*

*Love,*
*Rosie*

# CHAPTER FIFTY-ONE

'You moved back home, have you?' John said grinning, handing me my mother's house keys.

John wore the same circular wire spectacles that he had worn for twenty years. They were still trying to sit on the top of a nose that was not designed for spectacles.

'Thanks,' I said, taking the keys. 'Only for a few days.'

As teenagers, my sister and I had often knocked on his door when we were locked out. My situation now had strange echoes of those teenage mishaps, when I'd had dramatic imaginings of being stuck outside in the cold all night. But John or Sarah had rescued us. Just as they had done in the early days of my mother's single-parent status, when they had taken us in on the afternoons she worked late.

'What's it like having your mum living with you again?' He pushed the bridge of his glasses up and I watched them slip down again.

'Not as bad as I expected,' I beamed.

'Another one on the way, I hear.'

'Three months gone.' I looked down at my belly covered by my suit jacket, wondering when the jacket button would have to be left open.

'And I hear Noah likes chocolate muffins and Rosie never wants her hair cut.'

'Mum's informed you well,' I laughed, remembering that Imogen's friend had had such a terrible time with Social Services.

I wondered how much he knew about my situation now. 'Imogen still in New Zealand?'

He nodded with a glum smile. 'It's a long way for a cup of tea.'

I glanced behind him at the stacks of newspapers lining the walls. When Sarah was alive, the hallway was always swept and clear.

'At least you get a sunny Christmas every year.'

He grimaced. 'Anyhow, can't be helped,' he said handing me a tin of cat food. 'Minxy likes this horrible stuff. And don't forget to water the spider plants.'

'I might kill them off on purpose.'

He laughed conspiratorially. 'Those things'll out last us all.'

'Thank you, John,' I said, grateful to him for still living there.

Instead of going down the steps and around and up again to my mother's front door, I stepped over the low wall dividing their small front gardens, for old time's sake.

'Old habits die hard, eh?' John said, winking at me as he closed his door.

Inside, the old smells of childhood hit me in a comforting wave. Dusty books and cooking spices. Then the creak of the wobbly floorboard, third from the left, the crack that wiggled up the wall next to the radiator cover, the brush of the spider plants that dangled from the hallway table. I was home.

When I had brought my friends back as a child I had been embarrassed by the stacks of books in corners, the mish-mash of different patterns on the copious throws and cushions, the muted light that was sucked up by the dark blue walls and jungle of plants in the window. But now I saw bohemian charm and style, unaffected by the decades of various trends of interior design that have come and gone. When I thought of the fortune I had spent on decorating our house, I cringed. There seemed so little point to it when I thought of how often I had wanted to tweak and change it since, wishing I had chosen wood panelling instead of tiles, or slatted blinds instead of curtains.

In her kitchen, I opened her cupboards to look for provisions. I was hungry after my thwarted supper with Peter. I hadn't stayed in the restaurant. Our waiter had passed me as I wove through the tables towards the door, and I was too embarrassed to say that I was leaving. I supposed Peter and I could never go back to that restaurant. A slump of regret weighed me down.

It felt strange to be in a kitchen without having to think about what Rosie and Noah wanted to eat. It didn't feel liberating to be without what I had so often considered a burden.

I decided to make tea instead.

Among the usual array of mismatched cups, I spotted a mug that took my breath away for a second. *World's Best Dad* it said on the side. It had been a birthday present for Dad from Jacs and me, a few years before he had announced he was moving out to live with Jill – his secretary. After he left, I had hidden the offending mug under the sink in the newly painted pink bathroom, behind the loo rolls. I hadn't wanted to break it or throw it out, I had simply wanted to get it out of my sight.

I couldn't believe my mother had found it and kept it. It reminded me of the other possession of my father's that she had kept after he left.

Urgently, I climbed the stairs two at a time to the loft room on the third floor, which had been my father's workspace. My stomach was looping in anticipation.

I expected the room to be different – crowded with boxes or transformed into my mother's study – but it was almost exactly as it had been. My mother had never allowed Jacs or me to commandeer it for a television den or a bedroom, telling us that she planned to get a lodger. A lodger that had never materialised.

The strip of oak that stretched along one wall was empty of his music books and scores and HB pencils, but his stool sat in the same place, centrally, as though he had only yesterday jumped off it, leaving it twisting around and around for Jacs and I to play on.

The leather armchair was pushed into the corner, and my mother's guitar was resting against the arm. In the eves by the window, there sat the chest that I had come up to look for.

The smell as I opened it brought back memories of me sitting crossed legged at the spot where I now knelt, waiting for my father to choose a piece of music for me to play.

I had never been any good at playing the guitar, unlike Jacs who had reached grade eight, but I had loved the attention and patience my father had given me when his large, calloused fingertips had prized my clumsy little fingers onto the right strings.

When we were small, we had not been allowed to rifle through the music scores, in case we ripped something precious, and I felt a little sinful for going through it now, as though he would know somehow.

*Frets and Fingers* with its brown cover picture and the dog-eared *Easy Guitar Songs* were still there, on the top. Flicking through them felt like shaking hands with old friends. The surge of feelings and memories gave me goosebumps. I wished Jacs were here with me to rediscover them.

Further down into the chest, I found the music sheets covered in treble clefs, beats, note heads and stems in complex rhythms scrawled in pencil by my father's hand. Before computers, he would handwrite all of his songs.

I picked out a few randomly, most of them too complex for me to read. The 1970s pop songs that he had written were there, like 'Tears of Gold' or 'Flower Girl' or 'Temptation Baby'. The latter two were the only two European hits of his forty-year songwriting career, written for a Swedish female solo artist whose name escaped me now. However, there was one score that was notably simpler. It was written in fountain pen and there were no lyrics scribbled down the side or underneath the staff, as on the other sheets. I noticed at the bottom that it was titled *Helen, with love on your birthday*. My heart missed a beat. I had never known that he had written her a song.

Unable to resist, I sat down cross-legged with the guitar and tried to play it. I was more than a little rusty, but incredibly some of the notes came back to me. After a few practices, I got the gist of the song. It was melancholy, in a minor chord, but it was unquestioningly a love song. I wondered whether the whole of this room was a shrine to this very song, as though it was the sole reason she kept it as it was. I thought of how much they must have loved each other once. To write such a beautiful song was a testament to the depth of his feelings for her. It struck me that dealing with his abandonment of her must have been the hardest struggle of her life.

At the time, this would not have been obvious. She had been practical about our weekend visits to stay with him and Jill in their messy suburban flat. There were no shouting matches. My father was efficient about paying maintenance. Jill behaved herself. Ostensibly, the split was amicable. But after playing that song, I began to replay the reality.

I was reminded of the many times I had heard my mother being described as a stoic in the months after my father had left.

Indeed, my mother maintained a disciplined structure in her life, mostly. However, she was detached and self-absorbed, beleaguered by migraines, which acted like full stops on the flow of our lives, and on her mothering. Outside of the periods in her darkened bedroom, she resumed business as usual by imposing exhausting academic routines for Jacs and me, stifling us with her criticism and attention. I used to smell her skirt when she was bending over my work, and wished I could cry into it, for no particular reason other than indulging the sadness that lingered inside me. There was never time for hugs. And she was no less hard on herself, by taking on an unmanageable workload that she must have pressed down on top of her inner life, trying to suffocate it perhaps.

I put down the guitar. Strangely, I didn't feel sad, I felt joyful, that my father had loved my mother so much. In turn, I felt loved by both of them. Their separation had been the tragedy, for my mother at least, and I suddenly wanted to understand my mother's pain – the pain she had so efficiently hidden from us – as a way of understanding her love for my father.

I turned the lights on as I nipped downstairs and outside onto the small patch of garden to see if John's lights were on next door. A glow emanated from the equivalent room to my old bedroom on the first floor. This was his study, where he had always worked late into the night on his historical novels.

John wouldn't mind if I rang the doorbell, I thought, as long as I brought a bottle of red wine with me.

When he opened the door, he pressed his glasses back on his nose with a swift jab. 'Everything okay?'

'I wondered if you fancied a break from the bodice ripping for ten minutes?' I said, waggling the bottle of wine at him.

His face relaxed. 'A delightful idea, young lady,' he grinned, opening the door wider for me.

I pretended not to notice the stacks of newspapers and the squalor of the kitchen. Strange crockery covered the work surfaces. It wasn't clear whether they were clean or dirty. When Sarah was alive, the pastel blue surfaces had sparkled. It was a struggle to hide my shock.

If I had bumped into him in the street, I would have seen a functioning clean-shaven man, in his ironed plaid shirts and artfully threadbare slacks. How different the story was behind closed doors.

Nevertheless, he had cleared a space on the tiny kitchen table, lit a candle, which he placed on an embroidered mat, and brought out a wine glass, a tumbler and a carton of orange juice.

'I assume you're not sharing the wine with me?'

'Orange juice would be lovely, thanks.'

We sat opposite each other on the same plastic chairs Jacs and I had sat on as children, and the chaos around me melted away. How clinical my life had become. How easy it was to feel comfortable in a home that had a heart, however dysfunctional and chaotic.

I had wanted to launch straight in with questions about my parents, but instead we talked for over an hour about books and plays and music. It was like escaping to another world, where my cares were distant to me. My whole body seemed to steam, as though I'd turned the engine off after a long, arduous journey uphill.

'Your dad thought it was funny you went into the City.'

'He tells everyone I'm a banker, but I'm not.'

'He thought you'd go into the arts.'

'He doesn't understand anyone who isn't creative.'

'Jill wasn't.'

'But she facilitated his creativity. She always believed in him,' I reminded him.

'Unlike your mother.'

I laughed. 'She told him he should get a job in Woolworths.'

'I'd say that was the final nail in the coffin.'

We laughed together and I took a large gulp of juice. 'John...' I began.

He put his elbows on the table and his chin on his hands, ready to listen. 'Yes, Gemma.'

I smiled. I was taken back to when my sister was small, sitting here at this same table, when she would tell her long rambling nonsensical stories to John, who would listen with his whole being, even adding to the story here and there, much to my sister's delight.

'Did Mum ever talk to you about Dad leaving?'

'To Sarah she did.'

'I found this...' I said, unfolding the song onto the table.

'Oh, that,' he sighed. 'He played that at her birthday party.'

'Did she like it?'

'They snogged in front of everyone afterwards.'

'Yuck.'

He chuckled. 'They were so in love back then.'

'I don't understand what went so wrong.'

'Your dad wore his heart on his sleeve and your mum had hers in an iron box.'

I sighed, noticing my ragged out-breath. 'Mum never once cried after he left. Everyone marvelled at her stoicism.'

At the time, I had been proud of my mother for carrying on, for refusing to cry 'poor me!', and secretly proud that I could be as brave too.

'Do you know about the Stoics of Ancient Greece?'

'No,' I smiled, ready for one of John's special lessons.

'The Stoics did not advocate the stiff-upper-lip emotional detachment that they were often mistakenly known for – qualities that lots of people seem to admire in your mother – and they certainly did not believe in suppressing or denying difficult emotions. Cultivating the right inner attitude, paying attention to your own mind, was at the heart of all they taught.'

'So, you're saying my mother is the antithesis of Stoicism.'

'Kind of. But when you and Jackie were asleep, she'd come round to see Sarah.' He paused and looked at me with a sideways glance, possibly wondering how far he could go. 'I'd leave them to it mostly but believe me, your mother cried buckets.'

I shook my head in disbelief. 'I never knew.'

'Sarah would fret about you and Jackie. She said Helen was too hard on you both.'

I blinked rapidly. He'd spoken a truth that I hadn't consciously acknowledged, not fully, and I flapped my hands around my eyes to stop the tears. 'I don't want to cry.' I never cried.

'Your mum never wanted to cry either but Sarah forced it out of her.'

'Sarah was such a wonderful woman. I still miss her Christmas cake.'

John's eyes watered. 'I miss her every minute of every day.'

His possessions seemed to move in on us, as devastating symbols of his grief. I was overwhelmed and the tears began to stream down my face. I was crying for John's loss, I was crying for my mother's, and I was crying for mine. While John held me in the embrace that I had needed from my mother all those years ago, I didn't know if I would ever be able to stop the tears from coming. The well of sadness in the pit of me felt bottomless. How I had held on to that wealth of emotion for so long, I didn't know. As a child I must have existed with my fists permanently balled up. Now I felt like I was rolling sideways down a hill, letting the grassy hillocks and dips do their worst while I gathered speed and waited for the nasty bump at the end.

'Poor Gemma,' he soothed.

'I don't know why I'm acting like this,' I said, trying to talk through the subsiding sobs.

'You're going through a lot.'

'Did Mum tell you?' I sniffed, wiping my nose with the back of my hand.

'She tells me everything.'

'I made her swear not to,' I said, angrily, before I remembered that actually I had made Mum swear not to tell my father, rather than John.

'It's not like I'd tell anyone. I never go anywhere.'

It was true. Somehow, it was a relief he knew.

'What am I going to do, John?'

'When's the CPS thingy?'

'The hearing. Fourth of December.'

'What exactly happens at a hearing?'

'I'd plead *not guilty* and then we'd all go away again to prepare my defence.'

'It beggars belief,' Peter said, letting out a loud sigh.

'But I'm hoping it won't come to that.'

'Isn't it inevitable now?'

'The whole thing can be dropped if Rosie changes her statement.'

'You need to go home.'

'If I stay away, maybe she'll come round.'

'I don't think it works like that.'

'But when I'm around her I'm making it worse,' I cried, breaking down again, into my hands, pressing away the terror, gulping into the hole that was forming in my stomach when I thought of losing my three children.

'If you run away, you'll definitely make it worse.'

I wiped my face and stared at him wide-eyed. 'But she hates me.'

'Because you're lying to her.'

His words were like a slap in the face.

'She doesn't know that.'

'Children pick up on much more than you think. When Sarah was dying, Imogen and I tried to fob Evie off by saying she was going to get better and Evie turned her little face up to us and said, "It's okay, Grandad. When Grandma goes to heaven, she can look after Hammy," who was her hamster who died. She was only three.'

'Mum doesn't think I should tell her.'

'Helen's wrong,' John said casually, confidently, as he refilled my glass.

I gulped thirstily, feeling a charge of courage build in my chest.

'But the timing is really bad.'

'It might be *why* she's lying to the police. Not consciously, obviously,' he added, taking another sip before continuing, 'Deep down she might know something's not as it seems but can't work out what.'

It sounded right.

'Today she told me she thought she was adopted,' I said, pained by the reminder. I ached with remorse.

'What does Peter think?'

'Peter doesn't think she's lying about me slapping her.'

'Rubbish,' he spluttered.

'Seriously, he's starting to doubt me. I know it.'

'Perhaps you're doubting yourself.'

I couldn't talk for all the air that I had sucked into my lungs too quickly.

'I do think I'm a good mother, you know.'

'Of course you are.'

'I try my best.'

'That's all that matters.'

'It's not like I'm trying to be perfect or anything,' I said, tears spilling down my cheeks.

He paused mid-sip. 'Perfect's a tall order.'

'Impossible,' I groaned.

'Good enough is more achievable.'

'Mum always told us to strive to be the best in life.'

'And she was the perfect mum, was she?'

I couldn't answer him.

'Don't you dare believe your mother's hype.'

I wiped my eyes with the back of my hand and stroked my father's song-sheet. 'She was so brave when he left.'

'She is a formidable woman, and always has been, but she was also vulnerable and sad and angry when your dad left, as anyone would be. Her heart was broken in two.'

'She protected Jacs and me from all that.'

'That's what parents do.'

'Somehow I thought of her as a superwoman.'

'Who you could never live up to?'

'Kind of.'

'That's her competitive spirit, Gemma. I love your mum, but, Jesus, nobody is ever better than her at anything.'

'So true,' I grinned.

'If you Campbell women are all so intent on being so bloody perfect all the time, why don't you sell Rosie the fairytale, like, um...' He looked up to the ceiling as I imagined he would when he was writing his books. 'Okay. Here's one. Ready?'

I nodded.

'There was once a little baby who was only a twinkle in her parents' eye. Even before she was born, they loved her so much that they wanted to find her the perfect mother, so they searched the whole world, far and wide, through dark tunnels and busy cities, risking everything on treacherous journeys across the oceans, meeting tall mummies and short ones, kind ones and mean ones, rich ones and poor ones, until they found her one mother who they knew was just perfect to bring her to life. When she was born she was the most beautiful baby girl in the land and they knew they had chosen right. And they lived happily ever after. The End.'

I was moved, in spite of his tongue-in-cheek delivery. 'That's lovely.'

'Yes, it is lovely, so stop stamping down on it in a panic,' he said, slapping his hand down emphatically on top of the pile of newspapers that was nudging at our thighs. 'Or you'll end up fucked up like me.'

'You're not doing so badly,' I smiled, so sorry for him, wondering if his hoarding was a natural reaction to the loss of Sarah, the love of his life. He was literally filling the gaping hole that she left when she died.

He pushed his glasses up his nose in the nick of time. 'Don't worry, I'll take my own advice one day, when I'm feeling brave enough.'

'When you do, I'll help you through it.'

He smiled at me. 'You know you haven't changed a bit since you were little. You were always so polite when you came round and you always helped Sarah wash up the cups while Jackie and

Imogen tore the place up. You were so keen to do a good job for her.'

'I remember feeling like a burden on her.'

'You weren't, believe me. She thought you were an angel.'

'That's nice to hear.'

'But now I think it's time to throw the halo off and be really rubbish, just like the rest of us.'

'Okay,' I laughed, through a spring of new tears. 'Here's to being really rubbish!'

And we clashed our glasses so hard in agreement that they almost shattered.


The following day, I went into work feeling upbeat, refreshed after my night away. In my head I was phrasing how I might tell Lisa that I was going to put a request in for a few weeks' leave. I was going to take John's advice, and head back home.

But then Miranda Slater called me.

She informed me that a Child Protection Conference would be held the following week, which I was obliged to attend along with representatives from the Police, Health and Education, and any other agencies involved in the investigation.

I didn't know why they had called this meeting and I called Philippa Letwin to find out.

Philippa had not hidden her disappointment when I had called her to pass on the news. Apparently, the meeting was a crucial, and unfortunate, turning point; somewhere she had hoped we would never be. If, in this meeting, it was decided that the children's names were to be put on the Child Protection Plan – which was basically a list of 'at risk' children – the prospect of my prosecution at the CPS hearing would be a foregone conclusion.

'Did you call Miranda?' I shouted at Peter down the phone.

'Calm down.'

'Don't tell me to calm down, you fucking bastard.' I was hysterical, beyond terrified.

'I didn't call Miranda, Gemma.'

'Did you tell her I caused Rosie's head injury? Is that what you told her?'

'No. You're being paranoid.'

'Are you fucking surprised?' I yelled.

'Look, let's sort it out after the meeting tomorrow.'

Panic shot through me. 'I'm coming home.'

'It's not fair on the kids to come and go whenever you feel like it.'

'I'm not "coming and going". I've only spent one night out of the house.'

'Rosie was much calmer this morning.'

My mouth hung open. I didn't know what to say. I tried to swallow.

'Are you telling me to stay away from my children?'

'It's not like that,' he sighed.

'What is it like?'

'I think you're under a lot of pressure and I think it's getting to you.'

'Peter, how many times do I have to tell you, she rolled away from me. I didn't push her that hard.'

'Listen to yourself. You didn't push her "that hard"? You shouldn't have pushed her at all.'

'Fuck you, Peter.' And I hung up.

Peter had turned against me. I couldn't comprehend it.

I was still shaking violently when Lisa came in to tell me I was late for my one o'clock meeting.

Peter called me again and again that night, and I ignored his calls. If he was against me, if he had turned my mother against me, he could fuck off and leave me alone. If they thought I was the bad guy, then fuck them.

# CHAPTER FIFTY-TWO

*TOP SECRET*

*Dear Mummy,*

*It is 7 days after you left. Granny Helen comes into my room to wake me up every morning but she doesn't know that I am already wide awake. I wake up early to look outside to see if your car is home. Daddy says that you are not feeling very well and that you need to get better before you come home. Did I make you ill, Mumma? I miss all the voices you use when you read to me at bedtime. Granny Helen sounds like the Sat Nav, all robotic and boring and she only reads three pages! Can you believe it? She gets really grumpy if I don't eat my supper. She shouts much more than you do. You shout more louder than her, but only when I'm really, really, really naughty and if I have a tantrum. I would NEVER EVER EVER have a tantrum with Granny Helen. I think she would send me to boarding school or something. You would never send me to boarding school.*

*Here are the things I promise cross-my-heart-hope-to-die-stick-a-cupcake-in-my-eye to do if you come home:*
  *- I promise to brush my teeth the very first time you ask me to. (The toothbrush is DRY!!! HA HA. Remember?)*
  *- I promise to be good all the time.*

- *I promise I won't cry when I do my homework (even when it is maths and even when I am mega tired).*
- *I promise never to eat chocolate again.*
- *I promise never to have another tantrum ever.*
- *I promise to find all my cardigans from lost property.*
- *I promise not to fight with Noah (I love Noah).*
- *I promise not to chat-back to you and be rude.*

*INVISIBLE INK ALERT: Mrs E sent me a note in the blue bucket to come to her shed tonight after lights out and I sent her a note back to tell her not to forget the hot chocolate. I want to tell her all about Miranda coming round after you left and all the horrible questions she asked me about my head. Like, seriously, Miranda's teeth make me feel a bit VOMITTY. They sit on her bottom lip like they are growing out of it and she breaths really loudly. Sometimes I want to stick her dangly pen up her nostrils. Mrs E would NOT laugh about that. She would say I was being mean but Mrs E listens to me, like more than any other grown-up ever. Miss Porter in Literacy says we have two ears and one mouth, that means we should listen twice as much we talk. She says a famous writer said that. But Miss Porter never listens. She just shouts just like all the other grown-ups. In The Little Prince that she reads us, the main character thinks he can't draw very well because when he draws a Boa Constrictor snake that has eaten an elephant the grown-ups think that the picture looks like a hat (it does a bit!) but now every time I see a hat I think of a Boa Constrictor eating an elephant. How upside down is that? Do you think I will see a hat as a hat when I turn grown-up? Answers on a postcard!*

*Love,*
*Rosie.*

*P.S. Daddy never laughs at my jokes anymore and I have to ask him ten times about everything until he hears me. I think I know how you feel when you ask me to brush my teeth, like TEN MILLION TIMES. #thetoothbrushisdry. P.P.S. I think daddy misses you.*

# CHAPTER FIFTY-THREE

I felt cold and sick as we sat around the large oval table in an institutional grey room to hear the experts decide whether my children were at risk: in my hands, under my care. My children. *My* children.

Everything rested on this meeting.

Philippa had advised me not to speak. That was okay by me. If anyone had asked me to speak I would have vomited. My mother held my hand under the table. Peter sat on the other side of Philippa and he would not look at me. Dr. Isobel Frayn spoke first. 'I found a bruise on her left arm, which Rosie informed me was the result of falling off the trim trail in the playground.'

DC Miles checked her notes. 'The playground monitor, Annie McLean, confirmed that a fall had occurred on November the second.'

I wanted to tell them how long it had taken me to dress Rosie when she was a baby, how gently I had pushed her chubby fists into her sleeves. I wanted to tell them how many kisses I had planted on her face when she fell as a toddler, when she had run ahead before her legs could carry her. I wanted to tell them how I, too, was winded when I saw her fall from a tree onto her back last summer. Why wasn't I allowed to tell them that?

Miranda Slater spoke next, while she flicked and dangled her smooth grey mane. She had serious concerns about the 'instability' caused by my 'alleged mood swings' and 'sudden departure from the home' coupled with Rosie's 'recent head injury and suspected concussion.'

She had rolled away from me. Hadn't she? Who could I ask to replay what had happened? Peter? What had he seen that I hadn't?

Philippa Letwin responded in measured tones. 'Gemma absolutely refutes the allegation that she has in any way harmed Rosie at any point, including that of the incident mentioned, but she feels strongly that the logistics of parenting under the levels of scrutiny and supervision drawn up in the written agreement was stifling and unsettling for the children. Quite selflessly, she believes that Rosie and Noah are now in a stable and secure environment until the hearing, dependent upon Helen and Peter's continued care.'

*But I want to go home now. I have so much to say.* Could they see me? Was I invisible?

Miranda nodded, of course, and shared a sideways glance with DC Miles, before adding that 'consideration should be given as to whether to hold a child-protection conference prior to the child's birth.'

I clutched my stomach as if she had the power to rip my baby from my womb.

The peripheral view of Peter's face began to blur, the whole room began to fizz around the edges as my heart leapt haphazardly in my chest.

'No!' I cried out, but Philippa held my arm and shot me a warning glance. 'No, no, no,' I muttered, under my breath, digging my nails into my thighs.

*You'll never take my baby. Never. Never. Never.*

My mother spoke up. I recognised her outrage. Her palm sweated through my trouser leg. Peter spoke. Or mumbled, waffling sheepishly. '...wonderful mother... under a lot of stress.' Numbness spread through me. His regretful ramblings about my 'uncharacteristic' behaviour made me cringe. Who was this man who said he loved me?

Philippa said, 'In terms of her unborn child, with all due respect, I suggest we wait upon the outcome of the ongoing assessment, pending the CPS hearing on December fourth.'

*I'll die if you take my children away from me. Don't you understand?*

Philippa must have seen the horror that had drawn the blood away from my face, for she scribbled on a notepad that she pushed in front of me. *Hang in there. It's almost over.*

I was drenched in sweat. I felt it rolling down my back, under my arms, between my swollen breasts. The breasts that had fed my children, that would feed the baby that grew inside me. My role as a mother was being rubbed out, but I held the sensations and memories in my body like painful reminders of the mother I would always be.

How I yearned for Rosie and Noah now. Their absence was an unbearable void.

But the chairperson, whose name escaped me, the police and the doctor and the social workers, all seemed satisfied with their officially agreed-upon decisions to put Rosie and Noah on the Child Protection Plan under the category of Physical Abuse. They now universally believed that Rosie and Noah were at significant risk of being harmed by me. The conference had been neatly tied up for now, enough to stand up and leave. Everyone had their duties and roles nicely delineated. Through their eyes, through the prism of their moral and correct judgement, the threat of me had been removed from the equation. I had chosen to move out of my own home and now somehow I was being forced to stay out. Within one hour of sitting in this drab, mean room, I had seen enough to know the tide had turned. DC Miles and Miranda Slater did not simply suspect I was guilty, they *knew*. Tick. Job well done. Their trajectory was now clear.

I couldn't stand up. I had lost all ability to move. Everything was moving around me too rapidly.

But Peter could move. It amazed me that he could. It amazed me that he could walk. Towards me.

'Don't come near me,' I said.

As my mother tried to coax me out of the room, I thought back to the ranting and raving of that young woman in the police station and I envied her, spitefully.

I needed that fight in me, but at the same time I didn't trust it. Spitting abuse had landed that woman in a cell. My temper, my lack of patience, my lack of self-control had brought me here, to this awful room. Finally, I knew how not to be, but I didn't know how to be. I didn't know how to fight for my children, without fighting.

A silent scream reverberated around my body, perhaps trapped forever inside me.

A shaft of sunlight lasered through the crack in the curtains, stubbornly, cruelly rejecting my pleas for darkness. I fumbled for my laptop by my bedside. In one line to Lisa in an email, I could not convey how ill I was: how pointless my breathing had become, how useless my body was to me or my baby, how my thoughts tortured me. My phone lay switched off. I had crawled away from the outside world, tired of the spotlight, worthless in the life I used to own.

At night, I writhed, wide awake, moving from bed to sofa and back to bed again. My eyes ached with exhaustion and misery. I paced from room to room, as though walking towards something, and ending up nowhere, letting one fruitless step follow the next, finding no pathway, no answers. The anxiety crippled me: Were the children safe? What were they doing? Where were they? How were they feeling? Did they miss me? And then the anger came, towards Peter, towards my mother, towards Mira, towards the police, towards Miranda. For holding my children away from me, as though lifting them up from the snapping jaws of a crocodile. I was bitter with loathing and I beat my fists into my mattress, over and over, until I collapsed and curled up in a pitiful ball of self-hatred and powerlessness.

My whole being moaned and twisted at the threat that loomed, the threat that I could never really reach in my thoughts consciously, knowing the very concept of losing my three babies was intolerable. A blinding shot of white blanked out that future. I could not conceive of it, I could not endure it.

Each day was a delirium: an overpowering, endless torment that I had to survive somehow, as the authorities planned my family's future, without me in it, as the clock ticked towards the fourth of December, when I would hear whether the Crown Prosecution Service had overwhelming evidence to prosecute me for child abuse.

# CHAPTER FIFTY-FOUR

Mira opened the dining room door to reach for the meal that Barry had left outside it. There was a sticky note on the top plate, *I love you*, and one stuck on top of the bowl that covered her pudding with a felt-tip drawing of two hearts overlapping. 'Off to the Crown tonight,' he'd called.

Since their fight, Mira and Barry passed each other in the house like ghosts from different eras.

Mira was looking forward to seeing Rosie after Barry had gone to the pub.

Before meeting Rosie, Mira was determined to complete the photograph album. Over the last few weeks, she had begun to slowly but surely fill it up. Not with all the good memories, as one might expect, but with all the bad.

She had ripped out the photograph of her teenage self, looking happy and carefree, and replaced it with a photograph of her as a baby, crying on the sofa with chocolate smeared down her front. She looked small, dirty and neglected, just as she had felt.

This album was the new truth. Gone was her desire to push it away into brown envelopes or burn it on the compost or shove it back into plastic bags. She didn't want to tie the knot closed on the worst injustices of her life. She now wanted to smear shit over her mother's memory. The album was to act like a knife poking into Deidre's thick guts in revenge. There was going to be no rewriting of history. For posterity, Mira was going to uncover the travesty of her upbringing and castigate those she blamed for it.

However, the album was not going to serve as an excuse – Mira didn't believe in grovelling excuses – it was going to be an explanation. The photographs spoke for themselves. Somehow, the ugliness of them made her feel better, more like herself, and less like the woman she had been pretending to be all of her adult life. She was sick of pretending. Now the truth was out, she could not put it back.

If Barry understood the circumstances around the forced adoption, if he understood the backdrop of her family life, he might understand why she still yearned to meet her son.

Her joints creaked and snapped as she stood from the floor where she had been picking up the rejected cuttings. She was ready to take Barry the album.

He was sitting with his dinner on a tray in front of the television. She turned the television off and replaced his tray with her album. 'Before you go to the pub, I wanted you to see this.'

He looked up at her, as though asking permission to open it.

She sat down next to him. 'Go on. Open it.'

At every photograph, he asked her questions. Her sad stories tumbled out of her.

One page was of Deidre, at five years old, on that sofa, scowling at the camera, brandishing a fistful of sweets.

The next page was of her mother lying sprawled out on that same bloody sofa in her holey, puce leggings with her eyes half-closed.

The next page was a collage of all of the photographs she could find of her mother's ex-boyfriends. There were six in total.

The next page was a crotch shot of Craig. It was the only one she could find that she hadn't burnt in the compost. She had been amused that it was of his crotch, considering that his loins were in actual fact more relevant to her life story than his face.

And on and on. There were many more choice moments that Mira thought worthy of the album. With each new page, came an unpleasant reminder of her past. She had reconstructed the reality of her childhood. If she had brought this out to show dinner party guests, they would not coo over how sweet she and Deidre were as babies, they would probably cry for her.

On the last page, she had fixed the final photographs. She had cut around the little blue rabbit from several photographs, discarding the faces of Deidre, Doug and Harry.

Carefully, she had stuck the rabbits into a beautiful flower pattern. It was the same blue soft toy that she had bought her son before he was taken away, the same soft toy that she had sent to Deidre's baby on his first birthday. At the time, she had thought it would help her feel better to pass it on to another baby, to rid the house of it. Of course it had not worked. The grief had only worsened in the days after she had sent it.

When she looked at the sad page, devoid of any real baby photographs, she longed for the day when she might be able to replace the blue rabbits with real photographs of her son.

By the end, by the last page where the blue rabbits danced, Barry was crying. They were both crying. Mira had forgotten what it felt like to have a lightness in her soul.

'I'm so sorry,' he said.

'You have nothing to be sorry about.'

They sat in silence for some time.

Barry asked, 'Do you want me to cancel the lads?'

'No, no, off you go. You deserve some fun,' she said, closing the album, realising the time.

She took the album back to the dining room, where it would be safe.

When she returned to the lounge, Barry sat staring at the blank screen.

'If you stay in, I've got control of the remote!' she threatened.

'In that case, I'm off,' he laughed, leaping up and pecking her on the cheek. 'As long as you're all right.'

'I've never felt better,' she said, truthfully.

But Barry took ages to leave the house. He was fumbling around in the hallway, stomping up and down the stairs, opening and closing cupboards and drawers, until finally the house fell silent.

On the way out to the shed, she passed the dining room and noticed through the open door that a white DL envelope had been neatly placed on top of her album.

She moved closer.

The Post-it said, *Forgive me*.

Alarmed, she picked it up and popped her head out of the room, double-checking she had in actual fact heard Barry leave.

'Barry? What's this?'

There was no reply.

In her hand, the envelope sat, tatty and yellowed. The flap to close it was no longer stuck down. The handwriting on the front was unfamiliar. Everything about it was disconcerting.

She tucked it into the pocket of her wax jacket and traipsed outside into the cold.

The key was stiff in the lock.

Inside, the window was mottled with intricate, feathery ice motifs.

She slipped her worn fingerless gloves over her trembling hands, then put her reading glasses on and pulled out the letter.

A photograph fluttered out onto the floor and her heart stopped beating. She couldn't pick it up to look at it closely yet. The letter was shaking in her fingers. The rest of the world spun away into oblivion. Every ounce of her being was directed at the words in front of her.

*May 7th, 2005*

*Dear Mira,*

*I hope you don't mind me calling you Mira. It didn't seem right to call you Miss Waters. Or maybe you are married now?*

*It is my birthday today, as I am sure you, of all people, remember. Or at least I hope you do.*

*Since I turned eighteen, it has taken me many years to pluck up the courage to write to you. I found your address from the Adoption Contact Register. Thank you for adding your details.*

*If you would be interested to meet me, I would really like to meet you. My telephone number is: 0207 224 5678.*

*Best wishes,*
*Oliver Ivory*

Mira read it over and over and over again.

The door rattled open.

'Hello Mrs E,' Rosie whispered, rubbing her hands up and down her arms to warm herself.

Mira glanced over at Rosie by the door, as if she had always been there, as if her presence was inconsequential. She bent down to pick up the photograph and her chest seized up with love. That face. His face. The face of the baby she had seen hanging from the midwife's hands, high in the air above her splayed legs like a newborn king.

'Who's that?' Rosie asked.

'That's my baby boy,' Mira rasped, holding it out for Rosie to see.

'Oh! He's soooo cute!'

'He's called Oliver Ivory.'

'So he wrote to you?'

'He did!' Mira cried, as though confirming a miracle.

'Now do you believe in unicorns?'

'I do!' Mira grabbed hold of Rosie and hugged her with joy in her heart.

Then Rosie began to chatter away on Mira's lap, while Mira's brain was working overtime, charging ahead to when she would call Oliver Ivory. Oliver Ivory! What a good name. She was thinking about where it would be best to meet him. In London? Or would it be cosier at home? She would bake a cake for him. Thirty-four cakes for every birthday she had missed!

She read the letter again, admiring how flamboyant his handwriting was, with his long *y*s and curly *f*s.

And then, for the first time she noted the date.

2005. 2005? That didn't make sense. It can't have taken eleven years to reach her.

'Mrs E?'

'What?' Mira snapped.

'I was telling you about my movie roll.'

'Were you, pet?' Mira said, looking at the date on the letter again, trying to find any other explanation than the one she liked least.

'I learnt it in drama club. Like when you clap your hands in front of the other actor's face, it sounds like they are being slapped, or when you hit here, like this,' Rosie said, thumping her chest, 'and it sounds like you have punched someone in the stomach.'

'That sounds nice.'

'But it wasn't nice! I rolled so fast I hit my head on the wall.'

'Silly girl. Now, I'm so sorry, Rosie Rabbit, but I'm going to have to go.'

Rosie looked crestfallen. It couldn't be helped, thought Mira brusquely.

'But what about my hot chocolate?'

'I know. Why don't you stay here and make it yourself. You're old enough now, aren't you? There's the chocolate powder,' Mira said, handing her the tub and clicking on the kettle. 'Wait for it to click off before you pour it.'

Mira scooped up the photograph and letter and slipped them back into her pocket.

'See you soon, Rosie Rabbit.'

Flustered, Mira shut the shed door and locked it with the key, as it was her automatic habit, and slowly made her way, shed keys dangling, across the crispy lawn. The timing of Barry's discovery of this letter was incredible. The coincidence was uncanny: just as he finds out about her son, he finds a long-lost letter from him. Perhaps he found it lodged under the matt when he was sweeping up today. Perhaps he stumbled upon it in the pocket of an old suit jacket, forgotten about, unopened. Barry could not have hidden this letter from her for eleven years. Could he? He wasn't capable of such deception. It was inconceivable. He loved and respected her. There was no way he could have betrayed her with such a foul duplicity.


When Barry finally got home, Mira was waiting for him in the kitchen. She had the letter in front of her on the table.

He stumbled in, coughing, steaming drunk.

She waited for him to notice her there.

Seeing her, he stopped, stock still, his jacket hanging limply from one arm.

'Come sit down,' she said.

Dutifully, he wove to the table and slumped in a chair.

The fumes coming off him made her eyes water.

She smoothed her hand over the letter. 'Tell me you didn't hide this from me for eleven years.'

Barry's sluggish muscles tried to form words from his lips, but failed.

He put his head in his hands. 'You lied to me,' he slurred.

'So you punished me?'

'No, no, no, no,' he repeated, swinging his head back and forth. 'I hid it from you to protect you.'

Mira's whole world tilted. 'No, I won't believe it.'

'You were the one who wanted to keep him a secret. I rrrr… respected that,' he stammered. He raised his head. His eyes were swimming. 'I love you,' he whined.

'If you loved me, you'd never have held this back from me,' Mira murmured, in disbelief, amazed by his warped logic.

'But I thought you didn't want to remember.'

The magnitude of his misapprehension began to hit her. He was right, in one way. Until the album, until Rosie, she had not wanted to remember. Not more than a split second, in case the trauma of remembering obliterated her. She looked at him, impassively. He had known her better than she had given him credit for. For eleven years he had been living with the secret she had smuggled into their marriage, and he had accepted it. More than that, he had lived with it in his heart, as though sharing it unconsciously was enough, that keeping it might protect her from it. It had been a misguided act of love.

But the thought of those wasted eleven years ignited a wild rage in her.

'It was not your decision to make!' she cried, banging her fist on the table. He jumped slightly, sobering for a split second, before sliding back.

'That album…' he stuttered. 'That album… it broke my heart in two pieces.'

If it was too late, if Oliver, her *son*, had been too hurt by a second rebuff – which she wouldn't blame him for – Mira would never be able to forgive Barry.

She clenched her jaw, pulling back her anger. Barry wasn't strong enough for the weight of everything she was feeling, really feeling. She had lived for decades under a crust of pain, and now she was breaking through, to feel life's sun warm her skin, and to feel the cruel burn of that heat. She wanted to drum the beat of her loss – every minute of every year of that loss – across the valley, over the hilltops, to rattle through window panes. Her chest had been prized open and her heart was a shiny, juddering mass of naked yearning and unsatisfied love. There was no way she could send her desires into the shadows again, no way she could pretend that they hadn't existed.

'I want to meet him,' she stated tearfully.

'I don't know, love, I don't know if that's right, after all these years,' Barry blubbed, wiping snot from his nose with his sleeve.

His pathetic snivelling was hard to stomach. She wanted to slap him. If he had been sober enough, she might have whacked him with all of her might, savouring the hot, satisfying sting in her palm. But it would be wasted on him in this state.

'Go rot in hell,' she spat, leaving him there whimpering in the dark.

# CHAPTER FIFTY-FIVE

I awoke with a start. There was a child screaming. The cries reverberated through my body, clearing out my head, taking precedence over every other thought or feeling that had plagued me for so many days.

I got out of bed, smelling the sourness of my pillows and pyjamas.

When I opened the window, there was an icy rush of wind, and I heard the piercing scream of a child calling out for his mother from one of the houses further along the terrace. This was the scream that had woken me up. It didn't matter that the child did not belong to me, it mattered that it was a child screaming for his mummy. Only his mummy would do.

It was still dark, before six o'clock, but I stripped the bed and then showered.

As I stood under the flow of warm water, I picked at a curl of white paint on the wall, which revealed a hint of the pink paint underneath. I wanted to keep picking and picking until the distressing pink was revealed in its hideous glory.

I was tired of hiding everything away. I was Rosie's mummy and she had been screaming for me for a long time.

I felt hungry. My system was free of the unidentifiable virus. It turned out that even despair and self-doubt could pass through my body like flu.

After wolfing down three pieces of toast, I scribbled a note of my sincerest thanks to John, for showing me the way. Then I scrubbed the filthy kitchen, tied up two bags of rubbish, and dropped the note into John's letterbox. The urgency to get home was overwhelming.

On the train – which was trundling along in the opposite direction to the press of commuters – I sat in an almost empty carriage. There weren't any other passengers jostling to distract or irritate me.

I turned my phone on, daring to read some of the emails from Lisa. The most recent of which was an internal group email informing us that an outside candidate from our rival firm had been offered the promotion Richard had promised me. I couldn't have cared less. I shut my phone down. There was nothing important there.

The vacuum allowed me space and time to think, to feel. I contemplated the cowering wretchedness that I had succumbed to over the last few days. I had allowed the anger and fear to engulf me. I had let them take me and I had discovered that they would not kill me. I had let go of the tight reins on my life; the life that I had failed so miserably to whip into shape. The so-called strength of the Campbell woman had crumbled away. But miraculously, in its place, I discovered that truth and courage had been hiding in my heart all along.

With that, came acceptance that Rosie might never change her statement, that the CPS hearing would probably take place in four days' time and that I had absolutely no control of the outcome. Whatever happened, I was going home to tell Rosie a real life fairy tale.

# CHAPTER FIFTY-SIX

*Help me, Mummy*

# CHAPTER FIFTY-SEVEN

I walked into the kitchen where my mother sat reading the newspaper in her dressing gown. She looked about ten years older than she had a week ago.

There were two advent calendars propped up on the cookbooks behind her, with two little doors open. I had quite forgotten that Christmas came with December. This time last year I had a wreath on the door with red velvet ribbons, and a stack of Christmas cards to write.

When my mother saw me she jumped, and patted her heart. 'You frightened the living daylights out of me.'

'Sorry.'

'What are you doing here?'

'I live here, Mum.'

She closed the newspaper.

'Peter's gone to work already.'

'Are the kids still asleep?'

'I let Noah watch a bit of telly.'

'Before school?'

'Just to keep him quiet while Rosie sleeps.'

'But they've got to be at school in half an hour.'

'Rosie wasn't feeling well last night.'

'What was wrong with her?'

'She said she was over-tired.'

We both smiled. 'I've never heard her say that before.'

'She even went to bed early.'

'Bloody hell.'

'It's probably okay to wake her now.'

'I'll just say hello to Noah first.'

But when I walked into the television room, he looked up at me blankly, his eyes circled grey. He stuck his thumb in his mouth and looked back at his cartoon.

I sat next to him and put my arm around him. 'I'm home now, okay? I'm all better.'

And he lay his head down on my lap. When I realised he was asleep, I gently put the blanket over him and snuck out.

'Rosie,' I knocked. 'Rosie?' I went in.

Her duvet was flat. Her pillow puffed.

'Rosie?' I called out of her door. 'Rosie?'

I checked all the rooms upstairs and then charged downstairs.

'Mum, is she up already?'

'I didn't hear her get up.'

'Her bed's made.'

My mother's eyes sank back into their sockets. 'She never makes her bed.'

'Exactly.'

'She must be hiding.'

'Rosie! If you're hiding, please come out, darling!'

The panic was disorientating. Both of us maniacally flitted around the house, looking in all the rooms, once, twice, even under beds and in cupboards, and out in the garden, right down to the bottom, where her den was frosted and empty, the tin kettle lying muddy on its side. The blue bucket dangling.

Back in the house, I wanted to shake my mother. 'Where the hell is she?'

'Let's be calm,' my mother said, tightening the belt of her dressing gown. 'Let's be calm,' she repeated, but her eyes were darting all over the room, as though Rosie might be perched somewhere unnatural.

'Could Peter have taken her into school early?' I was clutching at straws.

'No, no. He left at six.'

I took out my phone, slippery in my sweaty hands. 'Peter, it's me.'

Silence.

'Peter?'

'I'm surprised you remembered my name.'

'Forget all that crap for now. Rosie's missing.'

'What?'

'She's gone. It looks like her bed hasn't been slept in.'

'Call the police. I'm coming home.'

Before I called the police, I called Vics.

'Darling, I haven't seen her. Do you want me to come round?'

'No, stay there in case she comes over.'

After reporting Rosie missing, I charged upstairs to look in her drawers, as the police had suggested, to see if any clothes had been taken. Then I remembered her diary.

It was under her pillow.

'Mum!' I called down from the banisters. 'Come help me with this bloody passcode.'

My mother joined me upstairs and we sat her on her bed with the plastic pink toy on my lap.

'Let's go all through the birthdays again. Try Noah's.'

I typed it into the number keypad. The pink door stayed closed. 'Nope.'

'Try her birthday.'

Nothing.

'Peter's?'

Nothing.

'Oh God,' I groaned. 'It could be anything.'

'Yours next,' Mum offered.

'I've tried that already. I've tried all of them,' I sighed despairingly. But I typed it in again anyway, for the hell of it.

The door popped open to reveal the thick pink notepad.

I looked at my mother triumphantly. 'She must have changed it.'

I placed the diary between us.

'What's this?' Mum asked, unbending the flimsy plastic pink arm of what I had always assumed was a mini-light.

'It's a lamp for after lights out, I think.'

'But she always uses her torch.'

'That's true,' I said, picking the yellow torch up from the table next to her bed.

My mother waggled the extendable arm of the light.

The notepad was about half full. I flicked through the pages. *Dear Mummy... Dear Mummy... Dear Mummy...* on every page. My face flushed with shame.

'It's to me.'

'She loves you so much, Gemma.'

A lump formed in my throat. 'And I haven't been there for her.'

'By the time we have kids, it's too late to realise how inadequate we are for the job,' my mother said. She wrapped her arm around me in an awkward but heartfelt squeeze.

I added, 'You did all right, for a Campbell woman.'

'We're a substandard lot. But we try our best.'

'I love you, Mum.'

'Love you too, darling.' She twitched a series of sniffs, as though smelling the air for breakfast, and pinched her pink-tipped nose. 'Right come along. Time to get reading.'

Why are there so many gaps in the writing? I wondered as I skimmed through the paragraphs.

'Wait a second... Look there are two pens.' I unclipped them from their Velcro holders by the side of the notebook. One was black and the other was white.

'What?' Mum asked.

'I remember now. When I bought this for her the box said it had invisible ink.'

I scribbled the white felt-tip pen on a blank page, which left no markings on the page, and then clicked the switch to the mini-UV-light. 'Shit. It's not working. Shit!'

I was convinced that the blanks held the key to her whereabouts.

My mother turned the diary over. 'Triple AAA. I'll nip down to the shops. You start reading the rest.'

I read from the back. There were no dates.

*TOP SECRET*

*Dear Mummy,*

*It is 7 days after you left. Granny Helen comes into my room to wake me up every morning but she doesn't know that I am already wide-awake. I wake up early to look outside to see if your car is home. Daddy says that you are not feeling very well and that you need to get better before you come home. Did I make you ill, Mumma?...'*

My tears dropped onto her writing and I blotted the page with my sleeve. As I continued to read, I noticed that there were six lines left completely blank in the middle of her entry, which I guessed was where the invisible ink began. I checked previous entries, spotting more and more blank spaces.

By the time I heard Peter pull up outside, I had no information about Rosie's whereabouts, but I had seen sides to her that I had completely forgotten about, that I had neglected to see. Her sincerity. Her fear. Her vulnerability. I couldn't bear that I had not found time to listen, really listen, and really hear. She needed this diary to feel heard; my attention might have come too late. I pressed the diary to my chest, heartbroken.

Peter came into the room.

'Oh my God, Peter, where is she?' I cried, falling into his arms.

He hugged me tightly, and I hoped he would never let go. 'The police'll find her.'

'Peter, I didn't push her. I didn't hurt her head. She rolled, I swear to God.'

Peter drew away and took me by the shoulders. 'I know, I saw her do it again when Noah hit her and I have been trying to call you for days. Where have you been?'

'It's doesn't matter now. I'm back.'

'It's been hell without you.'

I smiled sadly, wishing I could feel vindicated, knowing I had stayed away too long.

'I thought you said she was calmer without me.'

'I have never wanted to hear her tantrums more. She's been so good it's been awful.'

'I came home to tell her about Kaarina. I'm not going to run away from it anymore.'

Peter nodded and smiled, and then he scratched his hands through his hair. 'Oh God, where the hell are the police?'

I looked out of the window and saw Mira and Barry Entwistle's house.

'Mira,' I hissed.

'Gemma, no,' Peter cried, following me as I almost tumbled down the stairs.

'I have to ask her.'

I sprinted over to their house and knocked on the door repeatedly.

Barry opened it. 'Hello Gemma. How can I help?' he asked, twitching his nose so that his glasses popped up and down.

'Where's Rosie?' I screamed in his face.

Peter pulled me back. 'Sorry, Barry, we're looking for Rosie. Might you have seen her anywhere?'

'I'm afraid not,' he said, frowning at me.

'Is Mira there?' I cried.

'She's gone to work. Do you want me to call her and ask her about Rosie?'

Peter answered, 'Yes, that would be really kind, Barry, thank you,' and he yanked me away. I tried to look over Barry's shoulder.

'He was hiding something, I can tell,' I sneered, as Peter frogmarched me back home.

'Behaving like that is not going to help Rosie.'

Chastened, I stopped writhing.

Before getting back inside, I heard a car. My heart leapt. I hoped it was the police, but it was Mum's red Mini.

'The batteries!' I cried.

# CHAPTER FIFTY-EIGHT

Mira had woken up that morning with butterflies. It was the day she would be calling her son. His letter was waiting for her on the bureau.

Her mind was alert, as it had been all night. But she wasn't tired. Her eyes were wide open to the beauties of the world around her.

The drive to Woodlands had taken her breath away. The pink sky, the frosted branches, the bunches of brown leaves scurrying along the road next to her seemed to be saying 'Good Morning Mira!' and 'What a wonderful day it is today!'

The children at school were a delight, even when they weren't. She hugged them and laughed with them and admonished them gently.

When Patricia politely asked her to come out of the classroom for a word, Mira was not worried. She was on a high. Nothing could bring her down.

'Mira, I'm afraid your mobile telephone has been ringing quite insistently from your coat. I would ask you to turn it off before it sends me to the loony bin.'

Mira's mortification was quickly replaced by terror. Barry never called her at work. Nobody ever called her at work. Not even Deidre.

Having apologised to Patricia, she scuttled off to find her phone.

Four missed calls from Barry in the last fifteen minutes.

She called him back.

'Mira, love, the Bradleys have been round and they're saying Rosie is missing.'

Mira was confused and spoke without thinking. 'But I only saw her last night.'

'You saw her last night?'

'Yes, she came to visit me in the shed and then she...' Mira's heart was in her mouth. She dropped the phone and let out a small cry.

Without a thought of Patricia or Year Two, she shoved her jacket on, checked the keys to the shed were still in her pocket, and fled from the school.

She sped recklessly through the lanes. The joy and beauty of the drive earlier was now a blur. Her fear seemed to be spreading and ripping through the landscape like a hurricane.

She screeched the car to a halt on the roundabout and ran across the drive and round to the back of the house. Forcing her legs to move faster than they were able to, she was stumbling over her own feet. Her mind worked overtime as she imagined the state she would find Rosie in. The temperature outside had dropped to -4°C last night. There was no heating, running water or food in the shed. The kettle was empty.

'Rosie! Rosie!' she rasped through the door, desperately short of breath.

As she fumbled with the key, struggling to turn it in the rusty lock, she noticed a white piece of paper sticking out of the bottom of the door. Her heart stopped. Filled with dread, she scanned the scribbled note that Rosie had written on the back of a seed packet. *Help me, Mummy...*

'Oh God, Rosie!' she screamed as she scrunched it into her pocket and tried frantically to force the key again and again. She was ready to kick the door down, but then the lock clicked open.

Rosie was curled on the floor under Mira's tartan blanket, her lips blue, her teeth and bones chattering.

'Oh my child, oh my Lord above.'

'Thirsty,' she croaked.

Mira shook a watering can, finding a small amount of water to pour into a mug, which she put to Rosie's shivery lips. As Rosie sipped, Mira pressed her fingers onto Rosie's wrist, to measure her pulse. She counted. The child's steady heartbeat and the process of counting calmed her. The panic subsided. Wisps of relief seeped into Mira's consciousness. Gradually, her own breathing became normal. She sat there with her, for a few beats, stroking her forehead, aware now that Rosie was going to be well.

'Let's get you home, Rosie Rabbit.'

Mira scooped up Rosie's juddering body and carried her across the garden.

Barry came out and trotted next to her. 'Is she okay?'

The sound of his weedy voice curdled her stomach.

'She'll be fine once she's warmed up,' she spat back at him.

Weighed down by the child's body, she staggered on. With each step, she became more and more fearful of letting Rosie go. She braced herself for the abuse she would receive from Gemma and Peter.

She looked down at this beautiful child, clinging to her for strength in such a dear, trusting manner, and she recognised the terrible errors she had made. Rosie's tantrums might have been coming from Rosie's mouth, but the real cry for help had been coming from Mira's past. By confusing the two, Mira had put Rosie in danger. She had torn a family apart. She did not deserve Rosie's trust.

When Peter and Gemma opened the door to her, Gemma's face crumpled and she let out a cry so piercing and full of heartache that Mira almost collapsed with Rosie in her arms still.

As Peter took her from Mira, Rosie reached out for Gemma. Her weak arms wrapped themselves around her mother's neck while Gemma kissed her daughter's face until there wasn't an inch of skin that hadn't been touched by her love.

'Thank you, thank you,' Peter choked. 'Thank you for finding her.'

'But it was my fault!' Mira cried, stepping back from them, waiting for retribution. 'I locked the shed, I wasn't thinking, she was in there and... oh, I'm so sorry. I'm so sorry for everything.'

Gemma's pale and drawn expression hardened. 'She's safe now. Thank you for bringing her home,' she stated tersely.

Her gaze returned to Rosie's face, her wide smile returned, full of happiness and gratitude and forgiveness. Through that smile, Mira recognised Gemma's absolute devotion to Rosie. Beads of sweat broke out across Mira's forehead, from the exertion of carrying Rosie, and from the searing sense of shame. Gemma's dignified restraint was worse than a punch in the stomach would have been.

Peter took Rosie from Gemma. In a huddle, they began to move inside. Mira watched on, at a loss, fixed to the spot. But before Gemma had a chance to slip through the door, Mira touched her shoulder and Gemma spun around as though ready to throw that punch.

Mira spoke hurriedly but gravely, 'I'm not asking for your forgiveness and I don't blame you either if you never give it, but if I could explain... I don't know how to say it... I'm not making excuses, but nobody looked out for me when I was a girl and I thought if I could look out for Rosie, it would make up for it somehow. I'm sorry, so sorry,' Mira paused, trying to hold back the tears. 'If I could take it back... Oh... I'm sorry... I tried to save Rosie when I should've tried to save me. I'm talking nonsense. Sorry, I'll go.'

Gemma opened her lips, as though poised to say something, but they pursed again, tears gathering above her lashes.

'Goodbye Mira,' Gemma said.

Faced with a closed door, Mira murmured to herself, 'Yes, sorry, yes, I just wanted to… Yes, I'll leave you alone now.'

Humbled and chastened, Mira turned away, to return to her own home next door, as though she was drawing away from them, up into the sky, pulling back the lens of a camera from close-up to wide angle. She found herself looking at the bigger picture. They were her next-door neighbours, but their stories were miles apart. She had her own life to focus on now. She had her own child to find. And his letter was waiting for her on the desk.

Barry was standing by the bureau. His eyebrow and top lip twitched in unison as though they were connected by a thread. Oliver's letter was pinched between the thumb and forefinger of his right hand.

Mira sensed danger. On her return from next door she and Barry had drunk a finger of brandy and eaten some sponge cake together. She had tried to talk to him about what had happened, but he had been snippy with her and she had found it difficult to seek out his eye contact.

'Can I have that?' she demanded now.

The letter was hanging at his thigh. It was like seeing a baby dangling out of a window in the arms of a mad-man. She knew she would have to be cautious with him, gently-gently wheedle and sweet-talk him into giving it up.

'Let's put it away, eh?'

'I should never have given this to you,' he said. He waved it in the air carelessly.

Mira wanted to lurch at him, to snatch it, but the risk was too great. The letter held precious information. There would be no other record of his contact. She tried to remember Oliver Ivory's address, but she could not.

'It's my property,' Mira stated.

'Because of this, you almost killed that girl, love,' he said, flicking at the paper.

'What happened to Rosie was an accident. It has nothing to do with the letter.'

'It has everything to do with it.'

'Give it to me,' Mira ordered, thrusting her hand out for it.

'NO! I WILL NOT!' he bellowed. The flesh on his face shook. 'I forbid you to contact him.'

'What gives you the right to forbid me, Barry?' A door in her brain opened and years of stored-up animosity began to spill out of her mouth. 'You know *nothing* about real life. You've cut yourself off from the rest of the world, just like your dear mother did, keeping this fusty old house "just so", and planting geraniums for all those bored housewives, and whinging on at me when they have petty complaints about molehills on their crochet lawns…' She wiped her mouth of spittle. 'And yet somehow you think you know what's best for me? I had a life before you. I carried a baby in this belly. *I'm OLIVER'S MOTHER, for crying out loud!*' She was panting and sweating so hard, she thought she might die.

'You're not his mother anymore. You gave him up!' Barry shouted back, clutching the letter to his chest.

Mira squeezed her eyes shut. 'I won't hear it!' She held her hands over her ears and yelped.

A moment later, she felt his hand patting her shoulder and smelt his breath as he spoke, 'My Mira Meerkat, leave it be. It's too late now. There, there now.'

Her eyes shot open. She looked down to his other hand for the letter. It wasn't there.

Malevolence swelled in her veins.

'Where is the FUCKING LETTER, Barry?'

His jaw slackened. He stared at her as though she were a monster. She felt like a monster. He retreated. His eyes began blinking at double-speed behind his darkened glasses. The back of his legs came up against the fireplace tools, jangling the shovel, the poker, the tongs, the brush, unbalancing the stand until it crashed down, letting the tools splay onto the carpet. Carefully, carefully, she moved towards him. If she approached too fast, he might run.

'Step back,' he thundered. His arm shot out towards the fireplace mantel to grab the box of matches. With an unsteady hand, he lit a long match and pulled the letter from his back pocket.

Cowed, Mira shrank back. 'Oh God. Don't, please don't,' she whined. 'Please Barry. You don't understand. He's everything to me, please don't.'

'He's everything to you, is he? *Everything*, you say?' Barry retorted, high and mighty.

Mira wailed, 'Why can't you understand that? *Why can't you understand that I need him?*'

'I understand more than you think. Just you watch!' he cried petulantly, holding the match to the corner of the letter.

'NO!' Mira screamed, flying at him. '*NO!*'

But it was too late, the flames licked at Oliver Ivory's letter, greedily eating the paper, consuming his words. Weightless, acrid remnants floated to the ground. She fell to her knees, picking at the fragments. They dissolved like silky dust in her fingers.

She wept into her skirt. Barry had performed a barbarous, needless sacrifice. Her baby had been snatched from her, once again. The echo of loss was too much to bear. Her heart seized, and then it began to beat a dark and merciless rhythm, as black as the burnt remains at their feet. Nobody had the right to take her son away from her. She reached for the iron poker and she rose up, lifting the weapon over her head like a Celtic hero, before bringing it down heavily onto the balding, pitiful crown of Barry's skull.

# CHAPTER FIFTY-NINE

Rosie and I sat facing each other on the sofa, both of us in a cross-legged position and blowing on our mugs of hot chicken soup.

The fire's warmth had heated up half of Rosie's face, so that she had one red circle on one cheek.

I reached out to feel her forehead for the hundredth time that day. The fever had definitely come down.

'I promise I'm better, Mum,' she said, taking a sip of soup as though proving it.

'Eating is a good sign.'

'The doctor said chocolate was good for me too, remember,' she grinned.

'Yes,' I laughed. 'After your soup.'

She began sipping her soup in a good-natured hurry. I waited, nervously, part of me wishing we could sit like this forever, suspended in time.

'Rosie, I want to tell you a story,' I began. My stomach lurched.

'What story?'

'It's a true story.'

'Who's it about?'

'You.'

She stopped sipping her soup and looked directly at me. Her big blue eyes blinking rapidly, her one rosy cheek paling with worry.

'Does it have a happy ending?' she asked.

'I hope you'll think so.'

'Go on,' she said, gulping the last dregs of her soup and lying down on my lap.

I stroked her hair as I told her about how Peter and I had searched high and low all over the world for the perfect mummy to bring her to life.

As I unravelled her story, she curled her knees to her chest and plugged her mouth with her thumb, just as she had in my womb. I felt the wetness of her tears through my clothes. She then asked many questions about Kaarina Doubek's eggs and about 'Daddy's wiggling sperms' and the science behind the process, showing real intelligence and thoroughness, too much almost, until I worried she was getting herself bogged down in the detail.

'But you and I are more than just science,' I said.

There was a long pause as she thought about this.

'I'm not sure it's a happy ending, Mummy,' she sniffed.

I pulled her up to sitting, held her under the arms, just like I had when she was small. I wanted to look her straight in the eye.

'The best happy endings promise the happiest of new beginnings. Nothing is neat enough for a bow, Rosie, although I wish with all of my heart that it could be for you.'

'But you're still my real mummy, aren't you?'

I placed my hand on her heart, and her hand on mine. 'We will be mother and daughter for ever and ever after.'

'The end,' Rosie said, throwing her arms around me.

'The end, my beautiful girl,' I whispered in her ear.


I pulled a blanket over her as she slept. She looked at peace.

Silently, I rose from the sofa and took our two bowls to the sink.

Over the running water and the clatter of porcelain, I could hear shouting. I turned the tap off to listen.

It was coming from next-door. I could make out Mira's raised voice. At first, I smiled to myself. After all of Mira's judgements, she, too, seemed capable of breathing fire.

I thought back to her ramblings on my doorstep earlier. They were obviously heartfelt, and part of me had wanted to put my arms around her. I thought of the traumas that were passed down through the generations, and how unconsciously we acted those out again and again. Mira and I had brought our own miseries into Rosie's life, in strange echoes of our childhoods. I wondered whether Mira's judgemental finger-pointing had, perversely, been her way of staying in her comfort zone, in a familiar childhood place, too terrifying to question, too horrible to confront, and more easily deflected onto someone else. My anger was her anger, dressed up in someone else's life, at a safe distance. And I wondered whether my need to control Rosie, to control the truth – and the binding straightjacket that the lie became – had been my own comfort zone. My parents' divorce and my mother's cold-comfort control and impossible expectations had taught me those same bad habits.

I might never know what Mira's past had thrown at her, but I could only imagine that she was a survivor of hers in the way that I was of mine.

As I dried the bowls, and thought about how difficult it was going to be to live next-door to Mira, I heard Barry's voice crescendo. The rumble of rage reverberated through the walls and sent shivers across my skin. Surely the mild-mannered Barry Entwistle, with such a nervous disposition, could not shout with such force. Maybe someone else was there? I began to worry.

I opened the window to try to hear more. The argument was heated and volatile, and it was definitely between Mira and Barry. There was something dangerous in it. Not simply because of how unusual it was to hear them argue, but because it directly followed Rosie's rescue. Having believed Mira's story, having been taken in by her distress, I began to wonder whether there was more to it.

Mira had been a gibbering wreck at my door, full of humble apologies and meek smiles, but now I was hearing a savage row. I began pacing the kitchen, deliberating, torn. The wrongness of what I was hearing throbbed in my bones. My gut instinct was to race over there, to check on them. Or to call the police. The irony of that was not lost on me. For a split second, I empathised with Mira. I was in her place, listening to Rosie's screams from the other side, worrying about her welfare, feeling a sense of community responsibility.

I snapped back to reality. Her interference in our lives had almost broken my family apart. Every family was entitled to shout and scream at one another in the privacy of their own home. Abuse should not be the first assumption. Most families were not violent and cruel to one another. Mira's marital argument was none of my business. I was not going to be a curtain-twitching busy-body who would pry into their lives, just as she had done in mine. I was not that person. I would stay out of it.

That night, I slept curled against Peter's body, feeling his warmth for the first time in weeks, and I wanted to feel safe, but I was repeatedly woken by noises outside. Had they been in my dreams or were they from next door? Each time I thought I heard something, I tip-toed to our bedroom window to listen out. There was rustling in the undergrowth, scratching of the earth, twitching of the leaves, a high-pitched yelp. The noises must be cats or foxes fighting or deer eating the fallen apples or field mice scurrying through the leaves, I thought. I climbed back into bed.

The next day, all was quiet next door.

In the sunny morning light, I made a breakfast of warm croissants and sugary coffee for Peter, Mum and the children. Our household was filled with kisses and laughter, and relief.

Still, the niggle of next door would not leave me.

When I was making Rosie's bed, I heard Mira's car pull up into their driveway. I peered out. She was lugging a huge roll of wire fencing out of the backseat of their small car. Barry's pick-up truck was in the drive. Why was Barry not helping her? Why had he not bought the fencing? Why had she squeezed it into their hatchback?

Small anomalies. None of them very serious. None of them adding up.

I could not rest until I had checked on them both.


Yesterday, Barry had answered the door and I hoped he would answer it today. I braced myself for a frosty reception. I had been hysterical and rude.

The squirrel knocker was half falling off. I wondered if I had broken it. I tried to recollect how hard I had hammered.

Nobody was answering now. I knocked again, feeling a little light-headed. It was surreal to be on their doorstep.

As I turned away to go home, the door swung open.

'Yes, what?' Mira barked. An unfitting greeting considering what had happened between us. Her stubby hair was clumped into grimy tufts. Her ruddy, round face was mottled and sweaty, and I noted that her fingertips were black. Everything about her set my teeth on edge.

'Hello, Mira. After yesterday's dramas, I just wanted to make sure you guys were okay.' I glanced over her shoulder, trying to adjust my focus to the darkness of her hallway.

She cranked out a mechanical smile as though someone had pressed a button on her back to turn her on. 'How's little Rosie Rabbit this morning?'

A gust of cool wind blew through the house, bringing with it a smell of cleaning fluids and bad eggs. 'She's doing really well. Sleeping a lot.'

'Good, good,' she replied, nodding absently.

'Is Barry in? I wanted to apologise to him for being so rude yesterday.'

'Oh, stuff and nonsense,' she said. 'He's quite over it, believe me.'

'Is he in?' I repeated, trying to sound conversational.

'No,' she frowned. There was menace in the slice of her blink. Fear crept across my skin.

'Okay then,' I began, but then I heard a pattering noise from behind her, and she jumped and swivelled around, plainly terrified. I wanted to turn and run. Before I had time to act, two feathery bombs burst out of the door and beat and bashed and fought in a flurry of noise and pecking at my feet. I screamed in shock. The chickens scampered off around the corner. I held my hand at my chest and tried to control my breathing. 'Bloody hell!'

Mira hooted with laughter. 'Scared of a couple of hens, are you love?'

Gathering myself, I realised how stupid I must have looked. 'Sorry, it was just the shock of it.'

Mira wiped her eyes. It seemed I had provided some much-needed light relief.

'I'm just fixing up the coop,' she trilled, but her expression darkened again. 'Those sly foxes won't be eating any more of my chickens, that's for sure.'

'I'll be off now then.' I was desperate to get away, wishing I could run further than next door.

'Right-o. Thanks for dropping by.' She waved and closed herself back inside.

I walked away as quickly as I could, fiddling hurriedly with the latch to their five-bar gate. By the time I got home, I was trembling all over.

I charged upstairs, straight to the family bathroom, where I knew I could get a view of her chicken coop.

I stood on the loo seat and pushed opened the small top pane of the window and managed to spy a slither of Mira's side alley.

Having never seen the enclosure before, I would not have been able to tell if she had upgraded it or not. It was large for only two chickens, about seven-foot by five-foot wide. The double-layer of chicken wire that was nailed to the thick posts would certainly keep out the wiliest of foxes. Within the wire, there was a wooden slatted hen-house and a stone angel statue next to it – an eccentric ornament for a henhouse – and the two chickens, now safely shut away, pecked at the freshly-turned earth.

My neck ached with the contortion, so I pulled back.

I was about to close the window, when the door to the bathroom swung open. I almost fell off the loo seat.

'Something interesting out there?' Peter asked.

'No.' I slammed the window shut.

'You weren't nosing into Mira's garden were you, Mrs Bradley?' he asked, raising one eyebrow at me.

'No! Of course not!' I jumped down and washed my hands, trying to act normally.

'For a terrible minute there, I thought you were curtain twitching.'

The memory of Mira's ruddy face and black fingertips provoked a swirl of anxiety in my stomach. Blood rushed from my head to my toes, a dizzying vision of the freshly turned soil in the chicken coop flashed before my eyes: a shallow grave.

I felt Peter's hand rub my back. 'Are you okay?'

My head was hanging over the sink. I opened my eyes and laughed nervously, 'Sorry, had a bit of a funny turn. I'm fine now.'

The macabre vision appeared again.

'It's the trauma,' Peter said sympathetically.

And again.

I chucked the hand towel into the laundry bin and pressed my fingers into my temples. 'Maybe we should move house,' I blurted out recklessly. I wasn't sure I meant it, yet. I knew I was being reactionary.

Peter groaned. 'I think I need to sleep for a year to get over it all, first.'

'When the dust has settled, I suppose. When the police cancel the hearing, and Social Services are off our backs and stuff.'

'Why do we have to move?' He glared in the direction of Mira's house. '*She* should move.'

I sat down on the edge of the bath. 'Maybe this house has never been right for us.'

'The bills have never been right, that's for sure,' he snorted.

I sighed, agreeing. 'The mortgage has been a real burden over the last few years, hasn't it?'

'And I've always said this close is like a ghost town. When I was little…' he began.

'Yes, yes, when you were little everyone had orange squash on tap and fairies lived in biscuit tins,' I teased.

'They were elves!' he laughed, and he pulled me into a hug and I buried my face in his neck. I was shocked by what I had conjured up in my imagination, saddened by what the family had been through and grateful for what we could now salvage. With the baby between us and his arms around me, I felt an overpowering rush of love. In this blissful lull, before real life would inevitably creep back in, my thoughts were clear – streamlined almost – where the worries and concerns and aspirations of our previous life became unimportant.

'What about finding a smaller house in one of the villages further towards the coast? We could both work less, and live a bit more,' I suggested.

I imagined a village where there was a shop and a church and a pub, where the windows were thrown open in each house, where the fresh air and chatter and good will could fly back and forth through our homes and across our hedges.

'I never thought I would hear you say that.' I could tell he was sceptical.

'I'm serious, Peter. Vics and Jim are always talking of moving somewhere further out. If we moved out, they would follow, I know it.' I checked myself, put the back of my hand against my forehead. 'God, do I sound mad?'

His gentle, grey eyes shone brightly. 'Only in a good way.'

'I'd still have to think about the commute. I don't know, we can work it out somehow. Maybe I could work from home more often.'

I could picture the home I wanted already. It would be filled with colourful posters and paintings. It would have an open fire that I would have time to read in front of on the weekends. There would be an aroma of browning onions and homemade plum crumbles – which I would learn to make – wafting from the stove. And there would be lots of extra chopping boards for when my sister and mother visited for Sunday lunch.

'How about a dog?' he grinned, pushing his luck.

'Why the hell not?'

'Next you'll want chickens!' Peter cried.

'No, believe me,' I insisted, feeling a little sick again, 'I will never, ever want chickens.'

# EPILOGUE

It felt different. *She* felt different. She, who didn't have a name yet. I felt love without fear. That was new. I wanted her to stay awake. To see her eyes' slow blink. When she rooted around my breast, her little lips opening and closing, searching my skin for a nipple, I let her, watched her, luxuriated in its sweetness, her clueless, instinctual need. How strange that I didn't want to press the panic button to call for a nurse when she cried, as I had done with Rosie and Noah. How unfamiliar to be experiencing her newborn wail – her distress – knowing it would pass, confident she would settle in my arms eventually, confident that I was enough, even as she cried. She slept. I slept. She cried. I cried. She ate. I ate. We were working together. There was nothing more than this simple ritual for us right now; in these strange hospital hours, in this small blue room, in between worlds, nothing else mattered.

The door opened a crack. I didn't cover myself. I wasn't embarrassed by my semi-nakedness.

'Come in,' I whispered to Peter. My throat was still hoarse. The midwives had laughed with Peter about how much noise I had made during labour. I didn't remember. I think I left my body. She had arrived quickly.

Peter's face melted at the sight of us. The pride of what I had produced spread through me.

'How was your night?'

'Noisy out there in the ward. But blissful in here. She's an angel.'

'She is incredible,' Peter said, placing his large forefinger in her tiny hand, which curled around him, knowingly.

'Where are the others?'

'They're outside with Helen. Are you ready for them?'

'Bring it on,' I grinned. I was a little anxious about Rosie's reaction to her new sister.

Peter smiled at me and pushed a strand of my dirty hair away from my face to tuck it behind my ear. 'Well done, Mrs Bradley.' And then at the door, before he left, he added, 'You're incredible too, you know.'

The door opened. Two timid smiles appeared. Rosie was holding Noah's hand. Behind her back, she held something.

'Hello, you two. Come and meet your new baby sister.'

'Wow. She's beautiful, Mummy,' Rosie said, stepping cautiously towards us.

Noah pulled away from Rosie and jumped onto the bed. I lifted the baby up, away from his bounce. Her newness, her smallness, was exaggerated by Noah's boisterousness. 'Careful Noah.'

'Can I stroke her?' Noah asked, peering into her face.

'Yes. But be gentle here,' I said, brushing my hand where her skull bones had not yet met.

'She's got greasy hair,' Noah noted, pressing his fingers across her bald head. She didn't have much hair. A few wisps of blonde, like Noah had had when he was as new as her, and so unlike Rosie's full, dark head.

I looked over to Rosie.

'Can I hold her?' Rosie asked, placing a little present bag by her feet.

I hesitated, wondering if I could depend on Rosie yet. And then shame shadowed my heart. I had been trying so hard to trust her, and here came the real test.

'If you sit down there on that chair, I'll hand her to you.'

Carefully, I heaved my battered body from the bed and placed the swaddled bundle of my youngest daughter into my eldest's arms. Rosie glanced up at me briefly, proudly. The newest Bradley woke up, taking for granted her big sister's presence, and closed her sleepy eyelids again, comfortable where she was.

A few minutes later, my mother arrived. There were gasps and balloons and presents. Distracted for a moment, I took my eye off the baby.

'I brought you some food. Hospital toast is the pits,' Mum said, pulling out one snack after another.

Then I heard the baby's mewling cry. I looked over. Rosie was pressing her index finger into one of her baby sister's tiny eye sockets.

'Stop that, Rosie!' I flew at her, and lifted the baby out of her arms. 'What were you *doing*?'

Rosie flinched, guilt flushing her cheeks. 'I promise I wasn't pressing hard.'

My instinct was to punish her, to send her out of the room, to ban her from holding the baby ever again.

'I was just seeing if she could wink.'

'Oh,' I sighed, catching Peter's eye. A flicker of concern and doubt crossed his face. We had asked the clinic in Prague to resend us Kaarina Doubek's profile information, which we had then talked through with Rosie. Now I feared it had been too much for her, too soon.

'She's too young, darling.'

'But *I* still can't do it,' she whined.

And again, it was all about Rosie, when it should have been about the new baby.

'Real ladies don't wink or whistle,' my mother stated, missing the point.

Rosie's chin wobbled and her eyes watered. 'I only wanted to see if she could do it, like you and Noah can.'

I had to remember that Rosie was taking her own baby steps, and it was a small measure of progress that she was communicating her real feelings to me, rather than bottling them up.

I pushed aside my resentment, handed the baby over to Peter and knelt down beside her. 'Rosie, it doesn't matter. You can do lots of other wonderful, clever things, which you'll be able to teach your baby sister in time. You will always be my big girl, and don't you forget it.'

When I looked into Rosie's face, I noticed that my firm reassurance had calmed her, as though a veil of anxiety had slipped from her face.

'What have you got there?' I smiled, nodding at the little bag she had put by her feet earlier, feeling relieved there was a distraction, but weary of the longer struggle ahead of us: managing Rosie, managing the baby, remembering that Noah needed me too. I hoped the full year of maternity leave had been the right decision. It was going to be a steep learning-curve.

'I forgot!' she gasped, presenting me with a dusky pink posy of sweet peas. 'They're from Mrs E. She left them on our doorstep. It's got a note.'

My empty womb cramped up. 'She knows where we live?'

I looked over at Peter, who shrugged, possibly wondering why it mattered. I had not told him what I had done. I had not told him about the call I had made to the police after we had moved away from Virginia Close; a safe distance away, to our pretty, beamed cottage in a village near the coast.

With a shiver, I read the little card.

> *Dear Gemma,*
>
>     *Congratulations on your new baby girl.*
>
>     *Sweet peas are happiest with their heads in the sun, free and innocent, and their roots deep in freshly-turned earth. I thought they might suit her, a spring baby.*
>
> *Love from,*
> *Mira and The Chickens.*

I dropped the note as though it had burnt my fingers.

'You look like you've seen a ghost,' Peter said, alarmed.

The references to freedom and innocence and freshly turned earth, and those bloody chickens, was a subtle message from Mira. She must have known that the anonymous phonecall to the police had come from me. Not that it had amounted to anything. Barry's doleful photograph was still languishing on the police's missing persons list somewhere in the system, alongside millions of other lost faces. One heated argument overheard by a neighbour – with a suspected grudge – was not enough to justify digging up her garden. Mira had covered her tracks too well.

'Has she said something horrible?' Rosie asked protectively, her face falling.

'No. It's nothing.' I discarded the flowers on the side table.

Peter picked up the note and read it to himself.

'Sunshine and strong roots. Sounds like she's trying to say sorry.'

'She's talking about her own freedom,' I mumbled.

'Why?'

'Never mind.'

'She was a weirdo,' Noah said.

'I agree,' I said, when usually I would tell him off for being so rude.

'She seemed much jollier after Barry left her,' Peter mused.

'Cruel thing to do, to leave her in the lurch like that just because she wanted to find her son,' Helen added.

'He should have known better than to come between a mother and her child,' I said cryptically. And I looked over to Rosie, who grinned at me, as though she, too, suspected what lay beneath the chicken coop.

And maybe she did. I have learnt that children pick up on so much more than we ever give them credit for.

# A LETTER FROM CLARE

Dear Reader,

I hope that you enjoyed *Little Liar*. Maybe it diverted you from real life for a few hours. I am an avid reader myself, and I find that the escape of reading is essential for my sanity! If you want to stay updated on what I'm writing next, please sign up to my mailing list here www.bookouture.com/clare-boyd and we'll keep you in the loop.

The writing of *Little Liar* was a different kind of escape. The process was harrowing at times, and quite unsettling. I had to go to places in my head that were more than a little uncomfortable.

The idea for the book took hold after a conversation with a fellow mother at a coffee morning. Sheepishly, she confessed to shouting so loudly at her children that she was worried the neighbours would be straight on the phone to Social Services. I admitted to having had that same fear. Thankfully, my neighbours have given me the benefit of the doubt, so far!

But in Gemma's case, the worst happens. Through Gemma, my aim was to unravel the volatile, stormy side of motherhood, and explore the extremes of emotion that children can trigger in a parent. I wanted to push that idea, and push Gemma, until she blows.

In our modern world, so many of us are struggling through parenting in our isolated bubbles, feeling inadequate, stressed-out and over-tired. Often, we are hundreds of miles from grandparents, and too ashamed to ask for help from our friends. If you are one of those parents – as I am – I hope that this book might provide some reassurance that you are not alone!

If you liked *Little Liar* please do write a review to encourage others to read it. If nothing else, it would make my day brighter. In addition, there is nothing like a bit of old-fashioned word-of-mouth to get a book into a reader's hands, so spread the word at your book clubs or at the office or on the bus.

Please email me if you like, or follow me on Facebook or Twitter or Instagram. See below for details. *Little Liar* is my first published book, and I would be thrilled to hear from readers outside of my immediate circle of friends and family.

Thank you for taking the time to read my book.

With very best wishes,
Clare

 @claresboyd

 @Clare Boyd

 @ClareBoydClark

# ACKNOWLEDGEMENTS

My thanks go to the many people who have helped me – in many different ways – to write this book:

Firstly, I want to thank my agent, Broo Doherty, whose faith in me continues to amaze me; without whom, I would have given up writing years ago. Thank you, Broo, for making me laugh when I wanted to cry. And to everyone at Bookouture, particularly Jessie Botterill, whose incisive editing skills pushed me to write a better book. And to Peta Nightingale for seeing the book's potential. I am so grateful to them for their enthusiasm and encouragement.

I am indebted to my friend Maria, who supplied invaluable information about police procedure in cases of suspected child abuse, and who inspired some key story twists. I would not have been able to write this book without her help.

Special thanks to Simon, my soulmate, who built me a writing shed all those years ago. His unerring belief in my work underpins every word that I write.

And to my two beautiful girls, whose supportive hugs keep me going. Neither of them are anything like Rosie (most of the time)!

The next thank you goes to a group of women who did not have a direct link to the editorial processes of this book, but they have been integral to its completion. I don't have to list their names, they know who they are. Thank you to those life-enhancing friends who have respected my shed routines, listened for hours to my whinging and celebrated with real joy when I found a publisher.

Lastly, I want to thank my mother. She is my inspiration. I want to thank her for reading every draft of every book that I have ever written. Her intelligence and sensitivity and talent continues to influence me on a daily basis. I will never tire of our lengthy 'book chats'. Thanks forever, Mum.

Made in the USA
Monee, IL
19 November 2020